FaCE THE MUSIC

MARIA DARNOULT

FACE THE MUSIC

MARIA DARNOULT

FACE THE MUSIC

© Maria Darnoult

Maria Darnoult has asserted her rights in accordance with the Copyright,
Designs & and Patents Act 1988 to be identified to be the
author of this work.

Published by:

British Columbia, Canada

Email: info@wibblepublishing.com
Web: www.wibblepublishing.com

First published 2016

All rights reserved. All images, texts, and contents within this book
are subject to copyright laws. No part of this publication may be
reproduced, stored in a retrieval system now known or hereafter
invented, or transmitted in any form or by any means, electronic,
mechanical, photocopying, recording or otherwise, without the
prior permission in writing of the publisher and the copyright
owners. Every effort has been made to fulfil requirements
with regard to reproducing copyright material, the author
and publisher will be glad to rectify any omissions
at the earliest opportunity.

Legal Deposit: Library and Archives Canada, Ottawa, Ontario, Canada.

13-digit ISBN: 978-1-987860-08-5

Printed in Great Britain

DEDICATION

For my misunderstood best friend, Hannah

AUTHOR'S NOTE

This is a work of fiction, loosely based on a scandalous true life love affair which rocked a small class-conscious community a hundred years ago. Names have been changed, and fictitious characters introduced, with much imagination applied to the few facts available.

ACKNOWLEDGEMENTS

I am indebted to cousin Chris, for her journal recording the attitudes of the time, as well as the family histories, all of which made a sound base for this saga. To Manx National Heritage iMuseum for the invaluable resource of access to old newspapers. Great big 'Thank You' to my husband and sisters, cousins, Jim and Jo; to Rosemary for historical input and Barb for so much encouragement, and to Dave Moore at Wibble Publishing for constant, patient, good humoured help.

PREFACE

This story is set in the Isle of Man in 1908. Queen Victoria had been succeeded by her son, Edward VII; the Crown representative in the Isle of Man, the Governor of the time, was Lord Raglan who had been reluctant to come to the island, and had not made himself popular. Electricity was not widely available for domestic use, and there were few telephones in the island. Even those could only be used for local calls.

Castletown was once the island's capital and, although now stripped of that status, the town remained proud and class conscious. The great Manx poet, TE Brown, is reputed to have claimed that there were more social levels in Castletown than rings in an onion. This, of course, included poverty and hardship, as well as some great wealth.

As urbanisation spread in Castletown, the school building was surrounded by many other buildings, such as almshouses and other hovels, and, over the centuries, the area became the overcrowded poorer quarter, and then practically a slum by the time of this story. The headmaster of the school was a prominent member of society. He and many others tried repeatedly to have better accommodation acquired for the purpose of education, preferably with outside space for exercise and recreation.

The school pupils were exclusively boys at the time, encouraged to take scholarships which would enable them to move on to the most prestigious public school, the nearby King William's College. Scholarships had been provided by local benefactors such as Henry Bloom Noble and his wife, Rebecca, and the author Thomas Henry Hall Caine, as well as from the school's own funds.

The schoolmaster was also the organist at St Mary's Chapel Royal, which was very close by the school. He conducted the choir, instigated a male voice choir and a philharmonic society, and had a powerful influence in many circles, especially musical and educational ones. He is depicted as a strict disciplinarian with a temper, and a confident, if not flamboyant attitude.

He had been married in his early thirties, but his wife died in childbirth and he remained a widower, living with his sister, Agnes, and her family, plus some boarders from his school. This continued for twenty years, until the young Hannah Corlett came into his life.

Although descended from numerous teachers and church organists, she was the daughter of a house painter, and Agnes, with class distinction in mind, suspected the girl's motives. She thoroughly disapproved of her brother's liaison and actively discouraged it.

William and Hannah experienced the opposition, which did not only come from Agnes, but they had fallen in love. This softened William's approach to life, and they resolved that, together, they would....

'*Face The Music.*'

Chapter One

Will was so lonely, he felt his loneliness like a pain. Surrounded by people, admirers even, and living in a busy, bustling household, yet he was alone. His sweet young wife died trying to bear his dead child, but that was twenty years ago, and William Waverley had simply thrown himself into his work at the School and his music through the Church. He was constantly in demand, and partook in all the social events of the town, was considered amongst the gentry. He was important, some said flamboyant, but above all he commanded respect. But now, in his fifties, his pain just kept on growing, and he began to see himself as a sad, hopeless, old man.

And then, Hannah happened. When he looked back, it was difficult to recall how it came about. He could barely remember a time when she was not the centre of his universe, but he had stopped being lonely when she soothed his pain.

She had always been there, in church, at choir practices, a faithful participant, a good singer. But she was thirty years younger, an upright, single, career-woman, he had imagined, working in her grandmother's shop. How could he have known anything more about her - and yet, how could he not?

"You look so sad," she had said, "are you quite well?" The choir practice had ended and he had sent everyone home, wishing he could spend half an hour on his beloved organ to calm his frazzled nerves. She was peeling an orange as she spoke, and offered him a segment. His confident voice, the voice that had been shouting "No! No! No!" at the singers just a short while before, seemed to have deserted him. "We really were trying to understand what you wanted," she offered, "but....?" and her eyes were repeating her first question.

He sank down onto one of the church hall benches, and felt himself deflating like a balloon, from his puffed-up, angry indignation at what he had seen as the stubborn, if not bloody-minded, ineptitude of the motley voices collectively claiming to be the Southern Singers. Or was it his fault? Is it possible for such a dynamo to crumple? She had taken a seat alongside, and very close to him, and suddenly, he was overwhelmed at the concern on her face, more than touched that, although almost a stranger, she was the first person to notice that he was a troubled soul, with feelings. When he found his voice, he took a deep breath and confessed, "Actually, I am lonely - no, I know you think that's impossible, when there is always so much going on, but...." and she stopped him there by putting a finger to his mouth.

"I don't think it impossible," she said, "I am lonely, too."

For a long moment, they gazed at each other, her finger still on his lips, which he found had begun to burn. And then she stroked his face, and before he knew what was happening, they were kissing. She smelled and tasted of oranges, and a ridiculous vision of a voluptuous Nell Gwyn occurred to him.

Appalled at his fall from grace, he stood up and started to apologise. He was realising the difference in their ages, in their social standing, in.... everything.

"It is I who should apologise," she said, rising to stand in front of him, "except that I am not a bit sorry," and again she stroked his face and kissed him. This time he explored the feeling more thoroughly, took her in his arms and felt her press her body to him. Wicked thoughts raced through his head, while his pulse quickened, and he knew the longing that had been troubling him for so long.

With his head spinning, he drew away from the girl and smiled ruefully, not knowing what to do next. As if she understood, she also smiled, half nodded, and turned away to leave.

"I am in confusion," he said at last, "but at least allow me to escort you home."

Her face fell a little, as she said, "I would like that very much, but it might be better if you do not. We will be seen, and for all their holy airs and graces, the women around here have tongues that wag like dogs' tails. Your reputation could be compromised." Her tone was slightly mocking, but the smile reached her rather pretty, turquoise-blue eyes.

It was so long since anyone had spoken to him as an equal, that he realised he really liked this young woman. "That settles it then," he declared, returning her twinkle, "Please to take my arm, Miss Corlett."

Will spent a restless night, wondering one moment how he had let such unworthy behaviour take place, and the next moment imagining how he could engineer another such encounter. He would be in real trouble with his strait-laced sister, was it worth it? He felt the firm, young body press against him again, smelled the faint fragrance of oranges and thought, oh yes, it would be worth it.

He drifted off to sleep eventually and found himself barging through huddles of old women in the town, all with angel's wings, and with wagging dogs' tails coming out of their mouths, and every one of them eyeing him with unmasked disgust. But on he went, ignoring the hags, until he was in an orchard of orange trees, where he gorged on whole fruit, taking them in both hands and burying his face in them, biting through the orange skin so hard that the juice ran down his chin. He awoke with a start, with his heart racing and sweat on his brow.

Was he mad? Was he bewitched? How long had it taken? Ten minutes, five? From 'Are you quite well?' to all but the most passionate intimacy, with a practical stranger. Yes, he was definitely mad. But as his pulse slowed and he regained his composure, he remembered that, until that mad moment, he had been incredibly sad and lonely. She was almost right, he had begun to think he was becoming ill, but now? Now he felt a rebellious wish to be with her again, and again and again. He tried to recall what he knew about her, but it was only through the church and the 'Southern Singers' and social occasions connected with one or the other. He knew she had several brothers, and there was a sister who was also in the choir, but he fancied that Hannah did not live with her parents and siblings, and briefly wondered why, before his thoughts returned again to her kind concern, her witty remarks, her mouth on his..... her body..... and he slept again.

His morning routine always began early with a brisk walk before breakfast, to the church, where he played his beloved organ. It was referred to as 'organ practice' but as he had been playing since childhood, practising was hardly necessary. But it was his way of charging up his batteries to face the day. He adored music, and the sound of the organ sent him into raptures of delight. This morning, it was not only the music that delighted him, but the vibrations through his body from the wonderful, deepest notes. There was the deep growl from one of the pedals that gave him the most exquisite frisson and raised the hairs on his neck. He had no idea afterwards what he had been playing, only that his whole being was alive, vibrant, looking forward - to what, he was not sure, only that he had to see Hannah again. In fact, he had to have her.

The verger, who also made a daily early start in order to pump the organ for him, regarded him thoughtfully. Waverley was usually authoritative, flamboyant, very much in control, punishing the organ into triumphant fortissimo, but today he was caressing the keys, using the softer stops at first, until he found that deep pedal note, and then he played that almost continuously. There was no recognisable tune, and yet the beast simply sang. The headmaster drifted away when his time was up, looking like a man in a dream. The verger had been going to complain about traces of orange peel he had found on the church hall floor, but in the light of this phenomenon, decided not to.

∞∞∞∞

Hannah had also spent a restless night. She knew that she was in love, but the difficulties she would face in ever being able to come close to Will again seemed insurmountable. She knew what people thought of her, 'twenty-eight years old and unmarried, there must be something wrong with her,' but she had been in love with William Waverley for years, since having a strange dream about him, and other prospective suitors just had no appeal for her. Until now, she had almost been content to worship him from afar, and think of him in her lonely bed, as if he were her lover. A world of make-believe. The opportunity to speak privately with him had never presented itself, so she had 'pretend' conversations with him before she went to sleep every night. That night, the conversation began with what had actually been said, in the church hall and then as they walked along the street, although they had actually spoken very little, seemingly reluctant to break a nervous but companionable silence. In her nocturnal reverie, however, a great deal more was said, and continued for several hours, throughout some delicious declarations, a great deal of kissing, and then..... becoming one with him. She had been staggered by his complicity in the church hall, and could hardly believe what had happened. Because she loved him, she had been genuinely concerned for his health when he seemed so out of sorts. They were quite used to him being angry – yet now he also seemed so sad – but she had not expected events to turn out as they did. What had happened was the stuff of her dreams, although all over far too quickly. She wondered, if she had persisted, might she have dared to let him take advantage of her? She was also a practical woman and knew Mr Waverley was an honourable and courteous man – and that, in any case, the church hall bench was not the place for this most intimate of experiences. She would have to imagine that the rest of the world had ceased to exist, and that he had come to visit her in her boudoir. She would have to give this matter more thought, but she knew in her heart that she could not go on pretending. Not any more.

∞∞∞

He went home for breakfast, feeling like a young man, with a spring in his step. As soon as he crossed the threshold, his sister's imperious voice shouted "William!" Oh dear, he thought, that did not take long. She only called him William when he was in trouble. He put on a suit of armour, consisting of an innocent, questioning smile.

"Agatha?" he responded, mischievously inflaming her indignation. She was Mrs Agnes Lacey, and he knew she hated all of his corruptions of her name. He sat down at the table and tucked his napkin into his collar.

"Have you taken leave of your senses?" she demanded, banging his breakfast plate on the table in front of him, but without waiting for a reply, continued, "I have already heard that you have been consorting with that Corlett strumpet – no, you need not try to deny it, you were seen last night."

A delicious memory almost choked him, but to be on the safe side, he asked, "Doing what, exactly?"

"Oh, doing what exactly?" she mimicked, "as if you didn't know. Walking the hussy home, arm in arm, after choir practice, that's what exactly – have you gone quite mad?"

With some relief, he smiled, half to himself, and mused, "Perhaps." He thought Agnes might explode.

"What?" she yelled.

"Calm down, my dear, Miss Corlett was kind enough to enquire after my health, she thought I looked sad," he began.

"You will look more than sad if you take up with that predator. Thought you looked sad, indeed. You pursue that madam and I will leave this house. After all I have done for you, is this the thanks I get?"

"Oh my goodness, Ag, you will do yourself a mischief if you go on like that. Be careful you don't burst your stays." Agnes' teenaged daughter got up from the table, trying to stifle a laugh.

"Sit down, Christina," commanded her mother, "and in future, you will stay at choir practice until your uncle comes home, and you will walk with him."

"Oh, Mother, I usually do, but Uncle Will got so angry last night, he was roaring at us all as if we were deliberately singing badly. He just couldn't explain what he wanted of us," protested Christina, "and when he fairly threw us all out, we just went, gladly. But where is all this anger coming from - it seems to be in both of you?"

Agnes seemed hardly to hear, she was back on her high horse. "After all Mother and I did to provide you with music lessons, and get you into that good school ..."

"Right, that does it!" William stood up, throwing down his knife and fork. "That is so unfair. You know how much the music means to me, it has always been and always will be my first love, and I have always appreciated your efforts in my behalf, for half a century, you know I have. But I had to work hard at it too, and I am not thinking of ever giving it up. I don't understand why you are being so unreasonable."

Agnes was going puce in the face. "Unreasonable? Unreasonable? You are seen walking out with a girl who could be your daughter, and not just far too young for you, but a tradesman's daughter. For heaven's sake, William, what on earth will people think?"

Will had sat down again, deeply hurt at the mention of a daughter, but now he laughed. Part of his dream had come back to him when he remembered the old women with tongues like dogs' tails, and he thought how accurately Hannah had predicted the reaction. He knew his sister would be apoplectic, but he couldn't stop the laughter. "Walking out?" he spluttered. "I do the kind woman the courtesy of seeing her safely home, and that constitutes 'walking out'? I always thought you were a charitable woman Agnes, but you are no better than your coven of harridans, making such evil allegations. And what has being a tradesman's daughter to do with anything?"

"So you are not 'walking out' with the bitch?" Agnes was beginning to calm down a little, "I am only concerned for you. Will, you would be too stupidly flattered to spot a sycophantic gold-digger at work."

"If she is a gold-digger, she will be very disappointed in me" He tried to make a joke of it.

"Don't be obtuse!" spat his sister, "you know very well what I mean."

"I think this conversation has run its course," he said with finality, "I have never heard such ridiculous accusations." But was she right? Even as he was denying his liaison with Hannah, he knew in his heart that he was lying.

Having entered the house with a light heart, he left with a black cloud over him. Agnes was unaware that she had hit a raw nerve by reminding Will of his lost wife and child, and for a short while he wondered if, in the back of his mind, he saw Hannah as the daughter he had been deprived of all those years ago. Then he realised that his feelings for Hannah were not paternal. They were not paternal at all.

Did he imagine it, or did the old women look at him strangely as he walked to the school. Goodness, had someone seen what had happened in the church hall last night, or could they read his thoughts? He shuddered, and tried to clear his head in order to be able to begin the lessons. Euclid, he thought. Latin.... English Grammar.... Soft lips. No! Verbs.... Nature Study.... Oranges. God Almighty!

Chapter Two

Hannah worked in the grocery shop with her grandmother, Mary. It had not escaped her notice that young Hannah was distracted this morning, and it was not long before first one customer and then another could not help themselves gossiping. "I believe your Hannah is seeing Mr Waverley," said one. "Is your girl going to get a husband at last?" said another. "Must be getting desperate," giggled the last, and knowing looks passed between the womenfolk. Mary was aware of her grand-daughter's infatuation, but she did not know that the older man had walked her home last night. Now she began to watch the girl more closely, sometimes surreptitiously from behind the food displays. She was certainly day-dreaming, and now and then she seemed to be scribbling something on a notepad, but screwed up the paper and threw it away when Mary let her hear that she was approaching. She loved her grand-daughter, and nothing would have made her happier than to see the girl happily married to someone suitable, even give her some great-grandchildren perhaps, before it was too late for either of them.

Casually, Mary picked up the crumpled pieces of paper. Poor Hannah was mortified, bit her lip and waited for a reprimand. 'Hannah Waverley,' she read aloud. 'HC Waverley,' from another scribble. 'Mrs JTW Waverley' appeared on a third. Hannah cringed and held her breath as her grandmother raised an eyebrow. Then she pursed her lips and a dimple appeared at the side of her mouth. "You could do a lot worse," she smiled.

"Grandmother, help me!" gasped Hannah in relief, "Am I mad? What am I to do?"

"Yes, it is madness, you must forget the very idea," was not what Hannah wanted to hear. Then her grandmother smiled again. "But I do know what it is like to be in love, my darling. You may think it is a long time ago, but it doesn't seem long to me, I remember many delicious moments. However, I am hearing a lot of gossip, but is Mr Waverley aware of all this?"

"I don't know!" blurted Hannah, "but if all the nosey old women are shouting it out round the town, it will only be a matter of time before something must be done. Mrs Lacey will be furious for a start. But, oh Gran, I couldn't bear it if he should say it was all a mistake and I must never see him again. I would just die!"

"If what was all a mistake, dear?" probed the old lady, and Hannah blushed deeply and let out a long breath.

"We-ell, last night, after choir, he kissed me." There, it was said.

"Are you sure dear?" said her grandmother.

"Oh yes, oh yes, yes." Hannah was almost crying.

"No, I mean are you sure HE kissed YOU? Or was it the other way round, perhaps?"

Hannah gasped, "Grandmother! What are you suggesting? Do you think I would be so forward as to kiss him first?" Now it was her turn to realise she was in denial, but her grandmother knew her too well.

"I think you are entirely capable of going for what you want, you have been doing that since you were in the cradle, and I say, "all strength to you, my girl". So, whoever kissed whom, he then, being the gentleman he is, presumably escorted you home?"

"Exactly!" agreed Hannah, "He was just doing the gentlemanly thing, when some old witch obviously saw us and has spread her malicious gossip all over town already."

"Well, however you wish to convince yourself, that poor man needs some affection. It is a terrible waste of a good man, that he has not brought himself to another wife. That's not to say I entirely approve of your imagining yourself in that capacity, but you do look happy today, my child. And a young wife might even give him the children he always wanted."

That thought shot through Hannah's body and filled her with longing. She felt short of breath all of a sudden, so to hide her surge of emotion, she threw her arms round her grandmother and hugged her close. "Oh yes," said the old lady, feeling the young body against her, as Will had done, "that should do it all right!" They both laughed, and then fell to plotting the next moves.

∞∞∞

He was not imagining it. There were knowing looks in his direction as he walked home from school, and he dreaded encountering his sister again. He had survived the day somehow, he had a good crew of children these days and they distracted him with their enthusiasm for an archaeological project they were working on together. The boys had some good ideas for a display they intended to put on for Prize Day, and he forgot his carnal aspirations for a while. He had not seen Hannah today, didn't usually see her except at church or choir practice, but today he felt her absence keenly. When he had time for private thoughts again, she occupied every one of them.

He had to see her, he had to know if there could possibly be a future for them together. Had he been totally mistaken last night? Did he dream it? But what about all these 'knowing looks' from people he didn't even know. Oh Lord, had she told everyone what they had done? Would she do that? Surely not. But what if she was the gold-digger Agnes thought her, and was only out to make a fool of him? He felt crushed at the very idea. Was he to be lifted out of his melancholy for one night only? What a predicament. Yes, he was going mad, that was it, he was already mad.

When he entered the house, all was quiet. There was no sign of a meal being ready for him, which was a little annoying, as he had to go out again to a meeting of the Church Council. He found his sister in the parlour, winding wool with Christina. She did not look up as he entered, and he assumed that he was still in disgrace. He decided to jump in the deep end, and asked if there was anything for tea.

Agnes did not reply about the tea, but launched into another acid attack. "I knew that Mary Bickerstaff was up to something, she's far too cosy with her 'shop assistant,' more like a sister than a respectable grandmother. Why doesn't the strumpet live with her own mother, and her father, the house painter?" On and on she went. She had never been so humiliated in her life, everyone was talking about him and that woman, and how ridiculous a fool he was. Christina looked embarrassed but remained silent, as she continued to wind the wool from a long hank held up by her mother. He said he would go out to the meeting and hope there would be some tea and biscuits available.

"Why don't you go running to your little tart?" she said, "I'm sure you would get more than biscuits there."

"Do you know," Will said then, "that is a really good idea. I think I will do that," and he backed out of the room, enjoying the look of horror on his angry sister's face.

The meeting was not due to start for another hour and, although he did not really intend to do as he had threatened, rather than walking directly to the church hall again, he did find his footsteps taking him into the street where, last night, Hannah had thanked him for seeing her home, and demurely said, "Good-night." He would have loved to go to the church and play the organ to pass the time, he thought, but his steps slowed as he passed No 34. He walked on, but then turned and walked back, wondering how many lace curtains were twitching, and wondering also what he thought he was doing. He had no idea, and once again he turned and passed the shop.

Hannah had a little sister, Carrie, who was about eleven, and was now staying with the grandparents too. As Will passed the house door for the third time, Carrie came bouncing out, followed by her grandmother. "Oh my goodness, hello Mr Waverley," said Mary, and then to his amazement, "I am just taking Carrie to her friend's house, I won't be long, but I would like to talk to you if you can spare a few moments? Why don't you go on in. Hannah is in the kitchen," and with this shock announcement, she bustled off up the street with the little girl, who stared round at him, intrigued, as she was pulled along.

With his heart in his mouth, he knocked at the door, that had just closed itself, and Hannah came to answer the knock wearing an apron and wiping her hands on a cloth. She looked as if she had seen a ghost and for a moment just stood staring at him in disbelief. "I.... I was just passing," he began, "when Mrs Bickerstaff came out with the little girl. She said she wants to talk to me, and I should come in and wait for her to come back."

"Oh," said Hannah, and continued standing, staring at him. "Oh, God!" she said eventually, "come in, p-please come in," and she stood aside to let him pass, but not so far aside that he could squeeze through without touching her. She hesitated, as if to prolong the moment, but then shut the door behind them firmly. Then she flung her arms round him. He hesitated, but found he could do nothing but reciprocate, hardly believing what was happening, and they indulged in a long, wonderful kiss before a man's voice called, "Who was it, Hannah?"

Charles Bickerstaff was sitting in the kitchen with a newspaper spread out on the table. Will winced, noticing the appetising remains of a meat pie in a deep enamel dish that was only half hidden by the *Weekly Times*. "It's Mr Waverley, Grandpa, he's just called to see Grandma."

"She's gone out," declared the old man and returned his attention to the papers, while William stood by the table feeling uncomfortable, and distinctly hungry.

Hannah noticed his wistful glance at the pie, and knew instinctively what had happened. "Oh dear," she smiled, "are you being starved at home? Good job there is some left, then. Sit down, William."

The old man looked up from the papers and repeated "Mother's gone out," but Hannah assured him that she would be back directly, and placed a warm plate from the range, and a knife and fork in front of Will. His sister's words came back to him and he smirked. This was certainly more than biscuits. Grandfather had got up and taken his newspaper to the fireside chair, noisily turning the pages.

"Mmm, did you make this?" asked Will with his mouth full.

"What?" said the old man, peering over the paper, "Oh, are you still here? Aye, Mother makes a good beef pie." Thus he narrowly prevented Hannah from telling William her first lie and, realising this, she resolved never, ever to lie to him. There were things she must tell him, and she needed him to believe her.

"I made the gravy," she whispered, and then more loudly to her grandad, "Poor Mr Waverley has had no tea!"

"What?" said the old man again, but wasn't expecting an answer.

Mrs Bickerstaff had still not returned when all the pie was gone, and Hannah motioned Will to follow her into the parlour. Immediately, she shut the door and pushed herself against him. "You didn't come here to talk to my grandmother," she accused, "but I am so glad you are here. Am I imagining things, Will, or do you feel as I do?" In confirmation, he kissed her again, with more and more fervour as the notion became a reality to them both.

They heard Hannah's grandmother returning, and sat down on separate chairs to await her entry. "You really ought to have drawn the curtains before doing that," she twinkled, bustling to rectify the matter. "Now then, young fellow," and she raised her eyebrow, but seeing his embarrassment, she continued, "Hannah has confessed to me that she is in love with you, Mr Waverley. May I ask what your intentions are?"

"Mrs. Bickerstaff, I am taken by surprise myself. One kiss," then seeing that eyebrow raised again, "well, perhaps two kisses, and one walk home after choir practice, and the whole town seems to have made it a fact that Hannah and I, that Hannah and I, excuse me, did you just say that Hannah is in love with me? It has happened so quickly that I hardly dared to hope....."

Both women were nodding their heads. "Ah, my intentions..... I think I might need to come down from this cloud! I am in terrible trouble with my sister. Oh my goodness, I am due at a church meeting, I must leave. But I assure you that my intentions are honourable. Am I correct in thinking that we have your blessing? That would be so wonderful. I believe I may be falling in love with Hannah too, I have thought of nothing else but how to be with her!"

"Quite a speech, young man, quite a speech. If you have five minutes more to spare before your meeting, I will leave you two alone to say what you have to say to each other. It would be her father you would have to ask, but if indeed your intentions are honourable," the eyebrow went up again, "then you do have my blessing. Yes."

Will wanted to hug the intuitive old lady, and wished the meeting would go to hell and he could stay with Hannah for ever. "But," Mary had not finished, "you could always come back after your meeting, if you like, just for another five minutes, of course?" Will thought he could hear angels singing.

∞∞∞∞

Church Council meetings normally dragged on for hours, with gentlemen arguing heatedly, usually about money. There would be many digressions, and little groups would be talking about different matters. Will always found them tedious, and for this reason, with a heart like lead, he had thanked Mrs

Bickerstaff for her hospitality and kind invitation, but felt it unfair to accept, when it might be very late before he could return. She thanked him for his consideration, and he thought he detected just the slightest hint of relief on her face. He had no idea what the arguments were about at the meeting, as he was deeply absorbed by the events of the past twenty four hours. Thrilled and excited, but puzzled too.

How annoying it was, therefore, that the meeting was drawn to an abrupt and premature end, when the Chairman stormed out of the building after some disagreement. The Secretary asked for a vote on closing the meeting, and people began to disperse. Will sat on in his seat, still absorbed in his jumble of emotions, thinking about Hannah, her grandparents – and his bitter sister.

"Will you be leaving, Mr Waverley?" asked the Secretary, gathering his papers together and starting to turn out the gas lights in the vestry. "Oh, yes, of course," he replied, wishing he could go upstairs and play the organ, or better still, fall into Hannah's arms and disappear into her love.

Even if she was speaking to him, Agnes would not be expecting him home yet, so he walked round between the church and the school, leaned against the cold stone sea wall, and stared out across the water. It was a calm night, and the waves lapped quietly on the rocks upon which the town was built. Will thought he actually preferred to watch them when it was stormy, and the white foam crashed over the breakwater. That was more appropriate to his life right now. Agitated. Angry. Exciting. Powerful. Not tranquil and smooth and mirroring the few gas street lights in yellow pools. 'Powerful?' he thought. "Power-less, rather. In the grip of powerful desires, I am power-less. What on earth am I going to do? I am fifty-seven-years-old, a so-called pillar of the community, a respected citizen. Or I was. Now I am a quivering wreck, like a teenager lusting after a young woman."

Realising that his thoughts were taking him nowhere, he turned away from the wall and began to make his way home. As he crossed the Market Square, he heard a child's voice say clearly, "Look, Grandma, there's Mr Waverley again." He turned, and Mrs Bickerstaff joined him. They fell into step along the next street, with little Carrie trotting along between them.

"Your meeting...." she began, at the same time as William started to say, "The meeting finished early. I wish I had known that would happen."

"Never mind," replied the old lady, "perhaps it is better not to rush things, under the circumstances. Ah, this is where our ways diverge, good-night, Mr Waverley."

"Might I be permitted to escort you home? I feel I can talk to you," he ventured, "I am in such a quandary."

Mary looked down at the child, "Run along ahead of us, Carrie, but not too far ahead. Run from one street lamp to the next!" The child scampered off, and the two older people fell into the kind of conversation that skirts all around their major concern. The woman was well versed in diplomacy, listened to all the gossip in the shop, but never passed it on. William was intrigued as they chatted, and she told him about Hannah's life, and about her own. By the time they had reached her front door, Will felt that he had at least one friend in the town, and he continued on his way home with a clearer head and a lighter heart.

Chapter Three

He still had Agnes to face, of course. He almost began to feel sorry for his sister. What was happening to him was exciting, with promise for a future, whereas, for her, it threatened her long established way of life. It was true she had sacrificed much as a young girl, to enable him to have music lessons. Agnes had studied really hard to be trained as a teacher herself, and she and their mother had both worked hard, making up for the shortcomings of a profligate father, to ensure that he had the best education they could secure for him. But, he had worked hard too, and still loved working towards qualifications, even fifty years later. It was unfair of her to claim that he was forgetting all of that, just because he was now showing an interest in a young woman.

But he did appreciate all she had done, and he resolved to apologise to her and try to persuade her to see it from his side. Then again, she and her husband had not co-habited for twenty years. He had not given much thought to this situation, as Richard Lacey was often present at family gatherings, and they seemed affectionate enough, but Agnes was running her little school from home in Castletown, while Richard had taught elsewhere, and stayed locally. It started when he obtained the post of headmaster at Dalby school. It was difficult and tedious to commute between Dalby and Castletown, and he had lodged near the school, attempting unsuccessfully to persuade the authorities to provide a schoolmaster's house. Perhaps the little family would have stayed together, had such a house been granted. After that, he had taken a post even further away, in Kirk Michael, and Richard just never came back to live with Agnes, even after he had moved schools again, to Santon, which was so much closer, and on the railway line. By then, they had become accustomed to living apart.

This was the first time Will had paid the matter any attention, and he began to wonder if Agnes had a problem with marital relations. Oh dear, just thinking about marital relations sent a sensation surging through him. It was nearly twenty years since poor Ellen had died in childbirth and, at first, Will was so devastated that 'marital relations' had not occurred to him for many a year. Occasionally, a smart looking woman would attract his attention, and several had tried to get close to him, especially in the early years, when he was still young. But his work, and especially his music, were all that he needed for company. Until lately. Until now.

But again he thought of Agnes and how she must be feeling, after all these years of living comfortably with him. Agnes had married Richard Lacey in the same summer as Will and Ellen were wed, but they managed to start a family within two years, and their little boy, Douglas, was just starting to walk when Ellen shyly announced that she was with child. They were all overjoyed, as she and Agnes were firm friends, and Ellen adored the little boy, often spending time with him while his mother was teaching. Her pregnancy had appeared entirely normal, although she was only slight, and the whole family, household, street and town had been inconsolable when the happy young woman gave birth to a stillborn daughter after an incredibly long labour, and then died from the trauma. Because of the pain of his own double bereavement, it had taken Will until now to realise what this had done to Agnes, who had just discovered that she was expecting again when the tragedy happened.

∞∞∞

"Mr Waverley walked us home!" blurted Carrie as she bounced back into the house, sending Hannah into a turmoil of disappointment and indignation.

"I thought his meeting was going on until late," she complained, annoyed that he had just walked past her door without her knowing.

Mary sent Carrie off to get ready for bed. "Don't forget to brush your teeth, and that wayward hair – 100 times, mind!" Then she explained all that had happened, reassuring Hannah that she thought Will a genuinely nice man. Confused, worried, perplexed, anxious, but absolutely besotted with her. This was balm to Hannah's wounded feelings, and she went off to bed to talk to her lover, as usual.

∞∞∞

Will threw his hat into the hall in an attempt to lighten the mood, but the house remained silent. He went through to the kitchen and found himself some bread and cheese. The fire in the parlour had been left to go almost out, and he thought better of starting it up again. Whatever he might do would probably be the wrong thing in the present icy climate in the house, so he took his meagre provisions up to his room. Agnes and all the children (there were several boarders) must already be in bed, he concluded, so he must save his little conciliatory speech for the morning. This was not helpful when it came to trying to sleep, and he spent another restless night, fluctuating between confusion, remorse, sympathy and rampant desire.

Two things had given him hope, though. He was now confident that Hannah returned his feelings, and her grandmother seemed to be on his side. That was most encouraging, although she had advised him that, to begin with at least, he should restrict his contacts with Hannah to the usual choir practices and church services. He had joked that he thought the choir could do with a lot more practice, but she was firm. Your time will come, she assured him, but you must be circumspect. For herself she was not bothered about what the neighbours thought, but he had to admit that there was a large difference in their ages and, should he think of marrying Hannah, they must both be aware that one day she could be a widow. No of course he had no intention right now of ever leaving her, but 'time and unforeseen occurrence befall us all' and whether people were just busy being horrified, or maliciously predicting gloom and doom or were genuinely concerned about the disparity in their ages, they had to be patient, and realise that folk need time to acclimatise to extraordinary happenings.

"This is a gossipy place," she had said, "you walked Hannah home. As far as I know you did not even hold hands, but within twelve hours the news was the hot topic of the town, that the two of you were 'walking out,' and believe me, what they see as the unsuitability of the match, is only the fuel that made it so explosively newsworthy. It will be a five minute wonder. Well, seven days at the most. After that time, I suggest you walk her home again and that you do hold hands. Be patient, Will. You must take your time."

Although he felt that time was already running out for him, he acknowledged the wisdom of her words. Perhaps a few days would make the heart grow fonder, although he could not imagine being fonder, or waiting any days at all.

After his usual early morning organ practice the next day, Will approached his home with some trepidation, but was feeling more confident that he could come to a meeting of minds with his sister, of whom, after all, he was very fond.

"Where did you get to last night?" demanded Agnes before he could even say good morning. It was not a good start.

"What do you mean? I was home here by nine," he protested. "Where were you?"

"I took everyone to a little children's party at the Cubbons, down by the harbour. The Corlett child was there, but Mary Bickerstaff collected her before we left. I thought you had the church meeting, didn't you go to that? You were heading for trouble when you left here, I presumed you found it. We had no idea you were already here when we all got home, I left the door for you for hours."

"Ag, please can we start again, with, "Good Morning," perhaps? I need to have a proper conversation with you without having you go off like a pepper pot all the time."

"Finish your breakfast, everyone," she ordered, then, "I will talk to YOU later."

Looking forward to it, he said to himself, and had trouble swallowing his toast.

∞∞∞∞

Hannah knew what people said about her, and she found some of it hurtful. There had been suitors, several of them, but she had never been in love like she was now, and it was now that she knew why she had not been able to respond to certain advances that young men made. She had not been willing to abandon herself to anyone, the way she was eager to give herself to Will. She did not want to marry someone just to be married or just to have children, or just to be provided for. She knew she had so much love to give that her partner had to be someone worthy, who would really, truly love her in return.

She thought back to one of the young men that she had been walking out with for some time, and there had been a time when she thought herself fond of him, almost fond enough..... and kisses had become passionate and demanding. But kisses were never enough for young men. She hated and despised their propensity for pawing at her breasts or groping under her skirts, and could not understand why they were not satisfied with holding her in their arms and saying nice things.

As time went on and she noticed how people looked at her, she began to suspect that something had been said to suggest that she had given way to some of those advances, and then one day a man actually had the audacity to say he had heard she was 'free and easy.' Well, his hopes were dashed in no uncertain terms, but after that, she understood why people looked at her the way they did. She was horrified to think people had even been talking about her, never mind saying such iniquitous things – and, worse still, they were believed! She knew there was nothing she could do about it, except keep herself to herself, steer well clear of men altogether if possible, and bide her time. Perhaps one day she would get away from this town.

Her obsession with William Waverley had begun because of these injured feelings. She had needed a focus for her love, someone safe, who would not compromise her or tell tales about her. It started with a realisation that she saw him almost more often than any other man, and he was a good man, a nice looking man, well-respected, educated, talented, a mature man. And single. And then there had been 'the dream' in which a strange woman told her and William that they would be married. The oddly dressed woman, who wore her hair short, like a boy, had even claimed to be their grand-daughter. Hannah could not fathom what this was all about, but she had begun telling Will her secrets, alone in her bed at night, baring her soul and weeping into her pillow, pretending it was his shoulder. And he, of course, in time, had responded and fallen madly in love with her. Thereafter, their 'relationship' began to take on a more physical expression, and she writhed and wrestled with her quilt, pushing her breasts into 'him' and feeling his mouth on hers, and then his body......

She was not deluded. She was well aware that this was a fantasy, and a totally private one, so when she had gone to him after choir practice and enquired about his health, it was not on her mind. Because she had watched his every move for many years, she knew he was a troubled soul, and when he confessed to being so painfully lonely, her surge of empathy was spontaneous.

∞∞∞

Will set off for school feeling defiant and wanting to make his own decisions. Above everything on earth, he wanted to see Hannah, and saw nothing wrong with calling at the little grocery shop in Hope Street on his way to work. He was a teenager again, with nothing more in his head than setting eyes on the object of his desire, so he was already inside the shop and face to face with Hannah's grandmother before reality set in. "I see you are taking my advice, young man," she said, "but of course, you have come to see ME, just to say good morning, haven't you!"

"Ah – ah – ah pound of apples, please, Mrs Bickerstaff, and yes, of course, good morning, Madam. Is, er ...?" and he looked hopefully at the door into the scullery that served as a stock room.

"Not yet, what a shame! 'Er' clears up after breakfast before starting in the shop, she will be sorry she missed you. That will be one and tuppence, Mr Waverley." She looked up at him and flicked her eyes to show there was someone behind him. Will could have sworn there was a dog's tail on the customer's lips, and there was no doubt it would be wagging excitedly within the minute. Damn. But at least he would have something to eat today. He was surprised, and touched, when he opened the bag of apples later in the morning, and found two oranges in it as well.

Mary later advised her grand-daughter that she might want to be quicker about the washing up in future and, of course, Hannah was crestfallen at missing him by seconds once again. "Leave it," she commanded, as the girl was about to dash out into the street to see if he was still there, "he is long gone, but don't worry, he'll be back. I warned him to stay away if he could – but he can't, can he! I don't know what you've done to him, but you've done it with extraordinary speed and success!"

∞∞∞

Will came home to face the music after school, and Agnes sat him down across the table from herself and folded her hands in front of her. "Well?" she prompted.

"I want you to know," he began, "how much I love you, appreciate all you have done for me, and hope we can be agreeable with each other. I have realised how much you have been through, and how incredibly strong and supportive you are. Please can you countenance a compromise?"

She seemed to digest this little speech for several minutes, and then, emphatically, "No."

He stared at her, waiting for more. "No compromise," she repeated. "I hear you have been chasing after the barmaid's apron again, you can't leave her alone, can you. Am I right in thinking that you are determined to pursue the strumpet to the obvious conclusion? You're not the first, you know. Not by a long way, she is a tart and a whore, and you are no brother of mine."

"So much for my attempts at conciliation," he breathed. "Hannah...." Agnes winced at the mention of the name, "is not a whore, you are too quick to listen to gossip and to judge. And in any case, even if she is Mary Magdalene, I love her."

The biblical quotation incensed his sister ever further. "She is still a tradesman's daughter," she said curling her lip.

"So says the house servant's daughter," he reminded her, "what a bigot you are. Is there no worthy occupation in the world except being a teacher? It may surprise you to know that Mr and Mrs Bickerstaff were both teachers, and Miss Corlett at Victoria Road is Hannah's aunt. Hannah only helps in a shop because she is a good and dutiful daughter and grand-daughter, but she has qualifications in art and music and could be in a professional choir, she should certainly be in the church choir..."

"Huh, a chorus girl, maybe."

"With voice training, she could be a soloist, but she has a strong voice and would make an excellent first contralto in church. Also, she has perfect pitch."

"Well, she has made a perfect pitch at you, that's for sure," and Agnes got up to leave the table.

"Don't just walk away from me Agnes, please let us come to some conclusion."

"Will you leave this house, or will I?" she countered, "and take all the children with me?"

"That's your own unnecessary decision. Where would you go?"

"Back to Ramsey. I might have an option on a house there. I liked Ramsey, the people are friendly, and the sun shines a lot. Perhaps it would have been better if I had never left there."

This was a barb directed at him. She and their mother had come to the island some years before Will, and she had been headmistress at a girls' school in Ramsey. When he obtained the position with the Grammar School in Peel, he had invited her to join him on the staff there, and the family were reunited, remaining together when he then took the headmaster"s post in Castletown.

"It sounds nice. Perhaps I should go there and let you stay here, but I suspect you have already made up your mind to take that option."

"Yes," she said, "I heard about a house that might be suitable, and it has been at the back of my mind for some time, but your misbehaviour gives me very good reason to leave Castletown now. All the boarders can come with me, I could set up a school anywhere. I am not impervious to your words, Will, and I am grateful for the consideration you have attempted to show me, but I do not believe I could live in the same town and watch you completely ruined. Here come the children for their tea now, this is the end of the conversation. I shall write to my friends in Ramsey again and start making arrangements to move in the summer holidays." She broke off there with a slight sob. Struggling to regain composure, she touched his arm and whispered, "I wish with all my heart that you had found a suitable woman, but if your heart is set on this – this – harlot, then so be it. But, she will be the death of you, you mark my words."

Chapter Four

It was now Saturday, when Will had a number of private pupils for both classics and music lessons. He also had a regular round of golf, but today he could not settle to his normal routine. He instructed his first piano student to round up all the other boys and meet him at the church, and they would all have a lesson together at the organ. Despite Mary Bickerstaff's sound advice his plan had been to dispense with all his pupils in one fell swoop, and then to pay his respects at 34 Hope Street, although he had no idea how well he would be received, as it was a working day for them.

But his plan backfired somewhat, when the group of boys, who would separately have taken up four hours of his morning at the piano, had not only brought friends with them, but the whole gathering enjoyed their joint organ lesson so enthusiastically, that no time was saved at all. Will, in fact, also enjoyed the time spent in this way and was shocked to find that he had forgotten it was a ploy to allow him to go visiting. Every one of the boys, including some he did not know, wanted to help pump up the great organ, to hear the different stops being demonstrated and explained, to attempt to reach the foot pedals and hear, and feel, those resounding low notes. Those already able to play the piano, of course, were allowed to play hymn tunes for the others to admire. When eventually someone regretfully remarked that he had to be home for his dinner, the class broke up reluctantly, but with two new boys determined to ask their parents if they could have lessons with Mr. Waverley again.

Although he longed to clear his head with a round of golf, he had adult tuition commitments that afternoon, and he had promised to attend a private soirée in the evening at the rather prestigious home of his friends, Tom and Fanny Dodd. Between commitments, he tried to marshal his thoughts and plans. In a way, he felt that Agnes's decision to move away was her way of washing her hands of his affair. As he digested that, he felt liberated. She was the main stumbling block, he didn't care what anyone else thought about him, about Hannah, about anything. It was none of their business.

On Sunday, Will knew that he would see Hannah at church, but that he would never be allowed to have any time alone with her. Agnes would surely see to that. At the end of the morning service, he continued playing the organ until everyone had left the church, knowing that Hannah and her grandmother were the last of the congregation to leave. His frustration made him angry, he was not used to being manipulated, he was usually the one calling the tune in everything he did, and forcefully at that. But Mary Bickerstaff's words came back to him, and he begrudgingly accepted that she was probably right, and that if he could bear to be patient, the scandal-mongering would die down. It did make sense to go about his courtship in a decent manner, as becoming to people of breeding. So, he was trying to convince himself, but the word 'breeding' turned his thoughts back on themselves, to Hannah's body pressed against him, and he was resentful and impatiently angry again.

Agnes had hurried off home, but had left Christina to wait for him, as expected. He noted sadly that Hannah and Mary had drifted away with a group of other women, and he went obediently with his niece. Ever since Agnes's second child, Christina, had been born, Will had called her 'Baby,' and still did, although the girl was well on the way to her twentieth birthday. "Hallo, Baby," he said now, "let's go and get some dinner," and she put her arm through his. Sunday dinner had always been the one occasion when his family were able to spend some leisurely time together, with no classes or meetings, choir practices or golf, and he felt it best to go along with their usual routine in order to avoid Agnes's ire, if possible. Besides, he was hungry, and her roast beef was not to be missed. Will had never felt Sundays to be such a waste of time, but tried hard to look as if he was happily complying with tradition. Instead of their usual post-prandial stroll, he spent the afternoon in his room, preparing his class plans for school over the next few days, and thinking about Hannah.

She and her grandmother were at church again for Evensong, and he endured the service as well as he could, wondering if what happened afterwards would be a carbon copy of the morning. But when the time came, Mary and Hannah had stayed behind in the vestibule, and joined him as he left the church, just as Agnes and Christina also approached, having waited outside. Will shook hands with Mary, and saw Agnes flinch at their greeting as she hung back from joining them. In that way, he walked across the Market Place with Mary between him and Hannah, for the sake of decorum, as the grandmother whispered that Hannah had been driving her mad, pestering her to find some way for the lovers to be close to each other. But she still warned him to be patient, and he promised to try, thanking her as their ways diverged and they parted. He turned and allowed Agnes to join him for the rest of the way, although she declined to speak. Her silence was eloquent enough for Will.

∞∞∞∞∞

On the Monday, he started receiving letters. Some were horribly malicious, one actually claimed that Hannah was promised to him, but there was one, unsigned, that wished him luck! The two that did worry him a little, however, were the ones giving him notice that they would be removing their sons from his school. One gave reasons at length, but when he saw the signature, he was sorry for the boy who would be removed, as he was a tryer, who sometimes came to school showing evidence of bruising. My sister is not the only hypocrite in this town, he thought, and wondered if he should have referred the child's plight to some authority, a doctor, perhaps? But if he did that now, it would be construed as vindictive retaliation, and he had an unaccustomed feeling of shrinking from duty.

Feeling rebellious again, he now made a habit of calling at the grocery shop on his way to school, not caring who saw him or what they thought. From the Monday, Hannah was always there, and they had time for a few pleasantries, and for their hands to touch as she passed him his purchases and his change. He always made sure he would need change, when she would place the coppers in his palm, and stroke it with her fingertips. Only once did they steal a kiss, for the early morning was a busy time in the shop when the housewives called for their bread and provisions for the day. But a relationship was being established in the manner approved by Grandmother and, as she had predicted, the sidelong glances in the street died out after a few days.

The evenings early in the week were taken up with other commitments. Will had found so much musical talent and enthusiasm in and near the town, that he had started a philharmonic society. Some members met on Mondays, having formed a debating society, when they often discussed the music they were intending to perform for forthcoming concerts, then the following evening, they would put their ideas and interpretations into practice as the various instrumentalists joined forces. The outcome was normally exactly as William Waverley directed, but this week, he felt the need to acknowledge that there may be more than one side to some stories, and he allowed a number of variations and imaginative descants to be experimented with. All the musicians enjoyed this intercourse, and remarked to each other later how much Waverley's manner had softened. It was not long before they all knew the reason but, despite harbouring diverse opinions on the matter, not one member left the society.

Both Hannah and Will made a supreme effort to act normally at this Wednesday's choir practice, but Will was now so much happier than he had been for months, and had shed his exasperation with their timing in the new song they were rehearsing. He explained, much more patiently than usual, where the inflections should occur. "You are singing the words," he said, "but you're not reading them. Read the verse as if it were prose, and you'll understand the meaning, then you can sing it the same way as you would say it, and not just break it off at the end of every line. These are just songs, not hymns, you can leave those to the church choir!" After a full run through, he even complimented the singers, and everyone went home in a happy frame of mind. Except Will, of course, who was accompanied – chaperoned – by his niece, Christina; and Hannah, who knew the girl had been commanded to do so. She wondered how long she and Will could tolerate the situation, but knew she must let him take the lead.

∞∞∞∞

Next day, Will asked Mary if he might visit the house on Saturday evening and perhaps take Hannah for a walk, the holding hands one, he suggested.

Face The Music

Friday nights were choir practice nights in the church, accompanied by the organ, of course. Hannah would dearly have liked to be in the church choir, but the numbers were limited, and the places hotly defended, with a waiting list of people with more highly trained voices than hers. In any case, Friday was a busy evening for her, too, as she helped stock the shop with her grandmother for the busy weekend ahead. Mary boiled hams and prepared bacon joints during the day, and some of the cold ham had to be sliced up ready for sale. Huge cheeses were also brought to front of shop, ready to be sliced with the wire, as required. Their local supplier of butter and eggs delivered on Fridays, and butter was weighed out into pounds and half pounds and wrapped in grease-proof paper. Sugar, rice, lentils, barley and other dried goods were weighed out from sacks, and poured into stiff, blue paper bags. Hannah hardly had time to think about church choirs, or even about Will, except that, suddenly, now and then, she would remember all that had taken place between them, and her heart would soar.

Saturday was always a busy day for Will too, spent either at home at the piano, back at school for the extra Latin classes and so on, or in church for organ lessons, but several of the boys who had enjoyed the group lesson in the church the previous week had asked for the exercise to be repeated. He was always delighted with the lads who really wanted to progress, they reminded him of himself at their age, when he had been insatiable for knowledge and tuition.

The strains of the mighty organ made Saturday a joy, and the day passed pleasantly and quickly. Agnes, with plans to escape her intolerable predicament, had ceased hostilities and, so long as the despised name was not mentioned, managed to remain emotionlessly civil enough to prepare his meals as usual, and he enjoyed a lightly boiled egg for his tea. He knew the egg had not come from the Hope Street shop. Agnes had withdrawn her custom there, which was as much a relief to Hannah and her grandmother as it was to Agnes. But it was a nice egg, and he realised with a shock that if Agnes moved out, he would be without a housekeeper. He might even have to learn how to boil an egg himself! Or he could get married. Why did that thought punch him below the belt and thrill him right through?

∞∞∞∞∞

Having invited himself to the Bickerstaff home, he began to feel nervous about his first official appointment. Was he supposed to take a bunch of flowers? What could you take to someone who had everything in their shop? He racked his brain and stared around his room. Ah, would that be the thing? His eye had lighted on an anthology of poems. Well, they don't sell those in the grocery shop, he thought, and he placed it in his pocket.

Hannah rushed to answer his knock, and embraced him only briefly, as young Carrie had also rushed to gaze curiously at the schoolmaster, and she giggled when he bowed to her and said "Good evening, Miss Caroline, I trust you are well?"

He was ushered into the kitchen, where Grandfather was consulting a green coloured newspaper. "Mr Waverley has called to walk out with me, Grandpa," Hannah said loudly.

"Oh, are you here again?" said the old man, "there isn't any pie left."

Mary bustled through from the shop area, where she had closed up and cashed up, and heard this last remark. They all laughed at Grandfather's dry little joke. "That's quite all right, Mr Bickerstaff," assured Will, "I have had a lovely boiled egg for my tea tonight."

"We had boiled eggs. I did them!" chimed Carrie. "We didn't know whether to do one for you or not, so I didn't." Will was taken unawares by her candour, and answered too quickly.

"You did the eggs? That's wonderful. I shall know where to come when Mrs Lacey moves to Ramsey!"

He saw shock, consternation and incredulity on the women's faces, a blush on the child's, and Grandfather said "What?" but had already returned his attention to the sports pages.

"I will explain everything to Hannah as we walk," he said quickly to Mary, steering Hannah towards the door.

It was a pleasant evening, and they walked out past Hango Hill and skirted the golf course. Here, Will was hailed by one of his golfing friends. "It's true then, Waverley, you old dog," laughed the man, "we heard you were too busy being distracted to come for a round these days! How do you do, Miss Corlett? May I wish you both a very pleasant evening."

As they walked on, Will was feeling such a fool for having blurted Agnes's threatened move, as he was not sure he believed that she would actually move all that she had, her business and her boarders, just because of his liaison. He related all that had been said, and confessed how, although he loved his sister, he had felt liberated at the idea of being left to live the life he so dearly wanted.

Hannah held his hand, and squeezed it from time to time as he spoke, acknowledging that she understood. "Although all the harridans in town were casting aspersions on us, I do believe it was Mrs Lacey who was your major worry." She agreed. "All the same, she is your sister, and I am so sorry for you if she is determined to take such a drastic step. Oh dear, she must really, really hate me." They walked in silence for a while, both with their tumbling thoughts troubling them. Will had been about to tell her about the letters he had received, but realised that this would not be a good time. They simply added to his morose thoughts.

Suddenly, it occurred to him that this was the first time he had felt miserable since his initial encounter with Hannah. The thoughts of her had buoyed him up over all else, and brought him out of the despondency that was dragging him down, and he resented the fact that their first official appointment should be marred by his sister's venom. He pulled Hannah to him, embraced and kissed her and hoped the whole town, including Agnes, were watching. They had returned as far as Hango Hill and climbed the mound to gaze out to sea, and now he pressed her against the wall of the monument and kissed her mouth, her throat and all round her neck. She was crushed between him and the wall, and she wished the moment could last for ever. She shuddered with ecstasy as he licked her neck, breathed in her ear, and buried his face in her shoulder. "Oh, Hannah," he sighed, "I want you so much."

But, being the respectable citizen that he was, he allowed himself only this short interlude, before taking her hand and leading her back down to earth, along the promenade, round the harbour, heading back towards Hope Street.

Chapter Five

They strolled slowly, in silence, but frequently turning to gaze at each other. Then Hannah said, wistfully, "I've never been to Ramsey." Will told her he had been only a few times, it was such a long day out to get there and back, and still have time to see the town or do anything else, unless it was a long, summer day.

"We were living in Peel the first time we went," he began, then seeing a vacant bench on the harbour side, he sat, with his arm along the back of the bench, and indicated for her to sit beside him, while continuing with his story, "which was easier because there was a direct train, but when we went from Castletown a few years ago, we caught an early train to Douglas, got a horse tram along the promenade, and then took the electric tram on the new line to Ramsey. We had to get off the tram before reaching the town, though, because there is a deep ravine that it could not cross, and we were supposed to walk into the town by the road. However, where the tram stopped, there was a field on the cliff top, and we stopped to admire the view of the town and the whole sweep of the bay. It's very pretty, with its piers, promenade, whitewashed cottages, and the low hills of Bride in the background. It all spreads out just as it looks on the map."

"You paint a lovely picture with your words," breathed Hannah, "I dearly want to see the view from that field. Can we go, Will, please will you take me there?"

His arm had crept round her shoulders, and he squeezed her as he laughed at her childish excitement, then recalled the more recent visit in greater detail for her. "It was mainly an outing for the senior boys," he began, "to reward them for their hard work, then one or two of the lads who had younger brothers asked if they could come too, and it turned into such a party, that I persuaded Mrs Lacey and Christina to accompany us, to help supervise, especially with the smaller boys." Hannah was wondering how the boys may have felt about a day out with the hatchet-faced disciplinarian, but immediately rebuked herself for such unkind thoughts.

"After alighting from the tram at its terminus before Ballure, we explored that field and took in the view, and then we partook of the sandwiches that each boy had prevailed upon his mother to provide. There was plenty of running around and gay abandon, and a few noticed that we could scramble straight down onto the seashore, through the glen created by the ravine, and more than half of the lads voted vociferously for this course of action, in fact I believe one or two had already made a start down the slippery slopes. That's when Agnes stepped in and announced that any boys not happy with slithering around 'like wild Indians' could walk into the town via the road, with her."

"The 'wild Indians' option sounds more fun," said Hannah, her eyes shining, "tell me more." Will recounted the boys' excited scrambling, down into the glen and jumping across large rocks to cross over the river, with the inevitable wet foot for at least one of them. When they reached the shore, they spotted some rock caves, which had to be explored. They had a sandy beach at home, but the caves were much more exciting, and elicited squeals when there was talk of bats and ghosts and creepy crawlies. Some of them found sea creatures in the rock pools, and others enjoyed trying to skim flat stones into the waves lapping the shore. Some of the boys took off their shoes and socks and paddled in the shallows as they strolled the length of the shore to the pier head. They all marvelled at the iron girders of the pier which was so long that it seemed almost to disappear out of sight. They were all quite sad to leave the shore, but they trotted obediently along the promenade to the Market Place where they had agreed to meet up with the others. They stared at the hundreds of fish laid out on the cobbles, explored the other market stalls and inspected the harbour. Will told them about the swing bridge over the harbour, and how it had been constructed and installed, to save almost a mile between the main shopping centre and the north promenade. It was a marvel of modern technology, and he had hoped they might see the bridge open for boats to pass underneath, but the tide was out at the time, and all the boats lay against the harbour wall, their sails furled and masts leaning. Will explained that boys like that sort of thing, and they had written intelligently about it in school in the following days, some even drawing the swing bridge with surprising accuracy. Agnes and the other boys had been across the bridge and over to Ramsey's pleasure park, but now they all met up again in the Market Place. Then they still had to walk back up the hill to catch the Douglas-bound tram, and most of them were quite exhausted by the time they climbed aboard.

"Please, please take me to Ramsey, before Agnes goes there and spoils it!" blurted Hannah, immediately covering her mouth in apology. Secretly agreeing with her sentiment, Will ignored her outburst.

"They have built an impressive tram bridge at Ballure now, and the electric tram goes right into the town," he began, but Hannah was adamant that she only wanted to see the field he had described, and added excitedly that they must take a picnic there.

He told her he would never be able to refuse her anything, and promised that they would go to Ramsey as soon as it was possible. It would be the Whitsun holiday very soon, and he would try to arrange it then, as regular appointments were usually postponed on holidays.

While she had listened intently, and marvelled at how clever he was in making the boys' learning such fun, she was not interested in bridges, either for trams or horses or for ships to pass under. She was only interested in what she perceived as that Garden of Eden with the stunning view, as she was already forming a plan that involved temptation and forbidden fruit.

They were no longer alone, as other couples were also enjoying their Saturday evening stroll as couples do, although now and then there would be whispered remarks behind gloved hands. But soon they were back at No 34, where Hannah assured him they were expected back in the house.

He had not known what to expect, and was pleasantly surprised to find that Mary had prepared a light supper of pressed tongue sandwiches and cocoa, which she shared with them and Carrie in the parlour. They all chatted, getting to know more about each other, until it was time for Carrie to go off to bed. "Good-night, Mr Waverley," she hesitated at the door before asking, seriously, "Are you Hannah's boyfriend now?"

"Off to bed with you!" said Hannah, but the adults all laughed.

Face The Music

Will said, "I would like to think so, Carrie, would that be all right with you?" The child smiled shyly, nodded vigorously and scuttled off.

Mary was growing confident that it would be safe to allow the lovers some private time in her parlour so, after a further half hour of chatting amiably with them, she bade Will "Goodnight," indicating that she expected him to leave shortly.

After their first rush to embrace and kiss, Hannah began, shyly, "Will, you know you said you could never refuse me anything....?"

"I meant it, my love, I promise we shall go to Ramsey very soon."

"Oh yes, I must see Ramsey, and you already promised that, but I wanted to ask...." she blushed and inspected her finger nails, wondering if she should continue. He brought her fingers up to his mouth so that she had to look into his face, as he looked questioningly at her, inviting her to finish her request. "Would you consider...., oh no, I dare not ask it!"

"I would do anything for you, Hannah, I mean it. Whatever your heart desires....."

She took a deep breath. "Would you shave off your beard for me?"

He guffawed. This was not what he had expected. He didn't know what he did expect, had half wondered if she was going to ask him the very question he so wanted to ask her, but this was a surprise indeed. He was rather attached to his beard, it had been with him for many years. He cocked his head on one side and contemplated for several moments.

"I think it would make you look younger," she explained. "Not that I don't love you just as you are, but I think you might look like a new man!"

He could see that she might have a point, and looking a little younger might make their pairing a little less incongruous. He also knew that he had given her his word that he would not refuse whatever she might ask. Realising this had been rather rash, and feeling a slight reluctance to dispose of part of his identity, he knew he could not win.

"Well, I am a new man," he acknowledged, "and I admit to being nonplussed by your suggestion, but I cannot go back on my word. I did say I wouldn't refuse you anything, and I can see that in future I shall have to be more careful about my promises! Might I keep my moustache? Please?"

She could see that she had almost won, but considered the possible effect of the moustache with no beard, and found the idea quite acceptable. "Perhaps, to start with at least, then if it doesn't look right, that could go too at a later date!"

"Do we have a compromise?" he asked.

"I love you, Will," was all she would say, and they kissed good-night on their way to the door.

Now that they had 'an understanding' and were quite open about being seen out walking together, the whispering dwindled down to a few of the older gossips of the town. The 'new look' beardless Waverley gave them all something to think about for a day or two, but they were soon looking for tastier morsels of scandal. There were others, however, who held themselves to be of a different class, who simply refused to believe what they were hearing and ignored Hannah altogether. That group included Agnes, who was all the more convinced that her brother was on the road to hell when he appeared at her table almost clean-shaven after several decades of sporting a beard. This did not worry Hannah in the slightest. She was thrilled with his smart, new look, and she felt a little triumphant that he had complied with her very personal request. Her heart was set on marrying her man, and she was confident that he would ask her very soon. She had also begun to plan how their Big Day out to Ramsey would progress and was determined that, if he had not asked her by then, he would have done before they returned. Had he not said he could never refuse her anything?

∞∞∞∞

Will's busy life continued its fairly hectic routine, with his days at school, and most evenings taken up with various musical commitments and his private students. He had not realised how little time he had to spend on himself – or on his courtship. This was an unexpected cross-roads in his life, but it thrilled and excited him, and on any evening, he was welcome and expected at 34 Hope Street, either before or after his other appointments. On Saturday evenings, it was now commonplace for the pair to be seen walking out, along with many other couples, although Will could see that they thought his appearance among them amusing. He did not care. He began to realise that the loss of his wife and child in his thirties had deprived him, in a way, of a youth. The time when he should have been kept young by watching his own children growing up had been torn from him and plunged him into a middle age in which there was only work, and producing social events for other people, and their children.

He made his mind up to ask for Hannah's hand in marriage. He did not want to wait any longer. He doubted that there could be children for him now, he was probably too old, and certainly out of practice in the love-making department, but he knew Hannah made him feel so vibrant and alive, that he very much wanted to take her to his bed. Enough time had been wasted. He must do it now.

Before he went to sleep one night, he pondered about a meeting with Hannah's father, a man he had never had much to do with, simply because they attended different churches, and perhaps moved in different circles. He tried not to compare that fact with Agnes's disdain for 'tradesmen,' but whereas his own life was completely taken up with academic, church or musical activities, he was aware that William Corlett, the house painter, sometimes frequented the ale houses. An appointment with him could be an experience quite unlike any other. Will was not used to being nervous of other men, but he comforted himself with the thought that perhaps this was part of being young again. And being young again was so enjoyable and exciting. He must take the bull by the horns. He also had great hopes for the forthcoming Big Day out to Ramsey, anticipating that he and Hannah might be alone together for an entire day, and away from Castletown's inquisitive eyes.

∞∞∞∞

Hannah 'talked to him' all through one night, alone in her bed, working out what she must say to him when they went to Ramsey, and what he would say, and what would happen next. Then she would doubt the whole scenario and have to start again. She would begin with the same words, but what if he replied differently? What if he thought her too forward? What if he didn't want to get married? She was so aware of the effect that being close to him had on her, and she was fairly sure he felt the same inclinations. Fairly sure? She had to be very sure. Yes, she was quite sure. She was convinced that it was only because he was a gentleman that he had not pursued the same courses of action as her previous suitors. Yes, she knew very well that he wanted her. He had said so. "Oh Hannah, I want you so much," he had said, while their bodies clung together against the stones of Hango Hill, and she had wanted him to take her right then and there, with all her heart she would have welcomed his hand on her breast or behind her thighs, pulling her to him. But, he was a gentleman, damn him. In Castletown, he was a gentleman. So, all her dreams concentrated on the two of them being alone together, away from Castletown, as far away from Castletown as they could go. And as far away as possible from being forever the gentleman? That was The Plan.

Chapter Six

William did ask for an appointment to speak to Hannah's father. He knew full well that both of her parents were aware of the motive for his request, but had no idea how he would be received. From his own life experience, he felt he should take small gifts, and purchased a bottle of Castletown Ale and a bar of chocolate from Mr. Dodd's wine emporium, with a little encouragement from the proprietor, Tom Dodd, who was a golfing friend. "Good luck!" his pal had wished him on leaving, adding, "he's a pretty rough cove, your prospective father-in-law, tread carefully my old friend!"

His first impression upon being admitted to the Corlett home in Arbory Street, was that Mrs. Corlett, Hannah's mother, was the adult version exactly of little Carrie, of whom he was already fond. "Oh, ah, Good evening, Mrs Corlett, I, er...."

"Come in out of the draught, for goodness' sake," the woman was saying, and then shouted over her shoulder, "Billa! Somebody to see you." She ushered Will in to a back room, so similar to the rooms at Hope Street that he was almost nonplussed. Mr Corlett was even reading the newspaper, spread out on the table. But he rose from his chair when Will entered, and held out his hand. This was unexpected. "Good to meet yatlast," the man said, "We've been hearin all sorts." Will shook the proffered hand gratefully, and offered the beer, but did not sit until directed to do so in one of the fireside chairs while his host took the other, facing him.

"Well?" continued the father, inspecting the bottle, "say yer piece."

Feeling like that young man once more, Will was at a loss at first, but sensed that Corlett, unlike many others, was not antagonistic. The Carrie-lookalike mother hovered in the doorway. Her husband beckoned her to join them with a slight twitch of his head, and she sat down at the table. Will fished in his pocket and passed her the chocolate. She seemed embarrassed, and thanked him demurely.

"I know the whole town is outraged," began Will.

"Who?" demanded William Corlett. "Why?" Mrs Corlett inspected the chocolate bar, biting her lip.

"Because of our age difference...."

"We know about that. Yer owler than me, y'owl divil," said Corlett, "but in any case, it's herself y'll havtask – have yasked er?"

Will didn't know whether to laugh or cry. This sounded like approbation, approval, this was wonderful. He had not known what to expect, but it wasn't this amusing, almost friendly reception.

"I have not asked Hannah yet, but I am fairly confident that her answer will be favourable. I did not want to presume that she would have your permission, so thought I should ask you first," and then, just to clarify, "I love your daughter, Mr and Mrs Corlett, I have been so lonely for so long...."

"Hope ya know what yer lettin yerself in fer," said the man who was younger than Will but seemed to him a generation older. "She can be a spitfire ya know, allus gets what she wants does that'un."

Will smiled in agreement, then tried to recall the little speech he had rehearsed over and over. "Our paths have not crossed much before, Mr Corlett, but I am so pleased to make your acquaintance," and here he nodded also at Hannah's mother, noticing what a striking woman she still was, "and I am so pleased that it sounds as if you approve of my request for your daughter's hand?"

"What does Bickerstaff say?" asked the father.

Sensing some fellow-feeling, Will responded, "He usually says "What?" to anything, but I have not thought to ask Grandfather. D'you think I should? Mary is lovely, though, a very understanding and intuitive lady, and I believe we do have her blessing."

"Aye. She's a'right is Mary." said 'Billa' Corlett, and his wife smiled to the table top at this reference to her mother, and then also at Will.

"Aye," Father said again, "Put the wench out of her misery. Don't be expectin me to pay for the weddin though," he added.

"Oh, I had not thought that far ahead," admitted Will, "I can see no further than the end of my nose at the moment!"

"Enda yer dick, more like," responded the father, picking up his newspaper again, as Mrs Corlett gasped.

"How is our baby?" she asked suddenly, steering Will towards the door. "She is named after me, you know."

Grateful for her tactful change of subject, Will responded, "No, I didn't know that, Mrs Corlett, but you quite took me by surprise when you answered the door because you and Carrie are so alike, she is so pretty, and she is your image," and then, embarrassed by what he had said, "Oh, I'm sorry, I didn't mean...."

"Yes," said the mother, straightening her shoulders, "I was pretty once myself. Thank you for the chocolate Mr Waverley, as far as I am concerned, you are welcome in this family. We love Hannah too, and wish her the happiness that has eluded her for so long – she has been maligned and misused, and unhappy, but she has spirit and imagination, and she is too clever to be wasted working in a grocery shop. I always knew she was waiting for the right opportunity, and perhaps you are giving her that opportunity to spread her wings." She took his hands in hers and said, "God bless you both, William."

"Good-night, Sir. Good-night, Mrs Corlett, and thank you both for your kindness."

He heard the other man say "Pah!" as he left, and smiled to himself.

Outside the house, he wanted to run and jump for joy, and to shout out loud to the world that he was going to marry the loveliest girl in the world. Then he realised that he still had to ask her.

Hannah was expecting him at No 34, but he had only told her that he had 'an appointment,' so she would be unaware of the news he was bursting to tell her. He had already knocked at the door, however, when he heard the chatter and laughter of several voices, and his confidence quailed.

Carrie had run to answer the door and Hannah, on this occasion, had permitted the child to admit Will. As usual he greeted her formally and called her Miss Caroline, which always made her giggle and flush with pleasure, and she surprised him by announcing him at the parlour door, just as formally, to the gathering inside. The chatter ceased and all eyes turned to see the personage who, unknown to him, had been very much the subject of their conversation.

Hannah got up, and came towards him, gave him a peck on the cheek and took his hand. "This is William," she announced, turning back to the women in the armchairs. They all stared, and their tongues seemed to be frozen. Poor Will felt quite uncomfortable, but soon regained his composure by reverting to his normal, authoritative manner.

"Good evening, Mrs Bickerstaff," he greeted Mary and then, "I am honoured to meet you," he said, extending his hand to the next oldest lady. He had the uncanny feeling that he had met her before, and very recently, but looked questioningly at Mary, waiting to be introduced.

"William Waverley, this is my daughter, Emily Kaneen, and her daughter, Cissie." Emily shook his hand and nodded, as did Cissie, in her turn, as Mary continued, "as you can imagine Will, we were 'speaking of the devil' when you arrived, so you must excuse these two silly women, sitting there with their mouths open. Perhaps they were not expecting such a distinguished and well-mannered gentleman!"

"Oh, Gran, give over your teasing," said Hannah, laughing. "Aunt Em, this is the most wonderful man in the world, and you are both going to love him. Treat him nicely and he will write a song for you!"

"Really?" said Emily, now looking at Will in admiration. Still in some shock, but valiantly trying not to show it, she wondered why the obvious age difference had not been mentioned, but perhaps they would then have had a pre-conceived prejudice. They knew that poor Hannah had longed to meet the right man, and if this was he, then she was happy for them both. She would get used to the fact that he was even older than herself.

"Let's have some more tea," said Hannah, brightly, "Will, come and help me put the kettle on."

He knew this was a ploy to let the other women discuss what they had just discovered, but perhaps it was also an opportunity for a kiss and a cuddle. It was not, as Hannah's grandfather was at his usual post by the kitchen range, with newspaper on his knee, but slipping off, as the old man was nodding with his eyes closed – until he heard them enter the room.

"Ah, a man!" he said, "Welcome, brother, save me from the squawking hens in there."

Will was now on good terms with Charles Bickerstaff. "Have you left me any pie, Grandad?" he teased. Hannah rinsed out cups and saucers that had obviously already been used, and warmed the teapot while the kettle sang on the range.

"We had cake tonight," quipped the old man. "The hens brought it in. Em was always good at the baking - 'confrectionery' she calls it, I'm not sure what the difference is. Good though."

While Hannah took the tray of crockery into the parlour, Will quickly told the old man that he had spoken to William Corlett about marrying Hannah, and asked if they might have his blessing too.

To his surprise, Grandad also got up from his chair and offered Will his hand. "You're mad," he said, "but you're good for each other. We have noticed changes in both of you, and I wish you good luck, lad."

It was a night full of surprises, and Will was feeling happier than he had felt in over twenty years. When Hannah came back for the teapot, he took it from her and carried it into the parlour ahead of her. The women did not stop chattering this time, and he felt a breakthrough had been made. He was right, and Hannah's aunt and cousin were soon chatting with him as if they had known him for years. They passed a further half hour in general conversation, and eventually Will plucked up the courage to announce his news.

"Ladies," he began, "I have a very important announcement to make." There was a chorus of "Oooh!" and they all looked knowingly at each other. Hannah blushed and stared, holding her breath. "This evening," he continued, "I have obtained Mr and Mrs Corlett's permission to ask for Hannah's hand in marriage."

There was a general babble of delighted sentiments as they all spoke at once, before he mentioned that, of course, he still had to ask Hannah.

"Go on, then, ask her!" said Mary.

"Oh yes, let's hear it," echoed Cissie.

"On your knees!" demanded Emily. Poor Hannah didn't know where to look, but Will got up from his chair and reached for her hand.

Then he did as commanded and as was only right, bent down on one knee, and then got up again, feigning confusion. "Oh no! I can't do this without a ring. I haven't got as far as obtaining a ring!"

"Doesn't she have to say yes before you produce the ring?" asked Cissie. "It might be seen as presumptuous if you have it all ready in your pocket. And what if she says no? That would be the waste of a ring, wouldn't it!"

"Oh, do get on with it!" said Emily, "all this prevarication has us on the edge of our seats. Let's hear the answer before we worry about rings!"

Hannah was beaming, as her dreams were becoming reality. She could hardly believe it was happening, but having her grandmother and her favourite aunt and cousin right there to share the precious moment made it even more special than she could ever have imagined.

Will knelt again and said "Miss Corlett, please will you do me the honour of becoming my wife. Forsaking all others, will you keep yourself only unto me, so long as we both shall live?"

Hannah pretended to have to think about this, and then she said, "No."

There was a stunned silence, and then she laughed at Will's stricken face. "I will not keep myself only unto you as long as we both shall live – I will keep myself only unto you so long as I shall live."

∞∞∞∞

Charles Bickerstaff had heard the squeals of delight and a round of applause, so, assuming what had happened, he now appeared at the parlour door brandishing a bottle of sherry. "Get the glasses, Mother, it sounds as if there is something to celebrate." He kissed Hannah and shook Will's hand.

The sherry idea met with enthusiastic approval all round, except from young Carrie. "Ew, that's horibubble," she declared after only wetting her lips from her grandmother's glass, "I don't know how you could swallow it." She was yawning by this time, and announced that she would have to go to bed. She kissed everyone good-night, but hesitated when she reached Will. He took her hand and kissed that. "Ooh! That tickles!" she said regarding the moustache. Then, she bounded back to Hannah and said, "Can I be a bridesmaid? Pleeeease?"

Assured that she could, she trotted off to bed, although her grandmother doubted, in her excitement, that she would sleep. "You may come back down if we disturb you," she promised, knowing full well that both the disturbing and the coming back down were probably going to happen anyway.

The sherry bottle was soon empty, and more tea was brewed, as the question of a date for the wedding took on an urgency, so that new hats may be purchased. "How about your birthday in February, Hannah?" suggested one. "Not much of a time for a honeymoon," declared another, "And where will you live?" queried a third. But Will's head was just spinning. Hats? Weddings? Bridesmaids? Honeymoons? Houses? Everything was moving much too fast for him, and he grinned as he remembered William Corlett's remark about how far ahead he had seen. He admitted that his plans for the future had consisted only of fleshly gratification, and was realising how differently women approached such things.

Chapter Seven

Hannah was allowed to finish work early sometimes, so one afternoon, after school, Will and Hannah took the train into Douglas to look for an engagement ring. While they travelled, Will presented her with the anthology of poems that he had totally forgotten to give her in the excitement of their first time walking out together. And it had been exciting, he remembered every moment well, and the promises she had tricked him into making. The little coquette. He adored her. He had put a marker in the book at a poem by Christopher Marlowe, which began and ended with the words "Come live with me and be my love," which sentiment was now suffusing his whole being. His days at school, evenings so busy, and far too brief moments with his Love were only things to pass the seemingly interminable time until he would be able to take her in his arms for ever. Hannah's February birthday had been settled upon as a 'decent' length of time to wait, but not only did he not want to wait, he felt less and less like being 'decent,' and he found the waiting, and the self-control, tedious.

Hannah read the poem, pointed out that it mentioned a May morning, and reminded him that the coming weekend was Whitsuntide, and they were Going to Ramsey on Monday, when for the whole day she would 'live with him and be his love.' Because they both had secret hopes for that Big Day out, they were glowing with giddy anticipation. She flicked the pages of the poetry book, and found Shelley's poem about Love's Philosophy. "As the sunlight clasps the earth," she read aloud, "and the moonbeams kiss the sea – What are all these kissings worth, if thou kiss not me?"

She looked up and found that all the other passengers were staring at her and Will. Then one of them broke the silence by saying that he liked the one about the daffodils, whereat another chimed in with the Autumn one, and then "Tyger, Tyger burning bright," and a general chatter comparing lines of poetry filled the rest of the journey companionably.

At the jewellers, Hannah could not decide on a ring, looked at her hard worked hands and declared that, after all, a wedding ring was all she wanted. Will was perplexed, and began to survey the gold bands, but her eye fell on a pair of aquamarine ear-rings. "Oh Will, those are just beautiful, and just my favourite colour," she wheedled. She held one up to an ear, so that it caught the sun from the doorway as it dangled against her neck, and he knew he was going to fall for her tricks again.

"Whoever heard of engagement ear-rings?" he smiled, but she knew they were already hers, and declared that it would be their secret. They would know that the jewellery represented their pledge, but no-one else would suspect or be able to make any remarks, complimentary or otherwise, as they might of a ring, and she was tired of hearing the 'otherwise' type said about her. "Silly girl," he said and handed over the money.

While they were in Douglas, they paid a visit to Emily Kaneen, where they had been assured that they would always be welcome. Will was introduced to her husband, John, and the few of the large family who happened to be home by then, and they were invited to stay for tea. The youngest children, Ada and William, had put their homework away to come and stare at Will, who, being so used to dealing with children, put them at their ease, asking about their school work and offering advice. As Cissie and other brothers came home from work, they too made acquaintance with Will and all found him a 'regular good chap.'

After tea, someone started to play the piano and so began an evening of party pieces, songs, piano duets and recitations, with some reading from the new anthology, until Hannah looked at the clock and declared they must hurry now to catch the last train home. Now that it is light until so late, we don't realise the time, it was agreed, and the party, reluctantly, broke up.

The train home was almost full, and Hannah sat in the corner of a compartment, while Will sat close with his arm around her shoulder. It was convenient to sit this way, as the carriage was crowded. His spare hand held hers in her lap, and he longed to let it wander across her waist and under her blouse. Now that they were engaged, he was plucking up the courage to explore the delicious possibilities if only the opportunity would present itself. He wished that everyone else in the carriage would get off at the first stop, but nobody did, and he felt that all eyes were watching his surreptitious stroking of her hands, as he allowed the rhythmic rocking of the train to make gentle movements in her lap. She was sitting demurely with her eyes closed, enjoying every second. He hoped they would be more private on their long journey on Monday, and he could hardly wait for the Big Day to come.

The next few days seemed to drag interminably, but Will made time to visit a small antique shop that was actually the front room of a cottage on Queen Street. He had noticed jewellery in the window when he had passed that way some time previously, but had not given it any more thought at the time. That was Before Hannah, before time began, beyond living memory, but he was sure he remembered a certain item that had been on display, and he was impatient to see if he remembered correctly, and if the item was still available. He peered through the mullioned window, and saw the elderly shopkeeper peering back at him. She was beckoning him to enter the tiny room, and for a moment the story of Hansel and Gretel crossed his mind. He hesitated on the threshold, but the bony finger was still beckoning, and he was obliged to duck his head to enter the low-beamed parlour. "Come into my magnificent emporium," she cackled, "it is an Aladdin's Cave of priceless treasure."

Noticing that the aquamarine ring was no longer in the window where he thought he had seen it, he explained his quest. "Ah, you have a discerning lady," the crone crooned, "with beautiful blue eyes, no doubt." He confessed to her that his fiancée had thought her poor hard-working hands unfit for a delicate ring, but he was sure that the one he had seen would change her mind. "It must have had your lady's name on it, young man," she winked at him, "another customer asked to see that ring only a few days ago, which is why I had to take it from its display, but he was reluctant to pay the price I have on it." Will had never been a rich man, and his heart sank a little at this news. But at least he had not told Hannah about it, so had not been coerced into promising anything. He smiled at the thought of her, and asked what price the woman did want. He was surprised at the figure she quoted, and asked if she knew why the previous customer had not been happy with that. "Because," and she winked at him again, "that's not the price I quoted him. I just didn't like the look of him, the way he held it up looking for flaws." She fished about and found the ring. Holding it up to what little light pierced the tiny window frame, he saw it sparkle, just as Hannah's ear-rings had done, and he knew it was perfect. "This stone," she pointed out, "is not perfect, it has a tiny flaw, but it is at the back of the stone, against the setting, and it makes it look as if it has more facets than it has."

"This ring," said Will, "IS perfect. I love it myself, and I am sure Hannah will love it too."

The woman wanted to know who Hannah was, and was intrigued when he told her, as she was a customer at the Bickerstaff shop. She already knew William Waverley, everybody knew him, and she knew that he had been a widower for many years, but thinking of taking a wife who was so much younger was a concept she thought very brave. "Well," she decided, "if you love the ring, and she doesn't, she will not be the woman for you, will she! You should only need to bring it back if it doesn't fit her finger, but I know the girl, and I think it will. I wish you success and happiness, in fact" and she looked into his eyes for a long moment, "I assure you of both, and you will have children. I may not live to see them, but when you do, remember me, Dorothy Kinrade. Good Luck, young man, make the most of this belated happiness."

∞∞∞∞

Having the ring in his pocket made him all the more impatient for Monday to come. He hoped he would be able to contain himself on their walk out on Saturday night, as he didn't want to spoil the surprise on the Big Day. To keep himself from jumping the gun, he left the tiny box on his bedside cabinet, so that he could look at the ring a few more times before he gave it to her.

This was how Agnes, delivering freshly laundered pyjamas to his room, came to know that her brother was well and truly bedevilled. Had he already asked her, or when was he going to do it? Ugh, she shuddered, still having difficulty believing that he would go through with it. What was wrong with men? Their father had gone off the rails, chasing after a younger woman, Richard had seemed incapable of behaving decently, even though she had given him two children. Surely that was enough for any man? Were they all just animals? "Ugh," she said out loud, imagining her darling brother in flagrante delicto with that tuppenny tart, "No, no, no!" and it was all she could do to stop herself taking the ring box and flinging it out of the window. What she could not stop herself from doing, however, was to take a peep at the contents of the box, certain that the ring would be a tasteless, monstrous, expensive affair. She was taken aback on seeing the understated single aquamarine. It was charming, disappointing, and very nearly softened her stony heart as she had to admit to herself that William must be deeply in love. Well, of course, he would have chosen that ring, not her, he had nice taste. Agnes was a tiny bit envious, and she hated the infernal woman even more. "Oh, Ramsey, here I come," she vowed.

∞∞∞∞

Their Saturday evening walk was taken up entirely with their plans for Monday. Hannah had promised to provide the picnic, but would leave studying the travel timetables to Will. They would make a good start, and follow the same plan as Will had described taking with the school, starting out from Castletown on the early train. She insisted that she only wanted to go as far as 'that lovely field,' not admitting to him that, in her imagination, it was the Garden of Eden. Will thought that, if they were back in Douglas early enough, they might have their tea in a café there, and Hannah thought this must be how royalty felt.

They had taken their now usual route, which allowed them to stop at Hango Hill, but tonight they were disappointed to find another couple already lounging on the grass and leaning against 'their' wall, but Hannah also sat down on the ground at a discreet distance from the other young people, and lay back on the grass, inspecting the clouds. Will sat down behind her, so that she could lean against him, and she described the shapes in the sky and how they kept changing, as he stroked her hair and her neck, feeling the dangling ear-ring against her skin. This was a pleasant distraction reminding him that they were engaged, and he found that she did not flinch, except for a furtive glance at the other couple, when he slid his hand around her waist and cupped her breast, caressing it with his thumb. She did stop him when he more boldly attempted to pull up her blouse, but he contented himself, for now, with stroking, now her breast, and now her abdomen, and now her thigh. By this time, he was leaning over her, and kissing her upside down, whereupon they both fell over, laughing. The other couple glanced at them briefly, but were also intent on their own explorations in the semi-privacy of the site, overlooking the bay.

Returning for biscuits and cocoa at No 34, Will asked Grandfather about the weather forecast for the holiday on Monday, and they told the old folk about their plan to visit Ramsey. "Don't tell Carrie," warned Hannah, "or she will want to come too," then realising how this could be interpreted, especially by her all-knowing grandmother, she added, "it would be a long day for her. Perhaps we could take her to that new Silverdale place tomorrow afternoon as a treat, instead." She looked at Will pleadingly. "Help me!" her eyes told him.

Being a spur of the moment cover-up of their intentions for Monday, they had not discussed this before, but Will thought it would be a good way to absent himself from the icy silence of his home that was his usual Sunday penance. Grandmother's famous eyebrow was eloquent, she nodded, and advised them that Carrie already had plans to go on the train to Port Erin for the day on Monday with her little friends and one or two mothers. She would be far better entertained on the beach.

Having dived in with an excuse, Hannah now felt annoyed with herself, as she and Will would be out together, but have Carrie to look after as well all Sunday afternoon. But, as it turned out, they all had a lovely time at the pleasure park, pushing the girl on swings and roundabouts, and all taking a boat out on the lake. Will bought them all ice creams before their walk back into Castletown, and was Carrie's hero for ever. They passed through Rushen Abbey grounds, then followed the banks of the Silverburn all the way back to Castletown, Will and Hannah holding hands as Carrie trotted back and forth finding primroses in the grass, or watching the swallows darting over the water and seeing fish jump in the river, ending up for more swinging in Poulsom Park. They were only just back in time for Evensong.

Will had been obliged to confess to Agnes about his outings planned for both days, which he approached with some trepidation, as historically, they had always gone out as a family on holidays, but she was tight-lipped and dour. Douglas was now away at university, and some of her pupils would be finishing their schooling this term, including Christina, and it seemed that their days of holiday leisure *en famille* were all in the past. Agnes was imagining the lovely ring being placed on the strumpet's fat finger, and the only remark that escaped her was a click of the tongue. "Tch!"

Chapter Eight

The day dawned at last. Both Hannah and Will had expected to toss and turn all night in anticipation, but the excitement and planning, and the afternoon in the open air being active with a child, had exhausted them and they both slept extremely well. Will always woke early for his organ practice before breakfast, and he did not forsake this precious routine, but offered up some silent prayers from his organ stool. He had every intention of offering prayers of penitence by the next day, but it all depended on Hannah.

Hannah was busy preparing their picnic. They would be using public transport for most of the journey, but she was mindful that the picnic basket had to be carried from home to railway station, and from train terminus to Douglas Promenade to catch a horse tram, and she didn't want Will to be wearied from carrying a heavy load. She had other plans for channelling his energy. She had no idea how energetic a man in his mid-fifties could expect to be, but thought it safer to assume he might not bound around like a teenager. But he had seemed, all along, to be enthusiastic about this day out together, and she felt a stirring in her body that demanded she take some deep breaths to calm herself. They were betrothed now, so there was nothing wrong with their being alone together, but first, there were things she had to tell him, and she rehearsed, yet again, what she had to say.

Grandmother, bless her, had been up even earlier, as usual, and had made them some fresh bread rolls. She also donated two small bottles of ginger beer towards the feast, and prepared hard boiled eggs. Hannah divided up some of a meat loaf, and took three oranges from a wooden crate, using a handful of the wood shavings to protect the goods and bottles in the basket. She wrapped a quarter of cheese, and tore off a corner of the grease-proof paper to make a twist for some salt. This was a meal fit for a king. For her king. For her husband.

Two oranges went in the basket, and Hannah ate the third with her breakfast, smoothing some of the juice behind her ears, as she often did. She would not wear her engagement ear-rings today, for fear of losing them, and instead inserted her everyday pearl studs. She was wearing a high-necked, white blouse with a lace insert and tiny pearl buttons, a tight cummerbund and a long, dark blue, tiered skirt and two petticoats. She chose shoes suitable for walking in a field, she hoped, and was quite satisfied with her appearance in the cheval looking glass in her bedroom. She wondered if she would be looking at the same woman ever again. She hoped not.

∞∞∞∞∞

Even though it was an early train, the carriages were crowded with townsfolk off to enjoy their holiday, and Hannah contented herself with watching the scenery they were passing by. She had travelled this way numerous times in her life, but today everything looked so much more interesting, the trees coming into new leaf, sheep with baby lambs at heel, cows with little replicas of themselves frolicking in groups. They passed through a wooded area, where the light fell only fitfully through the trees, darkening the bluebells carpeting the forest floor to the exact shade of her skirt, and their fragrance came through the open window, mixed with the oily, smoky steam from the engine ahead. How full of life everything seemed, with the sun shining from a cloudless blue sky and a day stretching out ahead of them. On such a day, anything could happen, the world might change for ever.

At Douglas, they left the station and walked along the quayside, and round onto the promenade to wait for a horse tram. A few other passengers were doing the same and, for a nasty moment, Hannah envisaged the Garden of Eden being crowded too, which was definitely not in the plan. The first horse that arrived was called William, and they thought this a very good sign. When they remarked on it to the driver, he said, "He's a good horse, is William. Fast." Definitely a good sign, go William, fast as you like! They passed several others going the other way, and having noticed their interest, the conductor told Hannah and Will each of their names. She was sorry to hear that there was not one called Hannah in their current stables. There was an Agnes, but Hannah didn't want to know about her. She imagined it would be a sour and bad-tempered animal!

The horse took them all the way to the terminus for the electric railway to Laxey and Ramsey – or up the island's only mountain, Snaefell, if they so wished. It would be a fine day to do that, but that would have to wait for another time. They had their whole lives ahead of them, and it had to begin according to The Plan. Neither of them knew that the other had A Plan, each kept their own secret, and neither did they realise that most people who saw them assumed they were father and daughter.

They boarded the Ramsey-bound tram, which had a bench seat all the way along each side and, once again, Will placed his arm around Hannah's shoulders. When the conductor asked them if they were 'going all the way,' they looked at each other and giggled. Will saw the passengers on the opposite bench looking askance at them, realised what they were thinking, and quipped, "This is my Granny!" This seemed to lighten the atmosphere and the journey was spent in jovial conversation with all and sundry, although, happily, all people they did not know.

Many passengers left the tramcar at Laxey intending either to change to the mountain railway, or to visit the Great Laxey Wheel or one of the many other attractions of the village. New passengers joined them, heading for one of the spectacular Northern Glens, or for Ramsey. Hannah was amazed at the views from the tram, the line in places seeming to be perched on the very edge of the rocky cliffs, and she felt like a child, staring about her in wide-eyed wonder. As they turned inland again, while the scenery was still breathtaking, she knew they were getting ever nearer to their destination, and she felt very much more a woman, as her plans raced through her head over and over again.

The car stopped for some passengers to alight at a crossing called Belle Vue, and Will pointed out why it was so called. "There it is," he pointed ahead, "that's Ramsey, Shining by the Sea. What do you think?"

She had heard the song about Ramsey Town at a concert somewhere, but it was not in the Southern Singers' repertoire. She recognised the sentiment, however, and she craned her neck to see more. "Just a few more moments," Will assured her, "and we will see it properly, in all its glory!"

"We're going to walk along the shore," Will lied to the other passengers as they got off the tram, and they were wished a good day.

"Are we?" said Hannah, watching the noisy vehicle trundle off over the new bridge, "I thought...."

"Not unless we get very bored, my Love," he replied, "I just said that, in case anyone thought it a good idea to get off here too. We wouldn't want that, would we!"

"Oh, you're wicked," she replied in relief, "Wicked, Wicked Waverley!" She pushed him playfully as he picked up the picnic basket, then she hitched up her skirts and ran ahead of him into the little paddock that had been at the centre of her dreams for over a month. At first glance, it was disappointing, there were no apple trees, for a start, but then she took in the view and ran closer to the cliff edge to drink it all in. A couple of schooners in full sail were crossing the bay, which drew her eye northwards to a long, iron pier. Beyond that there were two more, shorter piers, and landward were the white buildings of boarding houses and hotels. Sure enough, the coastline swept round the bay exactly as she had seen on the map of the island, and low hills rose up between the town and the furthest point on the horizon. All was bathed in sunshine, and Hannah was captivated. For several minutes, she simply drank in the view, before realising that this was the perfect place for The Plan to be put into action. It was, truly, the Garden of Eden.

Will stood back, just watching her, watching her fall in love with the view he had described to her, and knew this would always be a special place. He thanked God for her reaction, and was now confident that his own Plan could come to fruition at last. If only..... his only reservation was that he had not made love for over twenty years, and was not sure exactly how things would work out. Once again, it all depended on Hannah, but he was as excited as a teenager. He could not remember being this impatient for intimacy, ever in his life. When he was a young man, he would not have dreamt of expecting Ellen to do this until they were married. She had not given him the kind of signals that Hannah did, with her searching kisses and writhing body. But then, as rumour had it, Hannah was experienced, and knew how to stimulate him. Oh yes, she knew how.

∞∞∞∞

Now that the moment had almost arrived, Hannah found that her heart was thumping and her mouth was dry. It must also be at least noon, so she asked Will if it was time to open the picnic basket. After seeing the view, that was what they had come for, wasn't it, and she could really do with a drink? They found a large shrub, quite close to the edge of the cliff, alongside a huge rock, both of which afforded them some shade and a little privacy, should that be needed, although the place was totally deserted. He unscrewed the lead stopper of one of the bottles for her, and looked in the basket for a glass. She laughed, and explained that their rustic fare did not run to a silver service, they must use their fingers to eat with, and drink straight from the bottle but there was a bottle each if he didn't care to share! He declared that he wanted to share everything with her, every morsel, every moment, every emotion. He kissed her savagely. His Plan had no specific timetable, but eating was not his priority, and he had imagined a leisurely picnic, but not yet.....

Whereas, unaware that he had a Plan, hers, she found, was changing by the moment. She took a long draught of the beer, but then so needed to belch, that she couldn't stop it happening, and she covered her mouth and spluttered with laughter. He laughed too, and threw himself on top of her, rolling over and over on the grass, still laughing. He was mightily aroused by this cavorting, and was desperate to continue right there and then, but she got up, wagged a finger at him and told him they needed sustenance, and he must behave himself. She returned to their flattened patch, and reluctantly, he followed. She divided up the meat loaf, offering him the half that was still in the wrapping. "Your silver platter is a bit limp, I'm afraid," she said, and burst into giggles again. Did she know that he felt anything but limp? "Here, have some nice crispy fresh bread to smarten it up."

He had taken a swig from the bottle, and also needed to burp. "This stuff is all gas," he pretended to complain.

"Oh, it must be a man!" she chortled. And so on the banter went.

"This is delightful cheese," said Will, when he had, resignedly, calmed down a little, "Where do you obtain it?"

Hannah told him about the farm at Pooil Vaaish that supplied their eggs and milk. "Mrs Costain makes all her own butter and cheese, and ours is the only shop she brings it to. We can sell all she can make of both, so you are honoured to have been afforded a chunk of that!" Hannah was beginning to wonder if Mary had put something more potent into the ginger beer. They were both so full of giggles and nonsense, could it just be holiday high spirits? Even the idea made her laugh out loud again, and she took a hard boiled egg, and, staring into Will's face all the while, bashed her egg against the rock and peeled the shell from it. He saw its naked whiteness, and found he had difficulty breathing, but when she slid half of it into her mouth, he thought he might expire altogether. She came up close and pushed the other half of the egg into his mouth. Mouths full of egg, their lips met and he felt sure this was the moment at last. But she drew back again, yet again.

"Will, there is something I have to tell you," she began, her mouth still full of egg.

"There is no need, my darling," as his trembling hand reached the hem of her skirts," I don't care if you are not...." and here she tucked her legs underneath her and put her finger to his mouth to stop him, just as she had on the occasion that had started it all.

He was beginning to get a little frustrated with all these false starts. She was just teasing him, surely, and while it was exciting to get a little closer each time, he was wondering how long it had to go on.

"No, Will, I have to explain," she begged. "I need you to understand and to believe me." He sighed, and withdrew his hand from her skirt's hem and folded his arms, as she told him about the former suitor, how she had thought herself fond of him, and how 'it' had almost happened, but that she was not happy with the pawing and the groping. Then, having rejected the fellow, he had spread rumours about her, which had been believed, and therefore she had 'a reputation,' which although unjustified, had almost destroyed her.

While she was speaking, he looked as if he was listening, but also began stroking her knee, and her thigh. That was when she told him how long she had been in love with him, playing out their fantasy affair in her lonely bed for years. And she confessed that she had planned to yield to him today, here in this beautiful field with the lovely view, but that now the time had come, she was nervous. "But with you, Will, I long for you to touch me in those ways, I want you to do it all, I have wanted you for so long, and it has to be you. It has to be you. But I don't want you to think I'm a trollop!"

"Oh, my precious darling trollop," he laughed, "I believe you have found the one derogatory word that Agnes hasn't called you!" and he told her that he had also planned to try and 'go a bit further' with her here, today, and how she inflamed his passion, and he felt that their anticipated wedding date in February seemed an eternity away.

"But, what if I were to get pregnant?" she asked.

"Oh, I'm sure I'm too old to be dangerous! But in any case, we are already engaged, we will be married, sooner or later – sooner would suit me just fine!" he assured her.

To his delight, he noticed that she had begun to unbutton her blouse, and when she then unlaced her bodice, her breasts were liberated, and he remembered his dream about the oranges. He could not stop himself diving at her and burying his face between them. He kissed her mouth, her neck, her breast, wound his tongue around a nipple, and she gave a little moan. "Oh God," he groaned, "I have to have you, Trollop, you can't tease me this way with impunity!"

He also knew that he would not be able to control himself much longer, she appeared to be willing, eager even, and his fingers were all fat thumbs as he wrestled with his buttons. He somehow kept himself from biting her breasts, while his free hand pulled up her skirts. Finding that her legs were stocking-free, and she still was not discouraging him, he could contain himself no longer. The moment had come at last. She was panting too, and gripping his shoulders so hard that he could feel her nails digging into him through his shirt. He had believed for so long that Hannah was what Agnes called 'damaged goods,' without caring in the slightest, he only knew that he wanted her, and with all the talking, he was simply on fire and could wait no longer. Her gasp was more of a slight sob as he lunged, and he knew immediately that she had told him the truth; she was a virgin – or until now, she had been – and a few seconds of this realisation was just more than he could bear. He uttered such a great roar, and an expletive that she had not heard him use before, that she was alarmed. He collapsed across her, feeling like an idiot. "Hannah, my darling, forgive me, you trollop, you witch, I fear I am already spent. What on earth must you think of me?"

Chapter Nine

She did her best to understand, while also wondering if that was how it always was, and if that was all there was to it. Her heart was still thumping. "Well," she faltered, "if a sort of scalding dampness 'down there' means being spent, then perhaps I am already spent, too." She was feeling a little disillusioned, but then realised that he really had wanted her, in the way that he had said, and that now he was hers. He was her man, and this was what she had wanted, wasn't it?

Hannah had heard women say that 'it' was something that seemed far more important to men, and began to wonder if it was true. Was pawing and mauling and gasping the extent of it? She had found her quilt more exciting, and had felt sure 'it' should be more mutually rewarding.

He apologised over and over, realising that, contrary to popular belief, she had not known what to expect, and he promised her that it would never be like that again. He had just been so overcome that it was happening at last. "Believe me, that was not how I planned it, but I thank you so much, so very much, for trusting me with your precious body, and proving your love, and that you.... oh, my sweet love, you have been so maligned. What a disaster for your first time, but when I get my breath back, with your permission, I would like to try and show you how it is supposed to be."

This sounded encouraging, so to mask her confusion and apprehension, she sat up and reached for the picnic basket. It was closer to him, and he took out the two oranges. He held them up close together at his chest and said "This is you, Mistress Nell Gwyn, Trollop extraordinaire."

She grabbed one of the oranges from him and bit savagely into it without peeling it. "And this is you, Mr Wicked Waverley!" The allegory made him quiver with excitement. He was puzzled that, for an inexperienced girl, she seemed to know how to push all the teasing buttons. Or was she truly unaware how easily a man could be inflamed?

They lay back on the grass, eating the fruit and staring at the sky, each with emotions choking them, and unable to speak for a while. Then Hannah said, "Ramsey is very beautiful, and will always remind me of this very special day. It's a pity it's such a long journey to get here. We could do with being able to stay overnight, if we were to come again some time, so that we could spend longer looking round the town. Ooh, tell you what! When Agnes comes up here to live, we could stay with her!"

The idea was so ludicrous that they both guffawed, and then found they could not stop laughing. He turned to her to kiss her and they rolled over in the grass again, kissing and laughing. He was re-aroused as they rolled, and then he found he was able to take full advantage of the opportunity. Her breasts were still exposed, and his buttons still undone, and this time there was no virginal resistance. They were both panting, and she was thrusting her body up to him in time with his gasps.

"Oh, ... you are not..... too old.... at all!" she gasped, "I want you.... to make me pregnant," she was breathing hard, "give me a baby, Will,.... do it,.... do it all,... I want.... to have your baby.... I want...." and he knew that this time, justice was being done properly. Then, as he surged at the last 'I want' he felt as if he might have spawned an entire cricket team. It had never been like this before, for him, any more than for her, and he wanted to stay there for ever, coupled as they were still. They lay panting for a few minutes, and Hannah closed her eyes. This must have been what her grandmother had meant by 'delicious moments.' She saw herself surrounded by babies, each one representing a lovemaking such as this had been, and she thought it was no wonder that there were so many children in the world. Her disappointment had been a very temporary thing, and she understood, in a way, that his previous loss of control was rather a compliment. She had not realised she could drive him to such an extreme and uncontrollable level of desire!

When she opened her eyes again, Will was lying across her, but was so still and quiet that for a moment of horror, she thought he was dead. "Will!" she gasped. and stroked his hair. He stirred, and opened his eyes.

"Aargh, I thought I had died and gone to Heaven!" He rolled onto his back, then raised himself on one elbow, and surveyed the wreckage of his handiwork. Some of her hair had escaped from its pins, and a couple of tendrils clung damply to her temples. Her breasts were still exposed to the sun, her skirts bundled up around her thighs, and one shoe was missing. He looked down at himself and said "God. Give me strength!" But God told him that it would take a little longer this time.

He reached down, found her shoe and gently fitted it back on. Then he straightened her skirts, and pushed back her hair. He had no idea how to go about lacing up her bodice, and knew he dare not fumble around in that area, or they may never get away from this magical place. He found his jacket and secretly reached for the ring box, then, while Hannah did up her blouse, he gathered the debris of their picnic and replaced it in the basket, keeping aside only the second bottle of ginger beer.

She stood up now, and pinned her hair up again as well as she could, and only Will could see the difference in her from the girl who had stepped off the tram only a few hours ago. Before she could pick up the basket, she saw Will go down on one knee again. "I know you said you did not want a ring," he began, "but this afternoon you became my wife – perhaps even the mother of my child – and you will now love, honour and obey me!" When he opened the box, tears came into her eyes and rolled down her cheeks. She was unable to speak, and he took her in his arms while she regained her composure. Then he took her hand and placed the ring on her finger. It fitted perfectly.

"It is so beautiful," she whispered, "I don't deserve...." He stopped her with another kiss.

"You are so beautiful," he corrected, "and you deserve the world. I can't give you the world, but I saw this and felt sure it would match the ear-rings you loved." He opened the second bottle of ginger beer, tipped it towards her and said, "To my wonderful fiancée, the girl of my dreams, my lover," and he drank, and then passed the bottle to her.

"To my lover,' she smiled, "Father of my baby, lots and lots of babies!" And she drank, and then had an attack of hiccups.

"We had better think about catching the next tram back," he warned, once she had held her breath long enough.

She leaned back against the rock, pulling him with her, then she kissed him hard, parting her lips and inviting his tongue. "You make me so happy, Will. I went to heaven, too, and I do so want your babies," she confirmed, "Let's just make sure of it!" She put her hands behind him and pulled him against her, so that she was crushed against the rock. Pulling up her skirt, she urged him to take her again, like this. Now the button-fumbling delighted them both, and she was pushing herself against him and then pulling him into her. "Will, I so wanted this to happen, that first evening on Hango Hill," she confessed.

"Oh, so did I," he agreed, "and every day since," and once more they experienced 'delicious moments.'

As they reluctantly pulled apart eventually, they were interrupted by a voice from above them. "Chackat.tt.tt.tt.t!" it said. They both looked up, startled, and saw a magpie on the top of the rock. "Oh my goodness, 'The Thieving Magpie!'" said Will, "Keep your ring safe or he will have it taken away to his nest!"

"Oh, Will, it's only one magpie – One For Sorrow! She looked stricken, but then the bird hopped off the rock and flew towards a thorn tree, where its mate greeted it. "Oh, no, it's not alone. Look, Will, It's Two For Joy!

∞∞∞∞

What a day, they agreed, when they were comfortably seated on the Douglas-bound tram at about 4 o'clock. For the holiday, there were extra tramcars in service, and this time they boarded Tram 20, which was one of the new 'winter saloons.' It had upholstered seats in pairs, and they were lucky enough to find one left unoccupied, immediately in front of a dividing partition, which afforded them privacy from behind. Being on the left hand side, it was closer to the sea and took in the views from the cliffs.

Where Hannah had been nervous on the outward journey, she found they were now even closer to the edge of the cliffs, with a sheer drop to one side, down to the rocks and the sea far below. But she wasn't nervous now. With Will's arm around her, she was not afraid of anything.

Once again, she noticed everything around her, and pointed out wild goats perching on the brooghs, and primroses in the verges. They did not chat with other passengers as had been so easy in the vehicle whose seats faced each other. These seats were arranged for everyone to face the direction of travel, and it felt more private that way. Just the way they wanted it to be. Hannah kept admiring her ring, and felt like pinching herself to be sure she was not dreaming all this. After all, she had dreamed this day over and over so many times, but she had never imagined that everything could be so perfect. The only flaw was that it could not be like this every day. How could she wait for another holiday? When would there be one? Tynwald Day, perhaps, but that was weeks away. She set to plotting when and how she would be able to see Will so privately again, as she was eager to repeat today's performance any day. Every day. Ten times a day!

Will was having similar thoughts, but in fact was a step ahead. He knew he could not take Hannah to the home he shared with his sister, but Agnes was going to be leaving for Ramsey in a couple of months. He would not need that large house, even when he was married, so he would look around for an apartment where he would be able to entertain his lover privately, perhaps even take her to his bed. Today's exploits, however, had been so exciting, that he was racking his brains for further outings. Her childlike wonder for all the new things she saw, he found quite charming. Then he realised he had taken the child out of her this afternoon, and made her a woman.

With a further gush of excitement, he wondered if he had also put a child into her, and the thought only tortured him, wanting her again, right now, on the tram! He was holding hands with her in her lap, and now he brought both of their hands onto his own lap. She looked at him, startled, then, realising what he was doing, she turned her face to look out of the window to save herself from giggling again. He tried to enjoy the gentle rocking of the tram, but could only stand it for a few seconds before realising that it just inflamed him all the more, and he was in danger of trying to lift her skirts again. Today had reassured him of one thing; he had not lost his appetite. He would always regret the premature end to the embarrassing first attempt, although it had been exquisitely exciting for himself, but he would make it up to her. Over and over again, he would make it up to her. It was gratifying to have found how quickly she rallied from that disaster, and how completely she had participated on two more wonderful, incredible occasions. He doubted that she really wanted a baby – not yet – but after so many celibate years, her words had easily set him alight.

Then, thinking of babies, he remembered the old lady who had sold him the ring, and he told Hannah to remind him to tell her something when they got off the noisy tram. They were in

Douglas by tea time, and they went into the Strathallan Hotel for a meal.

"There will never be another meal like the one we had earlier," he said ruefully, "I will never forget that one, but look at this menu, you can choose whatever you fancy. I'm going to have a beer, would you like some wine?" She had rarely tasted wine, but was quite sure she had been intoxicated enough by the day's events, and she opted for lemonade. They ordered, and then she asked what it was he had to tell her. "Oh, yes, it's about your ring," and he recounted his encounter with the old lady, how she had not wanted to sell it to a previous customer, and how it had a tiny flaw.

They held it up to the light, and could see how it seemed to sparkle all the more for its imperfection. And then there was her strange prediction before he left her that they would have children. "Remember me, Dorothy Kinrade," she had said. Hannah was charmed with the story, and also loved the name Dorothy. We could call our first daughter Dorothy, she suggested, and Will thought again how lovely Hannah was.

Afterwards, they hardly remembered the journey home. They were both re-living their actions and their declarations, and thinking about the future. Nothing seemed to matter now, except being together. Living their dreams. Hannah cradled her belly and wondered if there was already new life inside her. What an incredible feeling that gave her, and she hoped and prayed that it was so. Then they would be married, and live happily ever after, just as in all the best stories. Being practical, however, she knew that they would not know if she was pregnant for several weeks. Her monthly 'curse' was never reliably regular, so there would be an agony of waiting for the proof. But then, they could always try again. And keep trying. Every day.

∞∞∞∞

It was quite late by the time they got back to No 34. Little Carrie had already gone to bed, having had a wonderful day on the shore, and 'caught the sun,' as Mary put it. Remembering that certain parts of her body had never seen the sun before, Hannah subconsciously touched her top buttons, a gesture that did not escape her grandmother's all-seeing eye. "Gran, look at this," Hannah gushed, holding up her hand as only those showing off their rings ever do. She then shot off up the stairs to throw off her shoes and to get the ear-rings 'to make sure they match.'

Mary looked at Will, her eloquent eyebrow quivering. "You've done it then." It was a statement, not a question, and Will wondered how grandmothers always know. But he was proud, and so excited, and desperately in love.

"Don't be hard on us," he said, embracing Mary, "I didn't know if I was capable, but she is so lovely. Don't worry, I will never let her down. And, by the way, I didn't know she was a virgin. All I've ever heard is from Agnes, who is adamant that poor Hannah...." he had to stop there as Hannah started back down the stairs. Still embracing Mary, Will whispered, "Sshhh," in her ear, and Hannah pretended not to notice their closeness.

The procedure of comparing the ear-rings and the ring did not take long, it was as if they had been made as a set, although they knew that the ring was antique, and the ear-rings were brand new. Between them, they told Mary about Dorothy Kinrade and the prediction she had made.

"Oh, I went to school with Dottie," she exclaimed. "She was always a bit odd! But she seems to have a sixth sense. She is always predicting the future, and has an uncanny knack of telling people what they want to hear! I wouldn't take too much notice, but of course, she could be right!"

Hannah told her she thought the whole story so charming that, should they be lucky enough to have babies, she was determined to call her first daughter after the old crone, and then assured her grandmother that they both really, really wanted to have children. Poor Will had missed out the first time around, and she was determined that he should enjoy fatherhood 'before he was finished.'

Mary looked at the man in his late fifties and thought, well, he could have thirty or forty more years, but on the other hand, if Hannah over-taxes him, he might be 'finished' before Christmas.

Chapter Ten

They were both back to earth with a bump as life had to go on as normally as possible, he to the school and all his commitments, and she to the shop. But now, in her bed which felt so much less lonely, as her dream man was well and truly her man, she no longer needed to make love to her quilt. She was a woman now, not a silly girl, and she must act properly, even when she was alone. What they both did at night, however, was to write little notes to each other, which were exchanged in the shop on Will's way to and from school. "Your grandmother knows." said his first note. "Of course she does, she knows everything!" said the reply. "Agnes has no idea," said the next one, "In your dreams!" said Hannah's reply, and she did a 'Dorothy Kinrade,' and predicted that Agnes would call her a prostitute before the week was out.

They were both trying to find ways of being alone together somewhere, without having to go to the extremities of the island, and Will had enquired about accommodation for himself. Nothing was available immediately, so they racked their brains for ideas.

The obvious first resort was Hango Hill. Because they were often seen on that route, their presence did not arouse curiosity any more, and they could see for quite a long distance in either direction, so were unlikely to be disturbed suddenly. It was late May and the evenings were long, full of spring-like promise, and they acted out their earlier fantasy against the wall of the monument on numerous occasions. It continued to be exciting, as they were aware of what people would think, but really, the people of Castletown in general, still held very Victorian views, and it probably did not even occur to them what might be going on under Hannah's long skirts.

On another evening, finding their favourite spot already occupied, they walked further, and found a nook at Derbyhaven among the rocks and dunes on the shore. After they had gorged on lovemaking in the sand, they rolled back and noticed that there was a man on a boat in the little bay. He seemed to be pottering about, making far off tapping noises that they had taken to be the sound of rigging on masts in the breeze, but it looked for all the world as if he might have been looking at them. "Oh dear!" said Will, "What do you think we should do about him?"

"Do you think he saw us?" asked Hannah. "He's a long way away."

The extra frisson of excitement appealed to Will's rebellious streak. "Well," he decided, turning himself back on top of her, "if he can see us, he has already seen us, and if he didn't, let's give him something to look at!"

"Wicked Waverley!" she mumbled through his kiss, but was as willing as ever to comply. By the time they were 'spent' again, they spotted the little boat sailing out of the bay, and Will waved to it. "Farewell, little boat, what a lovely evening for a sail."

"Yes, farewell, Captain Peeping Tom, go and watch the ducks doing it!" said Hannah mischievously.

The man in the boat turned and waved back.

∞∞∞∞

When Sunday came round again, Hannah wore both her engagement ring and her matching earrings to go to church. It was the first time she had worn both, and she was aware that now she and Will were permitted to be seen together, without quite so many sidelong looks or whispers behind gloved hands. As before, though, Will walked with Hannah and Mary only as far as the square where their ways diverged, and Christina attached herself to the group. Agnes had gone on ahead to prepare the dinner, and Christina tried to be included in conversation. She admired Hannah's sparkling ear-rings and flattered, Hannah took off her glove to show the girl her engagement ring.

Knowing that Christina must be very much affected by the domineering Agnes's opinions on everything, Hannah took the opportunity to whisper to her that her Uncle Will was the most wonderful man in the world and that she loved him very, very much. The girl smiled wanly, almost apologetically, Hannah thought. If only she could get away from her mother, she might

Face The Music

be able to form opinions of her own, but here, in Castletown, there was so much prejudice and class distinction, it would be difficult to have an original thought.

Sunday dinner, the most divine meal of the week, was ruined today. There was the usual appetising roast of beef, excellent roast potatoes, beautiful vegetables and tasty gravy – and indigestion. Acid fell from Agnes's tongue and pervaded the whole house. Everyone picked at their food, longing to be anywhere but at this table.

"How you have the audacity to ask for God's blessing on this house when you then go out whoring, is beyond belief," she spat, after Will had said Grace, and that was just the beginning.

"What is she talking about, Baby?" Will asked of Christina, who blushed like a beetroot.

"Buying favours! That's what it's about. Flashy jewels in exchange for a prostitute's services. How disgusting. The sooner you are out of my sight, the better."

"How dare you!" Will was in danger of becoming as angry as his sister. "I have given presents to the woman I love. We are betrothed and will be married within the year, how does that make her a prostitute?"

Without waiting for a reply, his temper well roused now, he felt he had to defend his beloved. "You would not understand, but Hannah," he watched her flinch again at the hated name, "refused an engagement ring because of her working hands, but fell in love with the ear-rings, and would have been perfectly content with those, which were nothing like the price of a ring. Then, when I saw an antique ring that matched..... Oh, trying to explain to you is just casting pearls before swine, you are not listening. Cast the first stone if you are without fault yourself!"

He knew Agnes did think she was faultless, and more biblical quotations would fuel her fury. He watched with some satisfaction as she puffed out her chest and floundered to find a suitable reply. "Now you are accusing me of something?" she demanded indignantly, "are you comparing me with that strumpet?"

"Comparing chalk and cheese," he was calming down a little, but felt compelled to tell his sister a 'home truth.' "Hannah comes from a loving family, where husbands and wives stay together in a normal, happy household."

"Get out! Get out! Get out!" she exploded. "The fault in my marriage is all down to Richard."

Will got up from the table, thinking, sarcastically, 'of course it is!' He was certainly not going to get embroiled in that argument. "Is the piano yours or mine?" he asked, knowing what the answer would be, although he was fairly sure he had bought the piano, as he used it almost daily for giving lessons.

"Just leave everything. Take your dirty, filthy underwear, and get out."

Where could he go? Sleep in the schoolroom? In the church? The idea of No 34 was very tempting. He was in his room now, attempting to pack his few possessions into a trunk that had been under the bed ever since they moved to Arbory Street from The Crofts. Then, suddenly, Will regained his accustomed persona, and told himself, 'No!' She had no right to throw him out of the house that was as much his as hers.

More his, perhaps, since it was his income that paid the rent. Agnes fed him and arranged for the cleaning and laundry to be done, but actually, if there was any throwing out to be done, he could do it. He was the tenant, and he could throw her out. The spiteful, vituperative witch that his sister had become? He didn't know her any more. She had more to lose if he evicted her, as her pupils and boarders were her means of support, and if she went, her youngsters would have to go with her. She was going to do that anyway, come the summer holidays, so why not now?

But Will could not do that. Agnes couldn't do it really, he felt sure, it was only a knee-jerk reaction to Christina's tittle-tattle about Hannah's engagement ring. He knew she could not cope with his determination to marry Hannah, and if he lived to a hundred, he would never understand what she had against his lovely fiancée. Only that she was taking Will away from her, and in a way, he understood. He tried to think how he would feel if it were the other way around, and Agnes was all set on marrying someone he thought unsuitable. But the whole concept was so ludicrous that he had to laugh. Sitting on his bed, surrounded by his shirts and socks, all ready to be sent packing, including himself, he laughed out loud.

When he went back downstairs, the dinner table had been cleared, with a criminal waste of good food now emptied into the rubbish bin, and Agnes was in the kitchen with Christina, crashing the dishes in and out of the sink. "Why are you still here?" she rounded on him, her hands dripping suds.

"I am still here, because this is my house," he said calmly, "and next month, it will be Hannah's house too. She will live here, with me, as my lodger, until we are married." He knew this might kill her.

"Over my dead body!" she shrieked. "I have already given notice that this house will be vacated on the 17th of July," she added triumphantly.

"Well, thank you for giving me plenty of warning. Good grief, anyone would think you were 'a woman scorned' the way you're acting. What histrionics for a grown woman!"

"SHE will not live in this house. They already have new tenants waiting for our departure, so tell that to your little gold digger. Shame, isn't it!"

"Nevertheless," Will strove to keep his temper, "I shall not be leaving until I am ready to leave. I thought we were civilised people, and am saddened to see you reduced to such vitriol. You will just have to live with it until the 17th of July – or earlier if you would like to leave first?"

∞∞∞∞∞

In need of fresh air, he went outside and found that it was raining. Wonderful, he thought, just wonderful, how appropriate. Taking an umbrella, he marched off along the street, out past the church and the school, and out the length of the pier. It was not stormy, only raining, so the waves did not crash against the breakwater to match his emotions, they just lapped against the stones as if in submission to whatever might hit them.

Perhaps that was how he should react. Just let the waves wash over him, emerging wet, but just as strong. What useless thoughts. What was happening to him? Once again, he realised that his life had been transformed since knowing Hannah, and it was only Agnes who changed his lightened spirits. But how to ignore a woman with whom you shared a house, and a lifetime? Ah, well, with whom you had shared a house until today. Today he must think about alternative accommodation.

Leaving the pier, he followed the harbour, crossed the bridge and then doubled back on the other side, into Douglas Street, leading into Bowling Green Road. This was where he had been told that there would be a property available soon, but not yet. However, as he strolled he noticed a small sign in a window, in the end house, advertising the use of an apartment. Was his luck changing? He knocked at the door and was admitted into a sitting room by a servant, and introduced to two elderly ladies, Miss Jane Clague and Miss Janet Walkington. "Mr Waverley!" Miss Janet greeted him, "We almost didn't recognise you without your beard! What brings you to see us on a Sunday afternoon?"

"Ladies," he responded in his usual flamboyant fashion, "I don't know if you have heard, but my sister, Mrs Lacey, has decided that she wants to return to Ramsey where she spent some happy years a long time ago. Obviously, my work is here in Castletown, so her leaving requires me to find some alternative accommodation for a short while. and I noticed your advertisement."

"Mrs Lacey leaving Castletown? Why ever would she do that?" asked Miss Clague, but the other lady admonished her that Mr Waverley had already explained that she wanted to go back where she had been happy. What was wrong with that? "Sounds strange to me," insisted the first, so before she could probe further, Will asked about the accommodation.

They called the housekeeper back to show him up to the first floor, where he found a comfortable apartment in an extension at the rear of the house, consisting of a sitting room overlooking the road at one side, with a distant view to the Southern hills, and a connecting door to a bedroom at the back from which he could see the sea. It was perfect, and he went back downstairs to talk details with the landladies. They had other boarders, and breakfast was provided at 7:30am.

A mid-day dinner would be available, extra if required, and supper at 6pm. He was shown into the dining room where the meals would be served and he was delighted to notice a piano in one corner and a harmonium in another. The ladies were proud to mention that there was a bathroom on the first floor too.

The terms were very reasonable and Will thought he had drifted out of a nightmare into a dream. The apartment was furnished, so he could actually walk out of the Arbory Street house whenever he felt like it, and right now, he felt like it. He felt like getting Hannah into that apartment right this minute and....

He told his new landladies that he was captivated with the views from both sides of their lovely house, and that he would be pleased to move in during the coming week, which day he would confirm when he had made his arrangements. He paid them a deposit, without being asked, and the ladies were delighted with his good manners.

As the servant showed him out, he heard the elder woman remark, darkly, that there was 'something funny going on there, he's got a fancy woman you know,' but the other lady scolded her for 'listening at the village pump.' He smiled and would rather have liked to hear the rest of this conversation, but the big front door was closing behind him.

Chapter Eleven

The rain had stopped, but his mood had lightened now anyway, and he swung his umbrella on its handle, whistling a little tune. Instead of going home where there would probably not be any tea for him, he knocked tentatively at the door of No 34 Hope Street. He found that several of the Kaneen family were visiting, and he was welcomed into the crowded parlour. They had all been shown Hannah's beautiful engagement ring, and the ear-rings, and had been told all about both, so were full of congratulations, hand shaking and back-slapping.

Hannah told everyone that she and Will had enjoyed the most lovely day out to Ramsey, but it was such a long journey with all those changes of transport, she didn't know if it was worth the trouble to do it again (she knew in her heart that their first visit to magical Ramsey could never be repeated, and could not imagine having the time to do the same trip another time, without that very special purpose). Everyone said it was a lovely little town, and Aunt Emily suggested that they could stay overnight in Douglas, with them, if they could find another suitable holiday, in the school summer holidays perhaps, or what about Tynwald Day, that was coming soon?

"What a kind invitation!" said Will, "What do you think, Hannah? We would have time to see more of Ramsey if we were setting off from Upper Douglas to start with." It was agreed that would be lovely, until Cissie said perhaps she would come with them. But how could they refuse, after Emily's kindness! They would all think about it in the next month.

Then Will told them that Agnes had 'kicked him out' today. They were all scandalised, until he said that he had refused to leave until he was ready. She would be leaving shortly, but had relinquished the tenancy of the Arbory Street house without telling him, so he was obliged to find alternative accommodation. They were all agog to know what he planned to do next. With a half-smile in Hannah's direction, which Grandmother did not fail to notice, he told them that he had just come from a boarding house run by a Miss Clague and a Miss Walkington, where he had secured an apartment for himself. The house further along the same street would be coming available soon, but probably not until September, so he would see how things went in the meantime. He might move as soon as the other house was available, so as to have it ready for when they got married.

There was always plenty of food in Mary's house, and the inner man, who had been denied his dinner, was ravenously grateful for several rounds of baked ham sandwiches, and more than one slice of home-made cake provided by Emily. After this, they all walked together to the church for Evensong. Going with Will meant being there early, so that he could be at the organ before anyone else arrived, but they were a happy family, and all quite pleased to have time to chat quietly while they waited for the service to start. The mood changed slightly when Agnes and Christina, and some of her other girls, marched in, crocodile fashion, but only slightly, as they were all of one mind regarding that woman.

Will was so grateful to his 'new family' for their hospitality, and could hardly believe his good fortune in being taken into their warm hearts; but Mary and Hannah understood when he ruefully remarked that he had better walk home with Agnes tonight, just to make sure she didn't lock him out! He promised Hannah that he would see her at the shop early the next morning, and kissed her good-night right there in front of anybody who was looking. There were now very few who would take exception to that gesture, Mr Waverley's obvious newly-found happiness had begun to be accepted. By some, although not all.

As usual, Agnes did not speak to him on their way home, although Christina tried to break the silence by asking, "Are you all right, Uncle Will?"

"No, he is not all right," snapped her mother, "he is all wrong. Have nothing to do with him Christina," and all the young people with them, except for Christina shrank back, frightened. Christina was walking on the other side of Will from Agnes, and she slipped her hand into his and squeezed it, looking up at him apologetically. He nodded back to her with a half-smile in acknowledgement and whispered, "Yes, I am all right, Baby, thank you for asking," as she removed her hand and followed all the others into the home that they, for the moment, shared.

Once indoors, Will decided to make a stand, and asked if there was to be any supper. He announced that he had found an apartment at Miss Walkington's, to which he could move as soon as she liked, but that while he was under the same roof, he would be grateful if she could be civil.

She said he would find some cold ham in the kitchen. Well, since cold ham was all he had had to eat all day, he would have liked something different, and he asked if 'Baby' may be permitted to show him how to boil an egg.

Agnes snorted at his incompetence, but as Christina was already getting up to comply, she did not stop her. Poor Will felt like a schoolboy, but when had he ever had to cook a meal? Things like that were always attended to by the womenfolk, and the thought occurred to him that this represented a glaring omission in the male upbringing. It gave him an idea for some interesting experiments at school, it might be fun to see what the boys could do. They couldn't all expect to get married or afford housekeepers, or to stay at home with mother for ever. Yes, this plan appealed to him, and he drank in all that Baby told him. The girl seemed happy to help him, and he had the impression that she was more understandingly disposed towards him than her mother. He thought it quite possible that everyone else in the world was probably that.

He learned which end of the eggs to pierce with a hat pin so that they would not break in the water (he was being treated to two eggs), and how long to let them boil, according to his preference. That was when he learned that if they were left boiling for ten minutes, they would be hard-boiled, and he remembered such an egg on Hannah's lips in the long grass at Ballure. "Would you like toast, too?" Christina asked, and pierced a slice of bread on a toasting fork, which he had to hold close to the coals of the fire. "Oh dear, you've held it too close!" and she grabbed the burned bread and threw it in the bin, hoping that the smell would not have reached Agnes's sensitive nose. This was a vain hope, and her strident voice ordered the girl to 'leave him to find out for himself,' which, of course, he just had. Will tried again, and experienced such pride in having prepared food for himself, that he felt a peace and happiness that had been missing from this house for a long time.

On his way home from the church the next morning, he wondered if he might be expected to prepare his own breakfast, but was gratified to find that his porridge was all ready for him. Agnes did not speak to him, but she did not halt the chatter of the young people, and the atmosphere was almost as it used to be. It was unnerving, and he wondered what his sister was up to.

"I will pack up some of my things at dinner time," he ventured, "and move out after school. I'll ask Joe Garrett to bring his hand cart round."

"Why? what on earth do you think you're taking that requires a cart?"

"All I own will go in the trunk," he replied, "but I would not be able to carry that even if it were empty. There is only my clothing, really, but I must have my gramophone and records."

"I bought some of those records!" she snapped.

"Then you must keep whatever you think is yours, but the gramophone is mine. You are keeping the piano, I will take the gramophone." He knew that records would be no use without the machine for playing them, and he had the awful suspicion that she would try to keep him from taking it.

She simply sulked, and he took his leave earlier than usual, as he had promised to see Hannah early, and now he must make these other arrangements too.

Hannah was very excited about his sudden decision to move to Miss Walkington's house. She had not even had time to walk that way to see which house it was, and hoped to be able to help him move in later in the afternoon.

He called first at the big house in Bowling Green Road to confirm that, with the ladies' permission, he would bring his belongings later, and his tenancy would begin today. They were happy with this news, as it was the first day of June, which seemed a very appropriate day to issue his rent book. The room was already prepared, and they would now ensure that the bedding was aired and that everything he needed would be in place. A place would be laid for him at the table for supper at 6pm It was kippers tonight, and was that all right?

He thanked them, and then called at Joe Garrett's to ask for his services with the hand cart. He left his request with Mrs Garrett, Joe's mother, with details of the addresses from and to, and felt that he had done all he could to facilitate a swift departure.

At dinner time, grateful again to be served with anything, and especially as it was broth and bread, and not kippers, he quickly packed his clothes and shoes into the trunk, along with the depleted box of records, and he carried the gramophone downstairs in readiness to be collected later. He expected that Joe would help him down with the trunk. So, he went back to work, feeling excited in anticipation of this rather unexpected and sudden development in his topsy-turvy life.

∞∞∞

The afternoon flew by, and Will began to feel quite nervous, which was an unaccustomed feeling for him. He had always been in control, but now things were moving far too fast.

He went to the house that had been his home, found that his bed had been stripped, and he felt like a stranger. He checked all the drawers, but if he had left anything, it had been removed, although he was fairly sure he had decanted all his possessions into the trunk.

He was expecting Joe with the cart at four in the afternoon so there was nothing for it but to await his arrival. He was sitting in the dining room where he would see Joe pass the window, but the clock crept on with no sign of the handyman. Will kept going to the door to see him coming up the street, but there were no handcarts in sight. He wondered about going to meet him, but then thought Joe might come from another direction and they would miss each other. Joe must have another job on. When four o'clock became five o'clock, however, Will was very anxious, and he set off to the Garrett home to make enquiries. His knock was not answered, all was quiet, and he returned towards Arbory Street expecting at any moment to bump into the carter. But as he passed the Union Hotel, here came Joe staggering out, already very much the worse for ale. Will thought twice about accosting him, but Joe saw him first, and looked belligerent. "Did you get my message?" asked Will.

"I got yer message all right, yer cheeky bugger. Ya needn't be expectin any favours from me, y'll have to carry yer bloody stuff yer bloody self!" and he wobbled off towards The George.

Will was furious, but knew it would be unwise to attempt to get any more sense out of Joe. For a moment, he was stumped, and with his new landladies expecting him for supper at six, time was running out fast. What should he do? Go and make his apologies to them or try to collect some of his belongings first? He was dithering on the Market Place, when 'Billa' Corlett and his son, Sydney, emerged from the bar. Seeing the perplexed look on Will's face, Corlett did a double-take and stepped back to look at him. "What's up, Son?" he enquired kindly, and Will thought this sounded so amusing from a man who was his junior, but then realised that one day soon, he could be his father-in-law.

Will explained all that had, and had not, happened, and both the Corletts guffawed. Then Billa went on to explain that Joe Garrett had been walking out with Hannah years ago, and had caused a lot of trouble round the town when she 'finished with him.' It was down to that man that poor Hannah was hardly able to hold her head up for several years. Obviously, Joe was a sore loser, and was still bearing the grudge, even though the fault had been his own all along.

"Oh, Lord, if I had known that, I would never have asked," said Will. "He must have thought I was rubbing his nose in it! But what am I going to do now?"

"This is not a problem," young Sydney chimed in. "We have a hand cart, we'll just have to make some room on it, come on, let's go."

Sydney went on ahead to clear their cart and bring it round to Arbory Street, while Billa accompanied his prospective son-in-law to collect the trunk. Within fifteen minutes, the trunk and the gramophone were safely aboard the cart, and all three men set off to Bowling Green Road. Sydney helped Will heave the trunk up to the first floor, and Father Corlett followed with the gramophone. "Not sure if I didn't draw the short straw there," he puffed as he arrived at the top of the long staircase, "this is a brute of a thing! Oh, this is smart, isn't it," he remarked, seeing the sitting room. "This'll do ya until ya get wed, just the ticket."

Will didn't know how to thank Hannah's father and brother enough. "Think nothing of it," said Billa, "what are families for? But drop off another coupla bottles of that Castletown Red Label next time yer passin, and we'll find a use forrit!"

The smell of kippers brought them all back downstairs and Will bade the Corletts a very grateful farewell, and promised to see to the Red Label question forthwith. Then he remembered that Hannah would not know what had just happened, she had been going to help him with the move, but he must stop for supper right now or be in more trouble. Sydney promised to call at the shop on his way home and bring her up to date. No doubt Will would call on her later? Yes, but not until after the Philharmonic meeting, so probably about 9:30pm. Goodness, but life was fraught, all of a sudden. So much to do!

∞∞∞∞

Will was not usually keen on kippers, but the cook here obviously had a different method of cooking them than Agnes's daily help, and he found them quite delicious. In the light of his idea of sharing housekeeping tips with his pupils, he resolved to ask how these were done. He was also more than pleased to be given a glass of beer to accompany the meal, and began to feel that the rest of his life was just beginning. He should have done this years ago!

He just had time after the meal, to go back up to his apartment and put his clothes away in a wardrobe and a tall-boy, and lay out his pyjamas on the bed in the back room. Again he admired the views from both rooms. Not seeing bookshelves, he left his books in the trunk, and so the last item to come out was the box of records. The gramophone had been carefully placed on a small table, and he toyed with the idea of playing just one record before setting off for the music meeting. That is when he found that every one of his precious records had been smashed. This could not be down to the handling of the trunk, as he had been very careful with it at both ends of their journey, and the box was well cushioned amongst his clothes. This vandalism had occurred before they had collected the trunk, and that could mean only one thing. Agnes.

Chapter Twelve

Just as he was feeling happy, liberated and optimistic, she was still there, making his life a misery, and for a couple of hours he brooded about the broken records. Then, uplifted by the company of musical enthusiasts, he decided to put her venom behind him, and turn over a new page. He could replace the records, in fact it was high time he bought some new ones. There was only one that he had considered really precious. It was a recording made by the great composer, Grieg, playing the piano composition he had created for his own Silver Wedding celebrations. Will had obtained it on one of his rare trips off the island, and it might not be easy to replace that one. Ah well, what did it matter? He had Hannah now, and being secure in her love made everything better.

After the philharmonic meeting, he called at No 34, as promised. Hannah had been happy to see her baby brother, and he had stayed for a while. "So, you can be sure he knows all about you now!" Sydney had only just left school and taken apprenticeship with his dad in the house-painting business, but he already seemed so very grown up. He whispered to her that he thought their brother, Frank, was seeing a lady friend, but he didn't know who she was. Ooh, another family intrigue, how lovely, she thought, and was happy for Frank, too.

Then she wanted to hear all about Will's house move and his new lodgings, and when would she be able to come and have a look? Desperate though he was to take her to his own private place to make love to her, he had a distinct impression that it might not be seen as 'seemly' to the two elderly spinsters. "Let me get my feet under the table," Will suggested, "and I will see what is expected of their boarders, or what is not! There are two other single men, much younger than I am, of course, and I could tell they wondered what on earth I was doing there, but we will get to know each other in no time, I'm sure. I was in such a rush to eat my tea after all that palaver over the handcart. Oh, God, yes, I'd forgotten that bit. Or did Sydney tell you?"

"Yes, he did, and it brought back painful memories. It's my fault perhaps, for not telling you who the cad was who tarnished my reputation, but I had only wanted to forget it all, and had sort of got over it years ago. I have just found it very hard to trust anyone. Until I met you. You have changed everything, Will, and I love you so much."

"I could, and do, say the same, my sweetheart. I was thinking exactly that earlier. Can you imagine what my vindictive sister did, even when I was on my way out of her life? Do you remember that I had asked her who owned the piano? Well, I said since she was keeping that, I must take the gramophone. She doesn't listen to the gramophone, but she did buy me a couple of records, as presents, I thought. Now she wanted them back, and I told her to keep them, but I would take the machine and the rest of the collection."

Hannah was nodding as he spoke, and looking expectantly for the end of the story.

"When I took all my belongings out of the trunk, I found that all the records had been broken. They are brittle things, but in a pile, in a box, and wrapped in my clothing, they would never have suffered such damage in the trunk, and I can only assume that she took each one and broke it deliberately. It really saddens me that she could hit me where it hurts, my music. I can't believe it of her."

She could see that it troubled him deeply, so she embraced him, kissed him, kissed him again and took his mind off Agnes and broken records. As always, her kisses inflamed his passion and he wanted with all his heart to make love to her here on this comfortable sofa, but with a supreme effort, he dragged himself off her, told her she was a witch and a trollop, and lightened the mood. Mary would appear at any moment with the usual cocoa, and then he must get back to Bowling Green Road. He had omitted to ascertain if there was a curfew, but had the feeling there would be some strict house rules. It would not make a good impression to break any of them on his first night!

After a lingering, fumbling, writhing, good night kiss in the hallway, he took his leave and headed for what was now going to be his home. The door was not bolted, but he found one of the elderly ladies hovering to make sure everyone was home before she locked up. He asked about the house rules and she said she would give him his own key in the morning, but they did keep

'Christian' hours, if possible, and would appreciate being warned if he knew he would be in late. He agreed that this was absolutely correct, but he did have a lot of evening commitments, oh and early morning too. He told her about his organ practice before breakfast. She was surprised, but thought that his requirements could be accommodated without any disruption to the household. She wished him a very good-night, and hoped that he would be very comfortable there.

It was not what he considered to be very late, and a nasty thought had occurred to him that he felt he must check up on. Could Agnes have damaged the precious gramophone as well as the records? He flicked the catches and lifted the lid, with his heart in his mouth. He had stuffed the case with an old waistcoat, hoping to protect the turntable and workings, and was so relieved when he found it as he had left it, but better still, he had not realised that he had left a record on the turntable, and that it was the Grieg recording of the Wedding at Troldhaugen! The one that got away. Like me, he laughed, jubilantly. Yes!

What William could not, and never would know, was that Agnes had spent the entire evening alone in her room, weeping for the poor, lost soul she still regarded as her little brother. She was also full of remorse for her final, spiteful act, she knew he had not deserved that, and now it was Agnes who was thoroughly miserable.

It took a while for Will to calm down enough to sleep, and he tossed about a bit in the unfamiliar bed, his thoughts leading round in circles. He noticed that the bed creaked almost at every breath, but certainly at every move, and he knew that he would never be able to entertain Hannah in this room. He wondered what the room below was, and made a mental note to find out, but right now was conscious of every twang of the springs, which would wake him up again every time, just as he was dropping off. Eventually, exhausted, he did sleep well, and was ready for action by six, as usual. He let himself out quietly, cringing to find that the stairs also creaked, and he made another mental note to check which steps made the most noise.

The verger was checking his pocket watch when he arrived at the church, and Will apologised, and had to explain about his new arrangements. He would allow a few extra minutes henceforth, as it was a little further to walk than from the Arbory Street homestead. He also asked if it would cause a problem if he had piano pupils in the church hall, since he had had to relinquish his piano to his sister. The verger promised to find out officially, but he had no objection himself, especially if the times were regular, so that he knew when to open and close up.

Will played in his usual assertive fashion this morning and, knowing Agnes Lacey, the Verger could almost feel Will's release into the wild. It was always a privilege to pump the organ for this master of the machine, but today the music was divine. He could feel the benefit of those low notes through his body, too, and he wished his friend all the luck in the world. A middle-aged bachelor, but a little younger than Will, he felt that perhaps there was hope for himself yet!

Breakfast at 30, Bowling Green Road had to be experienced. The landladies had taken a shine to Will, and assumed that he would probably not come back mid-day for what they called dinner. Neither of their other gentlemen came home mid-day, and they had decided that they would all therefore have a proper meal to start the day, and 'dinner' when they came home at night. While there was the porridge he was used to, that was only one course. It was preceded by a half grapefruit, and followed by ham, eggs and toast. And coffee! He was not sure he would be able to move by the time he had finished, but then he remembered that he had quite a lot further to walk to work now, plus the fact that Hope Street was in the opposite direction, and he hoped that all the extra exercise might help to burn off all the food. All three 'gentlemen' chatted over their breakfast and quizzed each other about life in general. The two younger chaps were quite different, one working in a lawyer's office, and the other at the timber merchants, but both were single, with every intention of remaining that way! They were fascinated to hear that Will was engaged, and looked at him curiously.

It was now going to be a triangular route to call at Hope Street on his way to school, but he always longed to see Hannah, even if only for a few moments. Whenever the evening was fine, they would take their walk after his musical commitments, and he looked forward to the summer holidays, when they also took a break from choir practices and orchestra meetings, and would have more free evenings. They took every opportunity to find a spot secluded enough to indulge in their favourite pastime, but they were also happy just to be together, especially in the Hope Street parlour, with or without Mary or

Carrie. Will never abused the privilege of their privacy there, despite being sorely and frequently tempted, and tempted shamelessly by Miss Trollop, as he called Hannah. Sometimes they had to be content with companionship, but they were both very happy.

Occasionally, Miss Clague and Miss Walkington went visiting and, when this happened to be during the evening, Will's hopes would soar. He would not abuse the Hope Street home, but he couldn't wait to do it at No 30, although obviously not on that noisy bed! As soon as the old ladies announced that they would be out for the evening, on a blessed rare evening when Will had no other commitments, Hannah came to see his new home.

He felt almost as excited as he had the first time. The danger of being caught made the thrill all the more palpable, but he was fairly sure that they could have a couple of hours, at least, before he would have to smuggle her out again.

He was kissing her before they were through his door, and clawing at her blouse. But Hannah now took her blouse and bodice off completely while he undid his trousers. Before anything further, she unbuttoned his shirt, and that came off too. Still kissing and licking and biting each other, the skirts came off, as did the trousers, and for the first time they stood in front of each other, completely naked. Down onto the sofa they plunged, groaning and moaning and pumping, until they slid off the couch onto the carpet and continued until they were both completely exhausted. Panting from the effort, despite only wishing to continue with the same, over and over all night, they agreed that it had been so very wonderful, that it would be a tragedy to get caught now, and they began to get dressed. But they didn't get very far before the kissing started again, with clothing half on and half off. "Do you realise," she panted, "that was the first time we've done it indoors?" and she dragged him into the bedroom. He had told her about the bed but she didn't care. "Isn't it time we went to bed together?" she teased. The other boarders were out tonight too, so they assumed they were alone in the house, and those bed springs got a workout they had not witnessed for a long while.

She no longer begged him to make her pregnant, she was sure she already was, and that thought made her want him all the more. She would not tell him yet, she thought it might spoil things, and she wanted to be certain. But she had so wanted to be, she had wanted to force him to marry her, and yet she knew that, before there were any children, she would have him all to herself, and she wanted it to remain like that, too. However it would turn out, she was deliriously happy right now.

They did dress eventually, and crept down the stairs, shaking, whispering, giggling. Freezing when stepping on the creaking stairs, and saying "Sshhhh" to each other. They left by the back door, and along a passage that brought them out on College Green, and then onto the well-trodden promenade, and Hango Hill. Again! Oh yes, again.

So, the days and evenings passed, and in due course, Hannah discovered that she was not pregnant. She didn't know whether to laugh or cry, and she toyed with the idea of telling Will that she was, so that the wedding would be brought forward. 'Something' could always 'go wrong' before he discovered the truth, and she held conversations in her bed to this effect. But in her heart, she knew she couldn't do that. She would not lie to him. They would just have to keep trying!

She was unaware that Will had given the pregnancy possibility even more thought than she had, and he had also done a fair bit of tossing and turning, and churning things over in his head. Half of him was convinced he was beyond fathering age, and he remembered that it had taken over three years before Ellen fell pregnant, and that was when he was young. He was also terrified that the same thing might happen to Hannah as had befallen Ellen. What if it was his fault?

The other half remembered Dorothy Kinrade and her positive assertion that they would have children. Stuff and nonsense! Old wives' tales. But, what if....?

Hannah might be pregnant by a couple of months by the time they knew it and could arrange a wedding, and soon enough, everybody would know, and fingers would be pointed at poor Hannah all over again. Possibly not at him, but she had already endured enough, and he couldn't countenance the ignominy for either of them. It was not a good way to start, so he determined to approach the matter from a more practical direction. He enquired again about the house that was to become vacant further along the street from his temporary home.

Chapter Thirteen

June drifted by in a dream, as they had more time to spend together, and the daylight seemed to last for ever. One evening, Will said he would like to put some flowers on his mother's grave at Malew, and they strolled out to the church yard. Hannah let him have a few private moments at the grave, and she walked up and down, reading the inscriptions on the other stones, remembering some of the departed, and feeling a little sad. But then, she noticed a recurring theme to the epitaphs, and felt strengthened. Will was still kneeling in the grass with his head bowed when she returned to the Waverley grave, and she realised that his first wife, Ellen, was also there to remember. He looked up as she approached, and said, "This is where I will be one day. Will you bring flowers for me?"

She didn't want to think of his being gone from her, and she pulled him up from his knees. "Come and look at these," and she led him away from his mother and his wife. She pointed out several memorial inscriptions, and remarked how often the word Love featured. "Until now," she said, "I have regarded these sentiments as a bit trite and repetitive, as if that is just what is always said on a grave stone, but Will, now I understand what love is, I realise that all these people, yes, all of them, who are buried together, with some of their children in a number of cases, they all made love! They all 'died and went to heaven' long before they ended up here! Don't you think that is a happy thought? Oh, darling, I hope they all enjoyed each other as much as we do, and isn't it wonderful that two strangers can come together and become one?"

As he had thought a thousand times before, he just so loved this girl, and it was typical of her to have put that slant on this morbid place. Besotted as he was, he had not noticed that she was steering him towards the boundary of the yard, until he found that they were under a large tree, where the edges of the yard had not been trimmed, and the grass was long. At first, she pulled him to her against the tree, but they were soon in the grass and emulating the action that all the names on those stones had obviously taken many times. He did wonder if they were the first to do it in a grave yard, but it wasn't new, they hadn't just invented it, it was the most natural, common practice, and he also hoped that all those now lying peacefully around them had indeed known so much pleasure. When he thought about his mother, he was not so sure, but even she must have indulged at one time. Two times, even.

They repeated the No 30 experience only once, as they were very nearly caught out, and remarks were passed that warned Will to be more circumspect. He often recalled Billa Corlett's succinct summary of how far ahead Will could see, which would always bring a private smile to his face. In a way, however, his belated discovery of his own sexuality had brought him closer to his pupils. He remembered now, exactly how teenage boys felt, and he introduced some subtle references into biology lessons, which were not lost on some of the more astute lads. He felt that the more they knew about it, the less mystery, mystique and, possibly, ignorance, would surround it. One of the boys contributed to the discourse by saying that his father had been out on his boat one night, and saw a couple 'doing it' on the shore. "Going at it like rabbits, they were!" he asserted, and Will tried to discourage the sniggering, explaining that procreation was the most natural thing in the world and that it was an essential part of life, but he conceded that perhaps humans should act more responsibly than the animals. Then he thought he had better stop there, and practise what he was preaching. He did not tell them how excruciatingly marvellous and fantastic it was, especially on the sand.

After the second proof of non-pregnancy, Hannah was quite disheartened in one way, but also exhilarated in another. This was their time for being together, just the two of them, but she did wonder how long they would 'get away with it,' before a wedding was precipitated. Then she had the most frightening thought of all. What if she were to conceive, and Lord knew there were hundreds of opportunities, they were both insatiable for each other, but what if she were to find she was pregnant, but not have time to get married before Will died? This realisation brought her up sharp, and she was suddenly terrified. She remembered their first time, and how she had drifted off momentarily, waking up thinking that he was dead. Lying across her so still and quiet, she really had thought the effort and excitement had killed him. And what if it had? Just that once, if she had conceived his child in his death throes? She had been so caught up in the realisation of her dreams, that such a possibility, a real possibility, had never crossed her mind before. No, but this was silly, he was not an old man. He had begun to believe he was because there didn't seem to be any hope or future for him, but he was a young man, a very virile man, a very athletic man, and such a wonderful, amazing lover. She could not even countenance trying to keep herself from him, she just wanted him all the time, and he was always willing, eager, exciting, oh, so wonderful. She thought of the various places that they had made love, hardly ever indoors, now she came to think of it.

Hango Hill hundreds of times, on the beach, in the grave yard, that first unforgettable and wonderful time in the Garden of Eden. She wondered if there was a place, or a time, that they could do it where she couldn't get pregnant. But she did want his baby. She did. She wanted a little Dorothy, she had set her heart on a little Dorothy. And Will.

Tynwald Day was coming up early in July, which was another holiday, and the idea of going to Ramsey again excited and thrilled them both, even though they knew a 'first time' could not be repeated. They took up Aunt Em's invitation to spend the night before at her boarding house in Douglas, although Cissie's threat about accompanying them put a slight dampener on their enthusiasm. It was easier for them in Castletown now, than it had been at first. They were almost accepted as a couple, by most people at least, and the need to be private and away from the town was not as pressing as it had been in May. But the prospect was still stimulating, and they both looked forward to it eagerly.

Technically, Tynwald Day this year was on a Sunday, and the 'holiday' was taking place on Monday. They took the train after the evening service on Sunday, and spent the rest of the evening in the Kaneen household. This was always a joyous affair, with all manner of party pieces being performed. They could hardly believe their luck at having Will join their family, being the consummate musician, and the party went with a real swing. Cissie was looking particularly glowing, having confirmed her resolve to come with Will and Hannah to Ramsey the next day.

After an uproarious breakfast, everyone in holiday spirit with out-of-the-ordinary plans, Will, Hannah and Cissie set off on foot for the Electric Railway terminus. Before they reached it, Cissie told them how thrilled she was that this opportunity had been afforded her, and she was so grateful to them for not squashing the idea of her joining them. Then she shyly confessed that this was because 'her young man was coming too but don't tell Mother!'

Intrigued, they could hardly wait to meet the object of the girl's affection, but were more than surprised to see Hannah's brother, Frank, striding confidently towards them. Was it to be a whole family affair thought Hannah?

So much for getting away from everybody! But apparently, despite being cousins, Cissie and Frank had been quietly 'seeing each other' for some time. Frank embraced Hannah and shook hands with Will. "Han," Cissie confided, "it's so marvellous that you and Will are together. You have inspired us to declare our love for each other. People would frown on us because we are related, just as they frown on you because of the age difference, but you don't care, do you? And we don't care. We are so happy, and today is going to be just wonderful!" Hannah embraced them both again and confessed to some surprise and shock, but wished them the kind of happiness that she and Will had found.

"If you don't object," whispered Cissie once they were on the tram, "we wouldn't mind separating once we get to Ramsey. I'm sure you really want to be alone with Will, I know Frank and I want to be alone, away from the prying eyes of people who know us. You do know how it is?"

"Oh, we certainly do," agreed Hannah. Here was a release from their company. Much as she loved them both, she loved Will more, and now a day together, just the two of them again, seemed to be about to happen. What joy!

Studying the timetables, they decided to meet up again for tea, in time to go home on the last tram back to Douglas, but for the rest of the day they could go their separate ways. "Well, in that case," said Will, "shall we go up the mountain from Laxey? We could see the Laxey Wheel on the way."

Hannah thought he had the most lovely ideas, and they agreed to do this and travel further on to Ramsey later. They bade farewell to the delighted Cissie and Frank as they disembarked at Laxey, and waved to the tram as it rattled off towards Ramsey. They climbed aboard a different type of tram, and were carried up a steep incline, around the side of a mountain, from where they could see the Great Laxey Wheel across the valley. It was turning slowly, pumping water out of the mine-workings, where miners were working way underground, hacking lead ore out of the rock. No public holiday for them, then, thought Hannah.

Their tram continued to climb, up and around the highest mountain, where there was a hotel at the summit. They left the tram and stared round at the amazing views. It was legendary that from here on a clear day, seven kingdoms could be seen, and Will pointed them out for her. Looking back across the Laxey valley, the distant land mass was England, which became Wales if they turned and looked south. Over in the other direction were the Mountains of Mourne in Ireland, and when they climbed to the summit, they would see Scotland off the top end of the island! Hannah had counted four as he spoke, and asked about the rest. "Well," he smiled, "you are standing on the Kingdom of Mann, then all around us is the Kingdom of Neptune."

"Yes? and the seventh?" Hannah was still counting, but looked up at the sky where Will was pointing. "I can't see anything but sky!" she complained.

"Well, that's the Kingdom of Heaven!"

"Ah yes. Mmmm, I've been there lots of times, but not recently enough!"

They bought some lemonade, and then walked over the top of the hill to overlook the whole of the north of the island. Hannah could see the shape, just as it was on the map, even more so than from the Garden of Eden. She could also see plenty of the coast of Scotland, and she was captivated. Of course, by now, it was high time that they made love again and, forgetting her pregnancy fears, having made sure that they were well out of sight of other passengers, she initiated an intercourse that was to transport them both far beyond the view or the map, or heaven. They were both certain that 'Dorothy' was conceived that day, as it was an experience more beautiful than ever before. With the world at their feet, as it were, or the island at least, they may have been able to see seven kingdoms, but they saw only each other, and paradise.

Staggering back to the tram, they descended back to Laxey and walked round to the Big Wheel. "Oh my goodness!" gasped Hannah, "You can read about dimensions all you like, but nothing can prepare you for the sheer size of it in real life close up. It is amazing." There were a few older men around, too old or infirm to go down the mines any more, but who were happy to explain about the mine workings, and they imparted a lot of information. Will determined to bring some of his boys here, perhaps when the new school year started, or maybe sooner, before this term ended. This was so worth seeing, and these ex-miners could tell them far more than they could read in books. Hannah's usual insightful observation had summed up its impact perfectly.

They had a light lunch back in 'Ham and Egg Terrace,' and then caught another tram to Ramsey. Very tempted to get off at Ballure, they really did toss up whether to do that, but knew that they could not repeat the first impressions, and they must go right into the town this time, or they might never get there. They walked the shopping street, all the way to the railway station, where the steam trains left for Sulby, Kirk Michael and Peel. They then turned back along the quayside, where Will showed Hannah the swing bridge he had told her about, that had so fascinated the boys, and they walked across it to visit the pleasure park.

After an hour here, they bought an ice cream and walked up the zig-zag paths and sat on a bench looking over the boating lake. Hannah remarked on the view from this direction, now looking at the mountain behind the town. "We must be facing almost the opposite way from The Gar.... em, Ballure, is that mountain we're looking at the same one that we.... went up this morning?"

Will said no, they had gone up Snaefell, but this was North Barrule, as opposed to the South Barrule that could be seen from his window in Castletown. Hannah was amused, "So, which was the Barrule referred to in that new song that we sang at the Guild?"

Will thought through the words he remembered, "O land of our birth.... O island so strong and so fair, built firm as Barrule," and admitted to himself that he didn't know the answer for certain, but he said that probably Ramsey people would think it was North Barrule, while Castletown people assumed it was South Barrule, but they were both 'built pretty firm.'

"Is that why Ramsey people and Castletown people are so different?" persisted Hannah.

"What makes you think they are?" Will was quite shocked.

"Haven't you noticed?" she smiled, "Not one person has looked down at us here, they are not judging us, they are all happy. And I hate to admit it, but Agnes was right about one thing, the sun does shine a lot!" Will chucked her under the chin and kissed her. She could always say something to surprise him.

So many people were enjoying the sunshine and the holiday, it was idyllic, and they wondered where Cissie and Frank were, hoping that they were enjoying it too.

They strolled on to the next bench, and could hear a courting couple among the bushes. "Good idea?" Hannah smiled at Will.

"Trollop!" he replied, but before they could slip down among the bushes themselves, they realised that the courting couple were Cissie and Frank.

"No!" said Hannah, "Don't let them see us, we must leave them to it." and they crept further along the path, until they came upon an even more inviting patch of bushes, and became a 'courting couple' again themselves.

They met the others back at the tram station, as agreed, but stopped to have tea together first at the Waterloo Hotel. While the men went to place the order, Cissie told Hannah they'd had a lovely time, and even confessed to having what she called a 'bit of canoodling' in the bushes of the park. "But wait 'til you hear this," the girl continued confidentially, "just further along, there was another courting couple and they were going all the way! Oh, believe me, they were! You should have heard the moans and grunts coming out of the bushes. We were so embarrassed!"

"Tch! Disgusting!" said Hannah, biting her tongue. "Ah, well, I suppose they were enjoying themselves. It is a holiday, after all!"

"Oh Han! I'm sure a girl can get just as pregnant on a holiday as any other day!" and Hannah was pensive again. Hmmm, she was right there, and for some reason Hannah was on the top of Snaefell again.

Chapter Fourteen

The following week, Will enquired again about the house further along Bowling Green Road from his lodgings that was still occupied, but was delighted to be told that it would be vacant from the first of August. The landlord arranged for him to inspect the house, and he could see that a certain amount of painting and decorating would be required inside. On an impulse, he agreed to take the tenancy of No 22 from that date, and he gave notice to his landladies that he would vacate his apartment then. They were surprised, and asked if there was anything unsatisfactory about their accommodation. He assured them that he was very happy at No 30 and thanked them so much for giving him a home when he so needed it. Then he explained that he was to be married within a few months, and as No 22 was becoming vacant now, he would move in during the school holidays, and see to the re-decoration and other preparations, to have it up to a standard suitable for his lovely wife-to-be.

"Ah," said the older landlady. "That explains it. Why didn't you say you were betrothed? We thought...."

Miss Janet interrupted her quickly. "Is it Miss Corlett that you are to marry?" she queried, and as he nodded, she gushed on, "Why don't you invite her to eat here with you one evening? How about Friday, we would be so pleased to meet her," here she gave a warning glare at her colleague, "and of course it will be fresh fish for dinner."

Will was delighted, as Friday would be the last day of school, and a very busy day for him. It would be lovely to celebrate the end of term, and he thanked them both for their generous gesture.

He therefore had two surprising announcements to make to Hannah that evening, both of which thrilled her. The taking of the lease on a house seemed such a positive step towards their being married, and there would be somewhere that they could be quite alone and private. She was more nervous about meeting the redoubtable Miss Clague and Miss Walkington, and felt quite guilty about their couple of surreptitious adventures in their house. She must be on her best behaviour and pretend to be seeing the house for the first time.

Agnes and the remaining family prepared to move out of the Arbory Street home the same day. She had done a lot of thinking since Will had walked out of her life, and she was broken-hearted at their rift. In one of their quarrels, Will had promised her that the Corlett girl was the innocent victim of malice, and explained how that all came about. She had hardly been listening at the time, but had since been able to mull over all the things they had said to each other. She had said nasty things about Hannah trying to elevate herself to the upper classes by lying on her back, and Will had been outraged at her mention of class distinction. "What gives you the right to fancy yourself as gentry?" he had spat at her, "you are nothing but a snob." He had brought being a Christian into the argument, too, and some of his reasoning had, with hindsight, made her re-think some of her entrenched ideas. She still resented the little tart, or whatever she was, but she also still loved Will and could see that, away from her, he was very happy, which just made her feel even more dejected.

Had she been hasty? worse, had she been nasty? She was certainly chastened by what had erupted into such unexpected assertions; 'home truths,' as he called them. She had shed more tears in the weeks since he had left, and just hoped that, now she was leaving Castletown, she would start a new chapter and feel better. Meanwhile, her penitence sent her into Douglas to buy a present for her baby brother. She didn't expect forgiveness, and in any case, she could not really forgive him, but she did love him. He had been everything to her for almost all of her life. She did not feel strong enough to face him, but left a package addressed to him with Miss Walkington on the morning of her departure.

It was the last day of the summer term, and although the thought had crossed his mind at breakfast time that it was the day Agnes was moving out, it was such a busy and important day in his own schedule that he didn't have time to dwell on the problems his sister had brought upon herself. The school's prize distribution would be attended by all the usual dignitaries, the boys must be scrubbed and immaculate, all of them, and they had their archaeology project to put the finishing touches to. That had been laid out in the lower schoolroom over the past week, with the artefacts neatly labelled, and several of the boys well-rehearsed in being able to explain about it and answer any questions.

There would be so much to do, that Will had reluctantly missed out his usual morning visit to the grocery shop, but reminded Hannah on Thursday evening that they would have a lovely meal at No 30 on Friday, and then, of course, it would be the school summer holidays. Sunny days and long evenings were all they could see ahead, and a Castletown without Agnes!

After the bustle of the Prize Day, Will called for Hannah and his heart soared when he saw her dressed for a special occasion in a silver-grey dress, her aquamarine ear-rings and matching ring sparkling, and her hair pinned up with ornamental ringlets at her temples. She took his breath away, and he was so proud to escort her to the big house at the end of Bowling Green Road, passing No 22 on the way. "Just two more weeks," he beamed, "and I shall move in there, and we will have our very own home!"

Arriving at No 30 they were greeted by Miss Janet, who professed to be delighted to meet Hannah, and wished her happiness in her forthcoming marriage. She said she and her colleague had become quite fond of Mr Waverley, could see how happy he was, and were sorry he would be leaving their home. She ushered them into the parlour to meet Miss Jane, who eyed Hannah a little suspiciously, her eyes flicking from her to Will and back, but Will soon charmed her with his usual bonhomie. He repeated how very kind they had been to him, and how he and his fiancée appreciated the invitation to dine, and that they had both noticed some very appetising aromas as soon as they entered the house.

Miss Janet ushered them into the dining room, where a separate table had been laid for two, with candles and a bottle of white wine. This was such a surprise, but then Miss Janet presented him with the package that had been left for him that morning. "We assumed it might be your birthday," she explained, "I think this is from your sister. Isn't that nice?"

Mention of Agnes reminded Will that his sister had been leaving Castletown that day. This was both sad and joyous for him and Hannah, but he wondered what the package could contain. Agnes had been so bitter for so long, what was this parting shot going to be?

"Well, perhaps you had better open it!" laughed Hannah, "I think it looks like a book."

Will was just as intrigued to see what sort of book Agnes might have thought he needed, he knew he had removed all his own books when he left Arbory Street, but she must have found something.

But Catherine, the housekeeper, appeared with bowls of soup for their first course. She also poured them each a measure of the wine, and the package was put out of the way under the table. Hannah was not sure she had ever tasted asparagus soup before. The Bickerstaff household was more of a broth family, with plenty of meaty influence, and barley and dumplings, so she found this a very delicate flavour. However, together with a sip of the wine, she thought how nice it must be to live in such a style. The fish was lemon sole with slices of lemon and slim French beans, and again Hannah wondered if there would be any real nourishment coming.

The other boarders had already finished their meals and left the room, and as they waited for another course to arrive, Will, after checking that they were quite alone confessed to being quite concerned about the possibility of Hannah becoming pregnant. "You aren't, are you?" but when she shook her head somewhat sadly, he continued, "I wondered how you'd feel about bringing the wedding forward, say to my birthday instead of yours?"

Her heart leapt. "You know I can't wait, my darling," she replied, "when is your birthday exactly?"

"The twenty-fourth of September and as I will be taking No 22 from the first of August, I'm sure it could be ready for you to move in by then."

"Oh, Will, that is a wonderful idea. But how would we explain the change of plan. It might look as if I am already expecting!"

"Just the fact that the house will be ready, and why waste more time? People will soon know whether it was premature or not, and as far as I'm concerned, it can't happen soon enough."

She thought she might burst with happiness, and took a bigger sip of wine, as Catherine returned with apple pie and custard. Oh that's more like it, she thought, things are just getting better and better. When that was followed by a selection of cheeses, she began to realise that it was a reasonably substantial meal after all. Just different.

After the cheese and wine had all gone, Will remembered the package and brought it up onto the table. What on earth could it be? His fingers almost trembled as he pulled at the string.

There were four gramophone records in the package. The two that Agnes had retained, which she had bought for him in the first place, were *The Holy City*, sung by Edward Lloyd because she had been unable to obtain the Caruso version at the time, and a part of *Gilbert and Sullivan's The Mikado* that came in a number of volumes, the rest of which, of course, were now destroyed. Will realised that she must have known that the discs were no use to her without the gramophone, but he was touched when he took the wrappers from the two new records. She had found him a recording of the great Caruso after all, singing a well-known song from Pagliacci, and another of his favourites, the famous Australian soprano, Nellie Melba sang *Sempre Libera* from *La Traviata* on the second one. Will smiled at his sister's choices, one referring to a fool, the other to a fallen woman, and freedom. He was temporarily unable to speak.

Miss Janet bustled in at that moment and saw the records. "Oh, how exciting!" she declared, as Will allowed her to inspect the labels. "Can you play them for us in your apartment?"

He told her how he had brought his gramophone, and that all but one of his records had been broken in the move. Miss Jane said she would listen from downstairs if they left all the doors open, while the younger woman led the way to Will's rooms, followed by Hannah. Both women sat on the sofa, where Hannah shivered with a frisson of delight, remembering her first collision with that piece of furniture. "Are you cold, dear?" asked Miss Janet, but Hannah assured her that she was just excited, and Will wound up the gramophone. All records were only a few minutes in duration, but Miss Janet insisted on hearing them all, and then some of them again. "Oh, it is so long since there was music in this house," she reminisced. "Jane used to be a wonderful pianist, but her arthritis prevents her from much movement these days, poor thing. Oh, Mr Waverley, please will you play the organ for us?" and she led the way back downstairs.

Will sat at the harmonium and inspected the stops. He pedalled air into the instrument and tried out a few keys, finding happily that the little organ had quite a nice tone, and that the stops all worked as they should. For a neglected instrument it was in extraordinarily good condition. He spoke admiringly, and remarked how good it was that it had a large room in which to perform. The dining room had once been two rooms, but had been opened out to take more boarders than were presently residing, and the acoustics complimented the organ well. When Will played organ pieces from memory, Miss Janet was transported, and even Miss Jane had managed to rise from her chair in the parlour and toddle in with the aid of her stick. There were tears in her eyes, and between them, they would not let Will stop playing for another hour.

Catherine brought a tray of cocoa, in bone china cups, naturally, for them all, and was invited to stay and listen, although she could not have failed to hear from the kitchen. Hannah wondered if anyone in the entire street had failed to hear Will's rendition of the popular songs he had resorted to after he had run out of sacred inspiration, and the old ladies were beside themselves with rapture.

"Mr Waverley!" declared Miss Jane. "It would please me enormously if you would accept that harmonium as a wedding gift from me, or as a present for your new home. Take it when you move, and remember us when you play it."

Neither of them would countenance any refusal, it was settled, and the poor organist had no say in the matter. The harmonium, it was a very good one, with its two manuals, deserved to be exercised and enjoyed, and they could no longer do it justice themselves.

Will thought that, with possibly one exception, this was the best day of his life! There was only one thing missing, but this was rectified when he walked Miss Corlett home, via a somewhat circuitous route. It was quite late after all the entertainment, and almost dark at Hango Hill.

Chapter Fifteen

Over the week-end, they discussed plans for their wedding. Now that it could be five months earlier, there was such a lot to arrange. Once again, Will's head was soon reeling as the women-folk pounced upon all the components such as dresses for bride and bridesmaids, flowers, cake, the reception and invitations. Obviously, Will would advise on the music, but there was a problem, how could he be the bridegroom and play the organ at the same time? Then came the deeper complications such as whom to invite, not just to the ceremony, but to the reception, and who would he trust to play his organ? And where would this reception be held, anyway? And what about a best man? Oh goodness, and a honeymoon! Will began to think that dresses and flowers were the easy bits.

After a sleepless night, tossing about on his noisy bed, he wondered if it was actually wise to think about getting married in Castletown. There were still some of the 'important' people of the town who were not impressed with his choice of bride. While their opinions mattered not one jot to Will personally, he eventually realised that it might be more discreet to tie the knot elsewhere. He had a few good friends, and he decided to ask John Qualtrough and Tom Dodd for their advice, as well as asking Billa Corlett what his thoughts were.

At breakfast, Catherine the housekeeper remarked that he had been restless last night, and he realised with a guilty rush that she must occupy the bedroom below his. That would be along from the kitchens, which made sense, and he should have thought of that before. Now he knew who had initiated the previous hints about his surreptitious activities. With a shock, he also realised that Catherine knew exactly what he had been up to with Hannah, and he wondered what he should do about it.

That rebellious streak surfaced again, and he said to Catherine, "You should have come up and joined me," and enjoyed her look of horror as he winked at her.

She quickly rallied and said that she would do that next time, to the great amusement of the two other young boarders, and one of them said, "Oh no, Cath, come to my room," and the other soon joined in with further suggestions. Thus, the tension was released, and the poor housekeeper knew she was outnumbered, but had enjoyed the male attention nevertheless.

John Qualtrough was headmaster at the Board School and had been a friend as well as a colleague for many years. He came to Will's apartment the following week, bearing four bottles of beer, and listened to his friend's predicament sagely. "I think you're absolutely right about having the ceremony outside of Castletown," he agreed, "there is strong feeling here. I don't subscribe to it, obviously, but we have to submit to our 'betters,' don't we? Two of your erstwhile pupils have been bequeathed to me by their snobby parents and I can only say that those boys are well ahead of the others in their year, so their social climbing mothers have not done them any favours, but that's the problem we face in this town. Will, I will be happy to be your best man, please do me the honour of asking me!"

Will embraced his friend in gratitude. "It is so good to hear your condemnation of those condemning me!" he said, "You have always been such a staunch ally, I could not think of asking anyone better to be my truly best man."

John asked if Will had heard any other opinions, and Will confessed that he wanted to ask their mutual friend, Tom, and his future father-in-law, Billa, what they thought. Qualtrough said he would be very surprised if either of those pillars of the community, in their quite different capacities, would come up with any objections. In fact, he was almost sure that Tom Dodd or his wife had connections in the diocese, and could probably suggest another suitable church.

"Well, we'll soon find out," said Will, opening their second bottle of beer each, "Don't go yet, Tom is coming at five. I didn't summon Billa. He's going to be my father-in-law, you don't summon fathers in law!"

Their second beer bottles were soon empty, but Tom Dodd arrived right on time, was shown up to Will's apartment, bearing two bottles of red wine! Having noticed this, Catherine arrived shortly afterwards, with a tray of wine glasses.

"Catherine the Great!" said Will, not used to having drunk two bottles of Red Label in quite such a short time, "Why only three glasses? Won't you be joining us?"

Catherine winked at him, which was not lost on the visitors, who were constantly being surprised by their middle-aged friend. "I'll see you later," she said, and now it was her turn to enjoy the moment.

Thank goodness there are no meetings tonight, thought Will, as Tom poured wine into all three glasses. Dodd was swiftly brought up to date with their previous conversation, and he agreed wholeheartedly. "My business," he confessed, "is mainly with the well-to-do, and they are the ones who have a problem with your private life. Not me, you know that, Will, I am so happy for you, and for that poor Corlett girl – oh, sorry – no, but things are heard in my shop, and I do know what people say. But truly, Will, my customers are the most awful snobs, most of them not even true nobility themselves. There is a lot of social climbing in this town, and I thoroughly recommend you looking elsewhere to get married. Personally, I think you're a bloody lucky man, and all strength to you, but what I might suggest is that you write to Fanny's cousin, the vicar of Braddan. It might mean one of you having to live in Douglas for a short while, but let me introduce you by letter, and I'll give you his name and address. Will, with all my heart, I would love to attend your wedding, but it may not be possible, I hope you will understand. I will supply all the beer and wine you want for your reception, wherever you decide to have it, as a wedding present from me and Fanny. You know we both love and admire you, and wish you only happiness and success, any maybe even children," he finished with a flourish and a refill of all the wine glasses.

The three friends drank to that, and then they emptied the second bottle, and Will started to feel decidedly naughty. They all left together and staggered along Victoria Road, and alongside the river, until they parted at the bridge; John to turn back towards College Green, while Tom had 'another call to make' at the Castle Arms. Thankfully, the cooler evening air was sobering them up a little, and Will turned into Hope Street, with hope in his heart. Unfortunately, in his inebriated confusion, he forgot where he was going, and ended up at the house in Arbory Street that had been his home for 20 years. Now he was really confused, but still had the feeling that he had intended to be wicked, and then he remembered how wicked he wanted to be. 'Aah!" he declared to the empty street, "Hey, d'you know what? I forgot to turn up for dinner. Oh deary me! Oh God, my head! Call those people friends? Aargh!'

Billa, Frank and Sydney Corlett found him draped round a gate pillar, and dragged him home to their Malew Street house. They poured water down his throat, and then Mrs Corlett made tea, but she was the one who realised that he had drunk without eating, and she pressed him with bread and cheese. After these ministrations, he began to come round, and then sobered up so suddenly that he was appalled at his behaviour. He had never been drunk in his life, and was mortified to have lost the control that was so important to him. "You are with family," soothed his prospective mother-in-law, "no-one else will ever know. Don't worry, I've seen it all before. There, there," and she cradled his pounding head, stroking his cheek. He opened his eyes to find himself in her ample bosom, and started to pull back, but regaining his wicked streak, replaced his cheek at her breast, and enjoyed the mothering for a while longer.

The Corlett men folk were mightily amused at Will's fall from grace. While the brothers tittered together, Billa announced that he was quite glad to see that his daughter's intended was human, after all. He had begun to think the man was some sort of saint, but then even The Good Lord had been known to consort with publicans and sinners, and to drink wine! Yet again, Will thought how warm and welcoming this family was, and he was reminded of Hannah's comparison of Castletown and Ramsey people. He wondered briefly how The Good Lord would have got on in Castletown. But, surely, it was not the towns that made them different, he thought, there are just some very different kinds of people everywhere and these are the best.

Will was feeling so much better after the bread and cheese soaked up his indiscretion, that he took the opportunity to mention the problem that had occasioned it. He confessed to drinking with John and Tom because they were discussing whether the wedding should take place in Castletown or somewhere else. Again the men laughed at his innocence.

"Good god, man, ya can't go drinkin with a wine and spirits merchant and expec to gerraway with it! Qualtrough's no better, they can both hold their liquor from years o' practice! Can ya remember what their conclusions were?" asked Billa.

"I think Tom's wife, Fanny, has some relation that's in the clergy, he was going to ask her for the name of a vicar. They both thought it might be wise to wed outside of Castletown. John is still hearing the hoi polloi whispering about me and Hannah. Did you know two fathers had taken their sons out of my school and sent them to the Board School? What sort of people are they, that their prejudices are more important to them than their children's education?"

"None so quare as folks!" agreed Billa, "it's their loss, isnit."

"Kind people, realisation is dawning on me that I am in deep trouble," said Will attempting to stand. "Hannah will be wondering where the devil I am, and I walked out of No 30 with those two reprobates, without going in for my dinner. All the women in my life will be baying for my blood."

"Aye, get mixed up with wimmin and that's what ya get!" Billa agreed again.

"Excuse me!" interjected his wife, "it was getting mixed up with so-called gentlemen that got him into this mess," and then to Will, "I always find an apology works wonders. Let us know if you hear anything more, then. I think Fanny Dodd is some sort of cousin to the Rev Moore at Braddan. That would be a grand place for your wedding. Did I hear that it might be sooner rather than later?"

"What?" shouted Billa, "Ya mean she's in the family way?"

"No, no," protested Will, hoping he wasn't protesting too much, "it's just that I'm taking the tenancy of No 22 from the first of August and hope to have it ready soon, so we'd just like to get on with the being married thing."

"And why not, indeed!" Caroline gave her blessing to the explanation, whether she believed it or not. "But perhaps you had better go and make your peace with her before it gets any later."

Will found that he could stand all on his own now, and managed to leave the house with a modicum of dignity. Much Corlett chatter went on after he left, but he was now trying to work out which way to turn for Hope Street. The cooler evening air helped him to sober up, and he knocked gently at the door of No 34. It was flung open, and Hannah embraced him violently. "Will, wherever have you been? We were about to send out a search party. Oh, thank goodness you're safe! Ah-ha, have you been drinking?" She hauled him into the parlour and pushed him into an armchair instead of his usual place on the sofa with her. "Well?" she prompted, and he confessed all.

"I'll tell you what we are going to do," she said, and he thought it best to concur with whatever she was going to say. "I will walk you home, and we will make your apologies together to Miss Walkington and Miss Clague. What more can they say if you grovel a bit?"

On their way back to Bowling Green Road, Hannah probed more about Braddan Church, because she also had something to tell him. For as long as she could remember she had been friends with a distant cousin who lived in Liverpool. She called her 'Elbie,' and the girl travelled a lot, but had met Hannah when she was looking up some other relatives on the island. The two wrote to each other frequently and were each other's confidantes. "I want her to be a bridesmaid, Will, she has heard all about you over the last few months, well, no, not all about you, don't worry! But she readily agreed to come over for the wedding and be bridesmaid, when the wedding was to be in late February. When I wrote and told her that it would be late September now, she was devastated. She is going on an extended tour of Europe, and she especially organised it so that she would be back in February, but she leaves on the tenth of September and wouldn't be able to come over for the 24th. Do we have to wait until my birthday after all?"

Will had followed all this quite well, but he especially understood the threat of putting off the wedding again, and he couldn't have that. He was now quite sober.

"Do you know, when I checked the calendar, I noticed that the 24th is a Thursday, and we would be back at school, so it would be much more convenient to have the wedding before the new term starts. As soon as I hear from Fanny about this vicar cousin of hers, I will ask when he and his church, wherever it is, would be free to marry us before the tenth of September, so El.... El.... what did you call her? ...... will be able to make it."

"Elbie," nodded Hannah. "She has numerous names, but she writes a newspaper column and signs herself LB, I think it's so people don't realise she's a woman. It was her colleagues who corrupted it into Elbie, and everybody knows who we're talking about. Elbie is just lovely, you will adore her."

They arrived at No 30, entered the hallway together, and knocked timidly at the parlour door. Miss Janet invited them both in, and Miss Jane looked up from her book, peered at them over her spectacles and remarked, "Brought reinforcements, have you?"

"Miss Jane, Miss Janet, I am sooooo sorry...." began Will, but Janet laughed at him.

"She's only pretending to be cross, Mr Waverley. Please sit down, both of you. Catherine told us what you and your friends were up to, and we saw you all leave. Don't worry, dinner tonight was cottage pie, so it was easy enough to give everyone else a little extra, and nothing was wasted. It was very good cottage pie, so you might well be sorry. Shall we have some coffee?" and without waiting for a reply she rang to summon Catherine.

Miss Jane now chipped in with wry advice to get all his 'bacheloring antics' over with before he got married, and they all grinned, as much in surprise as with amusement. The canny Catherine had anticipated that black coffee might be required, and it was already percolating.

Will told the ladies what his friends had been summoned for, but they were shocked to think that a great man of Castletown had to go to such lengths for the sake of what a few ill-mannered people thought. Both of these elderly ladies had been in service all of their working lives, and they knew that people of real breeding did not act in such an unchristian fashion. But of course, he must do as he felt best, and they just wished them both well.

They finished their coffee. Will apologised again, and said good-night to the landladies. He kissed his sweetheart in the hall, but all the naughtiness had seeped out of him and he only wanted to sleep. Hannah understood this, and made no demands, kissed his cheek and watched him to make sure he made it to the top of the stairs safely, and then let herself out.

Chapter Sixteen

The following morning, Will received a letter from his nephew, Douglas Lacey. He had arrived home from University just in time to help his family move out of Castletown, and they had been kept busy over the weekend, sorting out all their belongings. Dougie was distressed to hear about the terrible rift between his mother, Agnes, and her brother. He had been at Oxford all the time that Will and Hannah had been walking out, and he had not heard a word about it. Chrissie wrote to him regularly, but she must have been under orders not to mention it, so it had all come as a terrible shock upon his arrival home. He asked if he could visit Will to catch up on old times. Will was touched, and felt sorry for the young man who had once been one of his star pupils, as well as a dear nephew. The letter also gave Will his sister's new address in Ramsey, and now he could rectify an omission that had been on his conscience. He must write and thank Agnes for her parting gift.

That evening, Will and Hannah strolled in the opposite direction from Hango Hill, and he told her about Dougie's letter. "Oh, goodness, I had forgotten about Douglas," she said, "he is a nice boy, isn't he? Wasn't he one of your best pupils? I'm sure I've heard about him, although I'm not sure I have a face to put to the name. He would be a few years younger, I imagine."

"He's about twenty-two now, and studying theology at Oxford's St Edmund Hall. He is more of his father's disposition than his mother's, although both Agnes and Richard have always been avid seekers of knowledge. Richard especially is into all sorts of studies and researches and archaeological digs, speaks fluent Manx, oh – you name it, and Richard will know about it! I'm very fond of him, he's headmaster at Santon School now. I must write to him about our marriage too. Douglas wants to come and see me, so I will sound him out about attending the wedding, I would like him to come."

"When it comes time to send out invitations, I suppose it would be only polite to invite all the Laceys. I doubt if Agnes would want to attend, and probably wouldn't let her daughter come, but at least if they don't make it, they won't be able to say it was because they weren't asked." As usual, Hannah had surprised Will with the way she understood things, and he thought this a very kind, if brave suggestion.

Before long, they found themselves scrambling on the rocks at Scarlett. Will pointed out the striations in the rocks, and Hannah teased him about being always the schoolmaster. "I went to school once," she reminded him, and then suggested what might happen in one of those hidden grooves. He adored her anyway, but he always loved the way she made everything such fun. They found a very secluded patch, almost like a cave, and he beat his chest, saying, "Me Cave Man, You my Woman," and they indulged in much the same activity as any Neanderthal couple may have done. The noises they made were probably similar too.

"Are you all right?" came a voice from somewhere nearby. Will looked round and saw another couple leaning over the edge of their rocks. Remaining on top of Hannah, Will replied that they were fine, his lady had slipped and been winded, he was comforting her but she was recovering well, it would just take a few minutes. The people moved out of their sight, but Will and Hannah arranged their clothing properly again, just in case.

"What an accomplished liar you are." said Hannah. "Tch! Shocking! Wicked Waverley!" As they scrambled to their feet, the young man appeared again, having clambered down the rocks to help them.

"I see what you mean," he said, "some of these surfaces are really slippery. It could have been dangerous if you had broken something, with the tide coming in. Are you sure you are all right?" He took Hannah's hand and helped her back up to the grass bank. "Oh, what a beautiful ring!" he gasped, "I tried to buy one just like it recently for my Eva," and he turned to introduce the girl who had remained at the top of the rocks. "I'm Tom Cowley," he held out his hand now to Will, to help him up the last big step, and also to shake his hand, "and this is Miss Quilliam. We are getting married at Braddan on the twelfth of September."

They strolled back towards Castletown as a foursome, having shown Eva the aquamarine ring, and the girl said it must have been destined for Hannah and not for her, as she was 'over the moon' with her sapphire, which was her birthstone. Hannah told her she had often wondered if she must have been born a few days early, as she had always favoured the turquoise shades of March over the purple ones of the February amethyst. Then she remarked that it was such a coincidence about Eva and Tom's wedding date, as theirs was not quite finalised yet, but would probably be at the same church a week earlier. "Oh, I don't think so," said Eva, "We asked for the fifth because that is my birthday, but they are fully booked up. I hope they will manage to fit you in, but you've left it awfully late. What about the banns?" Hannah noticed that the girl was looking at her lower half. She thinks I'm pregnant, oh I just wish I were. Perhaps I am!

Hannah explained how they had intended it originally to be in February, but that a house had become available now, and also about her friend, the older bridesmaid, who had to be back on the mainland before the twelfth of September. Then she went on to tell her how excited her little sister, Carrie, was, and how important she felt about being a bridesmaid too.

Eva asked how old Carrie was, and looked sad when Hannah told her. "You are so lucky to have a little sister." she said quietly. "I had two, but Melinda died before she was four, and Dora...." she took a deep breath that was partly a sob, "would have been just ten now, but she died too, only three months ago. She was still with us when we first started talking about getting married, and she so wanted to be a bridesmaid but.... it wasn't to be."

Hannah placed an arm round the girl's shoulders and tried to think platitudes of condolence, but could only beg her to look forward to their new life, and probably her own babies. Eva admitted that they had thought about making their new life, perhaps in America or Canada, but Tom had no trade, he was only a labourer. But she brightened a little as she realised things could be worse. "But at least he is not a miner, like my Pa and so many others, such a lot of them had to go to faraway places to find the work when the mines here were dwindling, and they still died from the horrid conditions."

Hannah assured her that there were opportunities for all in the Americas and Australia, where a willingness to work was the important thing. Eva tried to smile her thanks. "My mother is a school teacher," she said, "and is not best impressed with my choice of husband, so we are under some pressure to prove to everybody that we can succeed."

Again, Hannah sympathised, and pointed out the difficulties she and Will faced, especially here in Castletown, and how there was opposition to their union too. "Let us all prove them wrong," she said determinedly, "and show that love conquers all."

Will had picked up on the 'school teacher' remark, and asked about Eva's mother who, it turned out, was headmistress of Dalby School. Will told her that his brother-in-law, Richard Lacey, had been headmaster there at one time, and he hoped that conditions were better these days. So, the conversation drifted round to other parts of the island and the world, and Hannah sank into her own thoughts. Eva's mournful tale and mention of banns had depressed her and she began to feel a little agitated that this wedding was never going to happen. She had not given a thought to all the legal requirements, only to being Will's wife, and she hardly noticed the rest of the conversation, which had now turned to the weather and music for weddings. Arriving back in the town, they bade their new friends good-bye, and all best wishes for their new life together, and promised to keep in touch, knowing that they probably would not.

When they were alone again, Hannah mentioned the question of banns. They have to be read out weeks and weeks in advance, don't they, and time is running out. Will calmed her down, assuring her that his best man, John Qualtrough, was ahead of this problem. They would be married by licence so that no banns were required, and their antagonists would not hear about their plans. In any case, he laughed, we don't have a date or a church yet. I have written to the Rev Moore at Braddan, and hope to arrange a meeting with him very soon. We are not confined to Saturdays for our wedding, so I am leaving it to the vicar to suggest a date. Your father has recommended the organist from his church, I think he said a Mr Cubbon, to officiate at the organ, in case the usual Braddan one couldn't do it, so we are just waiting for a letter to arrive.

They were hardly through the door, back at 34 Hope Street, when Carrie came bounding to Hannah asking, "Can I have my hair done up special-like with flowers like a little crown?"

"What, now?" Hannah teased.

"No, Silleee, for the Wedding!"

"A cap of flowers, and a kirtle, embroidered all with leaves of myrtle, a belt of straw and ivy buds, with coral clasps and amber studs," Hannah quoted from one of her favourite poems in the little book Will had given her, and she saw Carrie's eyes widen and her mouth drop open. "Carrie, you are a pain in the neck!" but she knelt down and hugged her sister so tight that the girl squirmed, "but I love you so much, don't you ever forget that, Carrie, I am so lucky to have you to be the bestest bridesmaid ever."

Now that Will knew how to contact Agnes, he took out the writing pad, dipped his pen in the ink, and then his mind went completely blank. He wrote several conciliatory attempts and then tore them up, wondering why he felt so nervous about writing to his sister. Then he took hold of himself and began to write politely as if to a stranger. By the end, he had relaxed into familiar mode.

30, Bowling Green Road,
Castletown
22nd July, 1908

Dear Agnes,

    I trust that you are settling in at your new home, and that the upheaval has not adversely affected your health.

    Douglas has written to me, giving your address, and I hope to be able to meet up with him some time soon, but first I must thank you for your thoughtful gifts. I was very touched to receive the gramophone records that you had retained, but the new recordings of Caruso and Melba are better than ever, and such good choices, both of them. I have always loved 'On with the Motley,' as you know, and I now find it hard to express my feelings, when we had parted under such bad terms. You had no cause to leave such a lovely gift, but you could not have pleased me more, as you were not to know that almost all my existing records were broken in the course of being moved. It must have been the bumpy ride over the cobbles. Thank you, so much.

There is wonderful news, Ag, the great Madame Melba is to perform at the Derby Castle next month, and I must organise my duties to enable me to attend that great concert. Perhaps you may like to experience that great voice at first hand too.

Also, I shall be moving again at the end of next week, just a few doors along to No. 22, where I have taken the lease, and will be furnishing and decorating during the school holidays. Because of this, Hannah and I have decided to bring our wedding date forward. It has not been finalised yet, but we are hoping for a date early in September, and I will let you know when it is confirmed.

Please would you thank Dougie for his letter and tell him I would be delighted to see him whenever it is convenient for him to come to Castletown.

Thank you again for your wonderful choices of music. Please try to be happy for me.

Affectionately,
Will

He did not expect, nor did he receive a reply from Agnes.

A few days later, he was delighted to have the Rev Moore's confirmation that they could be married at the Parish Church of Kirk Braddan on the morning of Monday the seventh of September. Their organist, Mr Cubbon, would be required, and welcome to officiate. William must procure a licence, and let the vicar know as soon as it had been obtained, and then they would arrange for the usual pre-nuptial advisory meeting.

Hannah was thrilled, and lost no time informing her grandparents and parents about the date. Mary was a little sad that she might not be able to make it to Douglas on a Monday morning, as it was such a busy day in the shop, but conceded that it may have been difficult for her whenever and wherever it was. Perhaps if she closed up early, she would be able to attend the reception. In any case, she would be making Hannah's dress, nothing would prevent that. Mary had been a needlework teacher in her day, and her fingers were still as nimble as ever, but the artistic Hannah could design her own dress, and those of the bridesmaids.

Billa said he couldn't afford a new suit, so wouldn't be able to give her away, and Hannah felt sorry about that, as Grandad Bickerstaff probably wouldn't make it either. However, her brother Frank, already good pals with Will, offered to stand in as 'giver-awayer,' and Mother set about finding a recipe for wedding cake, insisting on providing that, and the flowers.

Hannah wrote right away to Elbie, and within a few days had her friend's delighted reply. An old hand at making travel arrangements, she would book her crossing for the week before, and take lodgings at Athol House, on Broadway, in Douglas where she had stayed several times before. Hannah must stay there with her for as long as she liked, but definitely on the night before the wedding, as she must not be allowed to see Will on the Big Day until she arrived at the altar. Elbie also gave her measurements for the bridesmaid's dress.

She had met little Carrie before and was pleased that they would be the only bridesmaids. "Why don't we call Carrie the 'chief bridesmaid'? she suggested, "so she can feel even more important and be responsible for holding your train and your bouquet. I will sign the register as a witness and generally attempt to outshine the bride! Please, just don't dress me in navy."

They both knew this was a joke, going back to a revulsion of her old school colours, but Hannah took up the challenge and thereafter referred to Elbie's outfit as 'the uniform.'

In the meantime, Aunt Emily had insisted on providing the wedding breakfast, or reception, or lunch, call it what you like, she said, but it made sense to have it at her house, where there was plenty of room; since the ceremony was at Braddan, and if they were going away on honeymoon, they would be getting the boat from Douglas too. Hannah had not thought about a honeymoon, Will had not mentioned it. She would not have cared if they didn't have one, she just so wanted to be Mrs Waverley and start their life together properly at last.

Knowing that Hannah had never been off the island in her life, Will made some secret enquiries regarding a honeymoon. He had been born in London, by an accident of his parents' wanderings at the time, but had been brought up in Cheltenham, and had worked for a while near Brighton. He therefore planned to take his bride to London, which surely everyone ought to see at least once in their life, and then to show her the seaside resort of Brighton, which would still be enjoying its summer season. Cheltenham would be a convenient 'half way house' on the way in both directions. He would write to his cousin, Gideon, and tell him they would be coming. All the houses in his area took in lodgers. They might even take the opportunity to visit his father's grave, perhaps.

Hannah had told him what Elbie planned about staying in Douglas during the preceding week, and he thought the girl must be very fond of Hannah to give up her time. He had no idea how she made a living, and with all the travelling she managed to do, he wondered if she was a lady of private means of some sort. However, she could turn out to be a useful ally in arranging the honeymoon travel plans, and he determined to talk to her at the earliest opportunity. With a morning wedding, and then a lunch time reception with speeches and toasts, it would have to be a late afternoon boat to Liverpool for the first leg of their journey. That would probably occasion an overnight stop in Liverpool. Their first night. Their Wedding Night. He couldn't wait.

Chapter Seventeen

The marriage licence was duly procured and Will and Hannah attended Braddan Vicarage to complete the arrangements, and listen to the Rev Moore's little talk about the meaning and responsibilities of marriage. They nodded, promised and agreed with whatever he said, and then caught the late train back to Castletown. Being a midweek evening, there were very few passengers and they had a compartment to themselves. This was too good an opportunity to miss, and Will began to tease Miss Trollop about the promises she had made, and how she must remain virginal until the wedding day, his hand creeping up her skirt the whole time. She pretended to slap him away, stuck her chin out and reminded him that he had made promises too. However, his hand had reached one of those spots that always made her shiver with anticipation, and she bit his neck in her excitement. "Ow!" he yelled, "Right, you minx, you can forget all that stuff and nonsense," and he launched himself onto her, forgetting to undo his breeches. They both just rolled about laughing and squirming, and finding that even this was quite delightful. And it was just as well, as the train pulled in to a stop at Santon, which meant that people might walk past, or even enter their compartment, so they straightened their clothing and sat primly, trying hard not to burst with laughter. One or two passengers did pass by, without looking in, but their moment had come and gone, and they simply chatted for the rest of the journey. There was so much to chat about.

Hannah did not discuss the designs for her bridal gown with Will, but she hoped to take his breath away by creating something quite different from the current fashions. Wedding dresses had evolved from the off-the-shoulder styles of earlier Victorian times, and were now all puff sleeves, high collars, lacy frills and flounces and great, flowing skirts, and Will had seen them all in his capacity of church organist. Hannah was not a frilly sort of girl, and the last thing she wanted was anything ostentatious. She knew she would have her critics, whatever she did, and she was determined to give them as little as possible to deride, but she had an ace up her sleeve with the champion needlewoman who was her Gran. Mary had a stash of samples and examples, and the two pored over the various articles, wrapping here and draping there in front of the long mirror. As for the bridesmaids' dresses, the poetry she had quoted to Carrie, which had been spontaneous at the time, had given her inspiration.

∞∞∞

During school holidays, it was traditional for other activities to be reduced as well, and some of Will's private students also took vacations. He therefore, found more time than usual on his hands, and even helped out in the grocery shop from time to time, simply so that he could be with Hannah. Not that he could get much sense out of her or Mary, now all that was in their heads was dress-making, and Carrie was no help, being so excited about all the measurings and fittings for her new finery, finding some new shoes, endlessly arranging and re-arranging her hair, and boning up on all the responsibilities of a chief bridesmaid.

But on the first day of August, which was a Saturday, Will moved his few belongings to the little house four doors away from his temporary apartment.

He didn't require a cart this time, as first he dragged the trunk along, and then he carried all his clothing in one trip, then his gramophone, and lastly his records and toiletries. He had bought an expensive bottle of wine from Tom Dodd, who knew how to recommend something that the ladies would appreciate, and he presented this to his landladies together with his house key. They were so sorry to see him leave, and insisted on his staying for lunch with them, before he went. He was reminded about the harmonium, and he promised to have it moved as soon as one of the rooms at No 22 was ready to take it. When Miss Jane asked if he would like the piano too, he said he couldn't possibly.... but again, they insisted, if he had room, he must have it so that he didn't have to give his piano lessons in the church hall. Will had played this piano on a number of occasions and knew it was in good condition with a nice tone. The landladies intended to create two more apartments from some of the rooms now used for storage, and would be grateful for more space in the dining room to accommodate the extra tables. When they put it that way he said, he would be doing them a favour if he could relieve them of both instruments? Oh yes, they dearly wished him to have them, knowing that they would find a happy home and continue to be useful and give pleasure.

The house along the street had only been vacated a few days earlier, and was not cold, although the fire had been left to go out, but there was very little furniture and, with a gasp, he realised that there was not a bed in the house! There was an old settee in the parlour, and a small table and two bentwood chairs in the kitchen. He was pleased to see there was a gas stove, although he had no idea how to work one, and there were some utensils so, feeling something like a fish out of water, he took stock of what he thought was required. Perhaps he was going to need Sydney's hand cart after all.

First, he went to 34 Hope Street and related all the news. Hannah was released briefly from her shop duties to gather some items from the house that were surplus to requirements. Some crockery and bedding, towels and pans were collected into the hallway; meanwhile, Mary packed a box with some basic foodstuffs, so that he could at least make himself some breakfast on his first morning. Of course, he must come back to 34 for any other meals, he would always be welcome.

Will then went in search of Sydney or his father, perhaps even Frank. Any of the brothers might be able to show him where to find the handcart. He needed to see Billa anyway, to take stock of the decorating that was needed, and quote him a price.

The lads were all out watching football, but Billa was in, taking a nap. Mrs Corlett bustled about, upon hearing the nature of his business, put the kettle on and also produced some housewares that she 'had been going to dispose of anyway,' and Will began to feel that his house would be a home in no time. He said he would have to buy furniture when the shops opened again on Monday, and would be making a list, but when he told her that he would have to sleep on the sofa, she said, "You can't do that! You need to see Mrs Quine on Douglas Street. She has a divan to give away. She wants the room for a big dresser she has just inherited. Pop in and see her on your way back." Then she brewed a pot of tea and woke her husband. Billa Corlett was happy to see Will and hear all the latest. He said they'd have this cuppa and then take the cart round to Mary's.

At the shop, Hannah helped them to load the items she had gathered onto the cart, alongside the goodies from her mother, and now Charles Bickerstaff joined them too. So, it was a merry little band of older gentlemen who trundled the handcart along the quayside behind Hope Street, over the bridge and off into Douglas Street. Here they found that Mrs Quine had already heard about the requirement for a bed, and Will wondered how that had happened. Young Carrie had popped in at her mother's while out playing with her friends, just after the men had left, and was sent on the errand to warn Mrs Quine that they were coming for the bed. She had helped the woman to drag it to the door, then walked further along to see where Will's new house was, and was now returning, eager to join them all and 'help.'

The divan came complete with a mattress, two pillows, and a quilt, and Will didn't know how to thank everyone for such kindness. The woman said both he and Caroline Corlett had done her a favour, and she pressed a freshly baked gooseberry tart into his hands as well.

Everything was decanted into No 22, and Billa Corlett scanned the whole house for paint and wallpaper requirements. "The trouble is, we can't really fit y'in right away, unless...." and he rubbed his chin, looking askance at Will, "unless ya care ter muck in as well?"

How exciting! Will had never been asked to do practical things, his responsibilities were all either musical or brain-powered, and he found this suggestion heart-warming. He felt truly accepted into the Corlett empire, although he warned his future father-in-law that he had never held a paint brush in his life, well, not one that big anyway. Billa assured him it wasn't difficult, but he would be bound to find it boring, however, it was man-power that was useful, and he could help to make the job a lot quicker. He might even be trusted with working out measurements for the papering, he said, eyeing some of the oddly shaped nooks and crannies of one of the bedrooms. Old Bickerstaff said he would just supervise, and Billa told him to beggar off, or words to that effect, although Charles didn't budge until they all did.

Calling it a day by about four o'clock, they all headed back towards the town, and Will asked for Mr Corlett's estimate for the decorating. "Well let's think now," frowned Billa, sucking air through his teeth and scratching his chin again, "maybe in the light of ya doin' some of the labourin' yerself, I reckon we shud be able to manage it as yer weddin' present, yissir!"

"My cup runneth over!" exclaimed Will. "You people are so kind to me. Thank you, Billa, I am so touched."

Billa waved away his effusiveness with a growl, but was pleased enough with the response.

Will then found time to call at the furniture shop of another friend, Benjamin Kermode. He explained that he had just taken possession of No 22, and that he would need to lay new linoleum before he could think about furniture. Ben seemed more interested in the furniture he had in mind, and a long list was mentioned, which the experienced man whittled down to the real essentials, just to get started with, and showed Will some very nice pieces at various prices. They all shocked the musician, but he knew it was all necessary, however, it occurred to him that Hannah might like to make some choices and he promised Ben that they would be back early next week to take a closer look. His friend knew he meant it, and asked if he had left No 22 open (which was common), and promised to go over there right now and measure up the rooms. "Pick your lino now, and we will have it cut and ready to lay on Monday morning," he said.

"Oh, shouldn't Hannah have a say in that too?" Will prevaricated.

"Are you a man or a mouse?" teased Ben, "Oh, all right, Mr Mouse, we will be open until six, hurry back!" Will took a quick look at the few linoleum options, and had a fair idea which he disliked least, thinking that most lino would eventually be hidden by carpets, furniture and rugs anyway, but he hurried off to whisk Hannah back to get her opinion quickly.

Needless to say, Hannah found this all very exciting. She had been thrilled to help earlier by collecting the items Mary had listed, and she really couldn't wait to be alone with Will in 'their' new house. She was so pleased about the re-decorating arrangements, and straight away decided that they would visit her parents tomorrow afternoon to look at the wallpaper books.

It was just as well that the furniture shop was closing soon, as Hannah would have loved to browse for an hour, but she was called back to reality in the need for linoleum to be laid before they started piling furniture into the place. She perused the collection of tall rolls of floor-covering, and her mind was thinking of curtains, cushions and rugs, as well as the colour of the walls or the wallpaper, and found it was difficult to choose. She wasn't wild about any of them, and settled, in the end, for the one that Will indicated, which was a mixture of shades of pale brown. Brown paint was used a lot in most homes, but Hannah was adamant that she would prefer lighter coloured furnishings and, with a clean sheet to start on, she was delighted to have been invited to help with the design. She really was going to be the mistress in this house. This home. Their home.

Mary had insisted on giving them both their tea before they headed off to 'the new house' so, armed with a few more bits and pieces that she had thought about, such as candles and matches, and kindling for the fire, they set off at last to be able to close the door behind them and be together, in private, almost legitimately.

∞∞∞∞

The plan was to leave what furniture he had all in the one room until linoleum had been laid in some of the others, and then to decant it where appropriate. The divan and the old sofa were therefore both pushed together in what they might call the living room, and they lost no time in flinging themselves onto this makeshift double bed. "Oh, Will, we are so nearly there, aren't we! I can't believe it is all really happening," she mused dreamily between kisses, but as he began to undo her blouse, she stopped him. She was convinced that someone would find a reason to interrupt them. "As soon as we have a bedroom properly furnished, next week, I will feel happier about stripping off, but tonight I really feel we had better...." and she had not completed the sentence when there was a knock at the door. Will separated the sofa from the bed while Hannah went to admit their visitors.

Her brothers, George and Charlie, had come 'for a skeet' at the place, feeling they were the only ones who had not seen it. Hannah explored the kitchen, found a kettle and the matches and soon had water boiling merrily on the gas. She found that four beakers were the extent of the drinking utensils, and remarked it was just as well that the whole family had not arrived.

Charlie said he would like to paint a picture for their new home as a wedding present, and asked if there was a subject or a place that they were fond of. Will and Hannah smiled at each other, and Hannah said that there was a place, but he would have to take a whole day out to paint it. "When you go to Ramsey on the electric tram," she explained, "you come round a corner where you first see the town, with the whole bay sweeping right round to the Point of Ayre, just as it looks on the map, and little hills in the background. That view is really pretty on a sunny day with blue sky and a couple of schooners crossing the bay."

Charlie said she had already painted the picture for him, and she said it was how it had been described to her, and she was so delighted that, when she saw it, it was just exactly as she expected it. "I know," he assured her, "I have been to Ramsey. I believe the tram goes all the way into the town these days, though. We had to go the last mile by horse and cart when I last went, and some people just walked it."

"Will took some of the boys from school, and they scrambled down the ravine and through the river to get into the town along the shore," she continued excitedly. "As soon as he described it to me, I wanted to see it for myself, so we took a picnic one day." They all noticed that she then blushed, and smiles and winks were exchanged, but nobody said anything.

"I believe Frank went to Ramsey recently," added George, "we must ask him if he noticed the view!"

"Yes, we all went together on Tynwald Day, Frank and Cis...." blurted Hannah before remembering that it was Cissie's secret.... it was a sort of family day out!" she finished lamely.

"It's all right, Old Thing," said George. "We know about Frank and Cis. Mother and Aunt Em don't know, and Sydney knows Frank has a sweetheart, but not who it is, in case he tells Mother! Such subterfuge, but that's why I wondered if he had noticed the scenery, I dare say his eyes were only on Cissie!"

"Aye, and his hands!" chimed in Charlie. Hannah pretended to be shocked, and they all laughed.

Chapter Eighteen

The men stayed for a couple of hours, and they all enjoyed each other's company. Will confessed that he had never attempted to light a fire and didn't know how to start. This caused great hilarity, and the account that the brothers had heard of Will's drunken escapade was also made much of, but by the end of the day, they were the best of friends and Will knew how to start a fire. In fact they were able to warm themselves since the evening and the house had begun to feel decidedly cooler. The house could now be aired before the furniture, or the decorators, arrived. Hannah said she had been half expecting their father to turn up with tins of paint, to which George said the night was still young! Realising that there was not a clock in the house, Will consulted his pocket watch and found that it was almost ten. "I thought it looked as if it was getting dark!" he exclaimed. "You don't really think Billa would turn up now, do you?"

"No, not on a Saturday, he'll be too 'far gone' himself by now!" said Charlie. "Hannah, let us walk you home so this good chap can get his head down at last, he must be exhausted after all today's excitement."

Will assured them he would have been willing for a little more excitement, but perhaps they were right, and they could save him the walk to Hope Street and back. After invitations to 'call any time,' and a good-night kiss for Hannah, the little group left Will alone in his new domain.

He had more excitement that night, without Hannah's help, when he realised he was not alone in the house. It had now gone almost dark outside, and he lit an oil lamp with a taper from the fire. After everyone had left, the house seemed so quiet, and Will could not remember when he had last been so alone in any house. It was therefore at first a mystery that he could hear something. His musical ear could usually interpret sounds easily, but this was for all the world like someone tearing up paper. He tried to think where there was paper to be torn up, then remembered the kindling that Mary had given him. They had used some of the paper and sticks earlier to start the fire, but the remains were still in the hearth, where they had left them.

Will took the lamp to the fireplace and peered towards the old newspapers. "Aargh!" he shouted when he perceived two mice, busily shredding the paper and enjoying the warmth from the grate. His shout and movement startled them, and they scuttled out of sight. He poked about with the fire irons, but they remained hidden. Here was another new experience for the headmaster, the all-knowing, unflappable commander. He was frightened!

He didn't relish the idea of killing anything but there was no way he would be able to sleep in this room with animals roaming about. What was he going to do? For a moment he thought about the nice comfortable, if noisy, bed he had left behind at number 30, but then pulled himself together and tried to apply logic. Surely the mice were not in the paper that he had brought all the way from Hope Street? That would mean there were mice at Mary's, and that didn't bear thinking about, with all the food in the shop. Had they been in the bed from the neighbour? No, the mice were here before him, and therefore the previous tenants may have had some traps. How annoying that it was after dark that this problem had arisen. He took the oil lamp into the kitchen and opened various cupboards, until he came upon the one under the staircase that had obviously contained cleaning materials and now just a threadbare broom. But glory be! Two mouse traps. Now, how do these infernal things work? Several injured fingertips later, the two traps, baited with cheese, were secreted at either end of the hearth, and Will settled into the sofa to watch.

He kept very still, staring at the place where he had last seen movement and, after a quiet while, first one mouse and then the other, poked their noses out again. Will was fascinated at the way they moved. He could not see their feet move and they appeared to glide, as they dashed in and out of cover. Just like clockwork mice he thought! Damn them! Why weren't they going for the cheese? He continued to watch their antics, and began to think they were quite cute, the way their pointed noses and whiskers twitched, and their black beady eyes seemed to miss nothing. Will hardly dared to breathe, but against all expectation, he dozed off, still sitting comfortably on the sofa.

CLICK! rattle, rattle. Will awoke with a start, and had hardly worked out what had happened when the same noise came again. The oil light was guttering, and he got up to turn on one of the gas lamps on the wall. On the way, he walked on something soft. "Aargh!" he said again, and a few expletives also escaped him as he realised what had happened and what he had walked on. He gingerly picked up the traps and put them, and their limp contents, outside the back door. He assumed there would be a midden somewhere, but he would investigate all that in the daylight.

He backed up the fire as Charlie had instructed, and curled up on the divan, hoping that sleep might return before the morning – or before more mice turned up – and he listened intently for a long time. He was intrigued with all the sounds that came to him out of the darkness. A breeze had sprung up, making a shushing noise in the trees on the avenue, and an odd little whistle as a draught crept under a door. A door banged in a neighbouring house. He could hear horses' hooves quite a distance away and wondered what was afoot. Probably the constables taking some Saturday night brawler to the dungeons! A church clock chimed once, and he tried to work out if it was one o'clock or half past something. He got up and pushed a coat against the bottom of the back door, just in case dead mice had a knack of reviving and wreaking revenge, and he found a window that was open a fraction and rattling intermittently. A list of jobs was forming that grew as he tried again to sleep, but eventually exhaustion overtook him, and he was awakened only by a shaft of dawn sunlight coming through from the kitchen window at the back.

Rolling off the divan, which had been surprisingly comfortable, he found his watch and learned that it was a quarter to five. He knew he would not sleep again and, adding 'move the bed' to the mental list of jobs, he padded into the kitchen and lit the gas. The kettle was soon making interesting noises, and he wondered what else he could get to work. The fire would need some attention if he was to make toast the way Baby had shown him, but didn't these wonderful gas stoves do it somehow? He scratched his chin for a few moments, before deciding to attempt to make some porridge instead. He was sure it was pretty easy, although he soon found that it was not as easy as he assumed, and his first attempt went as solid as concrete and 'burned itself' to the pot. Should he try to make toast after all? Or how about a fried egg? Oh yes, a fried egg would be lovely. And it was. Even if it did involve a kitchen full of smoke and an egg that was curled up and crisp at the edges, it was delicious and he had achieved it all on his own, shunning the sneaking desire to toddle four doors along and beg Catherine to cook his breakfast for him.

He opened the back door to let the smoke out, and saw the two mouse traps. Something had eaten half of one of the bodies, and poor Will's egg nearly came back to haunt him. He covered his mouth with his hand, and remembered that he still had to shave. Oh, life was easier when he had his luxurious beard. Mmm. Easier but not nearly as exciting! He decided that shaving was a small price to pay, then wondered if anyone had thought of providing a mirror. He rummaged in the jumble of his belongings and found his shaving brush, soap and cut-throat razor, and was relieved to find a mirror of sorts in the bathroom. It was quite something that there was a bathroom, with a flushing lavatory, not every house boasted such luxury, but this house even had a wash basin in one of the bedrooms. How very modern.

Will was suddenly appalled to realise that he had slept fully clothed, and he stripped off in order to get a wash. This was when he realised that he should have boiled a kettle just for washing himself, as he might stand the cold water on a warm August morning, but it wouldn't always be like this. He was going to have to get pencil and paper for this ever-growing list of things he had to remember now that he was responsible for a whole household.

Eventually, the ablutions and dressing completed, he began to feel more human and thought again about a slice of toast. Now that it was light, he could see how the stove might work. He put the kettle on again for some fresh tea, and tried a piece of bread under the grill. Remembering the burned bread of his first attempt at the fire, he watched what was happening, and made a seriously good piece of toast without setting fire to anything. He fiddled with the gas taps and realised that the flames were adjustable. How clever was that!

Flushed with success, he ate his toast with butter from Pooil Vaaish and some of Mary's homemade marmalade and enjoyed the freshly brewed tea better than the stewed first attempt. The day was getting better with the daylight!

He explored the layout of the whole house. It was quite a fine building, double fronted, with a central staircase. What would be the parlour was a large room on one side, running the width of the house, which would certainly accommodate both the piano and the harmonium in due course, while the other side was the living room at the front, with a doorway into the kitchen at the back. Upstairs were four bedrooms, two at the front and two at the rear, with the small bathroom in the middle. Under the stairs, a large cupboard had been boarded in, accessed from the kitchen, which was where he had found the broom and the mousetraps. Outside, he found a lean-to against the back wall, which was open to the yard on one side. This contained a dolly tub, complete with wooden dolly, a wooden clothes horse and a mangle. Ah, a complete laundry room. Will was not sure how hot water would be obtained in sufficient quantity to use these domestic wonders, and a whole new chapter was added to his list of things to do and to learn. But then, some things really were for the women-folk to know about, and he was sure that Hannah would take it all in her stride.

He disposed of the dead mice at the end of the back yard, and took the traps back indoors, ran them under the tap and left them to dry on the window sill, intending to set them again before he tried to sleep tonight. Then he went right into the cupboard under the stairs to see whatever there was to see. Now that it was light outside, but dark in the cupboard, he could see a chink of light where the floor joined the outside wall. Aha! That would be how the mice could get in. Another job for the list, he would ask Billa Corlett how best to block up a hole in the wall. Hannah had said they would go to see her father that afternoon to look at wallpaper books. He would ask him then.

Will made another startling discovery. Time flies by so much more quickly when you have one of those lists of things that must be done, and when you are the head of the household, chief cook and bottle (or mousetrap) washer, and he was glad he would have time to acclimatise to all this before the school term started again. Oh goodness. By then, he would be a married man. Just thinking about Hannah gave him a little flurry of excitement in the trouser department, and he suddenly couldn't wait to see her. However, as time had flown so much, he was now required at Church for his morning 'practice.' Even on Sunday, he liked to stoke the great organ into life early in the day, and today he must clear his head of all these secular (and sexual) demands so that he could give the music and the instrument the attention they deserved. He would call at Hope Street after practice and before Matins. And perhaps tonight they might actually have some private time! Perhaps.

After his organ practice session, he walked to No 34, where Mary was preparing to put a leg of lamb into the oven, and Hannah was peeling potatoes. Will sat down opposite Grandpa, and Carrie appeared from nowhere and perched herself on Will's knee. The kettle was already singing on the fire, and very soon a pot of tea was brewed, but they all wanted to know how he had got on in the new house, looking after himself!

It was quite a tale that he had to relate, and there was much hilarity over his unexpected ignorance of domestic matters. "I could have made your porridge!" claimed Carrie, jiggling on his knee.

"Yes, but you are a w'... ..... a lady!" protested Will, "and ladies are so much cleverer at such things."

Carrie didn't recognise diplomacy, or flattery, so puffed her chest out with pride at being proved cleverer than he was, because everybody knew he was the cleverest man in town.

"Don't get too arrogant, Miss, or he'll have you cooking his tea and washing his vest next!" warned Grandpa, "and lighting the fire and killing the mice, and ....!"

"Stop, stop!" poor Carrie cried, "I'm only a little girl, not a servant!" and she jumped off Will's knee and went to lay out the cups and saucers on the table. Hannah was now peeling carrots, and Will looked at her hard working hands, noticing that her engagement ring was not being subjected to the water and peelings.

The banter was all only in fun, but the child's outburst had touched Will's conscience, and he resolved then and there that he would not expect his wife to attend to these menial and dirty tasks, any more than he would ask the child. He must acquire a housemaid, and he wondered where he could find another Catherine.

They drank their tea, the dripping was melted in the oven and the lamb and potatoes went in to be cooking while they were all at church. Will and Hannah went on ahead, so that he could be among the first to arrive, and start playing the voluntaries, while the congregation filtered in.

After the service, it was quite in order now for Will and Hannah to be seen holding hands on their way home. Most of the congregation had dispersed by the time he finished playing the concluding voluntaries, his favourite 'show-off' pieces, but as an engaged couple, so soon now to be man and wife, they were perfectly comfortable with most of the people of Castletown. They were able to smile, shake hands and engage in polite conversation with numerous townsfolk whose respect for Will overcame any prejudices or gossip. It was plain to see how happy the man was, some people had even noticed how unhappy he had become in earlier months. These were the folk who accepted his liaison with the younger woman, setting aside their own misgivings on the matter. When this group included men and women who were prestigious in their own right, such as the Dodds and the Geldards, Miss Corlett the headmistress of Victoria Road school, John Qualtrough the Board School head, whose brother was their Member of the House of Keys, well, they could not all be wrong, surely?

Will and Hannah felt the warmth now from many of their neighbours, and were most gratified. It was a very happy couple who arrived back in Hope Street. Will was also more than ready for his Sunday dinner, which had begun to smell so appetising before they had left for the service. Remembering that he had only had an egg and a piece of toast, and those very early in the day, his juices were making rumbling noises. It was the most wonderful aroma that met their noses as they entered number 34. Mary had gone on ahead of them from church and cooked the vegetables, made gravy, warmed plates, and Will thought perhaps he would just move in here and forget about Bowling Green Road with its mice and noisy trees and acres of floor needing new lino and furniture.

Chapter Nineteen

Once the inner man, and the rest of the family, had been fed more than adequately, Will would have loved to do as most older men did after Sunday dinner, and have a snooze. He had slept so little overnight, and now he was replete, and happy, and warm, and sleep would have been wonderful. He watched enviously as Grandpa's head began to nod in his fireside chair.

But, Hannah had decreed that they would visit her parents and look at wallpaper books. Oh, deep joy, what had he let himself in for? And then he saw her face. She had washed up while he was still chatting with Grandpa after the rice pudding (with skin on, mmm) and had now combed her hair and replaced her engagement ring, donned a smart little bolero and was ready to go choosing wallpaper. She was so full of life and enthusiasm, and love. Her eyes simply melted him, and he knew he was her slave. There was also the promise that, tonight, perhaps, perhaps, perhaps.....?

Knowing that her father would also be snoozing after Sunday dinner, Hannah suggested that they take a stroll to put some time in. They walked along the harbour side and round Poulsom Park, returning along the bank of the Silverburn, and then via Milner Terrace and Mill Street to the Corlett house in Malew Street. On another day or evening, they might have found somewhere secluded to stop for a cuddle, but on Sunday afternoon, the park was noisy with the squeals of children, some of whom would be on their way to Sunday School, and some of whom might not make it. Now that Hannah's head was full of designs for dresses, furniture and wallpaper, she failed to notice Will's disappointment that she was not making her usual suggestions about having some fun.

He told himself to be patient, but watching her lithe body skipping ahead of him, turning to smile and hurry him, he felt a tiny bit neglected, and wanted her all the more.

Billa had been warned by Charlie that Hannah would be descending on him to look at wallpaper samples, and had hauled several of the large books into the kitchen. He had marked some of them to show what he already had in stock, and Hannah was pleased with those. Will knew he would not disagree with Hannah's taste, as he had already discovered that they shared many preferences and tended to think alike. She obviously already had plans for colour schemes and curtains, and her enthusiasm soon brought him out of his doldrums. Remembering the mouse holes, Will told Billa about his nocturnal adventures and the holes he had spotted, and was promised that any holes would be stuffed with plaster and/or other materials when the decorating began. Meanwhile, depending on the size and shape of the hole, a tennis ball or an orange might suffice as a temporary measure. Oranges always made Will think of Hannah's breasts, and he went a little weak at the knees, thinking of mice nibbling at them. Bloody mice. Bloody lucky mice!

After the usual cups of tea, they set off back to No 22, armed with a few sheets of wallpaper to try up against the walls, with Will's desire burning and his thoughts still on oranges.

When they arrived, however, Hannah bolted the front door, threw the papers on the floor, and grabbed at Will, crushing herself to him as he had not felt her do for what had seemed a long time. She opened her blouse, (oh God, the oranges!) and his trousers, and pulled him down on top of her on the sofa. She was kissing him hungrily and he felt like a teenager again. How did she keep having this effect on him? He lunged at her and felt her lust, as she pushed herself at him with each of his thrusts. She was moaning as if she was in pain, as her body reached at him and gripped him. He had learned to try to control himself since that first disastrous, embarrassing attempt, but he stood no chance with this vixen, and she continued to pleasure herself long after he had been rendered helpless.

She was still panting after he had rolled off her and straightened his clothing. She seemed to be sobbing, and eventually she said, "Oh Will, that was the first time in our own home! I couldn't wait any longer. I was trying to be good, but I just want you all the time, and all these arrangements and things we have to think about are so distracting. I wish I could wave a wand and just suddenly be married, with all the trappings over and done with! Make love to me again, Will. Please."

He lay down beside her on the sofa and took her in his arms, gently, lovingly. Not passionately, just soothingly, as he stroked her face and her hair, and she calmed down and smiled. "You are amazing!" he said, "I adore you, and that was the most exquisite experience. Let's remember that as another 'first time.' There will be lots more first times, and I can't wait to be married either, but I think you're enjoying it really. I am too, in a way, it's an education to see you so animated about the furniture and the decorating and..... Oh hell!" he broke off as he heard the garden gate click.

They quickly made themselves presentable, and Hannah retrieved the strewn wallpaper samples while Will quietly withdrew the bolt and opened the front door.

It was Hannah's mother, Grandmother Mary and little sister Carrie. The ladies had decided it was time they had a look at this house for themselves, and they explored the whole place while Hannah put the kettle on the gas, and sliced up some of Will's gooseberry pie. They discussed colours and curtains and furniture, and Will could see that this was a very feminine pursuit. He would not have cared about colours or things matching, so long as he could take that woman to his bed every night. Hannah had soon made her choices from the wallpaper samples, and obviously had her plans in place for everything else.

They drank tea and ate Mrs Quine's pie, and then Will shocked them all, by taking part at last in the domestic plans. "We shall have a large table in that other room," he announced. "I have been given a piano and a harmonium, and will be able to take my piano pupils in there, so I think it would also be a good place for entertaining. I am going to engage a housemaid, as my wife's place will be as hostess to our guests, and as my representative at social events around the town."

He felt pleased with himself for having made such a decision, in the manner to which he had been accustomed 'before Hannah,' but he had no idea how deeply he had hurt two of the others. Little Carrie was thrilled, Hannah's heart had soared, but Caroline and Mary felt insulted. He saw their faces as the room fell silent, and realised how his remark must have sounded to them.

"Oh, ah, I didn't mean it to sound like that!" he attempted, "Agnes had a house servant, and there is a housekeeper at

Number 30," he took a gulp of air, floundering a little, "and, there will be two or three boarders from school and, God Willing, Hannah may have babies to look after one day...." and his voice trailed off.

"Just keep digging that hole,' said Mary. "We understand, don't we Caroline? And, bless you, we should be grateful that you want to give Hannah a better life than we could give her. And we are, aren't we Lina? Grateful?" She nodded at her daughter, encouraging her to agree.

"There's nothing wrong with our lives," began Caroline, still aggrieved, "but I take your point in a way. You are of a different social class, and have different values and expectations," then, wagging her finger at Hannah, she continued, "but don't you go getting airs and graces above your station with us, Miss."

Hannah embraced her mother. "I shall be 'Mrs' soon! But don't worry, you will always be my mam and Gran will always be irreplaceable. As for you!" she looked at little Carrie who was mystified by the talk and the atmosphere, "you will be my chief bridesmaid, but you won't be our servant! Not until you leave school, anyway."

It had to be pointed out quickly that this was a joke, but Carrie remained confused and cross.

Will bent down and picked her up. "Hey," he said, "I thought we were friends. I did a bad thing then, did you notice? I spoke without thinking properly and I am awfully sorry if anyone is upset. I love you all dearly and admire you. You will not be a servant, Carrie, you will be a great lady, but the most important thing is to be happy. Can you be happy, and forgive me for making you cross? Please?"

The child put her arms round his neck and nodded into his shoulder, and then he set her on her feet again.

They all returned to Hope Street together as it was now time for tea before heading off to church again. The Corletts attended the Primitive Methodist church in Malew Street, not St Mary's 'High Church,' and so Caroline, still tight-lipped, left them at the Quay and went off into Malew Street.

Hannah, too, was unusually quiet. Her emotions were in turmoil. There had been so much in her head, designing dresses, thinking of colour schemes for the house, wallpaper, furniture, and top of her list, simply being Mrs William Waverley. She had even forgotten about the possibility of babies, but the talk of servants, boarders and social classes had thrown her quite off balance. Will had never mentioned any such thing to her privately, and she suddenly realised that he would probably expect her to give up working in her grandmother's shop. That might mean that Mary would have to give up the shop herself, she couldn't be expected to do it all on her own at her age, and keep house as well. Oh dear, things seemed to be going awry, and Hannah felt a deep guilt that in her selfishness she had shown no regard for the impact of her marriage on the other people she loved.

But Mary had given her nothing but encouragement since the day she had confessed to the first kiss, and even seemed as excited as herself about the designs for her wedding dress and those of the two very different bridesmaids. Hannah began to realise how much of a struggle life must be for people like her mother and grandmother. The kind of life she had expected for herself, and was training for, was the same endless effort of making ends meet, one way or another, in order to put food on the family's table. She had not seen marriage to Will as a passport out of such a life, it had simply not occurred to her that there was any other way of plodding on, and she would have accepted that without complaint. All she wanted was to be Will's wife, and she had expected that to include cooking his meals and washing his socks and keeping his home tidy, as well as spending every blissful night in his bed. Having children with him would be the natural progression, as her mother, grandmother and every other wife had done all throughout time, although as she had not become pregnant after three months of frequent and wonderful and fulfilling lovemaking, she was beginning to wonder if it would ever happen for them.

Now, she remembered the polite society of Miss Clague and Miss Walkington, and the somewhat refined meal they had provided. To Hannah's homespun palate, it had been positively epicurean, and quite an education. And she remembered how she had felt, being served wine by a maid. Was this the kind of cultured living that Will was used to and expected? Never having been permitted to darken Agnes's doorstep, she had no idea how much his lifestyle had differed from her own. Well, being the Lady of the House with a maid might be one thing, and all very nice if she had a baby, especially if it was a lovely little girl that she could dress in pretty clothes, but boarders?

Having her house full of other people's snotty-nosed little boys? That was quite a different matter.

She remained quietly deep in these troubling thoughts throughout their frugal meal of ham, cheese and salad vegetables, while the others chatted spasmodically. Poor Will felt as if he had committed a serious crime, for which he would surely be punished, and he knew not how to make things right.

As usual, it was the perceptive Mary who knew how to retrieve a balance. "Will," she began, "I think we can all see that Hannah has had a shock this afternoon." Will looked up at her with his eyes pleading for help. "What none of us may have realised is that the gossips and trouble-makers of the town, and your sister in perhaps a different way, latched onto the difference in your social standing, more than the obvious age difference, thinking that was Hannah's sole purpose in becoming romantically involved with you." Hannah looked up sharply, and Will took a breath to speak, but Mary continued, "I know, and you know, that is just not true. We are privileged to be close to both of you, and we know how you feel about each other. But today, you yourself have pointed up one of the differences in people's expectations. Folk like us could never even entertain the idea of having servants. We are the servants in this life, but I do not have a problem with it if you want to give Hannah the opportunity to sample some gracious living. She is a lucky girl to have found you at last. And you are a lucky man, so don't you forget that!"

Grandpa had no idea what this was all about, and did not see fit to enquire. Carrie just didn't understand any of it, but she saw Will reach for Hannah's hand, and she saw Hannah brush away a tear. She got up and started gathering the used plates, so that she could be doing something she understood, and to hide her confusion. Perhaps she would ask Jesus about it when they got to church.

Hannah asked Will to go on ahead to church, and she would follow with the rest of the family. There was something she had to do. Feeling at a loss for the first time in months, the poor man could do nothing more than comply with her wishes, and he trudged sorrowfully to church alone. He was also realising that there were differences that he had not considered. Again he remembered Billa Corlett's succinct remark about not being able to see any further ahead than his carnal desires, and he too felt the guilt of having been so absorbed in his own delight that the realities of life around him had failed to penetrate his rosy glow.

Back in Hope Street, Hannah went up to her room, threw herself on the bed and wept. There was too much happening all at once. Just when she thought her heaven was so close, her world had turned to ashes. Why had she not seen this coming? Too engrossed in the trappings of a wedding and moving house, and simply besotted with her man and her new-found sexuality, the world around her had ceased to exist. Now she had some hard thinking to do, and perhaps some difficult decisions to take. Mary's explanation was now so blatantly obvious that Hannah could hardly believe that it had not occurred to her before. She thought 'people' were only concerned with the difference in their ages, and possibly the fact that he was a schoolmaster and important person in the town, but class was not a concept that had occurred to her for a moment, in her own present circumstances or any other.

In her way, she also appealed to a higher authority to help her see the way, but did not wait to be in church in order to do it. After the sickening sobs had subsided and her tears dried, she began to feel stronger. What a storm in a teacup she decided. Very little had changed, except that her mind had been opened up to a wider picture. She was still going to marry the man of her dreams, she still had a beautiful wedding dress to make, she would still be choosing new furniture and home decorations in the coming few days, and Will could still excite and melt her with a look or a touch. It was only the acceptance of the baggage that came with him that needed her attention, and she resolved to be less selfish, and take him willingly as he was.

And then she began to smile. All that had changed, she thought, was that Will had unwittingly managed to insult her mother and her grandmother. It was definitely not the first time he had insulted anyone. Since they had been lovers, she had not seen the brusque and inconsiderate side of him that he had been quite famous for in the past. Choir members, or in fact the entire choir, were regularly denigrated, and she had no doubt that his schoolboys would have been subjected to verbal abuse if not fury. His short fuse was legendary, and she had almost forgotten this characteristic which, now she really thought about it, had been one of the things that attracted her to him. His complicity had quite staggered her, and as for his falling in love, well, that had only ever been in her daydreams. Her tears were forgotten as she was now laughing quietly to herself. She glanced heavenwards and mouthed 'Thank You.'

Chapter Twenty

After church, she was her old self again. It was Will who was pensive and troubled. They returned to Hope Street as they had always done and partook of the usual conversation and cocoa in the parlour. "Stop worrying, Will," said Mary, "it is wonderful that you have plans for your house. We had not thought about boarders and entertaining and the like, because they are not part of our way of life, and it has been an interesting day. Hannah, don't fret about me or the shop. Clara is going to move into your room when you leave, and she will take on all your duties. Lina can manage without her now that the boys are all grown up and can help with the heavy tasks."

Hannah should have realised that for one thing Mary would be ahead of the game, and for another that her sister Clara had always been there ready to help wherever she was needed. She was certainly helping with the dressmaking, and Hannah had enjoyed spending some time with her and Mary on this exciting task. She decided that during the short time left before the wedding, she would stay home in the evenings to attend to the dress-making, and the curtain-making, while Will helped her Pa and brother with the re-decorating. On Monday, she would go with Will to choose some furniture, and then she would buy curtain material.

Will was also feeling better. Chastened, but better than earlier, and he whistled a strain from one of the voluntaries he had played in church as he strolled along the harbour side and back to his new home. He had reluctantly said good-night to Hannah in the doorway at No 34, remembering their earlier experience on the sofa and, as usual, he didn't want to let her go, but she said again that she had things to attend to, and she would see him in the morning.

He lit the oil lamp before it got dark, stoked up the fire a little and sat thinking about the linoleum and furniture that would be their project for Monday. Yes, a good long table for the parlour, so that some day they could entertain a number of guests. Any boarders there might be staying could use the table for their homework, too. There would still be room for a few armchairs, or would there? The room was beginning to look rather crowded in his mind's eye, and he thought perhaps the organ might be better in the living room. Yes, that would leave room for a sofa or two. If they had guests, he could not expect them to sit at the table all evening.

These were not the priority, though. What he was most anxious to procure was a decent double bed. One that did not make horrendous noises, preferably, with good, strong springs. He imagined that Hannah would be thinking about sheets and counterpanes and so on, but he must remember to ask her. Perhaps now was a good time to write a list, and he searched for paper to write on. The only paper he could find was manuscript paper, but that did not matter. He wrote 'BED' above the top stave, with a dash and then 'bed linen?' He anticipated Hannah's smile at seeing that at the top of the list, but it was soon followed by so many more items, that it no longer stood out so blatantly.

For tonight, he was still sleeping on the divan in the living room, and he took the lamp into the kitchen and made a thorough search for mice or evidence thereof. He re-set the traps, just in case, and placed one carefully inside the cupboard. Then, remembering the hole against the outer wall, he returned to look for an orange to use as Billa's suggested wedge. Mary had provided him with some fruit, and he now picked up one of the oranges. Then he picked up a second one, caressing one in each hand, and, thinking of Hannah's breasts he brought them up to his face and deeply breathed in their scent. He acknowledged how excited this made him, and he was suddenly extraordinarily grateful for this day, this week, this year. This thing that was happening to him at a time in his life that he had begun to acknowledge as his declining years, with nothing to look forward to but a weakening and ageing body, losing his teeth and his hair and eventually fading away. But now look at him. He was nest-building as if he was a twenty-year-old, making plans for a wonderful future, and copulating with a beautiful young woman at every opportunity. A woman who, unlike himself, was in the absolute prime of life. And how responsive was she? Lord, she was so amazing.

As he crept back into the cupboard, he kicked the baited trap, which sprang and somersaulted into the darkness. Once more, Billa's remark about his being only concerned with his dick came to mind, and he conceded that it did feature very largely in his thoughts, especially at that moment. He found the threadbare broom and fished about until the wayward mousetrap was located. He used the broom to push an orange against the wall and crush it into the hole, then he re-set the trap and placed it carefully on the floor as he backed out into the kitchen. The other trap went near the fireplace again, and eventually Will settled into the little bed. He remembered to climb out of his clothes this time, and even found some pyjamas in the trunk. He turned out the lamp, noticing that there was still the slightest trace of light in the sky. It was a quieter night, with no wind in the trees, and no revellers in the streets as on a Saturday. A cat called somewhere, and far away a dog barked, but soon all was quiet, and Will had a blissful, exhausted sleep. He had remembered being awoken by the sun, so he had closed the door into the kitchen, and he slept right through until six.

∞∞∞∞

Monday morning, Rise and Shine! He opened the kitchen door and let the sun shine through from the back of the house. Placed a kettle and a separate pan of water on the gas, and looked again at the packet of rolled oats. If little Carrie could make porridge, then he must be able to. Will decided that yesterday had been a false start, he had fallen into every hole, had dug himself ever further into another one, and today would be the new beginning of life at No 22. One day, he would employ a house servant, but first he would learn how to do all these menial tasks himself. If he was going to expect his staff to perform jobs, it would be because he wished them to, and not because he was incapable himself. What sort of Commander would that make him?

Aware that one job at a time might be wise, he put oats into a pot, sprinkled a pinch of salt over, and then tried a cupful of water, and then another cupful into the mix. Onto the gas, and he kept stirring and watching, until quite suddenly it looked as he wanted it to be, then he added some milk and stirred again. Then some more milk, and gradually, he learned – he taught himself – how to make porridge, and just the way he liked it. The kettle boiled and he brewed tea in a teapot, then he just had time to eat his porridge and drink a cup of tea before the large pan of water also boiled. The next bit, he had not actually worked out in advance, so he stripped off his pyjamas and had his wash at the kitchen sink, to save carrying hot water up the stairs. Then he dressed, and took a mug of hot water to the bathroom in order to have his shave.

The new man returned to the kitchen, all spick and span, and then tried cutting a piece of bread to make toast. He had left a strange shape from his effort the previous day, and now he made another startling discovery. In the cutlery drawer, there were different types of knives, and he inspected several large ones. Aha, he had massacred the bread with a straight bladed knife, perhaps he should try this serrated one. The loaf was now a day older and easier to cut but, the resulting slice being something of a wedge-shaped compromise, he thought perhaps he would try toasting it at the fire. Ah, just one problem. Baby had used a toasting fork with a long handle, and he couldn't see one of those, but the fire was just right for making toast, so he gripped the 'doorstep' with the coal tongs, and held it over the coals. He rather liked the smell of burning bread, he told himself, but the job was not a total disaster. He cut off the crust where the tongs had held it, and scraped off the burnt edges, lashed it with Manx butter and Mary's marmalade, and ate like a king. The tea was still drinkable, too.

Knowing it was hardly vital, he added 'toasting fork' to the manuscript list. He thought he had done rather well today. There were no mice around, dead or alive, and the trap in the cupboard was still armed. He pushed it gingerly with the broom towards the far wall, just in case Billa or Syd might tread on it by accident when they came to decorate, and then he remembered that Kermode's men would probably be the first to arrive with the lino. He would have to mention the trap to them too.

He left the house and hurried round to the church, made apologies to the verger, and confided all the new tricks he had learned by default in the last two days. The man enjoyed hearing about the great Waverley discovering his vulnerabilities, and they laughed together. The verger, Bob Bridson, was a single man and had been fending for himself for years, since his mother had passed away, and had forgotten that he had made some of the same mistakes himself. Then he commented to Will that he wouldn't have to be bothered with all that when he got married, and Will responded that there was more to having a lady in the house than having your toast made for you, and he urged his friend to look around him. The twinkle in his eye stopped the verger in his tracks, and certainly got him thinking.

∞∞∞

Hannah had been expecting him to call after his organ practice but there was no sign of him at the usual time. She thought back to all the adventures he had gone through the previous morning and wondered if he had set the house on fire or scalded himself in the bath. Then she recalled Ben Kermode's promise about the linoleum, and realised that Will had probably had to stay in until that arrived. Will had left the house open in case he was not back before the floor men arrived, but as it turned out, they all met at the gate at the same time.

The men lost no time in laying the lino in the parlour where there was no furniture, and then helped to put everything on top of it, while they covered the living room and kitchen floors. They decided to leave the large cupboard under the stairs until everything else had been done, as that could be filled in with left over pieces. One of the chaps remarked that this area would be large enough to organise a larder as well as the broom cupboard. Put the long handles and cleaning things in this high end, and shelves in the rest, perhaps with a marble top for keeping things cool. This sounded an excellent idea, and Will wrote it on the list.

The upstairs rooms contained nothing yet, and were quickly dealt with. Will added 'stair carpet and rods' to the growing manuscript, and the men manhandled the trunk and the little divan up the stairs and into one of the back bedrooms. Will's plan was to sleep any boarders they may have in the rear rooms, although until the new term started, he did not know if there would be any such requirements. He and Hannah would be sleeping – ah sleeping together! – in one of the front rooms, and he was going to let her choose which one. He would continue to use the little single bed until he could bring his bride home to the new one. They might try it out for comfort before that, of course.

Will called for Hannah and they went together to the furniture shop. Hannah had very definite ideas about the furnishing of her home, and she chose a pair of fireside chairs with a sofa in a similar fabric for the living room. They needed more bentwood chairs, although the existing table would do for the present. She felt that the dining room suite would wait until later, as she and Will were both anxious to procure their bed.

They settled easily on one with the latest all-over spring system, with a deep mattress and brass-trimmed bed-ends. They also both liked a large wardrobe with matching tallboy (Hannah had insisted that the cheval mirror in her room at Hope Street belonged to her and would be coming to No 22 when she did). After this, Will's duty was done with the exchange of cash and receipts. They would be needing much more, of course, before the wedding day, but for ease of moving about while decorating, they decided to leave the rest until Hannah had selected her curtain materials. Will arranged for an account to be set up so that they could add to their stock little by little. He found himself surplus to requirement now, therefore, as she wanted to have time on her own in the soft furnishings department, now that she knew what her larger furniture looked like to match curtains to, and then there was the bed linen.

He was more than happy to let her take over completely, as he also had an errand or two on his list. He was heading for Mrs Kinrade's antique emporium in Queen Street, but on the way, he passed the ironmonger's and he popped in to ask about a toasting fork. He had decided that this was essential after all, or perhaps he just wanted to make the decision. Yes, he would treat himself to a toasting fork. Needless to say, he noticed a good many other items that he liked, and in the end he had to ask if his pile of packages could be delivered.

Mrs Kinrade was not very well, but she opened up her shop for Will. "I'm a bit poorly, Mr Waverley," she apologised, stopped by a wracking cough, and she held a handkerchief over her mouth, "they are sending me away to hospital, not that it will do any good, but I am glad to see you. Can I take it that the ring was well received? Your demeanour suggests a happy man to me!"

Will was distressed to hear of her indisposition and wished her a speedy recovery. His fiancée was delighted with her ring, and they now had a date for their wedding. He told her when it was to be, and how they had met the couple who did not buy the ring, and what a coincidence it was that they would be married at the same church and in the same week. But this was not the purpose of his visit. He then told her about Mrs Quine and the acquisition of a Welsh dresser that had provided him with a bed. He wanted to buy the kind woman a small gift, and thought perhaps something nice to show on the new dresser.

Dorothy Kinrade knew Janie Quine, and all about the Welsh dresser and where it had come from. "Let's think what that dresser needs," and she fidgeted about among the jumble of treasures in the tiny room, stopping again with a fit of coughing. When she got over that, she handed him a green glass cream jug with a fluted rim, hand painted with lilies of the valley and a young boy.

"That is exquisite," said Will, "and quite a lot nicer than anything I had in mind!"

"Actually," Mrs Kinrade seemed to change her mind, "I would like you to have this as a wedding present from me. I will find something else for Janie."

"People are so kind," said Will, "I want to repay Mrs Quine's kindness, and end up with another present! What am I to do with you! Thank you so much. I think Hannah will love this, I know I do."

"Yes, I think I know what you might have had in mind for the dresser," and she produced a serving plate decorated with deep blue, and gilded at the edges.

"Perfect!" said Will. "You are a bit of a mind-reader, aren't you?"

"Oh, more than that, dear, now you remember what I told you. Within the year you will have started your family, you can count on it."

Chapter Twenty One

When the crone could hear him between her fits of coughing, Will related how he had told Hannah about her prediction and that they both liked the name Dorothy and, if they had a little girl, she would be called after Mrs Kinrade, who had been so kind.

The old woman turned away so that Will should not see the tear in her eye, as she croaked, "That is the nicest thing I have ever heard. Especially as you *will* have a daughter, Mr Waverley, in fact you may have to think of more than one name. I'm sorry that I will not see the little girl but, as I said, I am being sent back to Liverpool where I came from, supposedly to be cured, but that is not going to happen."

Will tried to protest, to persuade her that she may get better, but she insisted that she was done for. "But don't waste your sympathy on me dear, I have had a good life. I remember Mary Bickerstaff when we were at the Liverpool school for orphans, she was Mary Danson then, always a dab hand with the needlework. It's quite amazing that we should end up in the same small town in the Isle of Man but, as you can probably tell from the name, I married a Manx man. It's a long story, but he was a good man, no don't worry about me. I have been happy here, but old age only gets worse once things go wrong and I only want to get it over with. I am also very happy for you and Mary's granddaughter, I know this town will not be easy on you, but take no notice of them. Face the music together and you will see it through. Now, is there anything else you see here that you would like? I have to get rid of the whole lot before I go away."

Will's emotions were all over the place, and he wished he could buy her entire stock if it would help the old girl. Impetuously, he selected a number of items of crockery, knowing he was short of cups for one thing, then, realising that he had quite a way to carry all his plunder, he stopped and asked if he could bring Hannah to see her, perhaps the next day, as she would have more idea of what they could use. Mrs Kinrade nodded and shooed him to the door, unable to speak any more.

By the time he had hauled his cups, plates, cutlery and photograph frames all the way back to Bowling Green Road, Will was exhausted; but he had hardly had time to sit down when the delivery boy from the hardware shop arrived with his toasting fork collection in the large basket on the front of his bicycle, with a new broom perched precariously across the handlebars. Hard on his heels came the horse and cart from the furniture store. The next half hour was taken up directing the men where to put all his furniture purchases, knowing before they left that Hannah would want them placed differently, but at last he was alone.

Despite the excitement of brand new furniture on the brand new linoleum, his hands shook as he unwrapped the pretty green glass jug from Mrs Kinrade, that she had carefully folded in tissue paper. He smiled and felt sad at the same time, then he tucked the paper round it again, and placed it on the window sill to show Hannah – their first wedding present.

He lunched on tea and tongue sandwiches, and then set about finding homes for the small items he had bought. There was a broom that still had bristles for a start, together with numerous dusters, cloths, polishes and detergents. Before long there was yet another delivery, this time from the haberdashery department of Kermode's, consisting of some heavy bolts of material and a pile of bed linen.

As the afternoon wore on, he took stock of the food that was left from the box that Mary had given him. Was that only two days ago? A lifetime seemed to have passed, but everything was now running low and he was going to have to dig deep in his pockets yet again at the grocery store. He would be glad when this day was over, but had the feeling there was a long way to go yet. When he set off, he took the large plate to Mrs Quine on the way. He could have delivered this on his way home, he thought now, but he had been in a hurry to decant the whole collection as soon as he could. At least now he could present the lady with his gift without being encumbered with a dozen other packages, oh and he had better return the dish that had once contained her wonderful gooseberry pie, too!

Janie Quine was quite embarrassed when he presented the package, said he shouldn't have, and that he had done her a favour. Her eyes widened when she unwrapped the platter, and she exclaimed it was exactly what she had wanted to be the centre-piece of her display on the dresser. And it might even hold the goose at Christmas when she had family round! She fussed back into her kitchen, looking round for something more to give him, as she was sure he could relieve her of some items she no longer required. As he was just setting up home, she knew a lot was needed, there seemed no end to it. He agreed, but pleaded with her not to load him up now, as he was on his way to do some grocery shopping. She said she would 'see him again' and beamed at him until he was out of sight.

He was not to know that she was staring after him rather sadly. Janie was one of a number of Castletown widows who 'would have given Hannah Corlett a run for her money' if they had realised that William Waverley was actually available. He had always cut a dash wherever he went, and was among the most important men in the town, but had never given the slightest hint that he was interested in marrying again. However, the women that she gossiped with were his admirers, and would not have seen a problem with his choice of lady friend, if only she hadn't been so young and pretty. Drat the girl! But now, Janie was forging a nice little friendship with him as her neighbour, and that was a higher card than her other friends could play. She rebuked herself though, when she found her own heart beating a little faster at the thought that he was sleeping in *her* bed! The fact that she had never used that particular bed herself was not the point. A woman could dream, couldn't she?

Will went straight to Hope Street, as he could hardly patronise another grocery shop, unless he required something that Mary could not supply. If he went to Tom Dodd's high class emporium, he could buy beer or wine, but otherwise he only sold much the same items as Mary, except that he charged a lot more; good friend though he was, this made no sense to Will, who was new to housekeeping for himself, and constantly shocked at the price of everything. The mention of 'class' came back to him, and he wondered what was the difference between gentility and folly.

Mary, naturally, was ahead of the game and had already stacked another carton with the perishables such as butter, cheese, eggs and bread. She had wrapped a few rashers of bacon, but warned him that he would not need the gas on 'full tilt' if he was going to attempt to cook that. She had given him a pitcher of milk, and he should keep the pitcher ready for when the milk cart came round. "Find out what time he passes your door and take your pitcher out for him to fill up from the churn. The same probably goes for fresh bread, you'll soon learn their delivery times. Catherine at No 30 would tell you."

They had the Manx staple of 'spuds and herrin' for their tea. The herring were still available fresh from the quayside but would soon be put down in salt barrels for use over the winter. They would then be cooked with the potatoes, but while they could be obtained as fresh as this, they were fried separately, and the new potatoes were served whole. Much of the late herring catch would go to the smoke houses to be kippered, which would also preserve the fish for later use.

Will could not remember having eaten fresh herring in Agnes's regime, and declared that there could be very little that would be tastier. He was reminded that this was 'poor people's food,' and he was beginning to think that the so-called poor people might know how to be more frugal and actually be better fed, satisfied and happy. When he asked about obtaining fresh fish, Mary advised him to rely on the fishmonger, because the landings depended on the time of the tide and varied from day to day for quayside purchasing

He insisted on paying for his groceries, despite being quite surprised at the bill, but life was teaching the teacher something new every day. Again, he planned to introduce some real life economics and housekeeping into the school curriculum. His boys should strive to get on in life, but they needed to know where their food came from, and how many other people's lives were involved in providing that food. Thanking Mary for more than she realised, he took one box, and Hannah carried another basket, with all his shopping, and they set off for No 22 at last. Hannah could hardly wait to inspect all that had been delivered there.

Janie Quine smiled demurely at them as they approached. She must have been looking out for them, but she had another fruit tart to donate to the food basket. "Mr. Waverley has been very thoughtful and kind," she explained to Hannah, "and I bottled so many blackberries last year that I've been using up my stock to make room for this year's crop. I pride myself on my pastry, so I do hope you enjoy this." So the same pie dish returned to No 22 after much thanking and blushing.

Hannah looked sideways at Will as they walked along and said she could see that she would have to keep an eye on him, she hadn't realised he had such a way with the ladies. He smiled at that, but confessed that there was more to tell her yet. "A bit of good news and a bit of bad news," he warned. "I'll explain when we get inside."

She ran straight to the pile of curtain materials and bed linen, and inspected the heap critically. "Yes, it all seems to be there," she remarked, "but I thought I had asked for the curtain material to be sent to Hope Street, where Clara and Gran could help me to sew them. Well, not to worry, at least I can measure up properly here, and divide up the material according to the windows. Oh, these chairs look just right here, don't they. I'm not sure about the sofa. Oh, of course, it looks too crowded because that old sofa can go now that we have this nice new one. Shall we just push it into the parlour for now? Right – upstairs with these bed clothes then." She glanced at her man, but not in the coquettish manner he expected from the remark. Much as the idea of going upstairs with her appealed to him, he really wanted to tell her about his encounter with Dorothy Kinrade and, also, he was not sure when to expect Billa and Syd, if not more brothers and relatives, to make a start on the decorating.

"Let's just look through my other acquisitions before you go up, and I want to see what we might still require. But first, here is our very first Wedding Present," and he passed her the tissue-wrapped gift.

"Oh! Isn't this lovely!" she gasped as she turned it over in her hands. "That is so sweet, who is it from?"

Will recounted his day's adventures, but was choked up himself when telling her about Mrs Kinrade and how ill she was, especially when Hannah wept at the tale. They sat on the new sofa and he put his arm round her and stroked her tears away. "The poor old dear never had children of her own to be named after her, and she was so touched to think that her name would live on, and what about needing more names? Do you think there really are people who can read the future? You're not...." he pointed at her skirt, ".... already, are you?"

"No, I'm not" (pointing at her skirt) "already, and in fact we can't make love tonight. I wouldn't want to stain the brand new mattress and sheets before it is even the marriage bed!"

Now, of course, Will wanted her all the more, and he climbed on top of her and began to push himself against her, their kisses beginning to grow hot and dangerous, when once again they heard noises outside, heralding the arrival of company.

All hands were required then to decant the decorating materials from the cart into the almost empty parlour, but while Will expected them to ask where they were required to start, Billa was demanding a cup of tea before they did anything. This was only his joke, although the kettle was put on immediately, but he explained that there would be a lot of preparation work to do before paint tins were opened or paper measured, and they would need that hot water. He had brought his own favoured brand of cleaning materials; rags, sugar-soap and elbow grease, and every surface in the house that was to be painted must be vigorously subjected to these three. He expected this to take their first couple of evenings, unless Will was deemed efficient enough tonight to finish the job during the daytime tomorrow.

Sydney said he couldn't stay long tonight as he had promised to meet some friends, but he would come earlier tomorrow night, straight after work if Will would give him a bite to eat, so this was all arranged. Billa showed Will what was required, starting with the woodwork in the kitchen, and watched as the teacher had a go with the dirt. Another new experience for him, and one which he enjoyed. Manual labour, rolling up his sleeves, working up a bit of a sweat, seeing something for his efforts, although there did seem to be a lot of it to do, he found rewarding. This was his home, after all, his and Hannah's home, and it had to be worthy, so preparation, although an apparent nuisance, would make the whole job a good one in the end.

Billa went to look at the mouse hole in the cupboard under the stairs, and Hannah took the bed linen upstairs. She was quite happy with the room that the furniture men had seen fit to house the bed, and she set about dressing the mattress with a heavy sheet of ticking, and then piling on the sheets and blankets, and ending with the counterpane she had chosen – was it only that morning? Its design would echo the roses on the wallpaper they – she – had also chosen. She had asked for four feather pillows and a bolster, although she was not sure how many pillows Will used. They could use spares on other beds anyway, but now she placed these in pillow cases, and stood back to admire the finished product.

Damn the women's curse, she thought, it looks so tempting. But just one more month and they would be married!

Chapter Twenty Two

The milk cart came through The Green at an early hour, and Will made the acquaintance of the delivery boy, who was called Davey, and his horse that he referred to as Dobbin. He said the baker's cart was usually not far behind, and, sure enough, Davey and Dobbin were barely out of sight, towards Douglas Street, when the sound of another cart approached from round the corner on Shore Road. This was a hand cart, pushed by a young woman and an elderly lady. They were a little shy, at first, at meeting a new customer, but Will soon put them at their ease by confessing to being new at keeping house for himself and would have to be guided by their expertise. Mrs Crebbin and her daughter Emma took up the challenge right away, advising him to take his pitcher of milk indoors, put it somewhere cool, and then bring out his basket for the bread. They warned him against buying too much, but he could not resist some little Bakewell tarts, and the old lady popped a couple of extras into his basket, 'for new customers!' she winked.

Will spent the morning, after his breakfast adventures, organ practice and a brief visit to the shop in Hope Street, beavering away at the woodwork in the living room. Between them they had finished the kitchen the previous night, Billa promising that kitchens were always the worst to prepare, and some of Will's cleaning materials had also seen service. Once again, this morning he could see that there was a lot of it to do, with skirting boards, window frames, doors and picture rails, but he found that just cleaning it made it look so much brighter and it did seem a little easier to prepare than the kitchen woodwork. He had not paid much attention to furnishings before, and realised another omission in his education that he could share with his pupils, especially if he was trusted with a paint brush before they all returned to school.

He went back to have some lunch with Hannah at No 34, explaining that he was obliged to provide Sydney with something at tea time, and she said she would finish in the shop at four, and come over and help with that, as she had an idea to try out the gas cooker with something more ambitious than porridge. Then Will reminded her that he would like to take her to see Mrs. Kinrade, and she said in that case she would finish at three, and they could go and see the old lady first. She said they must take her something to say thank you for the glass jug, and they wondered what they could give her. "She could do with a good feed, but taking food might look like charity," suggested Will.

"She used to like a little nip of gin," put in Mary, "but that might have given her the trouble she has now. How about some of that tonic wine the Monks make?" This seemed a good idea, even if they did have to go to Tom Dodd's to obtain it, but Will said he would pick it up along the way.

"Wine the Monks make?" repeated Tom, "you'd have to go to the monkery for that! No, I've heard of it, they make great claims about its health boosting properties, but we can't get it here. *Dubonnet* might fit the bill?" Will explained that it was for Dorothy Kinrade, but warned Tom that the old girl seemed to be already dying. "In that case, give the poor creature what she really likes," and he brought down a half bottle of gin.

Another hour with the sugar soap was spent happily in the parlour, then Will took his shopping basket and called for Hannah, who came out with hers, and together they strolled over to Queen Street and Mrs Kinrade's tiny house.

The poor old crone was the picture of exhaustion as she ushered them into the Aladdin's cave, and she immediately sat herself down heavily on a velvet covered chair, coughing and telling them to take whatever they wanted. First Hannah embraced her and thanked her for the charming little jug, which they would always treasure. Will presented her with the gin and she snatched it and held it to her chest as if it were a hot water bottle. What they really needed was some more crockery, Hannah told her. Old Dorothy attempted to rise, but had to sit down again, and Will placed a hand on her shoulder. "Stay right there," he commanded, "and point me towards whatever it is you're thinking of."

"There is an almost complete bone china tea-set in a box somewhere," she said. "It's a brown box with blue writing on it." As Hannah was thinking that bone china might not be what they needed urgently, it did sound very civilised, and Will found the box, covered in dust, underneath a small copper-topped table. "Yes, that's it."

Peeling back one of the dusty flaps only revealed shapes wrapped in old, discoloured newsprint, but when Will handed the top shape to Dorothy and she unwrapped a fragile cup, Hannah gasped, and Will knew why. "Oh yes!" the old woman managed a weak smile, "I had forgotten they were your colour," and she turned the cup round in her shaky hands, showing all the aquamarine roses, picked out with gold leaf and the prettily shaped gold rim.

"We have to have those," said Will, "but I am also rather taken with this little table, how much would you want for that?"

"I want to be rid of everything," said Dorothy, "have a good look round, make a list of what you want, and I hope you will need more than two baskets to take it away. And then tell me how much you want to pay for the lot."

Will envisaged Billa's hand cart called into service again, and between them they chose a number of items, most of which they had not known they needed, but the situation was unique, and they felt that they must help this lovely old lady whose name was possibly destined to live on in their lives. He laid several bank notes on the surface in front of Dorothy, and she counted it and stuffed the notes into her apron pocket, waving her hand round the room to indicate that they could take more for that price.

Hannah could see that Dorothy had items that might interest Clara or Cissie, and promised to tell all her friends to come round as soon as they could. Then she remembered that she should provide small gifts for her bridesmaids, and asked to see what Mrs Kinrade left in the collection of jewellery, as she was particularly interested in coral or amber.

It came as no surprise that these presented no problem to Mrs Kinrade. "I think I must have been put on this earth to supply your needs," she croaked, as her hand found a bracelet of amber coloured stones. Hannah looked at it across the finger tips of both hands and declared it to be perfect for Carrie's chief bridesmaid's dress. She beamed at the old lady, wondering if she was real, or some sort of Fairy Godmother, then, almost in horror, she noticed that the bony fingers were attempting to undo the clasp of a coral cameo that was pinned to her own dress.

"No!" she cried out, "you mustn't do that!" but Dorothy was not listening.

"It's nothing to me," she lied, "I just put it there today to cover this blackberry stain, look." Sure enough, there was a dark mark where the brooch had been. Hannah took the brooch, which was still warm, and looked askance at the donor. She was not sure she believed the old lady, and she turned the gem over to admire the intricate handiwork. On the back were the letters D and M intertwined, inscribed in gold.

"All right, Dorothy!" she gave a stern look, and Mrs Kinrade flinched, "so tell me what this nothing means."

"Can't you just buy everything and go away?" she muttered, but, seeing that Hannah was still glaring at her, she confessed. "Marcus gave me that when we were betrothed," then as Hannah began to return it to her she held up her hand to stop her and went on, "and he was a good man Mark, but he was a lot older than me, and we faced a lot of opposition." Light was dawning for Hannah and Will. "Yes, that's why you people are special to me, I know all about it. They all said I would soon be a widow, but he was the love of my life, I have needed no other, and if I had it all to do again, I would still choose to be with Mark. But now," she sighed heavily, "I have no-one to leave my possessions to, and if this might bring pleasure to someone special, then Mark and I will be happy enough."

Hannah knelt down in front of her and took her hands, her eyes welling up, and she was at a loss as to what to say. Then she noticed the stain on the woman's blouse and knew it was not blackberry juice. Dorothy saw her gaze, covered her breast with her hand and said, "Now, please go, I am so tired. Take the tea set and the jewellery and come back tomorrow, or sooner if you can, for the rest. Just go. Go! Go! GO!"

Will and Hannah went. They knew Billa's cart was at No 22 anyway, so would ask to borrow it as soon as he arrived later. Hannah requested one stop, at the butcher's where she purchased some liver. She already had an onion in her basket, and now she was ready to do business with the oven.

Will had become adept at keeping the living room fire going in the range, and they realised now that in effect they had two ovens. The gas cooker in the kitchen would have been a fairly recent acquisition, and was very useful for cooking anything for which temperature regulation was critical, but for keeping things warm, the range oven was ideal. Will had even found that he could dry his shoes in it when he had upset his pail of water over them while he was cleaning the woodwork!

Hannah elected to use the gas oven, but first she lightly fried the onion and then the liver. Gravy was made from the juices and all went into a covered cooking pan in the oven, while she peeled and boiled potatoes and cabbage. By the time Sydney arrived, their meal was ready, and they all dined with lip-licking delight. Janie Quine's blackberry pie had warmed in the range, and Hannah now produced a jug of custard.

Will saw that his wife-to-be was at home in the kitchen, and this had been another tasty, homely dish that Will had not experienced before (Agnes would never have resorted to cooking *offal*). But again he saw her hands, chapped from the cold water and vegetable peeling, and tendrils of her hair hung limply at her cheeks from the steam. He knew this was not her favourite time of the month, but he was more determined that they would have a housemaid as soon as she would permit it. He wanted her to learn the social graces, and to accept them as her right, as his wife. It was not a matter of class, he told himself, it was just the way it should be.

Syd decreed that Will had done quite a good job on the woodwork, 'for a beginner,' and while Hannah washed up their dirty dishes, Syd got down to the skirting boards in the parlour, and Will continued where he had left off earlier, with the door frame and both sides of the door. Who would have thought there could be so much surface in one room. By the time Billa arrived, the large parlour was ready, and the men all set off up the stairs to make a start on the bedrooms and landing. Father was well pleased with the progress that had been made.

They had not yet replaced the stair runner, and Hannah sat on the bare wood of the steps and scrubbed at the woodwork exposed on either side. After an hour, she called the men down for a break, having boiled a kettle and made tea. She advised Will to ask for more milk the next morning, for the week or so while the workers were around, as it was running very low. She had found the Bakewell tarts, though, and these were much appreciated.

Billa then took some materials into the cupboard under the stairs and set about filling in the mouse hole with a rock and some plaster. He removed what was left of the orange, demonstrating that it had been nibbled from the outside, but had done the trick 'temporale,' as he called it. "What ya need's a cat," he decided. "They don't just catch the buggers, they keep 'em away, a 'detergent' like."

Will smiled at the man's slight mangling of the language and looked at Hannah. She looked at her lovely new furniture, pursed her lips and said she would think about it.

Then they remembered having promised Mrs Kinrade that they would return with the cart, so persuaded Billa to let them borrow it. The Corletts were quite interested in the tale and decided to accompany them to the old crone's 'emporium' just 'for a skeet.'

It was all Dorothy could do to call to them through another window to let themselves in and take what they wanted. They were all quite worried about her, and Billa agreed to help relieve her of some of her stock, despite not exactly wanting any of it. "She's in a bad way, isn't she, the least we can do is give her some money, it's the only way she'll accept any help."

Sydney went into the other room to find the woman on her bed and was shocked, but moved, and he told her that there was 'loads of stuff' that he wanted to buy. She wasn't fooled, but was too weak to argue. When he returned to the others, who were loading their earlier purchases onto the cart, he said, "I'm going for Doctor Sugden, he's the nearest, that poor woman won't last the night unless we do something."

The doctor came quickly, aware of Dorothy's condition. She would have refused to see him if she had had the strength, but all she could do was to cough and point a bony finger at the gin bottle. She had been too weak to remove the cork and the doctor decreed that this was the cause of her distress, but he fed her something on a spoon that he said would help her to sleep, and he would call again in the morning. Hannah stayed by her side until she did slip into sleep, tucked her counterpane round her and crept out, feeling helpless and very worried.

Doctor Sugden called at Mary's shop in Hope Street next morning to advise that Dorothy had rallied after a good sleep, but he was transferring her to the mainland hospital that was expecting her. She was not strong enough for an operation, and she and the doctor both knew it would not do much good, but she needed to be isolated, and to have the constant care of the sanatorium in Blackburn. "She will be at her house for this morning, and is anxious to speak to Mr Waverley or to Hannah or her father," he said, "as you appear to be very good friends and she has no-one else to care. I would be grateful if you could slip over there right away, Hannah." Will arrived from his morning practice just as the doctor was leaving and immediately thought the worst, but the doctor smiled and told him brightly that Hannah would bring him up to date. "I would like to see you both after you have spoken to Mrs Kinrade. Please call on me this afternoon."

Chapter Twenty Three

Hannah and Will looked at each other, both stricken by this turn of events, but set off right away to see old Dorothy. She really was brighter, although still weak, but her mind was as sharp as a needle. "You owe me money!" she said as they entered her house.

They could not help smiling. They knew this was her joke, as Will had paid her yesterday for all the goods they went later to collect, and they had all tried to give her more cash in the evening, but she had refused.

"I know, I didn't want to take it last night. I was worried what might happen to it if I passed out, but listen, this is an imposition when you have so much else to think about, but I want you to clear the house for me. Use what you can, sell what you can't and dump anything you can't find a home for. There is some good stuff here, and you can surely use the furniture? You're just setting up home, aren't you? It's all yours. All I ask is that, if I have any debts, you will pay them off. I do not owe anybody anything that I know of, but I am not sure about this hospital or the doctor's bill. Also, it would comfort me to know that I might have a decent burial. No!" she held her hand up as they both tried to interrupt, "no, it won't be long now. I'm glad. But I am also very grateful that you people came into my life just when I needed someone. You have brought joy into my dark hours, and I wish you happiness together, with all my heart – what's left of it!"

Will and Hannah looked at each other again, and back to Dorothy. Hannah was fighting back tears. "We shall be honoured to help you," Will said. "Billa Corlett can take the furniture on his cart, and we will do all we can."

"I knew you would," croaked the old girl, "the rent is paid up to the twelfth, I think that's another week. Please clear the place as soon as you can. I am being collected shortly and put on the afternoon boat. The rent book is in the drawer of the hatstand, go and get it now so I can see you have it – oh the key should be with it, bring that too." Hannah retrieved both, and showed them to Dorothy. "Good," she said, "Mr Cubbon's man comes to collect the rent. Would you get word to him as soon as you have cleared the house, but make sure you clear it first, or the old rogue will take it all himself."

"There's not much wrong with you, is there?" smiled Will, "you have thought of everything."

"Nothing like staring Death in the face to clear the mind! But now I have your attention, I have one last request. Well, not so much a request, as a bit of a little daydream."

Again Hannah and Will looked at each other, intrigued by the lady's faraway look. "Well, go on, what is it?" said Hannah, "you certainly do have our attention!"

"You two remind me so much of my time with Marcus. Our age difference must have been similar to yours, but I had loved him long before he knew it." Yet again, Hannah looked at Will, and the old woman smiled. "I came over here with the family I was working for, and he was the head groom on the nearby estate." She lapsed into her memories again for a few moments, drew breath and coughed again, but seemed determined to tell them something. "You will be married soon," she continued, "but one day, when the weather gets wintry and cold, I would like you to wrap up warm and take a walk in Colby Glen. It was the most wonderful day of my life when Mark first made love to me, on a freezing day in November. We had walked briskly to keep warm, and up at the far end of the glen there is a hidden place like a cave. We went in there for a bit of canoodling, Mark gave me that brooch and asked me to marry him. And then...." the faraway look turned to a sad smile, and she was unable to continue for a long moment, "So, by the time we came out into the winter sunshine again, we had been to paradise and back, and I knew he was all I ever wanted."

"Dorothy Kinrade, I do believe this is a confession!" said Will, in an attempt to quell the stirring he had felt as she spoke.

"Not at all," she countered, "I am proud to share my most intimate secret with you two. Now, you know what you have to do? You will be married by then anyway, but you have experienced the kind of thrill I'm talking about, haven't you? No need to answer, I know you have, your love is written all over you both. Now, this is good-bye," she stirred as an ambulance stopped at the door, "I will not see you again, but I wish you success and happiness, and lots of children. God Bless you."

The doctor came in with the medics, and she told him that all had been arranged, and thanked him for attending to the matter. He said, in that case, Will and Hannah need not visit him later, but he would keep in touch to let them know how their old friend got on. Hannah asked him to give her the address of the sanatorium, so that she could write to Dorothy, and he said he would do that.

The tiny suitcase containing the few paltry possessions she had packed in readiness was placed on the stretcher, and disappeared with her into the waiting vehicle. They both waved to the ambulance as it trundled away, and then sat down on the old lady's still-warm bed, emotionally drained and stunned. "What a woman!" said Will. "What an incredible woman!"

∞∞∞∞

He made a start on pushing Dorothy's few pieces of furniture towards the door, while Hannah ran off to see if she could find Billa. Her mother might know where he should be, but her mother was not at home. She stopped one or two people in the street asking if they had seen Billa or Sydney, and was becoming anxious when she found them herself, painting the outside of a house on The Crofts. She gabbled out all that had happened, and Billa listened bemusedly. "He brings us nothin' but work, that fella o' yours," he declared, but promised to bring the cart round to Queen Street when they had a break at dinnertime, about half an hour away.

Mrs Kinrade's house was thankfully tiny, so it would not be a big job to empty it. Since there was available space at No 22, they took two small sofas and a spare bed, together with the ornate hatstand on the first cart, and stacked them in the parlour there. They elected to leave the old lady's bed where it was, at least for the time being. When they returned, they found that one of the tables she had used to display her 'antiques' was actually a large table with leaves that folded down, and Will was delighted to see that it could become the very thing he had in mind for entertaining his friends at. Chairs would come later, but this was a bonus.

Smaller bits and pieces were easily collected in a few more cartloads, as Billa left the cart in Will's hands when he returned to Arbory Street, with strict instructions to deliver it back there before 4pm. There would be room in their back yard in Malew Street, however, if there was too much for No 22. They could take their time over how to dispose of it all.

Not for the first time, Hannah thought she was dreaming and that Dorothy Kinrade was a figment of her imagination. Now, she was a figment who had disappeared, making it all the more unbelievable, and yet, here they were, gifted with all the pieces of furniture that they had left on their list for a later date.

They were all too exhausted to do any painting work that evening.

∞∞∞∞

The pattern changed slightly on subsequent evenings, as Hannah stayed at home with the other seamstresses, Mary and Clara. Hannah had fallen in love with some lengths of crochet work from Mary's 'rag bag' and with many fingers flashing and crochet hooks brandished, several more lengths were being produced, towards making an over-dress and a train. Carrie was still learning the craft, but she was permitted to sew some of the pieces together. There was such a lot of needlework to do, Hannah wondered if they would have time to produce the garments she had designed, but both of the other women were adamant that they had plenty of time. Clara took work home with her too, in order to fill in any spare moments productively. Her mother, Lina, had given her leave to spend all the time she liked on this endeavour, and she would manage the house work on her own, as part of her contribution to the wedding arrangements. She also, of course, had her own 'Mother of the Bride' ensemble to arrange, as well as all the flowers, as she had promised. But the cake had been made. Cakes, in fact, as there were three tiers, and these were maturing in a cupboard, having a little brandy added in holes made with a knitting needle, about twice a week. All was under control.

The bridesmaids' dresses would be quite plain, but have large shawl collars of similarly crocheted lace-work. Carrie's little-girl dress had a twisted belt, onto which Hannah was going to twine fresh ivy leaves. The shawl collar would be clasped at the neck by the amber bracelet. Elbie's dress would be Empire line, quite fitted around her slim middle, and her collar would be held by the coral cameo brooch. Hannah felt a little reluctant to give the brooch to Elbie, now knowing its history. It had been Dorothy's 'engagement brooch,' just as she herself had been content with 'engagement earrings,' but it was for Elbie's dress that she had sought the coral, so on Elbie's outfit it must go.

Meanwhile, Will did whatever he was told by Billa, with young Syd also lording it a bit, enjoying having more experience at something than the schoolmaster. But while they worked, Will put on some of his records. The Corletts were not familiar with much in the way of what Billa referred to as 'arty farty posh singin,' but Syd tended to pick up the melodies quickly, and before long was either singing or whistling along to the music. He liked *On with the Motley* but his special favourite was the record of songs from *The Mikado*, and he requested this to be played over and over. Will found this a little tedious and would have preferred to play more of a selection, but Syd had found a new interest, and lines from Gilbert and Sullivan found their way into his conversation. Will thought he might be quite good in drama too, as he would mime the actions while claiming that he had someone 'on the list,' and whenever they talked about someone they didn't think much of, he would pretend to whip out his notebook, lick his pencil and write down the name, swearing 'he never would be missed.'

When the gramophone was not playing, Sydney would be whistling *A Wand'ring Minstrel I*, then when Billa told him to shut up, he would bow and sing *Defer-er! Defer-er! to the Lord High Decorationer*, and then carry on whistling, dodging a cuff round the ear. Then he would pretend to write Billa Corlet on his little list. Billa responded, saying he'd had Sydney on his list for years and 'shudda stuck his head in the water butt when he was a pup.' It all helped to pass the time companionably enough, and the work went with a swing. By the end of the third evening, all the downstairs woodwork had been undercoated, and after a week, all the paintwork had been completed in the house. Will did not ask the painters to stay longer than a couple of hours, knowing they had worked all day and would be at it again early next morning. He had to sleep with all the windows open, to try to get rid of the smell of paint, and he knew Hannah would not be persuaded to visit until all the work had been done.

Chapter Twenty Four

A list of wedding guests had been drawn up and, being free during the daytime, Will had volunteered to write to everyone. He had hesitated at inviting Agnes, but remembered Hannah's sensible approach, and he did want to invite Douglas anyway. He therefore wrote to Mr Douglas Lacey and Family in the hope that Dougie would open the letter first.

A few days later, Douglas turned up late one morning unannounced. He apologised for not writing in advance, but after an argument with his mother about attending the wedding, he decided on the spur of the moment to come and hear Uncle Will's side of things first hand. He found Will attempting to erect a wallpaper pasting table, which was an opportune moment for a spare pair of hands to arrive. One of the items that had found its way from Mrs Kinrade's shop was a coffee percolator, which had not yet been used, as Will had not had time to work out how to operate it; although he had purchased some ground coffee from Tom Dodd, relishing the aroma as the beans were ground up in the shop. Douglas was delighted to be able to demonstrate, and soon the smell of brewing coffee overpowered all remnants of the odour of gloss paint.

They settled into the fireside chairs and drank their coffee, while Will recounted how suddenly Hannah had happened to him, and the rancour he had endured from Agnes and, it had to be admitted, from some of the townsfolk, including one or two misguided parents. Dougie listened with an amused grin. "I think I can see it from both sides," he said eventually, "but wouldn't like to say if one is any more right than the other. I have encountered Mother's bitterness now, obviously, and Chrissie just repeats whatever Mother says, although I feel that my sister would like to be happy for you, for your sake. She would not dare to attend your wedding of course, but in any case, she is off to Dublin soon and will probably still be away. Mother will not stop me, though, I will be more than happy to attend. I suppose it would look a little incongruous if I were to be your best man?"

Will was heartened to have his nephew's loving approbation, but laughed at his suggestion. "Well, yes, it would rather, but in any case, I have a very good friend in John Qualtrough, who is already burdened with that duty. You remember John? Headmaster at the Board School, he's a bit younger, but not quite as young as you."

"It is all a bit of a shock, but I can tell you are really happy, Uncle Will, and I think you are a lucky man. When I think of my poor father, living apart from Mother all these years, marriage shouldn't be like that, surely?"

"Your mother's prejudices go back a long way son, and are so deeply ingrained, I would not even ask how she justifies her total belief that she is right in everything, and no, marriage is not meant to be like that. I very much doubt if mine will be. Hannah is a very loving girl, and very tactile. I feel sorry for Richard too, but he seems happy enough – happier without Agnes probably, although they still seem quite at ease with each other when they attend the odd function. They were a good team once. I do sometimes wonder if poor Ellen's death in childbirth put Agnes off that side of things, it would be understandable in a way, she and Ellen were very close."

"From some things that Mother has hinted, I fancy that your own mother's marriage was not a happy one. It sounds as if my mother and grandmother could not wait to get away from your father. What do you remember about that?" asked Douglas.

"Very little, son. I was away at schools for much of the time, and a child doesn't notice family tensions, or I didn't anyway. Mother and Agnes came to the Isle of Man while I was teaching over in Scarborough, and I was given to understand that Father had died. I have never had occasion to think about it, but I intend to look for his grave while Hannah and I are on honeymoon."

"Oh, a rather unusual quest for a honeymoon," laughed Dougie.

"That's what Gideon said," responded Will. "I wrote to my cousins in Cheltenham, to tell them about the wedding, and asking about somewhere to stay on our way through. Most streets have plenty of places that rent rooms out, and I was assured that accommodation would not be a problem. I've kept in touch with Gideon from time to time over the years, without really learning much about each other. All the news is about so many of the family that went to Canada. I know he lost Mary Ann a couple of years ago, and I fancy he might be thinking of taking another wife, but he surprised me by saying he would like to come over to the island to see me married. I would never have asked him to go to that trouble, but I really hope he can make it, as, apart from your good self, my family will not be represented at all."

"I hope he makes it too, but the day is all about you and Hannah, after all. What did he say about looking up your father's grave?"

"Just the same as you said, something like it being a funny thing to show one's bride. It's not so much to introduce Hannah to my dead father, as to kill two birds with one stone, while we happen to be passing so close by and since I have never seen his grave. I'm not seeing a funny side at all."

"Let me treat you to lunch," said Douglas suddenly, perhaps to change the subject, "I noticed when I got off the train that the old Station Inn is still in business. How about it?"

"That would be jolly decent of you, Sir," replied Will. "I was just wondering what I could offer you in the kitchen department. But first let me introduce you to Hannah, on our way to the inn."

"Perhaps she would like to join us," suggested Douglas, but Will declined on her behalf. This was partly because he knew that Dougie was only a student and had no money to splash about, and that he would probably be footing the bill anyway, but also, Hannah was a working girl, and when not busy in the shop, she was busy dressmaking and making endless arrangements. There was also a delight in having the company of this educated young man, with whom he shared so much, and he wanted to hear all about his studies and his progress at Oxford before he had to catch another train all the way back to Ramsey.

They called at the Hope Street shop, and Douglas was introduced to Hannah, her sister Clara, little sister Carrie and Grandmother Mary but, as anticipated, they were all too tied up in their endeavours to countenance much of an interruption. Hannah said she 'might pop over later' to see how things were going, and both gentlemen could see that they were being dismissed.

Laughing together on the way to the public house, they fell into easy conversation, then partook of a leisurely lunch with a glass or two of beer. As expected, Douglas allowed his uncle to pay, and then they consulted the timetable to see when he must return. Will joked that they could have done with him to help with the wall-papering, and Dougie said he would love to have a go, if Will could put him up for the night.

Having recently acquired a spare bed from Mrs Kinrade, it just so happened that Will was able to extend his hospitality to an overnight stay. "What about Agnes, though?" he asked in trepidation, but Dougie assured him that she would not be worried. She knew he was attempting to come all the way down to Castletown, so it was highly likely that he would not make it back in one day.

"She will be agitated at not knowing what's going on and what's being said," he laughed, "but she won't be worried about my safety. I'm a big boy now."

∞∞∞∞

With two new raw recruits to wallpapering, in a mixture of two young men and two more mature men, a somewhat uproarious evening was spent at No 22, with little progress on the decorating front, but Billa used the time to measure up and cast his eye over the wallpaper requirements, so that a good start might be made the next evening, provided they were free of the distracting influence of Douglas Lacey by then.

When Hannah did 'pop over' it was a brief stay. She felt outnumbered, did not understand the male humour that was bandied about, and was far too busy to be wasting her time.

"Oooh," said Dougie and Sydney together. "Bit of a spitfire there, William!" Billa made a rude sign at his lower half and the young men spluttered with mirth.

As soon as the painting and wallpapering had been completed, Will and Hannah were able to take stock of the furniture that was still required for their home.

Mrs. Kinrade's bed had been brought to join the spare one that Dougie had used, so now one of the back bedrooms could be fitted out as a twin room. They had destroyed the mattress, just in case her ailment could be deemed contagious, as had been suggested, and the bed itself thoroughly taken apart and disinfected. With a new mattress and more bed linen from Kermode's (and various other sources around the family, and the ever-obliging Mrs Quine), No 22 would be ready to take boarders, if required.

A furniture mart provided a fine set of six dining chairs, which almost matched two that had come from the Queen Street 'emporium,' and Will could envisage a house warming party when they would entertain guests who were, for one reason or another, unable to accept their wedding invitations.

Hannah and her co-needleworkers had made curtains for the living room and the back bedroom where Will was sleeping, but had then returned to bridal wear, which was reaching an urgent stage. However, with ten days left before the wedding, the bride's and bridesmaids' dresses were ready except for the floral adornments, and final fittings for Elbie when she arrived. Hannah then settled down to making curtains for their double bedroom, and for the parlour.

Will had a meeting with Willie Cubbon, the organist from the Prims, and invited him to 'have a go' on his precious organ at St Mary's. He was impressed with the man's explorations on the larger instrument, and could tell that he understood his music. They discussed the hymns, both played their interpretations of the *Wagner and Mendelssohn Wedding Marches*, and attempted to make an appointment to meet the usual organist at Braddan Church so that they could hear the organ there. The man had initially suggested they come to a service to hear the organ, which both the Castletown men thought insultingly thoughtless, and hardly worthy of the explanation, but in the end, they were told to go when they wished and try it out.

The new church at Braddan was only about thirty years old, although its spire had been blown down after a short while, and the tower still had an unfinished appearance. The organ, both musicians felt, left a little to be desired after playing Will's powerful new organ at St Mary's, but it was adequate.

The verger from St Mary's, Bob Bridson, was invited to attend Will's wedding, as he was seen as a personal friend. Will had thought of asking him when he had found the Braddan organist so unhelpful, and wondered if there would be anyone provided there to pump the organ, but then he felt guilty about this, and convinced himself that there would surely be a verger there, and wanted his early-morning cohort to share his Big Day anyway. Bob could see all of this for himself, and accepted his invitation, tactfully mentioning that he would be happy to help out in the usual fashion 'if necessary.' Will was reminded, once more, that there were different kinds of people, wherever one went. Bob was famed for his tall tales, weaving himself into the starring role of any story he was told, and was excellent company at any party. He would be an asset whether the organ needed his strong arms or not.

There seemed to be so much to do and to think about, on all sides, that Will and Hannah felt caught up in a whirlwind. One Thursday morning, when he called at the shop after organ practice, he whispered a suggestion that sounded to her like 'Goldilocks.' She frowned only momentarily before getting his drift, and she beamed at him, and nodded, and mouthed the words 'Two o'clock.' He left with a smile on his face, and could hardly contain his excitement for the rest of the morning. He had almost forgotten the anticipation enjoyed in early courtship, everything had become so serious and fraught lately.

On his way home, he bought a bunch of flowers, and some beef steak and mutton chops from the butcher, then stopped at Tom Dodd's shop for a bottle of wine. Tom served him himself, saw the flowers, heard the request for wine and said, "Oh-oh, there is some 'jeel' afoot in Bowling Green Road tonight, I believe!" Will said he certainly hoped so, and Tom went on to apologise again for not being able to accept the wedding invitation, but repeated his offer of providing the beverages. In fact, he had drawn up a list that he was prepared to have delivered to Aunt Emily's house in Prince's Avenue, which was so generous that Will could not imagine his small gathering being able to do it justice. Tom assured him that he would be surprised how easily it disappears once people get into the 'spirit' of things, and they both laughed at his pun.

Will brushed the floor, arranged and re-arranged the furniture, found a vase among the boxes of items brought from Dorothy's that had been stored in the cupboard under the stairs for the time being, and arranged the flowers.

He boiled an egg and made some toast, and dined even though it was too early, he just had to keep himself occupied. Then he washed up his plate and egg cup, generally fidgeted about, and felt like that teenager again. He wandered from room to room, taking stock of what they had and what was still required. He couldn't help thinking that, although he had now been living in it for nearly three weeks, it was still just a house. It was not a home. That needed a woman's touch. It needed Hannah. *He* needed Hannah.

Suddenly, he could smell oranges, and his feelings surged. He wondered if he could contain himself until two o'clock and thought perhaps he should think of sucking lemons instead of oranges. But the idea of sucking anything was overpowering, so that when he spun round and found her standing there, he really thought he was hallucinating.

"I couldn't wait for two o'clock," she whispered, "I got off early." Will grabbed her and crushed her to him so hard that she would have gasped for breath if his mouth had not been covering hers. Kissing and licking and tearing at clothing, they stumbled up the stairs and into the bedroom that Will was using. Neither of them could wait until they were completely naked, and they surged and pumped and moaned on his little divan until they were quite breathless and spent.

"Oh God," he said, "I had almost forgotten how wonderful you are."

"There has been so much to prepare and think about, I was wondering if we would find time to be alone ever again," she agreed. Then she stood up, removed her remaining clothing, and said, in a childish voice, "Well, that little bed was too soft! I had better try another one, what might there be in the next room?"

They lay, naked, on the first bed in what was now a twin room, and she traced a finger across his chest and down over his stomach and abdomen and up again, and down and up again, and then she leaned over him and wound her tongue round his nipples. "Trollop!" he roared, and threw himself onto her, and into her again. "You are such a tease, now you just take that, ...and *that*, ...and **that**, ...and THAT...."

"Do you realise," she pondered, "that this could be Little Dorothy's bed."

"Aargh!"

Chapter Twenty Five

They nestled together for a while, getting their breath back and talking quite sensibly about all the wedding plans. Hannah mentioned that Elbie would be arriving on Monday, and they might not get the chance to 'do this' again at such leisure, once they got into the final few days, and she was so happy just to be here with him. She also wondered seriously how Old Dorothy was getting on, and hoped that Dr Sugden would keep his word and let her know the address of the hospital, as she would really like to write to her. She knew she would not be able to write back, but someone would surely read a little letter out to her, and it might comfort her a little to know that she was not forgotten. They both still hoped that the old lady might recover, and live to see her namesake perhaps. But this was not possible, was it? Dorothy had burned her bridges and had no home to come back to. They were lost in their sad thoughts for a while, curled together, and they both dozed off.

Hannah woke with a start, feeling cold. Getting her bearings, she gazed at her lover, still sleeping, and thought how happy and relaxed he looked, realising she had not seen him like this since the very first time they had made love, over at Ramsey overlooking the bay. She was overcome with love for this man as she thought through all they had done together since that wonderful day. She loved him so much, and in a little over a week, she would be his WIFE. She still could hardly believe it was all happening, except that 'it' was taking up so much of their time and thoughts. Again, she traced a finger down the side of his face, and leaned over and kissed him. Then she attempted to get up from the bed, but her movements woke him and he stirred.

"What?" he said, blinking in the light. "Oh, I thought I was having the most wonderful dream – and here you are, you're real. Ah yes, I remember now, I know you. You are Miss Trollop Extraordinaire!" and he made a grab for her again.

But she had got off the bed now, and putting on the little Goldilocks voice again said, "Oh, no, that bed was too hard. Might there not be one in this house that would be 'just right'?" She padded through to their double room at the front, but hesitated on the threshold. She looked back at him and said, "Dare we?"

They both thought about this for a moment, reluctant in one way, and yet still wanting each other. He cupped her oranges, or rather, her breasts, licked and kissed and sucked them, melting her to his body, but he guided her back to the twin room and onto the third bed, old Dorothy's bed with a brand new mattress. "We may as well try them all," he mumbled into her neck, "but we will have all the time in the world in the big one. What do you think of this one, Goldilocks?"

The third time was a little more sedate, more gentle, more time consuming, more exploratory, and then Hannah found a way to roll over on top of him and tantalise him with her breasts in his face, and to sit back on him, mimicking his actions, gripping and squeezing him, making him groan repeatedly, until he thought he might explode. For the fireworks moment, she let him roll back on top, and then they continued to lie like that, still coupled, for several minutes. "You will have to marry me now," she whispered, "this bed is good," then she pushed him away at last and began to put her clothes back on.

Matter of factly, she went downstairs and put the kettle on. "I'm hungry," she suddenly realised. "Uh-oh, has that Mrs Quine been simpering after you again?" as she noticed yet another fruit pie on the table. "Oh Lord, she hasn't been giving you flowers too, has she, and wine?"

"No, Silly, I bought those for you, only Miss Trollop didn't give me time to present them to her!"

She pulled a face at him and helped herself to a slice of the pie, and then started to warm the teapot. "Oh, you told me about Douglas and the coffee maker," she remembered. "I would love a cup of coffee."

Will showed her how it worked and, as he had done with Dougie, they sat in the fireside chairs and enjoyed the brew. "Where do we go from here?" Will asked. "It's so comfortable right here, and just lovely to be alone in our own home. Your dad and Syd have done a lovely job of the decorating, haven't they? I enjoyed having them around, they are both such characters." He continued to recount Sydney's antics over the gramophone, and in particular the songs from *The Mikado*. "He has quite a talent for picking up a tune, and pretty good at the actions too. He should join the drama group or he could be a comedian!"

Hannah told him about her other brothers too, she was very fond of all of them, and hoped they would all attend the wedding but, with being on a weekday, they probably couldn't all come. Then Will told her his plans for the honeymoon for the first time. He said he looked forward to meeting Elbie, and that since she was such a seasoned traveller, she could help him make the arrangements. Hannah had given no thought to a honeymoon other than wondering briefly if there was to be one, but had left it entirely up to Will to arrange if he saw fit. She would be happy just to come straight back to No 22 and into that lovely big bed!

"Trollop Insatiable!" he laughed. "Are you trying to kill me?"

"Yes," she said, "I want you to die with a big smile on your face! Come on, finish your coffee. I have a hankering to lean against the wall of Hango Hill once more before the wedding!"

∞∞∞∞

Hango Hill held many happy memories for them, but as they approached, Will said, "Am I imagining it or is that wall leaning a bit more, like the Tower of Pisa? That will be your fault, Trol."

"It's you who does the pushing," she laughed, "but yes, it does have a bit of a drunken look about it. Perhaps we should go to the inside and push the other way!"

Having performed several times already, in the end they only kissed and cuddled affectionately against the wall, for old times' sake, and then sank down onto the grass and contemplated the waves lapping the shore. Hannah suddenly felt overcome with happiness and excitement, that turned to a feeling that it was all too good to be true and would end with August. Watching the tide ripple in over the sand, she thought 'those waves will continue to roll in over this sand long after we are gone,' and her eyes filled with tears at the realisation that her happiness was, indeed, a transitory thing. She stole a glance at Will and found him staring out to the horizon, as if he were entertaining similar thoughts.

"This won't do," she told herself, "that's just the way it is. We must get on with the present." That reminded her that wedding presents had begun to arrive at No 22, and at Hope Street, and some even at her parents' house in Malew Street. They must make a list so they could be sure to thank everyone personally, after they returned from honeymoon. Ah yes, the honeymoon. That was just another thing to be excited about. She had never been off the island before, and had no idea what to expect from the places Will had mentioned, or how she would occupy herself on what promised to be very long train journeys. But that was all a fortnight away, and Will would take care of everything. Oh dear, no he couldn't take care of everything, she must think about what she would be wearing, for travelling and while they were away. She must think about packing a trunk.

By the time they returned to No 22, and having only had a slice of blackberry pie for lunch, Hannah was ready to attempt another meal on the gas cooker. She explored the 'cupboard under the stairs,' part of which had been converted into a pantry by her resourceful father, with a marble slab counter for keeping food cool. This had been found among Mrs Kinrade's meagre stock of furniture, but she somehow continued to be a source of everything the Waverleys would need. Here, she found both the steak and the chops and asked Will which treat had been intended for today. He looked at the red wine and elected to have the steak tonight.

Agreeing that this might be one of the last times they could be alone like this while still single, they settled down for a quiet evening at home, and enjoyed the steak and the wine. They both wanted to make love again, but the food, the alcohol and the day's excitement, both physical and emotional, had exhausted them, and they nestled on the sofa, listening to Will's records. Hannah giggled at the songs in the *Mikado*, imagining Syd acting the fool with his 'little list,' but when it came to *Three Little Maids From School*, she laughed out loud. "Ah, that explains it! He came in the shop wagging his finger at me and singing, *Won't have to wait very long they say,* and then went out again. I wondered what on earth he was on about."

Eventually Hannah reluctantly insisted that she must go home before it started to get dark. Will walked her home anyway, and strolled out along the pier, as he so enjoyed doing, on his way back. He leaned on the wall and watched the waves turn to foam against the breakwater, as the light faded and the lamplighter came round to ignite the gas lamps along the pier and the quay. He remembered having done exactly this – could it only be less than four months ago? – when Hannah had first 'happened' to him. What a difference she had made to his life. She was everything, and he could not now imagine life without her.

As he turned his steps homewards, he wondered about her friend. She sounded very sophisticated, and did not seem to go out to work for a living, but could afford to do a lot of travelling. This usually meant wealthy parents, or a benefactor of some sort, and he found himself quite intrigued and looking forward to meeting her in a few days' time.

∞∞∞∞

The next day, Friday, Mary told Hannah that she could finish working at the shop on Saturday, so that she would have next week free to prepare for the Big Day, and spend time with her bridesmaid friend. In the family, it had been decided that Clara would move over from the parents' house and live with Grandmother, sleeping in what had been Hannah's room, but little Carrie would go back to Malew Street to help her mother out at home. This was all very neat, but Clara had tried Hannah's bed and declared that she could not sleep on it. She wanted her own bed brought over from Malew Street, and why couldn't Hannah take her bed with her?

Beds, therefore, were destined to exchange addresses, as Hannah's went to Bowling Green Road, completing the bedrooms there, Clara's would vacate Malew Street and go to Mary's house, and Carrie's would go with her to her mother's. Hannah was more delighted with this arrangement than the others could have known. She knew that she had been making love with Will (in her virginal imaginings) in that bed for some years, and would be able to fulfil that dream when they returned from their honeymoon. It would be one of those extra dimensions she was planning to keep the excitement bubbling. She realised that 'being married' had been the pinnacle of her desires, without much, or any, thought to what happened afterwards, and wondered if there would be the same level of anticipation and excitement once they were man and wife.

Will had found himself thinking along similar lines, but from the direction that, up to now, life with Hannah had all been during the summer months, when he had a great deal more time than during the rest of the year. As soon as they returned from honeymoon, the school winter term would begin, so he would be out all day, and all his other activities that had been reduced during the holidays, would re-commence in the evenings, some in an even more concentrated fashion as they rehearsed and prepared for the Harvest and then Christmas festivals. He had the feeling that his moments for being with his wife might be severely restricted. But restricted to being in bed with her! That was a comfort, and the build-up of worries before the wedding would all be behind them, along with all the house furnishing and decorating. What a time it had been. What a whirlwind she was. What a different man he was now. Who could have imagined it all?

∞∞∞

Hannah wrote to Elbie, suggesting that she take the train to Castletown first thing on Tuesday, and they would spend the day together there. She would meet all the family, and they could have dress-fittings and practise styling their hair. She was so looking forward to seeing her friend again, and she warned Elbie that Carrie was jumping up and down with excitement at the thought of meeting her and making up the 'team' of bridesmaids. She knew there was not time for Elbie to reply, as she would be travelling on Monday, and be on the island by that evening.

The week-end passed much as usual. All was as ready as it could be barring the final adjustments and the fresh flowers, but Will and Hannah did manage to spend Saturday evening alone together, finding that their excitement was palpable. As Goldilocks had found that the new mattress was 'just right' they tried it out again to make sure, and then, later, after more wine had been consumed, they agreed that their new double bed really ought to be tested.

There was more room on this bed to spread themselves and sprawl, and a lot of teasing was indulged in, with tickling and licking and stroking. They were both exploring each other in ways that had not been possible before, and their anticipation was reaching fever pitch. It was Hannah who gave in first and begged him to take her, but he continued to suck her breasts and lick in between, stroking lightly around the tops of her thighs with a fingertip, making her shudder and plead. His fingers explored everywhere, driving her wild, and ever more so as he reached down and followed his fingers with his tongue.

Much as he would have liked to continue this indefinitely (he was enjoying the pleading) he found that his own anticipation was overheating, and she, as always, was going to get her way very soon. Their marriage bed gave them a new sense of belonging, and there seemed to be more love than ever in the love-making. Sweet nothings were not necessary but, because he was learning to pace himself, he was able to continue to drive her wild at a leisurely pace, making sure she was completely happy before he indulged himself. She felt that she had found a new sort of lover, and she resorted to the old ploy of gasping, "Give me a baby, Will. Please make me pregnant, Please, Will, I want your baby, I want.... I want...."

"Witch!" he gasped, "Trollop. Strumpet! Impatient little tart!"

"Well!" she countered, "I've never known it take all night before!"

"Complaints, complaints. I'm only a beginner, you have to give me time."

"Beginner, pah! Actually, that was quite excruciating," she admitted. "Whew! You took me by surprise, but I'll be ready for you next time."

"This bed is going to be all right, I think, eh Sweetheart?"

"Oh this bed is perfect. It might be worn out quite soon, but right now I think it's the most wonderful place in the world!"

Chapter Twenty Six

Elbie arrived in Castletown on the first train, so eager was she to plunge into wedding plans. Hannah had planned to meet every train until she saw her, so was well pleased with her early arrival. The two young women embraced and looked each other up and down.

"Hannah, you have blossomed!" was the first observation. "You still have that Manx weather-beaten looking skin, but I am going to take you in hand now. Yes, and hands too, let me have a look. Oh dear!"

"Oh Elbie, it is so good to see you. Never mind my hands. They are hard working hands, that's all. I am not ashamed of hard working hands!"

"Well, you should be, as the wife of the gentry, you can't shake hands with the likes of your Lady Raglan with a paw like that. But don't worry, we will get you sorted out in no time."

They giggled and chattered like teenagers, and Hannah discovered that her friend had 'had another little windfall,' which, as usual, provided Elbie with the wherewithal to pursue further travels. Apparently, she used her visits to various places as research, and wove local geography and folklore into her writings, which made them popular with readers of all areas, but especially in the places featured.

"Oh, have you ever written about the Isle of Man?" Hannah asked.

"Not yet," replied her friend, "but I expect to be hearing some interesting local tales in the coming week, that could just be material for when I return from Europe."

"How exciting!" said Hannah. "All I have done this summer is fall in love!"

"All excellent material, I assure you. I can make falling in love very saleable."

"Have you ever done it?" asked Hannah innocently, and then covered her mouth. "Ooh, sorry, I meant have you ever fallen in love!"

"Hundreds of times," was the unexpected response, "and 'it' too, oh yes, lots – all in the cause of research, you understand."

"Elbie!"

"Oh come on, Goody Two Shoes, don't try and tell me you and Will haven't....."

Hannah drew in a shocked breath. "I am not telling you anything," she said adamantly, "if it's going to end up in a newspaper." She thought quickly, knowing Elbie would not let the matter drop. "I spent a long time waiting for the right man to come along."

"Huh! Wasted a long time, if you ask me."

Hannah wondered if she had a point. If Will had not admitted to being so lonely, that night after choir practice, she would still be waiting.....

"Well, all I can say is, you don't know the people of Castletown," she countered, "they all had me down as a strumpet and a whore years ago, after I rejected Joe Garrett. You should have heard some of the things Will's sister used to say about me! And other old witches of her ilk. I was a completely 'scarlet woman' long before Will and I...."

"Aha! You have! Well, so you should. What if 'it' had been a total disaster? You could have saddled yourself to a useless husband for the rest of your life. I can see that it obviously was no disaster. Mmmm, I will know more before long!"

"Oh, Elbie, that's private stuff, and I'd be really grateful if you could keep this all under your rather spectacular hat. Will and I are still getting to know each other, really, it has all happened rather quickly. I would feel embarrassed and disloyal to discuss such intimate things. All I can say is.... he is wonderful! "

"Can I borrow him?" Hannah aimed a mock slap at her friend.

"No you can NOT! If I see you so much as bat an eyelid at him....' She didn't know how to finish the sentence, but it was not required, as they had arrived at Mary's house and shop. Hannah remarked that she had been relieved of her shop-keeping duties at the weekend, so Elbie didn't need to worry about her hands any more.

"Yes, we'll see about that," said Elbie, "I have some 'preparations' in my bag, but can Aunt Mary let us have some oatmeal, do you think?" They entered the shop from the house, and Elbie was re-acquainted with Mary.

Oatmeal and one or two other products were acquired, and then she wanted to catch up with 'Uncle Bowman.' She flirted with the old man, stroking his long beard and enjoying his embarrassed reaction. Her Nanna had died before she was born, she said, so she liked to think of him as Nanna's baby brother, with a beard! Charles himself had only a dim recollection of his half-sister from his father's first marriage, but it was nice to think about the family connections.

Carrie hurtled into the hall as the older girls made to go upstairs. They had met before, but not for some years, and little girls grow a lot in that time, so there were the usual oohs and aahs about how pretty she had become, and how she was going to be tall, and then they all repaired to what was still, temporarily, Hannah's room. Hannah was grateful for her little sister's presence as she knew, or at least she hoped, that Elbie would cease her probing questions while the child was there. She set about showing both bridesmaids their almost-finished outfits. This was also the moment to give them their presents, so Hannah made Carrie hold her coral-coloured dress up against herself, while the lacy shawl collar was placed round her shoulders, and then the amber bracelet was presented, and affixed to the collar. The child admired herself in the long mirror, but was soon distracted, wanting to know how her hair would be done up.

Hannah then showed Elbie her bridesmaid's dress, or 'her uniform' as she had dubbed it, and felt a little envious at seeing how slim she was. Hannah was slim herself, but the rounded breasts that so enchanted Will, gave her a top-heavy appearance, or so she thought. This had been, and still was, fashionable, but Hannah preferred to hold herself in with a laced bodice. Allowing Will to undo that was always fun. Elbie's slim dress, in the same colour and fabric as Carrie's, was draped with the lacy collar, and fastened with Dorothy Kinrade's cameo brooch. Hannah had a lump in her throat as she gave the brooch to her dearest friend. Elbie chirped about how perfect it was and what a lovely gift it was, but was not oblivious to Hannah's slight change of countenance. She did not ask about it then, but determined to hear the story at some more appropriate time.

Both bridesmaids wanted Hannah to model her dress and, although Carrie had been present at all the preparation and had sewn many parts together, she had not seen the finished product. They both gasped when Hannah emerged from behind the mirror. Her slim silk dress was not white, but aquamarine. "That's not a wedding dress!" blurted Carrie, but Hannah put a finger to her lips, then produced the long, crocheted white lace over-dress, that was longer at the back to become a train.

"That's your job, Hannah pointed at the train, looking at Carrie, "You have to try to keep it from sweeping the church floor!"

Elbie had tears in her eyes. "Han, you look stunning. I have been to a lot of weddings, but I have never seen anything like this. Is it your own design?"

Hannah thanked her for her kind remarks, and glowed with pride. "Yes and no," she admitted, "these are samplers from Gran's work box. I just fell in love with the crocheted lace work, and there was so much of it, the job was half done before we started, but Gran, Clara and I, yes, and Carrie too, have worked our fingers to the bone (she broke off and hid her hands behind her back) to make enough to complete the outfits. I think it has been worth it. You don't think it is too different?"

"It is gorgeous. I almost wish I was getting married myself," said her worldly friend, then, seeing Hannah take a breath to comment on this, waved a hand and continued, "No, no, no, I take that back. Remember what I told you earlier (she glanced at Carrie) about 'lots of experiences,' I am totally content with the lifestyle I have, and a husband would be far too demanding! Maybe one day, when I'm old and decrepit and in need of company, I might give the matter some thought...."

"Unless the right man just happens into your life?" suggested Hannah, and she stood between them as they tried to see all three in the mirror. She couldn't help thinking, *Three little maids from school are we,* and she smiled to herself, knowing she wouldn't have to wait very long now.

"Right, off with the finery now," she instructed, "All we have left to organise are the head-dresses and the flowers. Carrie, you will have a little twisted belt round your dress, with ivy leaves and other flowers woven through. I'm not sure what the other flowers will be yet, it depends what Mother can find for us! I am thinking bronze and white chrysanths, or carnations if we go really splendid, but we will have to wait and see. Now let's design the hair styles. You want a little crown of flowers, don't you Carrie, and I think that is a good theme for all of us. My veil can tuck into a coronet, but there is no need for me to have a complicated hair style, because of the veil. Whereas you two.... we could start with a circle of flowers and then get creative, piling your hair up and inserting more flowers here and there. How does that sound?"

They spent a happy hour arranging and re-arranging each other's hair, and generally chatting and getting quite excited. Hannah reminded Carrie that the wedding was almost a whole week away yet, so she would have to contain herself somehow. Elbie put some oatmeal in a cup of water, and instructed Hannah to leave it overnight, and then cleanse her face with the resulting liquor. "You must do this every day for the rest of your life," she instructed, "Believe me, you will thank me for it. As for your hands, use the cream in this pot at night when you retire, and then put gloves on. It could take a little while, but make it a habit, and you will not regret it." Hannah looked at Elbie's face and hands, and could see the difference from her own, but then, Elbie had never scrubbed a floor or peeled a potato or gutted a fish!

After a light lunch, Hannah and Elbie walked over to Bowling Green Road. Hannah had a sudden thought that put her into a panic. Had she told her friend what to expect of Will? She tried to remember what she had confided. She may have assumed that Elbie would remember who William Waverley was, she was sure she had told her about his job, and the organ and the choir, but had she described him? At all?

She had not, so when Elbie set eyes on Will for the first time as Hannah's intended, she gulped, gave a little cough to steady herself, and embraced him, so that neither he nor Hannah could see her face for a brief moment. She had to clear her throat again to respond to Will's little speech of welcome, as he had taken both of her hands in his and had put one to his lips. Elbie took a sidelong glance at Hannah, who narrowed her eyes at her, and then placed herself between them, reaching up to kiss Will's cheek, as if to claim ownership.

"This is a nice house," Elbie said to break the slight silence that had fallen, "why don't you show me round, Hannah, I can see that it has been re-decorated. Did you choose everything?" and she began to wander into the parlour.

"Yes, she did," began Will, at the same time as Hannah was claiming that they had chosen everything together, whereat Will grinned and continued, "she is the artistic director around here, but I'm sure you will find that she has nice taste."

"I have already seen evidence of her creative powers this morning," replied Elbie, seeing Hannah put a finger to her lips to stop her divulging anything about the wedding dress, "but I do like the way everything tones, even in this living room. Yes, very nice. I approve!"

"Come upstairs," smiled Hannah, taking her elbow, "I especially like the wallpaper in the bedroom. Father and Sydney have worked so hard for us, and now even Will can turn his hand to papering and painting! He has been learning what hard work is like these past few weeks, he even had to start with the scrubbing down! I think he has come to appreciate that there are occupations other than teaching!"

"Ouch! I heard that!" shouted Will from the bottom of the stairs, then, to himself, "It's Agnes who needs convincing of that!" He had learned a great deal over the holidays and there was much that he wanted to impart to his boys when the new term started. He had not admitted as much to Hannah, but he had been impressed with the Corletts' approach to their work, their knowledge and skill, and their use, in their own way, of mathematics in measuring and calculating. There was not a scrap of paper or paint left over from Billa's estimates, and he liked the way Sydney willingly and eagerly applied what he was being taught. He was very fond of Hannah's family, and certainly appreciated the value of their 'wedding present.'

When the young women came back down, Will remembered that Hannah's brother, Charlie, had called earlier with a package for them. He had forgotten Charlie's promise to paint a picture for them, until he saw the shape of the brown paper package tied with string. Now, he presented it to his bride, who had not forgotten her embarrassment when she had blurted out her description of the place where Will had first made love to her. She knew that her flaming cheeks had given her away, but although there had been knowing looks between her brothers, no-one had mentioned it since.

"Oh, Will, isn't it perfect?" she cried once the wrappings had been torn away. "It is exactly as I remember it, which was also exactly as you had described it to me, and I couldn't wait to see it. Oh look, there are even the two schooners sailing across the bay! I love it, oh it is so beautiful. Isn't Charlie clever?" she had turned to show the painting to Elbie.

"It is a very pretty place," said Elbie, "obviously somewhere you have been? With special significance?"

"Too many questions, Miss. Yes, obviously a special place, but it really is exactly like that. Who would not think it an exquisite view? This must go in the parlour, where all our guests will see it," decided Hannah. "I would not be surprised if Charlie gets dozens of commissions when people see this!"

Will was beaming at her enthusiasm, at the attention to detail of the lovely painting, at the view itself, but also at the picture's relevance to them both. It had been a very special place, a most unforgettable day, and the consummation of their wonderful relationship. He wondered if he would ever be able to look at the picture without feeling a stirring in his loins. He decided to put the kettle on, for something to occupy his mind.

Elbie declared that she was tiring after all her travelling. Yesterday's crossing had been horrendous in the stormy weather, and she would now take the next train back to Douglas once they had drunk their tea. Her hotel would be providing an evening meal, so she would perhaps just take a leisurely stroll on the promenade afterwards, and that would be enough for one day. She instructed Hannah to catch the first train to Douglas in the morning, she would meet her at the station, and then they would go shopping! Hannah tried to protest that there was nothing that they needed from the shops, but she was told that was nonsense, and they must spend the day together anyway.

They all walked to the railway station, Hannah waved to Elbie for as long as her train was in sight, and then the lovers returned to No 22.

While they both wanted to make love, so much had happened and been said, that they found they could not settle without bringing up another remark. Will, of course, had not met Elbie before, and had found her both fascinating and terrifying. "She is so worldly," he commented, "I'm not sure she is a good influence for you!"

"She is perfect!" declared Hannah, "she is exactly what I need right now. I don't have any other friends who would know how to point me in the direction I must take as your wife, Will. Life is going to be different for me, isn't it? I had not realised it quite so much until today."

Will thought about this and reluctantly agreed. "What have I done?" he whispered, almost to himself, "Am I taking you out of your familiar lifestyle? Does it frighten you? You mustn't be frightened, I will always be here for you. I want you so much, Hannah, I love you so much. Our life will be whatever you want it to be, I promise. I don't want you to feel apprehensive about anything." They embraced, and remained holding each other, staring into the fire, both lost in their thoughts, going over all that was happening to them. Wondering....

Chapter Twenty Seven

The young women had their day together in the capital, and Elbie, at least, found numerous items that had to be purchased. Hannah had never been shopping on this scale before. Hannah had never had the kind of money in her pocket that Elbie obviously had, and shopping for knick-knacks and trivial items would never have occurred to her. As for buying clothing? Well, one made one's own clothing, surely.

But not Elbie, and she would not hear of Hannah using something home-made for her 'going away' outfit. Hannah learned that she needed something called a 'trousseau,' and before the week was out, she would have one. She would brook no objections she said, this must be done, and it was Elbie's wedding present to her dearest cousin. Hannah felt her life changing – changing too fast for her – but it was so thrilling that she was swept along on the 'worldly' girl's enthusiasm.

She was reminded that she would be away on honeymoon for at least a week, possibly two. Now what was she going to wear for two weeks? She couldn't flounce around in her wedding dress for a fortnight, don't be silly! So, even after a pretty, royal blue, two-piece suit, with long skirt and tight-waisted jacket, had been modelled and purchased, she was still being told that she could not wear the same clothes every day. The very idea! Now come on, you will need at least one more suit, and a number of blouses so that you can vary the effect. And shoes, you will need several pairs of shoes. And hats too.

Hannah drew the line at hats. She might suffer one, and only one, if there should be an occasion that would demand it for the sake of respect, such as going to church. She imagined they probably would attend a church service somewhere, but Elbie decreed that she must wear her 'one' hat to travel in, as it was the easiest way to carry it and avoid its being crushed. Hannah saw the sense in this, and suffered the purchase of one hat, just managing to talk Elbie out of the extrovert kind that she sported herself, which was, admittedly, high fashion. She settled on a pale blue 'pill-box' with darker blue and aquamarine silk flowers and net. This would tone with either suit, as she had rather fallen for a light greyish-blue outfit that matched her eyes. Elbie assured Hannah that she was getting there, and that she would make a Lady of her yet!

Elbie treated Hannah to an elegant lunch in a hotel, which was another first for Hannah. There had been one or two special occasions when she had eaten at an inn, sometimes at a modest café, but she had never even been inside a hotel such as this one, where the dining room was called a restaurant.

Restaurants? Trousseaus? whatever was the world coming to? she wondered. The meal was more exotic than substantial, but she liked it, and quickly learned to extend her little finger when raising her teacup, and to leave the clearing up to the waitress.

They could not possibly walk back to Elbie's lodging with all those packages, and Hannah had another new experience when a motor car was summoned to the hotel foyer, and their parcels collected and stowed by people she did not know.

In Elbie's room, the girls lounged on the beds and chattered about all sorts of things. Mostly about the wedding, of course, but Hannah also tried to probe for more information on Elbie's private life. However, she found it so hard to follow, it was so very different from any life she could have imagined, and she did not understand a lot of what her friend whispered so confidentially. She dropped names into the conversation as if Hannah was expected to know who the people were, and poor Hannah felt embarrassed and wrong-footed. She began to understand what Will meant about her being 'worldly' and, although the girl's knowledge and confidence were inspiring, she knew she could not be comfortable herself in such a life. Not yet, anyway. She would have to pick and choose the best bits, she told herself, but leave the rest to the experienced young woman. That woman who did not, after all was said and done, have a husband, and Hannah clung to that realisation as the one card that was almost up her own sleeve. Also, she lived in England, which was apparently on another planet.

Together, they surveyed their purchases, and Hannah's new finery was placed on hangers in the large wardrobe in Elbie's twin room. Everything may as well stay here, she had decreed, and we will arrange for your trunk to come up on the train with you. Which day will you come? Come on Friday, and that will give us time to organise everything. Put Will's wedding suit in the trunk along with all our dresses. He will come up on Sunday night, yes? and stay over at your Aunt Em's where the reception will be held. Can we go and meet her now? I'd like to get the street map in my head, so that I know where everything is.

Hannah's head was reeling, but she welcomed the suggestion to show her friend where Prince's Avenue was, as it was literally just up the road and round the corner, really convenient, and if Aunt Em wasn't at home, at least Elbie would be able to find the house again.

They walked up Broadway and found the place looking somewhat deserted, but their knock was answered by a good looking young man. Hannah introduced herself and Elbie and told him their business. He said he was a lodger, his name was Patrick, but he was the only person in the house at present. However, he ushered them into one of the rooms where, as had been done at Miss Walkington's, a dividing wall had been removed to make a large, long dining room running the full width of the house. This would be where the reception would take place, and the young man, whose accent betrayed Irish roots, asked if they would like some tea.

Hannah thought it was time she was heading back to the railway station, but Elbie flirted outrageously with Patrick and was accepting his offer of hospitality at the same time as Hannah was about to decline. So determined was she to stay longer, that she followed the man out to the kitchens at the back of the house. Hannah frowned to herself and decided to remain where she was, imagining one very long table, with a top table at right angles, and calculating where everyone would be sitting. She was sure that Aunt Em would have this all in hand, but she also liked to have a rough idea of what to expect. There were some gift wrapped packages on a side table, and she inspected the labels. These presents would presumably remain here until after the wedding, and then be delivered to Castletown to await their return from honeymoon. She was not sure about all the etiquette and timings of these things, it was all quite frightening.

Elbie returned, carrying a tray of cups and saucers, and was followed by Patrick bearing a teapot. Elbie's eyes were shining as she announced that Pat was going to come to the station with them, and then walk her back here to meet Aunt Em. She flicked her eyes imperiously at Patrick and then at the teapot, and he jumped to fill the cups. Hannah didn't know what to think. How long had it taken Elbie to seduce the poor man into being used in such a way? Five minutes? But it all worked to her plan. She hailed a motor cab to take them all to the railway station at the other end of town, and Hannah was dispatched as if she were now surplus to requirements. Elbie would come to Castletown again the next afternoon, to liaise with everyone else there, and then, on Friday, Hannah would come back and stay with her at The Athol for the three nights before the wedding.

Hannah sat on the train alone, feeling wrung out. She could not quite decide whether she was happy or furious at having everything worked out for her. She had certainly been floundering at all the arrangements, but Elbie had it all organised as if it were a military operation, ticking items off a list as she ploughed on with her plans. And what on earth were her plans for Patrick O'Riley or whatever his name was? Hannah had her suspicions but was reluctant to believe them.

It was teatime by the time she was back in Castletown and she went straight to Bowling Green Road rather than her home. She wanted to tell Will everything and yet she didn't know how. If he thought Elbie 'worldly' from a first impression, whatever would he think now? Well, she didn't care, she just wanted to be with him. Elbie was going to separate them for three whole days and nights, and that was part of what she found upsetting. She knew it was silly when they would be together for the rest of time after Monday, but she had got used to being with Will. The whirlwind that was Elbie was wonderful and lovely and exciting, but oh dear, one had to take her in small doses!

Having had a 'posh' lunch, she was happy when she found Will opening a tin of salmon to make a sandwich. His bread ladies had left some more of their little madeleines too, she noticed, and she thought, somewhat rebelliously, that the simple local fare was quite fancy enough for her taste. For now, anyway. He brewed her a cup of coffee, and she snuggled with him on the sofa. He did not press for information but left her to tell him as much or as little as she saw fit. He was aware that there were 'secret' things about weddings, and a girly day out with a street-wise woman from Liverpool was bound to have been a culture shock for poor Hannah.

Eventually, she told him that she had received her orders and that she felt like a schoolgirl. But he surprised her by advising her to just go with the flow. Elbie's timetable sounded very reasonable to him, and Hannah was lucky having someone to direct the traffic, especially a girl who seemed to have such a lot of experience in all sorts of things. Hannah wondered just how much he had divined, but decided against telling him about the Irishman just yet. She would wait to see what the outcome of that escapade might be. For now, she was so tired, that she fell asleep in his arms, and he was afraid to move for more than an hour.

∞∞∞

Elbie leaned towards Patrick, who thought she was inviting him to kiss her. And so she was, but only teasing, and she took his hand as they walked back towards the promenade. When they reached a bench facing the sea, she sat, and allowed him to put an arm along the back of the seat. She sat demurely, gazing out at a steamer approaching in the bay, as she idly placed a hand on his thigh and traced a light circle with her fingertip and then removed her hand, knowing he would react. He leaned forward and put his other arm across her waist, pulling her towards him for the kiss that, this time, she did not refuse. It was a long kiss, for a couple who had met less than two hours before. It was a long kiss by any standards, but they both knew what it meant. After a while, they got up and walked a little further.

As they walked, he was asking where she was staying and how long she was here for, which reminded her about meeting Aunt Em, and they wondered whether to go back there or spend the evening together first. After another lingering, exploratory kiss, they plumped for the spending the evening option, and walked the full length of the promenades to the far end, and up into a glen at Summerhill. He was well acquainted with this place, and it was obviously a popular haunt for lovers, overhung with many trees and shrubs, with a few street lights here and there, but plenty of dark nooks and crannies, some of them even with bench type seats.

They were soon getting better acquainted on one such secluded park bench, and Patrick's practised hand found its way inside her blouse before he followed it with his mouth and tongue. While she was moaning with pleasure at that, his hand stroked her thigh, moving her skirt up deftly at each stroke, and very soon he was entering her, gently at first and then, as her knees came up around him, less gently and more fervently.

"Holy Mary!" he said, "I wish all the girls round here were like you."

"Oh, I think you have done that before, Pat," she laughed.

"Well, yes, but it usually takes weeks to get where we were an hour ago! Aren't you worried about.... anything?"

"No, I don't worry about anything. I had an abortion years ago and now I can't get pregnant, so what's to worry about? I like doing it, and there is always a willing someone to do it with. You're very good! I'm quite sorry I won't be staying here but I might see you again before I go home."

They took a horse tram back as far as Broadway, and she took her leave when they reached her hotel, as she was expected for an evening meal. She knew she was late for this and should have gone on to meet Aunt Em after all, but she did not need him any more, so he was dismissed, and he returned to Prince's Avenue alone. She had to apologise for missing the meal, but because she was a good customer, a light supper was procured for her in her room.

She was not particularly proud of herself, but she chalked up another experience. How easy had that been? But she had had Irishmen before, what she really wanted was a local chap. Hannah had brothers, she must engineer a meeting with one or more of them, perhaps tomorrow. She had met them before but not for some years, and she wondered how much they may have matured. She supposed Hannah was getting it right now with her lovely old man. It couldn't be too difficult.

Chapter Twenty Eight

Everything was carried out according to Elbie's directions. She arrived in Castletown early on Thursday afternoon, announcing that she had walked up the road to meet Aunt Em in the morning. No, the Irishman was not up, apparently he was a baker and worked overnight in the bakery but she did not tell Hannah anything more about him.

She was anxious now to meet Hannah's immediate family again, so first they went to the shop in Hope Street where she caught up with Clara, whom she had not met on any previous occasion. She was quite surprised at how different the sisters were in appearance, although they had the same sense of humour and laugh. Not having realised how close Clara was in age to Hannah, she hoped that she had not upset her by accepting the invitation to be Hannah's bridesmaid, but Clara assured her that Hannah had suggested perhaps having three bridesmaids, which she had declined, and in fact she was quite glad that she would not have to perform any duties on the day, other than as a guest. She had really enjoyed helping to prepare the dresses, though, and would be asking Hannah to design *her* wedding dress when the time came.

Mary was going to close the shop on Monday afternoon, so that they could all attend the reception. The numbers witnessing the ceremony itself would be an exclusive little band, but the family would make up for it later when they all got together, and everyone was looking forward to it.

Having been invited to return at teatime, Hannah and Elbie moved on to Bowling Green Road, but called at Malew Street first to warn Mother that they would come later on, and hoped to see everybody then. Will was not at home when they arrived at No 22, so Hannah brewed some coffee and the two young women sat and enjoyed a brief break. He had been attempting to work out an itinerary and timetable for the honeymoon, and a newspaper had been spread out on the table with some advertisements circled, and some pencilled notes in the margin.

Elbie cast an eye over his scribblings and smiled. "It is not nearly as complicated as he is thinking," she told Hannah. "Travelling is so easy once you reach Liverpool, he doesn't need to make bookings in advance, but I'm sure he wants to have his schedule planned."

When he returned, she repeated this sentiment and he was grateful for her advice. She would be returning to Liverpool on the same boat as they were catching on Monday afternoon, and she would show them to a very convenient hotel where they could spend their wedding night. After that, they would be on their own, but next morning they could turn up at the railway station whenever they were ready, and step on any train they liked. "Cheltenham? I would imagine you could get on the Bristol train. You might need to change trains somewhere on the way but just ask at the station, everyone is very helpful. Make sure you have all the addresses you need in your notebook, and plenty of small change for carriages and so on. You've travelled before Will, don't be worried about it, just enjoy the experience."

Will smiled and heaved a sigh of relief. "I did intend to ask you," he said, "but wasn't sure when I'd get a chance to see you again. Have you met the family yet?"

They told Will the plans and he said he would come with them, and so it was that all three turned up at Hope Street for their tea. Carrie laid the crowded table, and Hannah helped Clara to prepare plates of sandwiches and a bowl of salad, being careful not to get her hands wet. She had begun the grooming régime as instructed by Elbie, so was especially careful about what she let Elbie see her do, and made sure that it was Clara who sliced the tomatoes which, according to her mentor, stain terribly.

After their tea, they repaired to the Corlett household, where Elbie was re-introduced to all the brothers. All the males in the household, including Billa, were charmed and intrigued by the sophisticated woman who flirted with all of them, hardly recognising her as the young girl she had been when they first met. She now thought Sydney the most fun, but knew he was far too young for her. They were probably all her juniors, if she were counting, but she was only hunting at the moment. "Ah, Charles, you are the artist," she declared, "I have seen the wonderful painting you have done for Will and Hannah. How clever you are," and she watched Charles's chest swell with pleasure. She found ways to compliment each of them, so that they were all her slaves, and she was enjoying the blatant adulation, calculating to herself which one she might be able to get on his own.

In conversation, however, she gleaned distinct hints that both Charlie and Frank were already 'spoken for,' not that they admitted it in so many words, but she was well accustomed to divining information. This only left George, and he seemed much too reticent and wary. She didn't have the time to seduce shrinking violets, so she decided to settle for having some fun with young Sydney. When she heard about his singing and acting capabilities, she led him on to perform the 'little list' song from *The Mikado* for them all and then asked him if he could dance. Of course he could dance, so she got up and held out her arms to partner him. They waltzed round the room as he sang *A Wand'ring Minstrel I*, then she steered him out of the room and into the hall, out of sight of the family. Here, as they both continued humming, she pushed her breast into the poor boy's face and laughed at his startled expression, then she put both his hands on her breasts and encouraged him to stroke her. Before returning to the family, she treated him to a very grown-up kiss, and then waltzed him back into the parlour, quite satisfied with herself.

"You've gone very quiet, Syd," remarked one of his older brothers, "you haven't had your wicked way out there with this poor young lady, have you?"

"Hah! I wish..." he replied. Everyone laughed at the ridiculous suggestion, and conversation resumed.

Had Elbie disappeared with any of the older brothers, Hannah would have been very suspicious of her motives, but did not think for a moment that she would have misbehaved with an innocent boy but right now her head was full of wedding preparations. She was quite anxious about leaving her home next day as a single girl and returning to the town as a married woman, so it was her own love life that was uppermost in her thoughts. But Will had wondered about the little episode, and had caught Lina looking askance too, and thought again that this cousin might not be the most suitable company for his wife-to-be, but it was too late to do anything about it except hope for the best. Or was it?

Both Elbie and Sydney were thinking about sex.

∞∞∞

It was Elbie who had decreed Hannah's timetable and therefore how everyone else should fit into it, but now it was Hannah's mother, Lina, who stepped in to clear up some of the grey areas. She had been thinking; since the ceremony would be on Monday morning with a brief wedding breakfast afterwards at Aunt Em's, before the happy couple left on the afternoon boat for Liverpool, 'certain people' who were obliged to be at work on a Monday would miss out. "Why don't we all get together for a party at Em's on Sunday?" she suggested. "That way, we could all celebrate together, wear our finery if we feel like it, then Will and Carrie and I could stay the night and be ready with all the flowers right there in Douglas for the first thing on Monday."

Will thought this not only a sensible sequence and a lovely idea regarding all the family, but also a chance to see a little more of Hannah. Elbie seemed to have intended to take her away from him for a precious three whole days. Before anyone could object, he was first to respond, therefore, with, "Brilliant, Lina, what do you think everyone? That way all of us," and he threw his arms out to indicate all in the room, "will get to celebrate together, and Mary and Chas too. I will arrange for Sunday Evensong to be replaced by evening prayers so that I don't have to be at church, and I can accompany the luggage to Douglas without having to ask anyone else to take care of it."

Now, for the first time, Hannah interjected with, "Mother, I love you, and Elbie, if you don't mind, I would quite like to spend Saturday night at home for the last time. I am so worried that we will forget something, there are so many things to think about. I will come to Douglas tomorrow morning and stay with you for that night, then come back down to Castletown on Saturday to clear all the odds and ends up. Then I can come back with everyone else on Sunday, and sleep at your hotel again on Sunday night. Oh, that would be such a relief!"

"And we can practise putting the flowers in our hair," put in little Carrie, to whom this was the most important part of the big day.

"I will go and see Tom Dodd right now," said Will. "His wedding present is 'all the drink we can drink,' but I'm thinking that he and Fanny might be able to join us after all if the party is on Sunday. That would be lovely, when they have been so kind. I had better see Qualtrough and invite him too! Will you see how the Thorburns feel about it, Lina?"

Elbie knew she was expected to object, but all she could think about was an unexpected free night, and what she might be able to get up to. Graciously, she admitted that there were lots of details to be attended to, and she realised that the other ladies were worrying about this and that, some things of course that she had not even thought about, so Cousin Lina's suggestion seemed to cover every eventuality, and she was grateful. Then her mind returned to de-flowering the boy, Sydney.

∞∞∞∞

So it was that Hannah took her wedding dress, and Elbie's bridesmaid's dress, to Douglas on the train on Friday morning in a trunk, which also contained Will's wedding suit and some of Hannah's own 'Sunday best' clothes. The rest of her trousseau had never left Douglas. Alighting from the train, she hailed a carriage for herself and arrived at Athol House on Broadway just as Elbie came down the steps to meet her. They prevailed upon the carriage driver to help the hotel lad up the steps with the trunk, while Elbie stroked the horses' noses and whispered sweet nothings to them.

Then the carriage took them back into town and the shopping centre. They spent another happy 'girlie' day together, browsing in numerous shops but while Elbie made a number of purchases, Hannah bought only a gift for her bridegroom. She had spotted a silver tie-pin with a single stone matching her ring, and she walked past the shop window several times while she considered making such a purchase. Spending money came so easily to her friend, but it was not a familiar feeling for Hannah, and she knew she would always be reminded of the turmoil of emotions that represented the decision to splash out on this quite unnecessary gift. But it was so perfect, and she was so happy and this whole experience would never be happening again.

They called on Hannah's Aunt Emily to make sure she was aware of the Sunday plan, and found that it had already been suggested, but not confirmed. She also thought it a lovely chance for all the family to get together, and meant that the wedding breakfast after the ceremony could be a light lunch rather than a cooked dinner, which would have to have been rushed through in order for the couple to catch the boat. Running a boarding house, Em was already organised to provide whatever meals were requested and this presented no problems at all. She looked forward to seeing them all on Sunday.

In the evening, they dined in Elbie's hotel dining room when, although they continued to chatter excitedly about the coming week-end, Hannah noticed that Elbie frequently looked out of the window. "Are you feeling claustrophobic?' she asked, "would you like to take a stroll after we've finished?"

Elbie only laughed it off, but they did take a walk along the promenade. They both received admiring glances from some passers-by, but Hannah was oblivious. Had she noticed, she would have put it down to the excited glow of a bride, as she was truly walking on air and still could hardly believe that all her dreams were so close to coming true. Elbie was still quite appalled at her friend's choice of husband, but acknowledged wryly to herself that, at least, she had no desire to steal him, as she had done with a couple of other friends' bridegrooms. Those poor chaps were taking themselves off the market, sometimes unwillingly, and they deserved a little treat before they were committed for ever. Elbie knew a delicious feeling of power on those occasions and felt slightly cheated if she was unsuccessful in tempting a groom to indulge. That was not an option this week, but there were still some challenges available to her.

They sat in the gardens for a while, listening to the band playing, and it was all Elbie could do to decline an invitation to dance when a good-looking stranger approached her. "Perhaps tomorrow night," she whispered to him, withdrawing her hand, and she and Hannah wandered back to her hotel for a nightcap.

In the morning, she asked if Hannah was sure she really wanted to return to Castletown as they could have had such a lovely day together; now it was Saturday there could be all sorts of entertainment going on. But Hannah could think only of spending some more time with Will and her family, where she was familiar and happy. Elbie was lovely, but she was such a whirlwind. "I just want to be sure that everyone is ready for Monday, I'm really quite nervous about it all. Did you say you would be leaving the island on the same boat with us on Monday afternoon?"

"Well, I did intend to go back on Monday, but I'm thinking that I would quite like another day or two here. When I get back, I will be getting ready for my European trip, and I don't want to be kicking my heels at home trying to put the time in. You have some nice shops here that I might go back to for some items for my trip. I was going to show you where to stay in Liverpool on Monday night, but you will find it easily yourself. I'll give Will the directions."

Hannah was a little non-plussed at this, but felt another frisson of excitement that, once they left the pier at Douglas, she and Will would be on their own at last, as man and wife.

Elbie accompanied her to the railway station, this time taking a horse tram along the promenade and walking the rest of the way. Hannah was thrilled that the horse was 'William' again, although it was a different driver and conductor from their day out in May. The day that had really cemented their relationship, the day she became a woman, the day she would never forget. William trotted eagerly along and the journey was soon over. "Don't worry about me," smiled Elbie as they parted company, "I think I might take a trip on the electric tram today, and if the band is playing at the Palace again tonight, I will find someone to dance with!"

It sounded like fun and Hannah was almost envious, but being with Will was now paramount, and she sighed to herself as the train rattled its way towards Castletown. Will had strolled over to the station to meet her, in the hope that she would be on the mid-morning train, and they embraced as if they had been separated for months. Knowing that, from Sunday, the Bowling Green Road house would be unoccupied until they returned from honeymoon, he had gathered together various bits and pieces of food that they could use up, and he called their lunch 'a picnic.' Hannah was reminded once more of their magical day out to Ramsey, and she proposed an idea to him that would pass a little while until it would be lunch time.

"Very well, lead on MacGoldilocks, your wish is my command," and he almost overtook her on the stairs.

Chapter Twenty Nine

Hannah and Will had both made lists of all that had to be done, although most of the preparations had already been seen to. The last minute items were largely down to her mother, Lina, so after their lunch they walked over to Malew Street to see if there was any help needed there. Hannah was expecting to see jugs of flowers waiting to be fashioned into bouquets, posies and corsages, but Lina had arranged for the flowers to be delivered to Emily's house in Douglas. What good thinking, this would save their having to transport them on the train, but would mean a busy Sunday morning for someone, or several someones, making them up into the required arrangements. One thing Hannah must obtain herself, though, was the trail of ivy that she had planned to twine into Carrie's belt. Hannah also decided that ivy stalks would make sturdy bases for the coronets, so she and Will went for a walk along the river bank beside Poulsom Park, in search of ivy, and armed with Mother's kitchen scissors.

When they returned, Carrie could wait no longer to have her hair twined and arranged, so that she could see how the ivy coronet would work. With the help of some cotton from Lina's work basket, they made the crowns, and used some crumpled crepe paper to stand in as flowers, and the child was enchanted with her reflection in the mirror. "I can't wait for Monday!" she trilled, and Hannah said she felt the same.

"Come on then, let's see you in your dress too, so I can work out this twisted belt I've promised." This entailed Hannah and Carrie sprinting off to Hope Street, Carrie still with paper flowers in her hair, to find the bridesmaid's dress; and they took the ivy with them so that Will would not see the dress in advance. They knew the superstition only applied to the bride's dress, but they decided that it was better to be safe than sorry, and they left Will helping Mother to prepare tea for everyone. Carrie was transported with delight when she saw the overall effect of her hair 'done up special-like' as she had requested, with its little crown of ivy and white flowers, and the posh frock with crocheted lace yoke. Hannah laughed at her and said anyone would think it was Carrie who was getting married. But she remembered Eva, the girl they had met on the rocks at Scarlett, a girl who would be married herself in another week, but whose little sisters had both died before they could be the bridesmaids she and they would have wished for. Once again, Hannah hugged her sister tightly, and was told off for dislodging one of the paper roses.

Carrie took off the dress, very reluctantly, not seeing why she couldn't spend the weekend in it, but helped to twist the long frond of ivy into the belt, adding another piece to trail down the front of the skirt. Hannah said she could see that she was not the only artistic designer in the family, and the youngster was pleased with both the effect and the accolade. She placed the dress back on its hanger, realising it was only until the next day when they would be taking it to Aunt Em's for the party and to stay the night.

They returned to the Corlett house in time to meet the brothers coming home from work, a little earlier on a Saturday than other days, and they all crowded round the big table in the kitchen. Carrie bragged about designing her own outfit – well, all right, just the belt – and the older brothers smiled indulgently at her excitement and at the crumpled 'flowers' in her hair. Sydney, on the other hand, who was only a few years older than Carrie, asked why she had had her head in the rubbish bin, and had to make hasty amends when he saw her lower lip begin to tremble. He picked her up and swung her round, saying he didn't realise it was Carrie who was getting married, he thought it was 'the Battleaxe.' He received a withering look from Hannah, but the tension was relieved, and they began their meal, chatting companionably.

Unguardedly, Hannah remarked that Elbie had been going to ride on an electric tram today, and would probably be going dancing at the Palace Gardens tonight. There was a brief silence while everyone grappled with their impressions of Elbie, until Lina said she was glad that Hannah had come home to spend one more night with her nearest and dearest rather than being out on the town with that flibberty-gibbet. Goodness only knows what that lady might get up to.

Hannah said, "Oh, Mother!" but no more, and each again kept their own counsel. Sydney especially kept his own counsel as a wild thought had crossed his mind. He always went out with his pals on a Saturday night, and he wondered if any of them felt like going to Douglas for a change....

∞∞∞

Hannah and Will repaired to No 22 and spent a happy evening cuddled on the sofa and listening to records. He reminded her that, as soon as they were back from honeymoon, most of the evening commitments would be starting up again for the winter, and worse still, he would be at school all day. She began to realise that her earliest aspirations towards him had looked no further than being his wife. The ramifications of that had not troubled her thoughts since, as in the beginning, she had thought it all only a pipe dream. Now it was so close to becoming a reality, the harsh light of day was dawning but she determined to enjoy every moment of life with Will. Even if it meant joining one or two of his societies, she only wanted to be with him. She had already begun to think that they were not going to conceive any children, regardless of what clairvoyant old crones might say, so her part in life would be as Mrs William Waverley, gracious hostess, patroness of the good works of the town, the headmaster's wife and tireless worker for every worthy cause. And, while she might permit him to engage a housemaid for the dirty work, she would cook him delicious meals, darn his socks and sew on wayward buttons, and she would warm his bed every night. For now, they had tonight, and next week would be so exciting that they hardly dared to think about it.

∞∞∞

Sydney obtained some wages from his Pa, and set off to find his pals. Two or three thought it would be fun to go to 'the bright lights' on a Saturday night, so it was a cheeky little band who boarded the train. Now, while the other boys would provide him with an alibi, should one be needed, he began to wish he had come alone, so he asked nonchalantly what they would do when they got to Douglas. "Head for the Dogs' Home" was the general consensus. Pub crawling was their usual pastime, and although none of them knew exactly how to find the Dogs' Home, they thought it sounded good. So, when Sydney suggested going dancing, he knew what the reaction would be.

"Dancing?" with curled lips. "With wimmin?"

"Well, much as I like you, Ginger, I don't fancy dancing with you, you nincompoop!" Sydney responded, and so it was that, after a first glass of ale at the Railway Inn, he excused himself and said he'd catch them all up at the station for the last train home.

He had begun to have strange feelings in his trousers as he sprinted along the promenade in the direction of the Palace complex. Sure enough a band was playing in the gardens, and couples were swaying to the music. He strolled around the periphery of the crowd, straining for a sight of Elbie. And he soon saw her. He did not notice that she was surrounded by several young men, he was only looking at her breasts and remembering how she had placed his hands on them. Yes, those two breasts there, he had had in his hands. Really, they were his property, but for several moments he simply gorged on staring at them, wondering what he had to do next about the stirrings between his legs.

Suddenly, he realised that she had bent down so that her face was in line with his stare, and she was waving a gloved hand at him. Smiling sweetly at the men around her, she excused herself and came over to Sydney. He took a quick look behind him to make sure she was not heading for someone else, but he was on his own, and she embraced him hard when she caught up with him. He was overpowered with the scent of some floral perfume, the feel of those hard breasts pushing into his face, and she pulled his head down onto them, panting a little. "You came!" she breathed, and he had a terrible, guilty thought. "How wonderful!" She pretended that they were dancing to the music, as they continued to sway gently until the music stopped.

"Buy me an ice-cream!" she demanded, "and then let's find somewhere else to go."

It occurred to him that they were not far from Aunt Em's, and there could be someone around here who would know him. Never having been alone with a female of any age, except for a normal teenager's clumsy fumbling among the bushes, he was floundering in his present predicament. He did wonder if he was dreaming, but he found an ice-cream stall and bought them one each. She suggested strolling along the shore with them, and he dreaded meeting someone there, but while they might know him, they would not know her, so perhaps he would get away with it.

They sat on a bench on the promenade and, when they had finished their ice creams, she turned to him, took his hand over her head and placed his arm round her shoulder. Then she cupped his face and kissed him. "You don't have any idea what to do, do you?" she smiled gently.

Naturally about to deny it, he took a breath, but she kissed him again, expertly, opening his mouth with hers and licking his tongue. He thought he might pop out of his trousers altogether but was powerless to stop anything that might happen. "I think you have great potential!" she simpered. "Would you like a few lessons?"

He knew that he was supposed to jump on top of her, but quite how the mechanics of it worked, he was not sure. He did think, however, that the middle of Douglas promenade might not be the place to find out.

"Let me show you where I'm staying," she was saying, and as she led him towards her hotel, she gave him lessons in foreplay. "You have to tell the girl that you are hopelessly in love with her. Oh I love you so much, yes, of course I want to marry you, all that sort of stuff. I doubt if girls around here normally let you have your way all that easily, but eventually you will meet someone special that you really do want to be with. Oh God, don't look at ME like that. I can assure you I am not *the one*, Sydney, but I would like to be one that you will never forget. Here's the hotel, come on, I'll show you my room."

He was definitely dreaming, as he followed her up the stairs. The room contained two single beds, and a small couch. Before they sat down, she embraced him again, and told him to do as she did. She stroked his face so gently that it felt like a tickle, and he tried to do the same to her. More kissing, the mouth, neck, ear. Stroking and squeezing the breast. He reciprocated each of her movements. "Now tell me you adore me." He kissed her this time and whispered in her ear that he 'had always fancied her.' She burst out laughing, sat down on the couch and patted the seat alongside her.

"No, Sweetheart," she remonstrated, "think like a woman. That's man talk! You have a lot to learn, but come on, let's try again, now think sweet nothings, silly things, not necessarily the unbridled truth!"

He was on fire by this time, and she was having a pretty tough time holding back herself, so she changed tactics and let him try it his way. She praised him when he said the right words, and rewarded him by exposing her firm breasts. When he fumbled, she helped him out, and showed him little secret fastenings and little sensitive places to stroke and to kiss. Then came the skirt lifting – gently, Sydney, no, really, much more gently – but it was amazing how quickly he learned, and before long, life would never be the same again for Sydney.

∞∞∞∞

Hannah and Will also made love again that evening, knowing this was definitely the last time before they would be man and wife. She wondered if they would feel differently then. She had the feeling that the supposed naughtiness of doing it before marriage might have contributed to the excitement. She also acknowledged to herself that in the very early days she had rather wanted him to make her pregnant, so that he would have to marry her, and she felt ashamed about that now. She had hardly dared hope that he could actually be in love with her, but now she knew that he was. He really loved her, and not only because she had shown him that he was not too old to enjoy lovemaking, but because they were kindred spirits in so many ways. They were going to have a wonderful life together.

It was fairly dark by the time Will walked her 'home' to Hope Street for the last time, but as they walked, they heard someone whistling the tune of *the Wand'ring Minstrel*. That could only be Sydney, they said together and sure enough, here came Sydney with a group of other young boys, looking as if he was the only one who was sober. Ah well, he certainly sounded happy.

∞∞∞∞

Oh, Sydney was happy all right. After that first incredible, amazing, explosive time, they had tried it again a little later, taking it more slowly, with more talking, kissing, stroking, teaching and learning. Elbie had frightened him at one stage by asking how he would feel if he had made her pregnant. Shit! he hadn't thought of that, knew he had not been able to think about anything but doing it. She pointed out that she was twice his age and assured him again that he was not to think of her romantically, except to remember this night. Even tomorrow they could not let anyone see that they had been intimate, but she let him stew about the pregnancy idea for a short while before admitting that it was impossible for her. However, he had to think about it very carefully before getting himself into that situation again, as most other girls might easily have got into trouble, even at their first time. Right now, he didn't care about other girls. She had said she was going to stay in Douglas for a few more days.

Chapter Thirty

It was Sunday morning, and while Will was obliged to be at church for the morning service, Hannah had elected to accompany him. The Corlett, Bickerstaff, Thorburn and Kaneen households were buzzing with activity and excitement. Everyone was scrubbed and smartened, and all their requirements checked over and over, so that by 12:15 they would all be present and correct at the railway station.

Lina felt as if she was conducting a military operation. Getting all her sons out of bed and polished up had seemed harder than usual, but whereas it was usually Sydney who was the last to appear bleary-eyed, today he was up and first at the wash basin. There was too much else to think about, or she might have been a tiny bit suspicious, but of course, she had no idea that she was not looking at the child she had chased out of bed the day before. Sydney had grown up in the last twenty four hours and was now so eager to be getting on with the day, when he would see Elbie again, and after the first hour he was restless and impatient. Even then, his mother was too preoccupied to notice.

But eventually they were on the train, complete with all the packages and bags, and their excited chatter filled their compartment in high spirits. Two carriages were required to deliver them all from Douglas station to Aunt Em's in Prince's Avenue, where everything had to be decanted again, opened up and sorted out. The flowers had been delivered, and Cissie had started to create Hannah's bouquet, ordering her young sisters, Florence and little Ada, to collect flowers in matching colours, ready to be made into the bridesmaids' posies. They were also permitted to attempt corsages for the older ladies, and buttonholes for the gentlemen. Their eldest sister, Lena, was in charge of the table laying and decorations, while numerous brothers of varying sizes were dispatched on little errands, intended to keep them out of the way, but generally ending up with them getting under their sisters' feet and causing mayhem.

Sydney offered to walk down to Elbie's hotel to collect her and escort her back. Hannah asked how he knew where Elbie was staying, but was too excited to listen to his stumbling reply. "Oh go on, then, get on with it, and mind you don't get lost on the way."

Lina had not heard this exchange, and was slightly concerned when she heard that he had gone on this errand. Sydney had held his breath in case one or more of his cousins would want to come too, just to get away from all the woman-stuff going on. Sydney was good pals with his cousin Thomas, but fortunately, he was not in the room when Syd left.

He contained himself until he was out of sight of the house, and then broke into a canter down the hill. Elbie saw him coming from her window and waved to him, indicating that he should come up to her room. She greeted him warmly, seeming amused. "How kind of you to think of me," she began, but he was already reaching for her quite roughly. She allowed him a very passionate kiss. "My, you are a quick learner," she smiled, "but you are too rough for me. Now, I know you are excited, but you really must try to pace yourself."

"Elbie, you are only going to be here for a few days, I just so want to be with you," and he reached for her again. "I will be gentle, I promise," but he grabbed her again, and was already groping for the hem of her skirt. She knew they only had a very short time and was actually finding this experience very exciting and rewarding. His adulation was gratifying although so predictable, and she did only have these few days. So, she reached for him, and started to undo his buttons for him. Then she stopped.

"Jesus, Sydney, you are all tarted up for the big do, we must not let you get all crumpled up. Just take your clothes off, carefully for goodness' sake," and she was removing her blouse while he complied. Then she bolted the door, dropped her skirt on the floor and spread herself of the bed.

He was all fingers and thumbs, but appreciated her presence of mind regarding his clothing. His mother would have noticed if her assiduous pressing had been ruined, and embarrassing questions would be asked. But right now there was an almost naked woman making herself very available on a bed, and he had nothing on. No-one had ever seen him like this. Naked perhaps when he was a child, but even his mother had not seen him like this, as he looked down at himself.

"Ooh, come and get me, Big Boy," she was purring, and he wasted no more time.

∞∞∞∞

The military operation was in full swing up the road at the Kaneen household. Those who would not be able to attend the wedding on Monday had mostly elected to wear their finery, or at least their 'Sunday Best.' Carrie, of course, demanded to be allowed to wear her bridesmaid's dress and have her hair done up with the flowers in it, so that the grandparents and guests would see her. Hannah thought it less dangerous to allow her this concession rather than to have a child in floods of tears spoiling the afternoon.

Will was pacing up and down rehearsing his speech, folding and unfolding a long piece of paper. There were things he wanted the whole family to hear, and had elected to make his speech today. It was beginning to look as if there would be nothing left for the Monday other than the actual ceremony at Braddan Church, but everyone was agreeable with this arrangement. Tomorrow would look after itself.

John Qualtrough, the best man, brought his wife along, both being friends and neighbours of Will. Tom and Fanny Dodd brought several crates of ale and a case of wines, but had left their teenager twins to their own devices at home. When Will promised to return whatever was not drunk, Tom insisted they only need return the bottles and the crates. He looked at one or two of the smaller children and said, "Who knows, if somebody collects all the bottles up and delivers them back to me, they might get the money back on the empties." The children were then looking for empty bottles even before anyone had started drinking. Not that there was long to wait, of course.

Sydney and Elbie turned up quite quietly, cleverly and separately mingling with the buzzing crowd so that their guilty faces were not noticed. Eventually, Qualtrough tapped a spoon against a glass and called for them all to take their places at the table. Lena had made place cards in her immaculate copperplate, and soon everyone was in their place.

Hannah's uncle, John Kaneen, being the head of the household, said Grace, and asked God's blessing also on the two special people who were taking such a big step.

John Qualtrough rose again and asked if everyone's glass was charged. Thanking Uncle John for his thoughtful words, and Aunt Em for her wonderful hospitality, he proposed a toast, "To tomorrow's bride and groom – Hannah and Will." Everyone stood and raised their glasses, drank the toast and sat down again. Then John proceeded to tell some anecdotes about the bridegroom, saying what a lucky man he was, but wondered if Hannah knew what she was letting herself in for. "He's a hard man, you know, just ask his pupils. He will have been on his best behaviour recently, well, I am assuming he has, since he has been conspicuous by his absence on the golf course!" He ended by thanking the bridesmaids in advance, realising that this reception was a little out of the ordinary, but he could certainly see that one of them was more than ready for duty, and what a picture she made. Little Carrie was bursting with pleasure and excitement, but bowed her head graciously to Mr Qualtrough – he was a headmaster, and he was talking about her!

Glasses were topped up, and then Will got up from his chair, amid cheers all around the table.

"Unaccustomed as I am...." he began, but had to stop and wait for the laughter and foot stamping to die down, "to speaking in public. Yes, well, all right, I am accustomed to speaking in public, I am quite accustomed to shouting in public...." more laughter.... "but this is a day, or tomorrow will be a day, such as I could never have dreamed of." The smiling faces, now without the noisy laughter, encouraged him.

"I am so grateful to Mr Qualtrough, who used to be my friend, for his introduction, and for reminding everyone that I can be 'a hard man.' It appears that I was already in possession of a reputation, which is something we know all about. I have heard such expressions as bad tempered?" he paused for titters, "self important?" he looked round questioningly and saw only grins, then continued, "and I now humbly admit these crimes...." he looked back at his notes but could not read a word of them. "I am here to tell you people that, six months ago, I was an angry old man. I was lonely, bored, tired and desperately unhappy. Hannah," he paused and looked lovingly at his wife-to-be, saved me. Here and there a handkerchief was suddenly in evidence. "I want you all to know how much I have learned from this very brave young woman, and the loving Corlett family, how honoured and blessed I am that they accepted me, despite the opposition there could have been, has been and will be. I have had a wonderful and happy summer getting to know them, never expecting to be so contented. I am almost eager to get back to work to share many new ideas with my pupils. In future, I will be encouraging their strengths and promise to try to be more patient. Some boys are good at languages, some shine at mathematics, one or two, bless them, are even musicians! Would you believe, I have one youngster who can hold a conversation in extemporaneous Latin but can simply not grasp the principle of ratios; another almost has difficulty stringing a sentence together in his own language but can work out angles and elevations in his head with incredible accuracy. Doctors and pharmacists may need Latin, but we also need some boys to learn other basics to be builders," he glanced round the room, and waved a hand in various directions, "home decorators," (laughter) "accountants and navigators. If I were on a ship at sea I would prefer to be with a semi-literate, brawny young man who can find our way home, than a college don who could get lost in Poulsom Park (sniggers now, as an unfortunate visitor had recently reportedly done this). So I will be more appreciative, and remember to think like the pupil, with it all there to be learned. We already started before the holidays by visiting a farm to learn about animals and the milking and growing vegetables, and the wheat and barley, then we got the boys to ask how their mothers obtained and prepared food, the youngsters even enjoyed exchanging recipes," the titters began again, "and having a go at the cooking at home. We have not had any reports of poisoning, not yet anyway," a few more titters, "but what I am so awkwardly trying to say is that I have learned more myself this summer, about strengths and weaknesses, about faith in the future, about happy, loving families, and I thank you all. SO much. Now, shall we eat?"

There was a round of applause, eyes were wiped, Lina's magnificent chest protruded even more than usual as she looked side-long at Billa, who placed a hand on her knee. Elbie had given up her bridesmaid's place at the top table for Mrs Qualtrough to sit by her husband, and engineered a place between Frank and Sydney instead. Now, she put her hand on

Frank's knee, just to see the reaction. Frank smiled questioningly, but placed her hand firmly back into her own lap, and then she laughed out loud as, still looking at Frank, she placed her other hand on Sydney's knee, and stroked his thigh. She felt the boy tense, and saw Frank turn to the girl on his other side, whisper to her and they both looked along the knees. By then, of course, Elbie had taken up her knife and was buttering a roll. Sydney was a little red-faced but was giving some attention to his glass of ale.

After they had all eaten, the ladies took to clearing the plates away, and Elbie helped, in order to find her way into the kitchen again, where she found Charlie, the Irish lodger, washing dishes in the sink. "Ah, were you not invited to the shindig?" she smouldered, tracing a finger down his back, making him shudder. He said he was quite happy not having had to socialise, since he didn't know any of the people involved. "You know me," she said, "rather well. Why don't I bring a few bottles up to your room? Where is it?" He told her, and a little later, she smuggled a bottle of wine out of the dining room and slipped up the stairs. Sydney was the only person to see her leave the room, and assumed that she intended him to follow her.

He sidled out of the room and followed the waft of her perfume up the stairs.

Chapter Thirty One

The tables were pushed back against the walls and a great family gathering enjoyed the rest of the afternoon, chatting with relatives they may not have seen for a while. Glasses were kept topped up, although tea had also been brewed for those who knew their limits, and the best bone china and silver tea and water pots appeared.

Hannah and Will were pressed to open the wedding presents that had accumulated on and in a sideboard, and one or other of them made little speeches of thanks, recounting anecdotes about each donor. Everyone admired the lovely painting that Charles had done for them, depicting the beautiful view over Ramsey, and Will was effusive in his thanks. He mentioned also, that Sydney had made the rather smart frame, and thoughtfully painted it to tone in with the furnishings in their new home, and everyone looked around, as he voiced their thought, "Where is Sydney?"

As he spoke, a flushed and very angry-looking Sydney burst back into the room, obviously about to blurt some terrible news. "That...." he began, but stopped when he saw all eyes on him. "I need the lavatory!" he mumbled and dashed back out again, to save having to make any explanation.

His mother was about to get up, but Billa held her back, shaking his head. He looked around still shaking his head, and raising his eyes to the ceiling, as if to say, 'boys - what can you do with them?' and the tense moment passed.

"Too much of Mr Dodd's fine ales, perhaps!" said Will and proceeded to unwrap the next gift. "Speaking of whom, of course, we must all thank Tom and Fanny for oiling the wheels this afternoon, and I am so glad that they were able to join us in our unorthodox pre-nuptial reception!" Tom raised his glass, and his wife smiled demurely. Will then thanked Fanny for putting him in touch with her cousin, the Rev Moore, who would conduct the service the next day, but expressed regret that he would not be able to attend either of their receptions because of other commitments. "We know how popular September is for weddings," he explained, "which is how we ended up with a Monday, so that we could fit in a honeymoon before school starts again – and there's a thought! How different my life will be when the new term starts."

Everyone smiled and nodded at that, as Will continued remarking on the wedding gifts, and then he also recalled a couple of regrettable incidents from the previous month.

"It is with great sadness that we remember Dr John Clague. He was not yet sixty-six, which is no age for such a man to die, except that he had been ailing, and somewhat out of circulation for some time. He was a man of many parts and will be sadly missed, not least by the Philharmonic Society. His contribution to the history of Manx music was immense and, of course, such was his approach to medicine, that many a complaint was cured entirely without drugs. He was a personal friend who shared my passion for the music, and was always genial, but adamantly refused my invitation to join us here today. He knew his time was up."

Heads nodded and a tear fell here and there as Will continued, "One more disappointment for us is the temporary loss of the wonderful new ship that was launched so recently. Hannah and I were really looking forward to sailing on the speedy *Ben My Chree*, but apparently, something jumped out at her in the Mersey and put her out of action for a while. My wife," he smiled at Hannah and beamed round the room, repeating for emphasis, "my Wife has not sailed before and is a little nervous of the new experience, so a journey of a little over two hours would have pleased her quite well. However, it seems to be quite a settled spell of weather, and I'm sure the trusty *Viking* will serve us well enough."

Hannah had hardly spoken, but her reticence was put down to nerves, and she was left to smile graciously at all the jokes and other conversation. She was actually wondering, with increasing suspicion, where Elbie was.

Someone started to play the piano, and those who could sing soon joined into the jollity. Will was begged to play them something grand, but he professed that his hands had begun to shake with nerves. "Nerves? YOU?" objected John Qualtrough, and Will said it must be 'the new me' but might pluck up the courage a little later. So, the party continued, with other musical instruments, well-practised close harmony, a solo or two and numerous recitations.

After a short while, Hannah realised that Elbie was back in circulation, chatting here and there as if she had not been absent, flirting in her usual fashion with any male, and eliciting dark looks from the women. But Hannah also noticed that Sydney was actually glowering in the direction of the bridesmaid, although trying to keep his eyes off her, and morosely downing more beer. She did not feel comfortable about this, but felt it unlikely that her baby brother would confide in her, so she took George, who was nearer in age to Syd, to one side and asked if he had noticed anything strange. George reminded her that teenagers are always full of anger, but admitted that it was not like their Sydney, and he would keep an eye on developments and try to find out what it was all about. Their cousin Thomas might winkle out what was going on. "You don't need young lads' problems to bother you today of all days, go and enjoy yourself, Han."

Hannah did have far more to think about than Sydney's moods, but she was going to be spending the night with Elbie, and she wondered if she could get at the truth diplomatically, or if she would be obliged to voice her terrible suspicions.

Those who were returning to Castletown that night were to leave by the late train, and the party began to disperse after nine o'clock. As they left, each one embraced Hannah and shook Will's hand, wishing them well.... until it came to Sydney, who looked sheepish and seemed at first to have lost his tongue. "What happened to our *Wand'ring Minstrel* tonight?" asked Will, "I was looking forward to your great party piece!" Hannah was about to suggest he was too busy 'wand'ring' but Sydney gave a theatrical bar-room belch, punched his sister playfully and mumbled, "Too much ale!" Then, regaining composure, he whispered, "I do love you, you old battleaxe, and I know this old bugger will look after you!" and he ran off before they could retaliate.

Will, Frank, Carrie and her mother were staying over at Aunt Em's in order to be ready early on Monday, and it would be a much smaller party that gathered back there after the ceremony. They were able to stay up later and have cocoa together after the others had left, but eventually, as it had now gone dark, Will suggested walking Hannah and Elbie down the hill to the hotel.

Elbie said good-night, kissed Will's cheek and went ahead to her room, leaving Hannah and Will holding hands in the cool evening air. She asked if he would like to find a bench in the gardens across the road, so that they could just sit quietly together for a while, and this they did. He put his arm round her shoulders and she leaned her head on his chest. "What's worrying you, my dearest?" he probed, "you have been very quiet all day."

She longed to tell him her fears, but in working out what to say, it all sounded so ludicrous and unlikely, and downright dreadful that she decided to assume she had been mistaken, reading too much into what she had seen. This was her time, hers and Will's, and she was not going to let anyone spoil it.

She sighed, and admitted she had been worrying about so many things, but now she just wanted to enjoy being with him; and was so excited about tomorrow and the rest of their lives together, that she couldn't help feeling it was all too good to be true and something terrible would happen.

He stroked her hair and kissed her temple. "I have all the same fears," he said. "You have made me feel young again, but it doesn't change the fact that I will be sixty before much longer, and we are taking an enormous step. Believe me I have asked myself over and over if we are doing the right thing, but I am so sure that we are, my darling, and, even if only for the sake of decency, we should conform with convention. I do feel it is a ridiculous suggestion, but remember Dorothy Kinrade and her prediction? We must be married, we just must!"

"Would it be terrible to say I wish it was this time tomorrow?" she asked tremulously.

"Yes, it would. Tomorrow is going to be the best day of our lives, and it will be wonderful. And so exciting. And soon over, too, so stop this nonsense. At once, mind – Wife, you must do as I say now!"

She smiled and thought, 'We'll see about that!' but was comforted, until their steps returned towards the hotel and Elbie. Hannah decided to ignore the gnawing agitation in her stomach. To hell with Elbie and her (possibly) wicked ways. "Good-night, my bachelor darling, I will see you in church!"

"Don't be late!" he watched her until she was safely up the steps and in the house.

∞∞∞∞

Elbie was already in bed and pretending to be asleep when Hannah let herself into the room. This certainly absolved Hannah from challenging her right now, but strangely also convinced her that she had not been mistaken. The sophisticate did have something to hide.

While Hannah fell into an emotionally exhausted sleep, Elbie wrestled with her conscience, and agonised over the way she had treated poor Sydney. She hated herself sometimes. Her desperate need to have sex was an addiction, but she exonerated herself by blaming circumstances. She had been taken advantage of and made pregnant when she was thirteen. The only way she could think of to get help was to flirt with another man, who claimed he would 'do anything' for her if she would let him have her first. He was quite kind, and much gentler, and he showed her that it could be enjoyable for them both. She did enjoy this lesson, but had already learned a lot about men and was soon learning how to manipulate them; and so a desperate deed was done with a sharp instrument that nearly killed her. At the time, a baby was the last thing she wanted, but after this, it was the last thing she could ever have. However, now she was able to indulge her own passions without that sort of fear, but she was never going to trust a man again. She simply used them.

Young Sydney was different. Relieving young lads of their virginity gave her a special sort of power, which multiplied her own pleasure in the act. She knew that every one of them would remember her long after subsequent lovers may be forgotten. But, she was actually quite fond of this boy, and she had treated him abominably. What must the poor kid be going through? It had not been fair to tease him, but then, she didn't know he was going to follow her this afternoon, she hadn't thought of that.

Oh, this was just exactly what she had always wanted to avoid. Getting involved with other people's feelings was a recipe for disaster, which was why she always kept her sexual partners at arm's length. They should be ships that pass in the night, and each go on their merry way without a backward glance. Because Sydney was so young, he would not know how to handle this, but what was her excuse? God! She hoped Hannah wasn't aware of what was going on. That would be unfair on Hannah too, wouldn't it? The more Elbie thought about it, the more wretched she felt, alternating between protecting what she saw as 'her private life' and the realisation that her actions could affect other people's feelings. She did like Sydney, though, and having sex with him was really good. She decided to wait and see what he was going to do next. She would go along with whatever he wanted. He probably hated her now anyway. Which would be a pity.

∞∞∞

Sydney shared a room with his brother George and, having gone straight to bed as soon as they arrived back home from the train, he churned everything over and over in his head, not realising he was also tossing and turning and keeping George awake.

"Syd, you are going to have to tell me what's bothering you, or neither of us will get any sleep tonight. You haven't been your usual carefree self all day, what on earth is the matter?" George whispered loudly.

"Oh God, George, it's so awful that I daren't tell you," whimpered the poor boy, feeling out of his depth with his situation, but probably trapped into confessing all.

"Well, whatever it is, it might help to talk about it. Things aren't usually as bad as they seem in the dark. What is it? You're not sick, are you?" said George kindly.

"No. I don't think so. I think I might be mad. Oh, no, I can't tell you! Oh shit, I am in such a mess, George."

"Are you in trouble? What the f*** have you been up to? Is it those Garrett boys leading you astray? Frank and me will soon sort them out for you!" George was beginning to be so anxious about his young brother that he was making rash promises. Tackling the local tearaways would have been the last thing he would consider normally.

"Aargh, it's nothing like that," and George felt a slight relief.

"Oh for Christsake spit it out then, you've got me all of a dither now too."

"Aw no, I've got to handle this on my own. I've got myself into it, I'll have to...."

George had slipped out of his bed and across to Sydney's, and he now took him by the shoulders and hissed, "TELL ME!"

Sydney was quite frightened. Now he was in real trouble, he had infuriated his mild mannered brother who had never been known to say boo to a goose. He thought he might cry, and had to gulp to stop a huge sob from escaping. Oh what a mess he was in, all through trying to be a man. He thought what had happened this weekend had made him an adult, but perhaps he wasn't ready for it all. In his misery, he suddenly wanted his kind brother to take the pain away. This wasn't going to be easy.

So he took a deep breath, and related what had happened – only last night and today. George couldn't believe what he was hearing. Not having got further than holding hands with a girl himself, he was shocked beyond belief, and then rather envious. He had climbed back into his own bed and, as Sydney described his adventures, he began to have stirrings in his body that he was not accustomed to. His mouth dropped open in the dark and his eyes opened wider every moment, until he was gasping for breath himself.

"You haven't gone to sleep on me, have you?" said Sydney, having got as far as being stripped naked when he went to call for Elbie, and suddenly realising it had gone very quiet.

"Ah, bah, pah, no, you've just taken my breath away, you lucky little bastard. I knew she was a dreadful flirt, but I thought she'd run a mile if anyone actually took her up on it! All those airs and graces, good grief, you just don't know people, do you? No, I'm not asleep, I don't think I'll ever sleep again. Tell me what happened next?"

"Well, what do you think happened next? Oh God, it is bloody mind-blowing, isn't it?" George was reluctant to admit he had no idea how mind-blowing it was. It was pretty explosive just hearing about it! "Anyway, after that episode, when I saw her sneaking out of the reception with a bottle in her hand, I assumed she expected me to follow her to a bedroom. I waited a few minutes in case anyone else had noticed, then I followed her up the stairs. I could still smell her perfume, and I was gagging for her by the time I reached the first door. It wasn't quite closed, so I tapped on it and pushed it open, and there she was, with her tits already out."

George found he was sweating slightly and having difficulty swallowing. "And...?" he prompted.

"Well, I've never been so embarrassed in all my life. She wasn't alone, George, that bloody Irishman was standing there with not a stitch on him!"

"Good God almighty. Did he have his tool in his hand, or what?" spluttered his brother.

"His hands were full of her tits, his tongue was half way down her throat, and his dick was in her hand!"

"Bloody hell! Is she a prozzie or what?"

"I think she is just insatiable, but I just stood there with my gob open, not knowing what had hit me. I was turning to scarper when, do you know what the f***ing tart said – oh so sweetly, as she does – "Why don't you come on in, Sydney, and try three in a bed? Can you believe that? I was so humiliated, I almost fell down the bloody stairs and just wanted to 'tell on her,' but when everybody seemed to be looking at me, I didn't know what the hell to do, just had to get out of there and try to calm down. Then back she waltzes into the reception as if butter wouldn't melt in her mouth. I could have killed her, but she wouldn't look at me any more and just went round flirting with every other chap."

"Hell fire, I wonder how many more she had after that!" George's heart was thumping, with indignation and anger as well as lust now. He was scandalised at Sydney's story, but was sure of one thing. He had thought Syd lucky to have had the experience at first but did not envy him this resulting predicament. "So what are you going to do now?" he asked, forgetting that this was exactly the question that had troubled his young brother to start with.

Sydney sighed. "Telling you has helped me, George. Thanks for forcing me into it. I suppose saying it all out loud does make you see it more rationally, but what to do now is still a good question. Jeez, just thinking about her, I want to do her again. There she is panting for it, and can't get pregnant, I'm not going to get a chance like that again after she goes back home, so do I pretend I wasn't bothered and take what's going, or try and forget all about it?"

"Do her again!" both brothers said at once, and then laughed into the darkness.

After a while, one of them said, "Three in a bed? How does that work, then?"

Chapter Thirty Two

Hannah woke early. It was just becoming daylight, and she blinked as she opened the curtains and saw the dawn light over the bay. It was going to be a lovely day. Well, of course it would be a lovely day, Will had promised her that. It was her Wedding Day, a day she had long thought would never happen, and she was filled with loving anticipation and excitement.

She watched a horse and cart turn up Broadway from the promenade, stopping at each hotel to deliver fresh milk, eggs and cream. She could already smell their own fresh bread being baked downstairs in this house, but other carts trundled past purveying goods, breads, cakes, vegetables and other fresh produce.

A groan from the other bed made her squint back into the room, where a dishevelled Elbie was rubbing her eyes. It was amusing to see this smart young woman of the world at her most vulnerable, with her hair tousled and hanging round her neck and shoulders. Hannah's heart softened. Elbie had been a good friend to her and a tower of strength in helping with the wedding arrangements. She must not interfere with the girl's private life. She was just a little concerned that it somehow involved her youngest brother, but today was not the day to dwell on other people's problems. They must sort them out for themselves.

Being early, Hannah was first to the bathroom, and she took her time over her ablutions. Her last morning as a single woman. She could hardly believe it. At last, at last, the day has arrived and she drew a long breath, filling her nose with the scent of her *Lily of the Valley* soap and dusting powder. She was not sure if she would be able to swallow any breakfast, but felt she should eat something to avoid having her tummy rumbling during the wedding ceremony. She went downstairs in her dressing gown to ask at the kitchen, which was already buzzing with activity. They kindly arranged to send up a tray for her and Elbie with boiled eggs, toast, orange juice and coffee, so that they need not change their clothes twice.

She dragged her friend out of bed and sent her to the bathroom, having relayed this information, and the tray had arrived before Elbie returned. Hannah breathed in the aroma of the coffee, and wondered if she was always this sensitive about the smells and sounds and sights of the early morning, or was this day special in some way? She smiled to herself, and hoped the early morning stirrings were afoot in Princes Avenue too.

They were, of course. Aunt Em had her second day of military operations to organise, as well as her usual few boarders to provide with breakfast. Carrie had been up since before dawn, worrying about her hair and her flowers, then could not find her shoes. A tragedy was averted when a leaf dropped off her ivy drapery, and was sewn back on with a few deft stitches. Will was accustomed to rising early, and had helped with boiling kettles for all the tea, coffee, washing and shaving that were required, and was already dressed in his wedding suit, having very proudly attached Hannah's silver and aquamarine tie pin. What a beautiful gift, he was such a lucky man.

The girls appeared one at a time and got on with the final adjustments to Hannah's bouquet, the bridesmaids' posies and the men's buttonholes. And Carrie's hair. There was still the light luncheon to be arranged, for an unknown number of wedding guests who might wish to attend. Emily knew there would be a handful of people she had not yet met, but also anticipated that some of yesterday's family members may turn up as and when they could get away from their workplaces, just in time to see the happy couple off, perhaps, and then wind down in her dining room for as long as they liked. This was exactly how Em liked it to be, happy, casual and relaxed. Or this was how it would appear to be, after her meticulous attention to details, and there was enough buffet-style food for half of Douglas to graze on all afternoon.

∞∞∞∞

Sydney asked his dad if he could finish work early and go and see Hannah and Will in their bridal gear and going-away outfits. Billa surprised him by saying they would all finish early. Mother was already in Douglas, but he wasn't fussed about going to Braddan Church himself, as Frank had volunteered to give The Battleaxe away, but they could get the mid-day train and join the official reception for lunch and all have the afternoon off. "Ya'll have ter make up forrit, mind!" he teased, but Sydney missed the point, and promised he would. All he was thinking about was engineering another encounter with Elbie, and he began to get excited again.

John Qualtrough and Bob Bridson met at Castletown station and shared a compartment on the early train with Hannah's uncle, Peter Thorburn, then they all took a carriage to Princes Avenue where Qualtrough collected the bridegroom. Frank had stayed at Aunt Em's overnight, several times 'accidentally' meeting Cissie on landings and in doorways, and stealing surreptitious kisses, so they were both in high spirits, as were all the youngsters. Some of them had also begged time off work, and the children were still on school holidays and generally running about excitedly. A charabanc had been hired to take them all to the church and bring them back (and Emily had already counted the driver among the extra mouths to feed); very soon they were all on their way to Braddan, leaving Frank and Carrie with the horse-carriage, which set off close behind, but stopped again at Athol House to collect Hannah and Elbie. Carrie was pretending she was the bride, and waved to people on the road as they passed by.

After their breakfast, Hannah had packed her trunk while wearing only her underwear, carefully placing her chosen going-away suit at the top. Frank had brought the carriage down the hill to collect it, deliver the bouquet, and to 'make sure that the ladies had remembered what day it was.' So by ten o'clock, all that was left was to put on her wedding dress at long last. One of Elbie's jobs was to help her arrange her head-dress and veil, and Hannah had to arrange Elbie's hair, coronet and flowers. "Oh, don't forget Dorothy's cameo," Hannah said as Elbie arranged her own large lace collar.

"Dorothy?" queried Elbie.

"Oh, sorry, it's not Dorothy's, it's yours, of course! She was the old lady with the antiques. I wanted something coral coloured to complement your dress, and she insisted on giving us this. It had been very special to her, but she was adamant that she wouldn't be needing it any more. It was hard to take it from her, but it was so exactly what I had in mind for you. You will look after it, won't you!" and she kissed Elbie and turned away.

"It's lovely," smiled Elbie. "It's so nice when there is a story attached. Now, I'm done, are you ready for this?"

They admired themselves in a long mirror. "Oh Elb," breathed Hannah, "I'm sure I'm dreaming."

The young women embraced again, clinging to each other for a long moment, and then Elbie led the way down stairs to the waiting carriage, where Carrie was already jumping up and down shouting, "Come on, we're going to be late!"

"No we're not, Carrie, and anyway, that's the bride's prerogative."

"What's per.. prog...." began the child, but was told to shut up by Frank, and to hold onto her hairdo as the horses picked up speed.

People waved to the ribboned carriage, shouted and clapped and whistled, and Hannah felt that her grin must meet her ears as she waved back. Several women remarked to each other about the unusual bridal dress, but all thought it absolutely lovely. Wedding dresses were not always white, but although her lacy overdress was snowy white, the full length under-slip was her favourite aquamarine, and the effect was quite stunning. She had placed her engagement ring on her right hand, ahead of receiving her wedding band on her left, but her favourite earrings dangled behind the two long ringlets she had fashioned at her cheeks to soften the effect of the hair pulled back from her face and swept up into the coronet of white carnations.

John Qualtrough had shepherded everyone into the church, including the charabanc driver, and Will had been delighted to be greeted by his nephew, Dougie Lacey. He was bursting with happiness, constantly asking if John had the ring, was he sure he had the ring? Then when John saw the horses approaching, he pushed Will into the church and closed the door. Their organist from Castletown, Willie Cubbon, was playing *Handel's Largo* quietly while the congregation chatted and waited, and Will started to sweat, standing all alone in front of the altar, wondering if his blood pressure would hold out for just a little while longer, and had he asked Qualtrough if he had the ring?

As Frank helped the ladies down from the carriage, the best man opened the church door and gave the expected signal to Mr Cubbon, then everyone eagerly rose and craned their necks as the great organ shouted out the beloved Wagnerian message, *Here Comes the Bride.* Will thought he might explode as he turned to see his girl. If he lived to be two hundred he would never forget that first glimpse of his radiant bride, looking more stunning than he had ever seen her before. Her white gloved hand on her proud brother's arm, her little sister importantly holding up the train of her amazing dress, with the sophisticated Elbie paled into insignificance bringing up the rear. They reached Will, Frank took a step back, Carrie took the bride's gorgeous bouquet of white roses and coral carnations, and Hannah beamed up at him through her veil.

The Rev Moore welcomed them all and gave what was probably his well-practised, usual speech about the meaning and importance of marriage, and there were some stifled titters when he mentioned the procreation of children. Most of them, including Will, thought this unlikely, but only time would tell if Dorothy Kinrade had psychic powers or not.

They all sang *Love Divine, All Loves Excelling* and there was a Bible reading. They made their responses in something of a daze. Handkerchiefs were brought out and eyes dabbed. Qualtrough did have the ring after all, and eventually Hannah lifted her veil as they were pronounced Man and Wife, and then Cubbon was playing *Schubert's Ave Maria* while they signed the register in the vestry. When they re-appeared, the organist struck up the *Mendelssohn recessional* and everyone was rejoicing as they trickled out of the church, some standing in little groups to pick over what they had witnessed, and that was that.

∞∞∞∞

Will and Hannah were conveyed back to Princes Avenue by horse carriage, while everyone else climbed aboard the chara. They had both prevailed upon Dougie Lacey to come back to Emily's, Cubbon the organist, Bridson the verger and both drivers made up the happy throng. Emily's buffet was available for all, with plenty of Tom Dodd's beverages left over from the previous day too. Will apologised that there would be no speeches today, things just weren't as funny the second time around, but if anyone had any anecdotes to relate, they should feel free to entertain them all. "Speak now, or for ever hold your peace!" he quipped.

Billa and Sydney had turned up, so Sydney was prevailed upon to do his *Mikado* performances. Billa explained to the throng how this amazing talent had been discovered, and painted an amusing picture of their illustrious headmaster, covered in wallpaper paste and splodges of paint in his ham-fisted attempts at home decoration. Thereupon, Will extended a warm invitation to all and sundry to visit him and his lovely wife as soon as they were back from their honeymoon; then people could see for themselves what a lovely job they had all done together, and he repeated his sentiment from yesterday, as to how much he had learned from the happy family that had welcomed him so readily. He whispered to Hannah that he hoped Douglas Lacey would convey that little epithet to his mother. "Mmm," mused Hannah, "I don't suppose he will!"

Now that the party pieces had been kick-started, Bob Bridson soon got into his stride. His escapades were legendary, although very few of them were true. He just made himself the hero of any story he happened to have heard. He claimed to have travelled the world, sailed with and even advised Nelson, with whom he hunted rabbits on the Dogger Bank, when everyone knew he had never been further off the island than The Carrick in the bay. Since Lord Nelson had lived and died in a previous century the inaccuracy of his stories was always uncovered by his ignorance of the reality, and all the more amusing for that. But telling his amazing tales made him very thirsty, and it was as well that Tom Dodd had been so generous.

Mary and Chas Bickerstaff made it to Emily's just in time, and Mary's pride was palpable at how beautiful her granddaughter looked in her rag-bag 'designer' dress. Who would have thought her handiwork would see the light of day after all these years. The look on her face would remain with Hannah for ever, and her heart overflowed with love for all her family. Food, drink and entertainment well under way, Hannah slipped upstairs to change into her going-away suit. Frank was given a spare key and instructed to return her gown and the wedding presents to Bowling Green Road while they were away, and keep an eye on the place for them.

When it came time to leave for the afternoon boat, the charabanc driver offered to take anyone down to the pier head who wanted to see them off, as he had to go past there to take the bus back to the depot, and those who still had the energy to walk back again jumped at the chance. Sydney and Elbie were among these passengers, but to Sydney's annoyance, so was Doug Lacey.

Hannah was nervous again now. She had not been on 'The Boat' before. She had heard a lot about it, and it wasn't all good, but it was still a lovely day, so the sailing should be quite smooth. In any case, she was with her husband now. What came next was all going to be an adventure.

∞∞∞

Smoke was billowing from the two great, red funnels, as the engines were stoked up for the voyage. Will and Hannah saw their trunk and bags hauled aboard while they waited with hundreds of other passengers on the pier. Much hugging, kissing and hand-shaking was going on as loved ones said their goodbyes to their departing family and friends. Many more people were returning from happy holidays in the island, going back home in time before the school terms started again the following week.

Soon, the signal was given for the passengers to cross the gang planks, and Hannah was frightened that she would lose hold of Will's hand in the crush, but he surprised her by standing back to let other people go ahead of them. "We have a cabin," he explained, "and don't need to worry about the scramble for seats." They turned and waved back to the family members who had accompanied them, and who were now retreating back towards the promenade, from where they could watch as the ship departed.

As the crowd subsided, Will guided Hannah ahead of him, stopping only to exchange words with the Purser for directions to their cabin. Once inside, Hannah threw off her hat and slipped off the new shoes that had begun to make their presence felt. Then they were able to relax a little, until suddenly there was an enormous deep-throated blast on the ship's siren. Hannah jumped, and Will laughed. "That's the signal that we are about to move!" he explained, and led her out onto the walkway, where they could look over the railings. Sure enough, it was happening so gently that Hannah could not have said they were moving, rather that the stone walls of the jetty seemed to be moving, giving her a strange unsteady feeling. Then when she looked up, she began to feel the vibrations from the vast engines far below, as the pier, the harbour and eventually the town, slipped past her. Once out of the harbour, the queasy feeling subsided, and they could see that people on the promenade were waving, although she could not make out who the people were. Their own loved ones would be among them, so all they could do was wave towards the shore in general. Similarly, their family could not identify them, but waved at the ship as it slipped out to sea, seeming to get smaller and smaller until it was just a speck.

Chapter Thirty Three

Sydney stayed close to Elbie and asked if he could walk her back. She said of course he could, and Mr Lacey was coming too. Drat Mr Lacey. Dougie was about twenty-two and home on vacation from Oxford University. Very charming, very eligible, very available, very annoying. Sydney sulked as the three of them sauntered back along the promenade, with Elbie in animated conversation with the student.

∞∞∞

Will and Hannah stepped back inside their cabin, and Will locked the door. Hannah gasped in surprise. She had not had time to think past the moment they were in. These were moments she had dreamed about for a decade, and now it was all coming true. "No more sneaking about and hiding," he said. "Now we are legitimate, and I can't wait any longer to experience my conjugal rights that you promised this morning!"

Will knew that it felt like a long time when they were confined to the ship for three or four hours, and that Hannah had reservations about the journey, so he told himself that this was just to distract her from worrying. The truth of it was, he had planned this moment and now he could wait no longer to make love to her. He took her in his arms and kissed her thoroughly, removing her smart jacket in the process, and enjoying the anticipation and the knowledge that she was his wife now. He had also had the misgivings that something would crop up that would prevent this wonderful day from coming to fruition, and now the relief was washing through him like a flood, as they sank down onto one of the bunks.

Hannah didn't realise that she was weeping, until she felt tears trickle past her ears and down her neck. She kissed her husband hungrily, the pent up emotions and worries of the past weeks exploding through her body, making her ache for him to consummate their union. She knew she should remove her beautiful new clothes, her carefully co-ordinated going-away outfit, but there was no time for such delays, her need was far too urgent for that. Will was mindful of their wedding finery, and lay beside her for a while, stroking her face and her hair; driving her wild with desire, and himself ever more impatient. But carefully he unbuttoned her blouse and slid his hand inside, and they both moaned with pleasure at the intimacy as he kissed her breasts, which still, as always, made him think of oranges.

He decided that his new trousers had better be removed, and Hannah also slipped off her long skirt. She then stroked him where she knew he liked it, and at last they hurled themselves onto the bed again, and were lost in mounting ecstasy for a long, long time. The vibrations from the great engines seemed to add a frisson of excitement for them both. The word 'multiples' came into Will's mind, and he realised he had not known it could happen like this. Goodness, gracious, but marriage was going to be exciting with this girl. After a while, they both slept, and it was only a change in the sound of the engines and motion of the ship that alerted them to the approaching end of this very special first part of their journey together.

∞∞∞∞

Sydney was getting more and more agitated as they strolled on the promenade, the three of them. Just being close to Elbie did things inside his trousers and he really wished Douglas Lacey would fall into the sea. He suddenly remembered Elbie's coquettish invitation to join her and the Irishman for three in a bed. Oh God! Was this her plan now? Jeez. He and George had not been sure what happened in such situations. Was he about to find out? Somehow, he couldn't imagine the refined Mr Lacey peering at him from the other side of Elbie's naked body. Sydney didn't realise he was walking along with his tongue hanging out at the thought. Not of a naked man in the same bed, but of Elbie, spread-eagled. He couldn't stand it any longer, and he blurted that he was going to get himself an ice cream. He had hoped they would leave him then, but Elbie cooed how wonderful that would be and they must all have one.

At this, Dougie expressed his regrets, but he didn't have time now. He must catch the electric tram home to Ramsey, but he looked forward to seeing them both again. His gaze lingered on

Elbie's face as he took her hand and kissed it, with a little bow. "Until tomorrow, perhaps," he beamed, then he turned on his heel and continued along the promenade. Moments later, he jumped on a horse tram and was gone.

"What a nice gentleman," said Elbie, and then, "I don't really want an ice cream, do you? I'd rather have a lie down." To Sydney's delight, she then took his hand as they turned onto Broadway and headed for her hotel.

∞∞∞∞

Hannah's first experience of 'going by boat' had been exquisite, and all her fears had vanished. Forgetting that she had slept through most of the voyage, she assumed that the crossing had been a smooth one. They dressed again and were ready to claim their luggage after gazing at the buildings on both sides of the Mersey as they approached the pier head. Porters with hand carts jostled for their business, but Will went straight for a horse and trap to take them to the hotel nearest to Lime Street Station, and they were soon checking in at the Midland Adelphi. Having slept on the steamer, they were not as exhausted as they had expected to be, and they enjoyed a leisurely meal in the hotel's restaurant, politely declining their famous speciality of fresh turtle soup! Their meal was followed by a short stroll around the block, when they found a choice of railway stations in very close proximity. Will elected to stick to his original plan, that advised by the much-travelled Elbie, but felt quite guilty when Hannah innocently asked where they were going. He had kept the honeymoon as so much of a surprise that he had forgotten to give her all the details, but now she was interested to know what lay ahead.

"I am taking you to London," he announced, proudly. "Not only because I was born there, I also studied there, but also, everyone should visit London at least once in their lives. After that we will have a few days on the South Coast, but our first stop, tomorrow, will be in Cheltenham, where I was brought up. I have family there, and it will be good to meet up with my cousin, Gideon, who keeps in touch. He hoped to come over to the island to see me married, but it would be expensive for him to do that just for the sake of it so we came to this compromise.

This way, I will get to show you off to lots of family members. You will never have seen so many Waverleys!"

Hannah was thrilled that he had gone to so much trouble. It all sounded quite wonderful, and she continued to walk on air, as they returned to their hotel room and turned in for the night. Their Wedding Night!

Without the throbbing of the ship's engines, Will was delighted to find that he could perform just as well in a luxurious and very large bed as he had on a floating bunk, and Hannah thought that they must definitely have conceived 'little Dorothy' several times over that day. She had been married for twelve hours, and marriage was wonderful.

∞∞∞∞

Douglas Lacey was enjoying his ride back to Ramsey on the electric tram. It was a scenic journey, and the late summer afternoon sun was beginning to cast long shadows. The island was his home, but he looked forward to graduating and carving a life for himself in the wider world. He had friends of both genders at University, and he knew flirting when he encountered it. He also knew about arousal and how difficult it could be to back out of a passionate situation, but he had the distinct impression that Elbie had been making him an offer. The kind of offer he didn't get every day, and he was in a quandary over the way she had made him feel. He was pondering what to do next as the tram rattled along, when he realised that the regular movements of the vehicle were influencing his thoughts regarding Elbie, her offer, and the word 'arousal.' By the time he reached Ramsey, he felt capable of taking Elbie somewhere secluded, if only she had come with him on the tram. As he walked from the station to his mother's house, he recalled what the girl had said. She would come to Ramsey herself, tomorrow, on the tram arriving around noon. She had been quite specific about it. It was an invitation, wasn't it? Oh, surely not. He must be imagining things. On the other hand, it could do no harm for him to saunter down to the tram station around mid-day.

∞∞∞∞

For the moment, Elbie had forgotten about Dougie Lacey. All her attention was focussed on Sydney. It had to be, while she had his penis in her mouth, but she was enjoying the rapturous noises he was making, and she wanted him like mad, although he might have to recuperate a little first. To give him time, she declared it would only be fair if he could do the same for her, with his tongue. She might not see Sydney again for years, if ever, and they had to enjoy each other as much as they could right now, and she really needed 'finishing off,' as she called it. He took to the experience immediately, and she reached a glorious finish, which kept her happy for about fifteen minutes. Then she showed him a few other tricks, until they were both exhausted, and the sun was going down.

Sydney had trouble walking normally as he reluctantly headed for the railway station. Who would have thought so much could happen in one weekend. How could life ever be the same after Elbie?

Chapter Thirty Four

After an early breakfast at the Adelphi, and being persuaded to at least have a look at the turtles, a carter was summoned for the transportation of their trunk and luggage to Lime Street Station, where Will procured their tickets, along with their instructions; they were required to change trains at Birmingham, but need not worry about their luggage, as that would be seen to for them. They were wished a very pleasant journey, and that was that.

Hannah began to feel nervous again. Having to be at a certain platform by a certain time seemed to be something that would have dire consequences if not strictly adhered to, and she imagined being parted for ever from their trunk. She half wished that Elbie was there to reassure her, but then dismissed that thought. She was still very concerned about that young lady, and not at all sure that she was trustworthy.

Feeling in her reticule for a handkerchief to dab at the frightened tear that was threatening, her fingers located a small package that she could not identify by touch, and she had to pull it out of the bag for a closer look. It was something in a small envelope. It was Dorothy Kinrade's cameo brooch, enclosed in a little note from Elbie. "Darling Hannah," she read, "I could see that this sweet brooch meant a lot to you, as it did to the person who gave it to you. It served its purpose admirably on your perfect wedding day, and while I am so touched by your gift, I could not possibly keep it. I hope you will wear it and remember all that it represents. Have a wonderful honeymoon, and write to me when you are home again. Thank you for asking me to be a bridesmaid, I was honoured to witness your marriage, and I wish you continued happiness for many years to come. I will welcome any opportunity to pop over to the island, so be sure to let me know when your babies start arriving! Much love, Elbie."

Now Hannah really did need her handkerchief, but had forgotten her original reason for seeking it. She scurried along after Will as he marched to the required platform, and then, having arrived in plenty of time before the train pulled in, they ordered cups of tea in the waiting room. Hannah had tucked the package back into her bag, as she did not want to start a conversation about Elbie right now. Will idly enquired what she had thought about the turtles swimming about in their warmed pool at the Adelphi, just waiting to be made into soup. In her emotional state, Hannah felt sick and faint at the thought. "How could they!" she blurted. "How could anyone point a finger at an animal and sentence it to death? It's... it's.... inhuman, that's what it is!" Will wished he had not mentioned it, and pressed her to drink her tea. He could not know that even thinking about the poor sentenced turtles was preferable to talking about Elbie.

∞∞∞∞

Sydney was back at work after all the festivities, and his life-changing weekend. Remembering Elbie would keep him going for a day or two, but what was he going to do then? Where would he find a girl he could have a bloody good romp with, without the danger of her getting clingy, or worse? He started daydreaming about all the girls in Castletown, one at a time, but he didn't come up with a valid answer. Hmmm, perhaps he should go into Douglas more often. They were sure to be more free and easy there. Or would farm girls be worth a try? Barns and haystacks came to mind, but there his reverie was cut short when Billa noticed that he had painted the same doorframe several times.

∞∞∞∞

At the other end of the island, Dougie told his mother that he had decided to have a day out by himself. "You were out all day yesterday!" objected Agnes, but he told her he would soon have to go back to Oxford and he wanted to enjoy 'his island' a little more, and perhaps be inspired to write some poetry. She made him a sandwich to take with him and warned him to be careful. He wasn't sure quite what she meant by that. You never knew with mothers, they had an uncanny knack of seeing right through you.

At first, he set off up the paths to the Albert Tower, which perched on top of a hill overlooking the town and the whole of the north of the island, where Queen Victoria's beloved Prince had admired the stunning view. He lay back on a patch of grass and tried to identify all the buildings he could see, all the way out to Andreas Church. He crossed a field and sat again, looking out to sea. From here, he was unaware that he was looking out over the top of Hannah's 'Garden of Eden,' where she had been captivated by the view, and lost her maidenhood. Dougie's thoughts may have resembled Hannah's on that memorable day. His fantasies definitely included sexual activity, and his heart thumped as he wondered if he had the courage to take Elbie up on whatever she offered. She had a pretty mouth for a start, and pert little breasts..... He could at least get a little better acquainted with those? He decided to eat his sandwich, just to get it out of the way, and to occupy his hands, that were in danger of making a fool of him.

He wondered where he could take Elbie where they would be private, and thought perhaps they might walk along the shore towards Ballure. It would just depend on how many other people were around. Or there was a field behind the little Ballure Church. Nobody would see them there.

With such plans half formed, he set off to the tram station, suddenly feeling foolish. What if she didn't come? Well, no-one would know he'd been stood up if he just happened to be sauntering through the station when the tram came in. He would just have to find something else to do. Or meet the next tram?

But Elbie was on the tram, and she ran into his arms and pressed her body to him as if they had been lovers already. He was delighted and thrilled, but looked guiltily around before shepherding her out of the station and along to the promenade. "It's lovely that you could come," he said. "Do you have a plan? What would you like to do? Do you know Ramsey, or shall I just show you round generally – see the sights, and the park, and just get to know each other a little better?"

"Oh do stop babbling, Dougie. I can't be bothered with all that pretending to be coy. My plan is to make love with you, and the sooner the better. Where can we go?"

He was flabbergasted, even shocked. Thrilled beyond belief, so much that he thought he must have misunderstood her. "I might not take you home to meet my mother just yet," he joked, playing for time.

"Oh God, no. I've heard about HER. What about walking out that long pier? There might not be anyone around at the far end?"

"I wouldn't count on it, but it is worth the walk. It's wonderfully peaceful out there, with a great view looking back at the town."

"Let's do it!" she cried and skipped on ahead of him. She put the pennies in the turnstile to let them onto the pier, and they began to jog along the half mile out over the sea. However, at the half way point, she pulled him onto a seat in one of the shelters. There was a tiny railway along the pier, and at the 'half way house' the tracks doubled to allow trains to pass in opposite directions. "Look!" she declared. "From here we can see anyone coming for miles in either direction. Let's do it!" she said again, and this time she was pulling up her skirts.

"Elbie!" Dougie's mouth had gone dry and it came out as a squeak. He cleared his throat and asked the usual questions, and she gave the usual reply about her inability to conceive, and then prevented more talk by sticking her tongue in his mouth and her hand in his pants.

'Bloody hell!' thought Dougie, 'I'm being raped! Gadzooks, she's a mad woman.' Numerous expletives entered his head, but couldn't get out because of her tongue. His hands clawed at her breasts, and she wrapped both her legs round him. Almost before he knew how it happened he was exploding inside her and wishing the moment would never end. It didn't end for quite a while, but then they could hear that people were approaching on foot from the seaward end, and they hastily repaired their dishevelled clothing. They continued their walk then, glad that those people had been leaving, and they now hoped to find the end of the pier deserted.

It wasn't, of course, there were always people fishing out there, but they seemed to be absorbed and didn't even look up when the couple passed them. The café was deserted, except for a girl behind the counter, waiting eagerly for a customer. Elbie insisted on treating Dougie to a meat pie and a cup of tea, while she tucked into a huge slice of chocolate cake. Suitably fortified, they wandered outside again and round beyond the café where, seeing that they were unobservable, she drew up her skirts again and brought his fingers to touch her. She groped with his buttons and pleaded with him to take her again. He had not expected anything like this, but she had such an enticing and irresistible way about her, that he soon found he was capable of the unexpected, this time opening her blouse and sucking her breast, while entering her standing up. He kissed her violently, finding she tasted of chocolate, which drove him to further frenzy, and they were both grunting and moaning, oblivious to the rest of the world. The rest of the world was not oblivious to them, however, there were some young boys fishing from a lower level of the landing stage, who looked up at the noises coming from above. They were most interested in seeing the woman's tits, and lost interest once they were covered up again, but they kept looking back in case there was any more entertainment coming.

"You're good!" said Elbie.

"You're bad," replied Dougie. "Wicked. Evil. Wanton. You're a very naughty girl!" They laughed together again and held hands as they strolled back along the pier, admiring the promised view of the town and the hills behind. "Would you like to walk along the beach now?"

"All right. Did the tram come in along there?" she pointed to the cliff top. "Perhaps I could catch one back to Douglas from up there somewhere."

"Oh, do you have to go back so soon?" Douglas was crestfallen.

"Well no, not just yet, but if I can catch the tram along that way, it would save coming back into the station again. That's all I meant."

The tide was far enough out for them to walk along to where the Ballure River tumbled down to the sea, under a private two-arched bridge in someone's garden, which was known to one and all simply as The Arches. They went under one of the arches and climbed along a wooded path, until they came out in a small field that overlooked the shore. They had arrived at Hannah's Garden of Eden, without knowing it, and they walked along and sat down leaning against the large rock that had seen life-changing activity in late May.

Elbie had flopped down and closed her eyes, but when she opened them she exclaimed, "My God!"

"What is it?" asked the startled Dougie.

"It's the view! That's the very same view that Hannah described, and Charlie painted for her. Did you see the painting?

He did it as a wedding present. She especially asked for a picture of this very view. I'm not seeing the two schooners today, but perhaps they'll appear soon. Doug, do you know what this means?"

He was still puzzled, not knowing the full story of the painting, or of Hannah and Will's courtship.

"Well I never," she was saying now. "Oh my God – you do realise what we have to do now? Oh yes!" and she was already opening her blouse, but this time she stretched out on the grass before lifting her skirts.

Douglas looked down at her incredulously. "You can't..... you can't want it again already?"

"No of course I don't want it," she lied easily, "it just has to be done. Don't you see? This is the spot where Will and Hannah ....?"

"Where Will and Hannah what?" Douglas was truly scandalised.

"Come down here and let me show you," she giggled, and show him, she did.

Chapter Thirty Five

The newlyweds alighted from the first train in Birmingham, and Hannah was nervous for their possessions all over again, while they waited for their second train to divert them to Cheltenham Spa. She need not have been so worried. When they arrived at their destination, their trunk and other bags had arrived there too, and they had hardly stepped off the train when they were hailed by Will's cousin Gideon.

Gideon was as unprepared about Hannah as Elbie had been about Will, but he hid his amazement well and hugged his new cousin-in-law warmly, trying not to compare the embrace with the day, a month ago, that he gave his own daughter away. He had brought his horse and trap, where the men hefted the luggage onto the back board between them, and then drove to his own house, in a street of lodging houses occupied and run by numerous other relatives. When they arrived, they found several families already waiting round Gideon's doorway to greet the travelling couple. Some were not so adept at hiding their surprise, but everyone was charmed with Hannah, and delighted for Will who had been a widower for so long. It did not take long for the womenfolk to predict children for 'Old Will,' and it was a happy crowd who celebrated together. Trestle tables had been laid out in the street, so that everyone could enjoy the party. Gideon's daughter, Amy, hoped they were hungry, and Will admitted to having had one rather stale railway station scone since breakfast, and he was ready to eat a horse, as he had to keep his strength up now. Everyone roared with laughter and clapped him on the back.

"You are an inspiration!" whispered Gideon to Will in a quiet moment. "I miss Mary Ann terribly. Annie and Elsie are both married now, the boys have stayed in Canada. There's only the teenagers left here, but I have a very dear friend, if you get my meaning. Emma lives with her mother, running one of the lodging houses down the road. I've been toying with the idea of, 'you know,' but she is a good fifteen years younger. What do people say?"

"People will say what they want, without thinking, wherever they are. The people of Castletown are scandalised, but what does it matter? They are not the ones feeling the pain of loneliness, Gid. I know exactly how that feels, and I can't tell you how happy Hannah has made me. I was so depressed and feeling like a tired-out old man, and then suddenly I'm a young chap again. And don't worry about, 'you know,' it will all come back to you very easily, and you can make up for lost time!"

"You didn't just start last night, then?" perceived Gideon. "You lucky dog. No wonder the stuffy neighbours are shocked! I might not have your courage, and I would hate to compromise Emma, but I will certainly pursue the matter more positively! Goodness me, you are a dark horse!"

They chattered on about family members, and Will was pleased to hear that his Uncle William was still alive, living with cousin John and his family in Toronto, having lost Gideon's mother, Sophia, about ten years ago. John had also been widowed and married again. "Lizzie's nearly 20 years younger too, come to think of it. It must sit well with our older men! Of course, your father did the same." Gideon stopped abruptly as Will twisted in his chair and looked askance at him.

"No, you're wrong there, Gid. I think you'll find that my mother was actually a couple of years older."

Dates and details were racing around in Gideon's head, as he quickly realised that his favourite cousin, the brilliant one with letters after his name, was ignorant of some of the facts of life. How was he going to break the news? Carefully he looked at Will and said, "After your mother went back to the Isle of Man...."

"Yes?" prompted Will, "Mother and Agnes went to the island after father died."

That confirmed Gideon's suspicions. "You weren't around when they went, you were teaching somewhere else, I believe?" Will agreed that he was away working in Scarborough while Agnes had applied for and secured the teaching post in the island. Suddenly, in his embarrassment, Gideon had a flash of inspiration. "You've never seen your father's grave, have you? Didn't you suggest that when you wrote to me weeks ago. I thought it a strange request at the time, but we will go and visit it tomorrow." Will's curious train of thought was interrupted then, as Gideon's 'very dear friend,' Emma, arrived on the scene.

Hannah was getting on like a house on fire with the many female relatives that Will had never spoken to her about. They wanted to hear all about the Isle of Man and her family and how she knew Will, and what the neighbours thought about their marriage. She had to admit to being a little nervous on this last score. The people of Castletown had not been kind to her, but that had been the case for years, and she tried to ignore it. She confessed to having been taken by surprise that Will had fallen in love with her. They all smiled knowingly when she said how prestigious a personage he was in their town, and how people argued with him at their peril, but that in general, the boys he taught loved and respected him. He certainly did his best for them, even if it meant pushing their boundaries a little, but they had a lot of success, and she was so proud of him.

It was a large and very happy street party, with much back-slapping and hand shaking, and embraces from the ladies. Hannah thought she saw a puzzled look pass between Will and Gideon, but she was soon distracted by having to describe her wedding dress, and how they had raided her grandmother's sewing basket for inspiration. She drew little diagrams describing the dresses and the flower coronets and, of course, her ring and ear-rings were much admired. They went on to ask where the newlyweds would be living, and Hannah recalled the fun they had all had decorating and furnishing their new home in Bowling Green Road, not forgetting to describe Charlie's wonderful painting. The memory of that landscape brought tears to her eyes, and Amy chided the women for tiring this poor girl to death. What a day she has had, now we must let this good couple get some rest – if they can! Hannah would have been shocked to know what was happening in her Garden of Eden at the same moment.

∞∞∞∞

This had been their first, exhausting, full day of marriage, and they were both instantly asleep when their heads touched their pillows that night. Hannah awoke in the darkness after the first deep sleep, wondering where she was, but as realisation suffused her mind and body, she luxuriated in the relief that her dreams had all come true at last, and she stretched contentedly, catlike, and was soon asleep again. When she awoke to a dawn light, it was to find Will leaning up on one elbow, regarding her with a happy smile. "I'm so used to waking early and going for organ practice," he whispered, "I still wake up at the same time every day, but I don't remember when I last had such a contented and refreshing sleep. How are you feeling, Mrs Waverley?"

Thrilled at hearing her new name, she felt a surge of excitement and love, and she stroked his face, just as she had done in the church hall months ago. Despite the absence of oranges, it had a similar effect again, and they began with tender kissing, followed by pressing bodies and finally the fulfilment that she had ached for, for so very long, but now, at last, legally, leisurely, in a large, comfortable bed. It was still a little furtive, and they continued to whisper, as they did not want to alert the rest of the household, but it was soon obvious that others in the house were going about their early routines.

They lay back thinking how wonderful life was, and wondering when they should make an appearance, when there was a quiet knock, and Amy's voice whispered that she was leaving some hot water at their door. Will was able to speak out loud at last, and he called their thanks. There was already a ewer of cold water in a large bowl on the dresser, as well as a bar of soap and some towels. Dressing gowns hung on the back of the door, and Will covered himself modestly before opening the door to collect the hot jug. Hannah lay back and watched him as he washed and dressed, and then followed suit while he shaved. She was aware that these honeymoon days would be unique, life would settle into a more mundane pattern once they were at home again, and the getting-up sequence more urgent, once Will was back at work. Back to a timetable, and being obliged to keep to it. Best make the most of this short time. It was already Wednesday, and the new school term would begin in one week.

There were other boarders staying in the house, but Gideon and Amy were a good team, and breakfast was ready whenever their guests required it. Will and Hannah rejoiced in being on holiday, and allowed those who were rushing off out to work to eat first, while they chatted with their cousins. Amy insisted that they partake of a hearty breakfast, to 'set them up for the day,' and she also prepared them a small package of sandwiches, to 'keep them going on the journey.' Gideon had already seen to the horse, he had to have his breakfast too, but he was harnessed to the trap at the front door as soon as they were ready to leave. Their trunk was hauled out again between the two men, and then, with good-bye and thank you hugs for Amy, they were off into the Cheltenham sunshine. There was a bus service into London at noon each day, which would be easier than changing trains again. Because it went direct to the capital it would take them no longer, and they would be at their hotel in time for tea.

But first, as promised, they would visit the cemetery. Hannah had not been warned about this little diversion, but she was delighted that Will was taking the time to remember his father. She understood that he had died before Will's mother and sister had gone to the Isle of Man to live, where Will followed when the opportunity of a headmaster's post came up in Peel. She did not even remember his mother very well, she had just been one of the old black-clad widow-ladies in the town, who had died before Hannah had realised that she was falling stupidly and hopelessly in love with William Waverley. The mother was buried at Malew, in the same grave as Will's young wife. Hannah recalled seeing their names when they had walked out to the church yard with some flowers a few months ago, and remembered feeling pleased that his mother's name was Charlotte Christian Waverley, because her own middle name was also Christian.

Gideon stopped the trap outside the chapel, and they all walked along a tree-lined avenue, scanning the many large headstones, until they stopped at the familiar name. Gideon was biting his lip. Noticing this, Hannah peered at the stone inquisitively. She and Will read the wording aloud, together, "In loving memory of James Maurice Waverley," they began, but Hannah stopped there, as Will continued, "Beloved husband of...." and there, he also stopped, perplexed. "Selina?" he blurted, frowning at his cousin. He looked back at the stone in disbelief, "and he only died in '94?" Again he looked at Gideon. "Who the deuce is Selina?"

"Yes," breathed Gideon, "it was obvious yesterday that you didn't know about this little episode. Apparently, the old rogue sloped off and left your mother, and was gone for so long that everyone thought he must be dead. I can imagine Aunt Charlotte being outraged at his treatment, but I don't think there was much love lost, as the saying goes. I suppose your women took the opportunity to leave the district themselves and make a new life back in the Isle of Man, where your mother was born and where she had met James. I understand they were working for the same household." Gideon realised that Will was not taking all this in, his face was a blank. Poor Hannah looked embarrassed and a little frightened.

"Then suddenly, he turns up back here with this young woman, announcing that she is his wife!" Gideon added, feeling that perhaps Hannah would work it out bit by bit.

Hannah gave him a wan smile and asked about this Selina. "Is she still alive? Where is she? Where did they live?"

"Woah, slow down. I don't have all the answers, and I really don't know where she is now. She seemed to disappear after James died. I haven't heard of her passing, but who knows? Anyway, it's all long in the past. What's done is done, it's not worth worrying about."

Will had remained silent and tight-lipped. Hannah addressed Gideon again. "I think I know how he is feeling," she explained. "Did his mother and sister know about this? He will be wondering why they kept it from him, and he will think of it as lying that they didn't see fit to confide in him."

Will re-joined the conversation. "You are absolutely right, Hannah, but when my blood pressure calms down a bit, it will probably explain a lot for us. I always had the impression that Mother wanted to get away from my father, and that Agnes hated him for some reason. Could the failure of her own marriage be down to some deep-seated mistrust of men? Could her antipathy about our marriage have been out of concern for YOU?"

"Oh, very droll!" snorted Hannah, "No, not that last bit, but I'm sure you are onto a thread that we can think about – some other time, perhaps? Do we have a bus to catch?"

"Lord, yes we do. Gid, thank you so much for this. I won't hold it against you. It's a revelation, that's all, and brings up more questions than it answers, but we had better get on our way. I intended to give this wonderful girl the time of her life. We will have to do as she says and think about it at some other time, although I fear it might occupy my mind on the long bus journey ahead!" Hannah groaned, and they all laughed.

Chapter Thirty Six

Elbie returned to the mainland that day, in order to prepare for her lengthy European touring holiday. She had been looking forward to this, but now she was quite reluctant to leave the Isle of Man. Her nine days there had been an unusual experience, even for her, and had made her stop and think about her behaviour. She knew her remorse would not last, it was not her way to look back, but from the deck of the *Viking,* that was exactly what she was doing. Looking back. The Irishman was good fun, with a ready wit and an infectious laugh, but it was the contrasting 'other two' that had, against her own principles (yes, she did have some, in her own way), crept into corners of her heart. Dreamily, as the ship went, stern-first to begin with, out of Douglas harbour she gazed back at the receding island and recalled her conquests.

The boy was so sweet. She so loved helping young lads into adulthood, knowing they would never forget her. But this one was her best friend's youngest brother. How could she! Oh yes, but he was lovely, and so grateful! It was always nice to be appreciated. But he was still a boy, and that was all. And then there was Douglas. If circumstances had only been different?

Douglas Lacey was indulging in a similar reverie. He had returned to Hannah's Garden of Eden, but in his mind the huge boulder was 'Peggy Creg' as he trawled his memory for the words in Manx for 'kissing' and 'rock,' corrupting them to sound familiar. He did not know the words for all that had happened, in fact, now that Elbie had gone, he wondered if it was all a dream. He leaned back against Peggy Creg, and sketched the pretty view of Ramsey Bay, forming also in his mind the words for a poem. He would write her a sonnet so that she would not forget him, and what they had done together.

After copying what she thought Hannah and Will had done there, they had caught a Douglas-bound tram right beside the garden, but had travelled only a short way before alighting at Dreemskerry. From there, they walked down the hill to Port

Mooar, where there was a tiny cottage almost on the pebbly beach that doubled as a café serving delicious, fresh home-made bread and thick Manx broth. Fresh bonnag, just out of the oven, meant that the butter melted into it before being spread thickly with farmhouse strawberry and rhubarb jam. Afterwards, hand in hand, they clambered along the headland, remarking on the sparkling, grey-green waves breaking and spilling white foam against the rocks, 'suggestively' according to Elbie; until they found a clearing that was secluded enough for her purpose, which of course was to enjoy one more slice of her new best friend, Dougie, before they would have to part.

"You are trying to distract me from my studies, aren't you?" he declared as she pulled him down again. "How will I get you out of my mind, Elbie? You do realise I am fall...." She stopped him by putting a hand to his mouth, followed by her tongue, while her hand groped for him, and she threw herself on top of him.

"Don't spoil it, please don't spoil a wonderful day, Dougie," she breathed into his ear as she moved back and forth on him. "After today, it's unlikely that our paths will cross again, but we have had some golden moments, haven't we? Just as we are now, amid the smell of turf and heather, and I will remember you too. With much affection. You are quite experienced, aren't you? Mmmm," and she kissed him deeply for a long time.

After they were both spent at last, and lying back on the grass, he said, "You have paid me two compliments, Miss Minx. I am flattered that you think you will remember me, but as for being experienced, well, I've done a little experimenting, but I am now more than twice as experienced as I was when I got up this morning!"

"A quick learner!" she laughed, just stopping herself from saying 'another quick learner,' realising he would want to know about the others, and feeling guilty about Sydney all over again. He had walked her back to the tram stop, pausing occasionally to kiss and stroke her, reluctant for their day together to end. In the gathering dusk, a skylark serenaded them, although they could not see it way above in the reddening sky. Inside the little shelter, the glorious, insatiable woman had demanded his services yet again, and he knew he would never know another girl like this. He had barely entered her when they heard the tram whistle blow, and knew their time was short. The previous crossing was about a mile away, and the tram had a slight incline to climb. The urgency excited them both so much that they almost allowed the tram to trundle on past them, but fortunately, it stopped to let other passengers alight.

Leaning against Peggy Creg again now, Douglas felt that excitement all over again, and thought what a wonderful thing God had given mankind to experience. Had poor Elbie not been barren, he might surely have known the joy of procreation, if not at any of the first attempts, then surely that last mind-blowing explosion in the Dreemskerry tram shelter! He had walked home along the tram line, feeling elated, but drained and a little bereft.

∞∞∞∞

Entirely as expected, Will sank deep in thought once they were on the London bus, and Hannah knew he had to revisit what he had learned today and explore all he had previously thought he knew about his late father. She had been shocked too, but was remote from the hurt that he was feeling at having been kept in the dark. Agnes had been unkind about her brother's new love, and Hannah had difficulty feeling kindly in return, thinking unhappily that it might be quite in character for Agnes to have withheld the information that their father had simply left their mother. Such ignominy! But now, perhaps, skeletons in closets! Was there a sniff of hypocrisy here? The more she thought about it, the more indignant she became.

Then she realised that, having been free of Agnes and her venom for a couple of months, she was back here, between them as she wanted to be, driving a wedge, without even knowing it. Hannah decided to keep her own counsel if she could possibly hold her tongue, but her anger simmered, just the same.

The bus had made a brief stop in Gloucester, when Will had roused himself enough to smile and pat her hand, but was back with the furrowed brow as soon as they were on the move again. Hannah decided to banish her strange in-laws from her thoughts, and go back to the people she knew, and knew she could trust. Ah, well there was a problem. Could she trust her best friend? Could she trust her brothers? She remembered asking George to quiz Sydney about his strange behaviour, but she was left to wonder if he had divined any information from their *'Wand'ring*

Minstrel' because, of course, there had not been time to see either of them again before they were on their honeymoon.

Well, some honeymoon this was turning out to be! While they were alone, things were just lovely and loving and wonderful, and she had been so happy on waking up in the wee small hours of the morning, realising all they had been through and that now they were Mr and Mrs Waverley. Her dreams were fulfilled, and when she thought of their lovemaking, she was almost sure their further dreams must have been initiated. But as soon as they were with other people, things started to go wrong. Oh, Gideon and his family were lovely and had been so welcoming and hospitable and accepting, she could not deny this. They were her new cousins-in-law and she did like them all. But the secrets! Secrets and Lies, people say, don't they? Yes, secrets breed lies, and lies weave such a tangled web, and more lies. She was so glad she had confessed all she could about herself to Will before ever she had allowed him to be intimate with her. She thought yet again about the Garden of Eden, and the lovely view over Ramsey and the North. That bay was so pretty, and they could see all the way to the Point of Ayre from their big rock.

∞∞∞∞

"Golden moments," said Dougie to himself out loud. "She said we had golden moments. That carnally obsessed woman has poetry in her soul," he mused that perhaps they were not so different after all, before realising that, apart from an incredibly physical intimacy, they had not shared much else. He did not know how old she was, where she lived (apart from 'on the mainland'), or how she made a living. And apart from saying he was at Oxford, he had not talked about his life. He learned something about himself that day and also about human relationships. Yes, they had enjoyed each other's company, she had loved the views he showed her and laughed at his jokes, but what would he remember about her, except her easy ability to arouse him, and to satisfy him, and then to want it all again? He was used to requiring brain power to forge a relationship, a meeting of minds, possibly and hopefully, a superiority of mind. He expected a woman to look up to him. Elbie didn't look up, except when she was on her back, which of course was as frequently as she could engineer it, but she was always in control of the situation. She got what she wanted, and that was all. But they had shared golden moments, and even thinking about her aroused him, again and again.

In the few days that he had left on the island, he returned frequently to Peggy Creg, to Port Mooar and round the rocky outcrop to Maughold Head. From the headland near the lighthouse, he could behold the entire sweep of Ramsey Bay, all the way to the Point of Ayre. The words simply flowed as he recited his poem for Elbie, and he was pleased with it. She would recognise the message in it, and no-one else need know.

∞∞∞

"I won't mention it again," promised Will as the bus drew in to the terminus in London. "I have thought it all over and over and, obviously there are a hundred questions, and I will just have to write to Gideon and ask some of them!"

"We must write and thank them all for their kindness, anyway, as soon as we are home again," remarked Hannah, hoping she would not find herself drawn into a discussion now.

"We may find we have to pay another visit?" Will looked nervously at his wife, but she reassured him.

"From what I have heard of Cheltenham Spa, it is a place that would be worthy of a lot more than a one-day visit, and not just to find out about family history," she said. "It is so popular for the healthy element. I've heard a lot about it, and you just had to notice that every house in that street was a lodging house – they must have a huge demand for accommodation for some reason! Perhaps, when we go again, you and Gideon could follow up your ancestry while the ladies and I partake of the waters, or the shopping."

"You are an incredible lady!" said Will. "So understanding. We will do that. Soon."

She knew it would probably never happen, but was happy that perhaps the subject could be closed, at least for the rest of today, and hopefully for the rest of their honeymoon. They were alone together again, after all.

∞∞∞

Elbie had wandered about the ship, taking more of an interest in her surroundings than she had ever done on previous voyages. Almost every other time, she had found herself a man within the first hour, and then a quiet corner somewhere. Men were so predictable, she had hardly ever encountered a problem getting what she wanted from them, and a voyage was so blessedly short that she could vow to meet again, or keep in touch, and then melt into the crowds upon departure. This time, her Isle of Man encounters were refusing to recede into the distance, as the island itself was doing. As the purple shape began to fade from sight, Elbie found herself leaning on a rail and weeping. It was so long since she had felt such sadness that at first she could not identify what was wrong with her. When she felt a gentle hand on her arm, and heard a man's voice enquire if he could do anything for her, she recoiled from his touch, sobbed, "Leave me alone," and fled out of his sight. Now she was even more confused. She had not resisted a man's touch like that since she was thirteen.

∞∞∞∞

Dougie was so pleased with his 'Golden Moments' poem, that he even showed it to his mother. She saw a light in his eyes and was straightaway suspicious of what he had been up to. She read the words over and over, and admitted defeat. It was simply charming, describing nearby beautiful areas and views in an understatedly poetical way. She would not have been able to scramble around rocky promontories or tramp through the bracken as she may have done when she was young, but she was glad that her son was appreciating his homeland, and that such memories would stay with him wherever he might go in life. Dougie watched his mother's face soften, saw her heaving chest subside as she read and re-read the lines; and he smiled a secret smile to himself. That was when he knew it was too late. He was already in love.

∞∞∞∞

Sydney had decided to take his bicycle and explore the neighbouring parishes. He knew he wouldn't find another girl like Elbie. In fact, with hindsight, he wasn't sure that Elbie was quite 'nice,' and he certainly would not want any girl of his to be so easy. On the other hand, he wasn't looking for a wife yet. Lord no, not for at least ten years, he had wild oats to sow, didn't he? But he would be careful about where he sowed them, hence the decision to start looking a few miles out of town.

He stopped in Arbory to admire the sunset and the amazing colours in the clouds, and at first he did not notice the girl in the garden, unpegging the washing from a clothes line. She was beautiful. Elbie was sophisticated and smart, but she was skinny, and she was not beautiful. This girl's fair hair hung down unpinned, and swirled in the breeze as she bent down to put the sheets into a large basket. As she bent, her ample breasts looked almost in danger of escaping from her peasant blouse, and Sydney felt an indecent urge to have one of those in his mouth. "What are you staring at?" the girl demanded, suddenly noticing him leering over the wall.

"Jeez, I'm sorry – I actually stopped to admire the sky – isn't it brilliant? Hey, can I help you with that?"

She had glanced at the sky, but then looked again and cocked her head on one side. "That cloud looks like a man on horseback," she remarked, as he vaulted over the wall and advanced on her. As she turned back, she gave him two ends of a sheet to fold up with her, and as they came together, it was all he could do not to kiss her. He already had a familiar feeling in his trousers. She stared at him in horror, and then a man's voice called out wondering what had happened to her out there.

"You"ve got me into trouble already," she pouted and he thought, 'if only!'

Hurriedly, as she piled the last of the washing into the basket, he asked if he could see her again. What was she doing that night? She seemed puzzled, before realising that he had paid her a compliment. Then she looked crestfallen. "Oh, I don't get out at night," she said at last. "Except to chapel on Sunday."

"What chapel? Can I come?" he blurted, as an older man appeared at the door asking again what was going on.

"Can't stop you," she shrugged, and the breasts heaved again as she turned away. Then over her shoulder she whispered, "chapel on the corner," and she was gone.

Sydney took a deep breath and thought, well, that wasn't too difficult. God, those tits will haunt me.

∞∞∞∞

"Where are we going now?" asked Hannah, gazing round in awe at the bustle of traffic. She had never seen so many motor vehicles in amongst all the horse drawn carriages, and the noise made her quite nervous. She clung to her new husband's sleeve as he hailed a motor taxi, answering her question in his request to the driver.

"The Westminster Hotel," he called, and then to the driver, "that's all right, I know it is not far, but we have heavy luggage and I wish my WIFE to arrive in style, if you please."

The driver looked from one to the other, smirked and nodded as Will helped him to heave the trunk on board. Once seated, Will explained to Hannah that, because his parents had been keeping a shop in the Westminster area when he was born, he considered himself a Londoner, and wished to share the London experience with her. He had returned to study close by, in order to obtain his degree, and had been re-acquainted with the scene which, he promised, would offer a great many sight-seeing opportunities for the few days of their holiday. As she looked askance, he continued to outline his plans for a further few days on the south coast, near Brighton, in order to revisit a small town nearby that had captured his heart during a short period as a student teacher.

"Oh yes, you did tell me about that once before. But, goodness me, you have been busy, making all these lovely plans." And then, narrowing her eyes suspiciously, "I hope you didn't have to get too cosy with Elbie to work all this out?" but as he made to deny it, she laughed out loud and pushed him playfully. "Oh forget Elbie, forget everybody. We are alone together at last, and we are on honeymoon. Ooh, is this the hotel already? Let the adventure begin!"

End of Part One

Nobody could have foreseen how much their lives were about to be disrupted. Will imagined that his routine would continue much as it had been since Agnes left, but with the added delight of a lovely young wife to come home to. Hannah had longed to be Mrs William Waverley for so long that she saw no further than the moment she was in. She had achieved her goal without getting pregnant, but she still hoped that Mrs Kinrade's prediction would come true one day.

Elbie was about to be made a startling offer, even before she embarked on her European tour, and on her travels she would experience a life-changing encounter.

Sydney's only thoughts involved sex, but could lead to a dangerous romance. He would know real fear before long, whereas Douglas would have more fun being miserable than he could have imagined.

First, though, there was the well-planned honeymoon, which had already been set somewhat awry by the revelation on the grave stone. That would entail a long investigation, and involve meeting more new people.

And, of course, there were the people of Castletown. There would be much more music to face before long.

Face The Music